WolfWalkers

The Graphic Novel

WolfWalkers
The Graphic Novel

Based on the film by
TOMM MOORE & ROSS STEWART

Adapted by
SAM SATTIN

Little, Brown and Company
New York Boston

About This Book

This book was edited by Rachel Poloski and designed by Ching N. Chan, Maria Caritas, Dwi Febri Novita, Dies Caya, Marsela Giovani of Caravan Studio. The production was supervised by Bernadette Flinn, and the production editor was Lindsay Walter-Greaney. The text was set in Jacoby, and the display type is Wolfwalkers.

Illustrations by Tomm Moore and Maria Pareja.

Cover design by Ching N. Chan.

Little, Brown and Company
Hachette Book Group
1290 Avenue of the Americas, New York, NY 10104
Visit us at LBYR.com/Wolfwalkers

First Edition: December 2020

Little, Brown and Company is a division of Hachette Book Group, Inc.
The Little, Brown name and logo are trademarks of Hachette Book Group, Inc.

The publisher is not responsible for websites (or their content)
that are not owned by the publisher.

Library of Congress Control Number: 2020937579

ISBNs: 978-0-316-46178-8 (hardcover), 978-0-316-42953-5 (paperback), 978-0-316-42949-8 (ebook), 978-0-316-42951-1 (ebook), 978-0-316-42950-4 (ebook)

Printed in China

APS

Hardcover: 10 9 8 7 6 5 4 3
Paperback: 10 9 8 7

To the amazing wolf pack of artists and production staff who made the movie and this graphic novel possible.

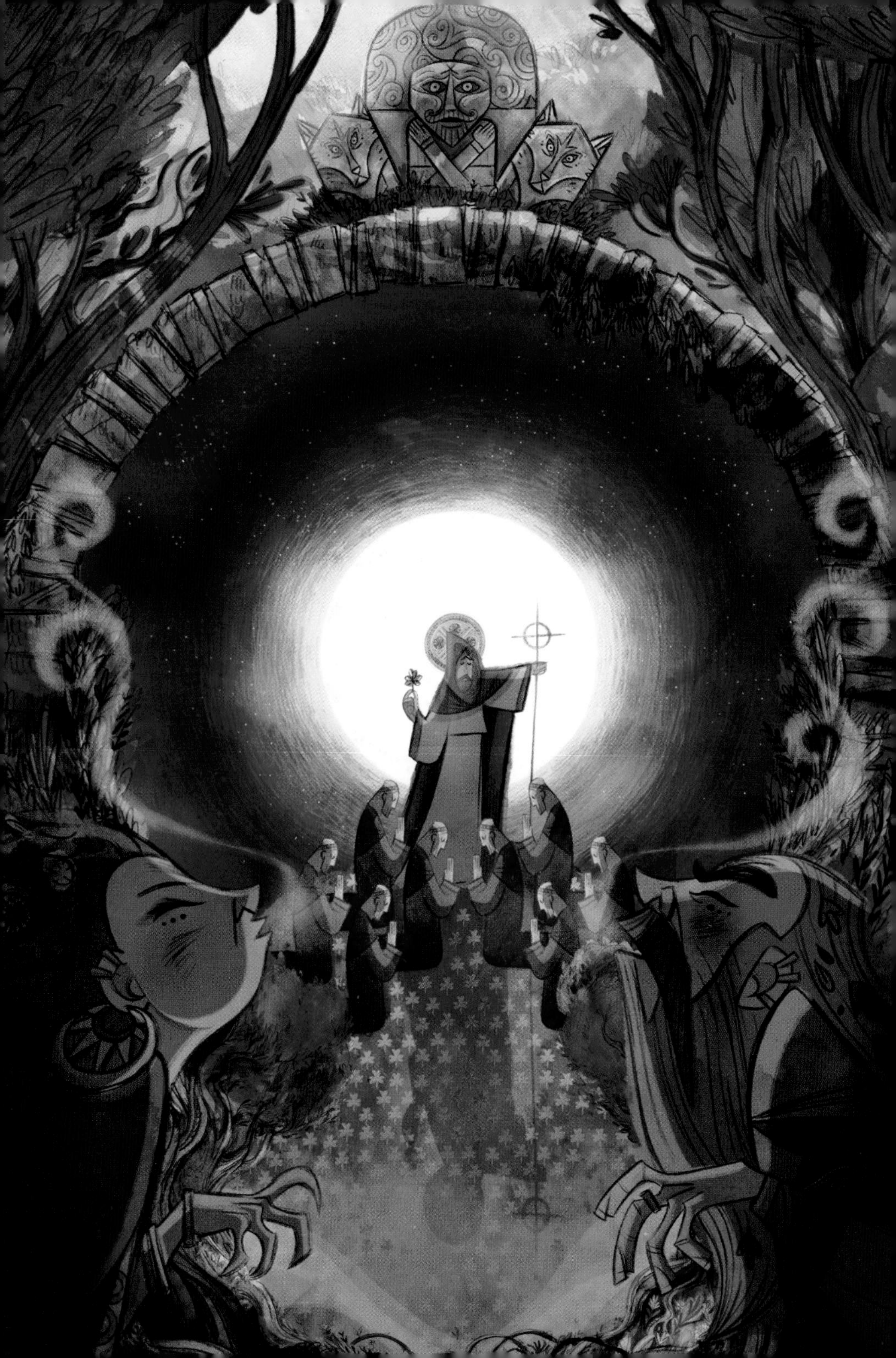

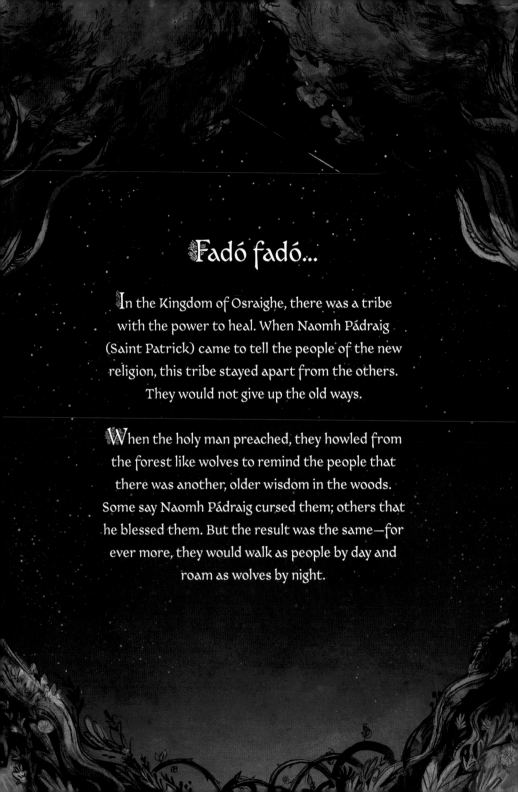

Fadó fadó...

In the Kingdom of Osraighe, there was a tribe
with the power to heal. When Naomh Pádraig
(Saint Patrick) came to tell the people of the new
religion, this tribe stayed apart from the others.
They would not give up the old ways.

When the holy man preached, they howled from
the forest like wolves to remind the people that
there was another, older wisdom in the woods.
Some say Naomh Pádraig cursed them; others that
he blessed them. But the result was the same—for
ever more, they would walk as people by day and
roam as wolves by night.

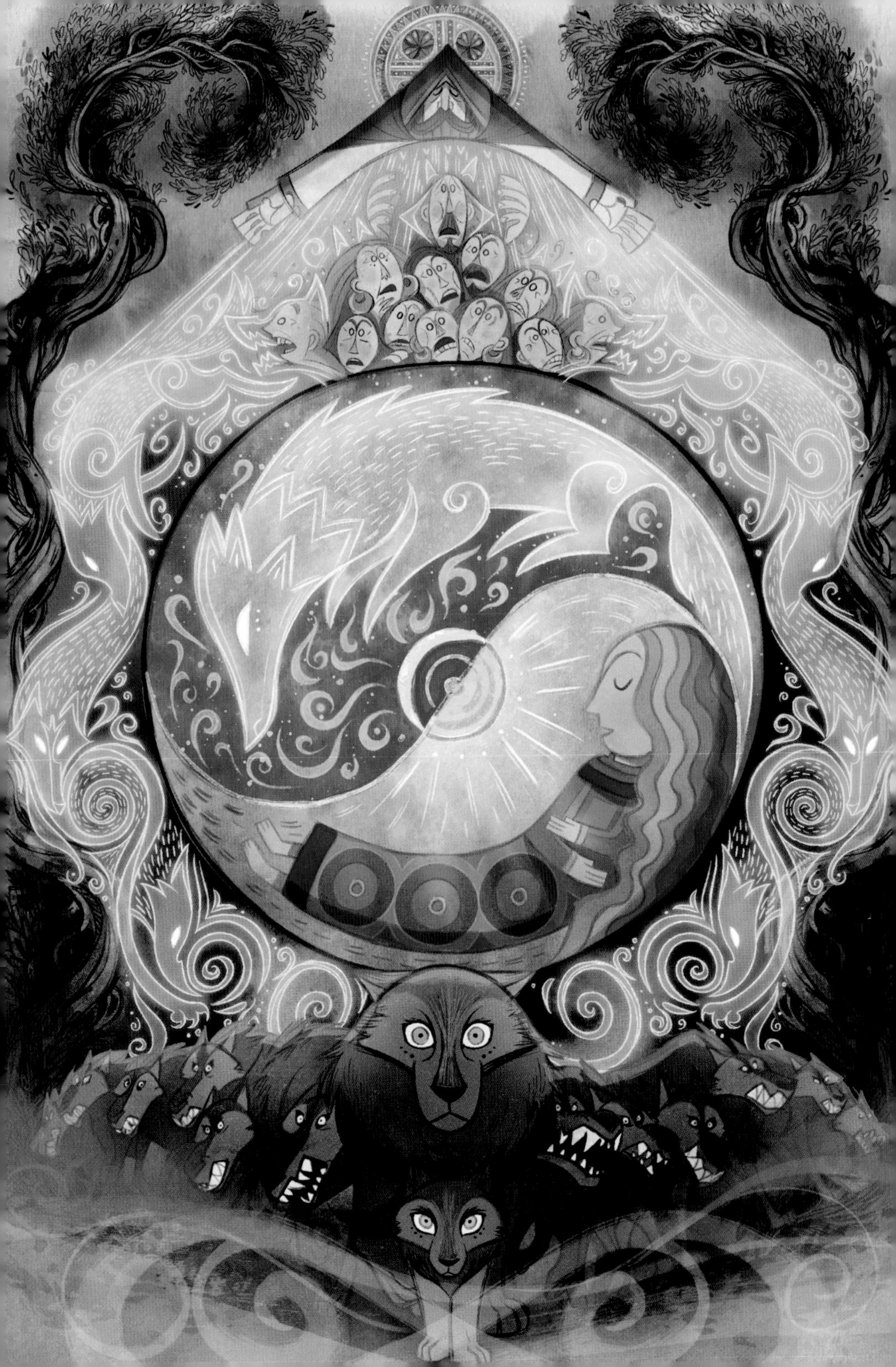

Leaving their human form behind, any harm or good that befell them as wolves, they felt in their waking form, too. They were a proud breed living with the wild wolves, keeping the peace between man and the wilderness.

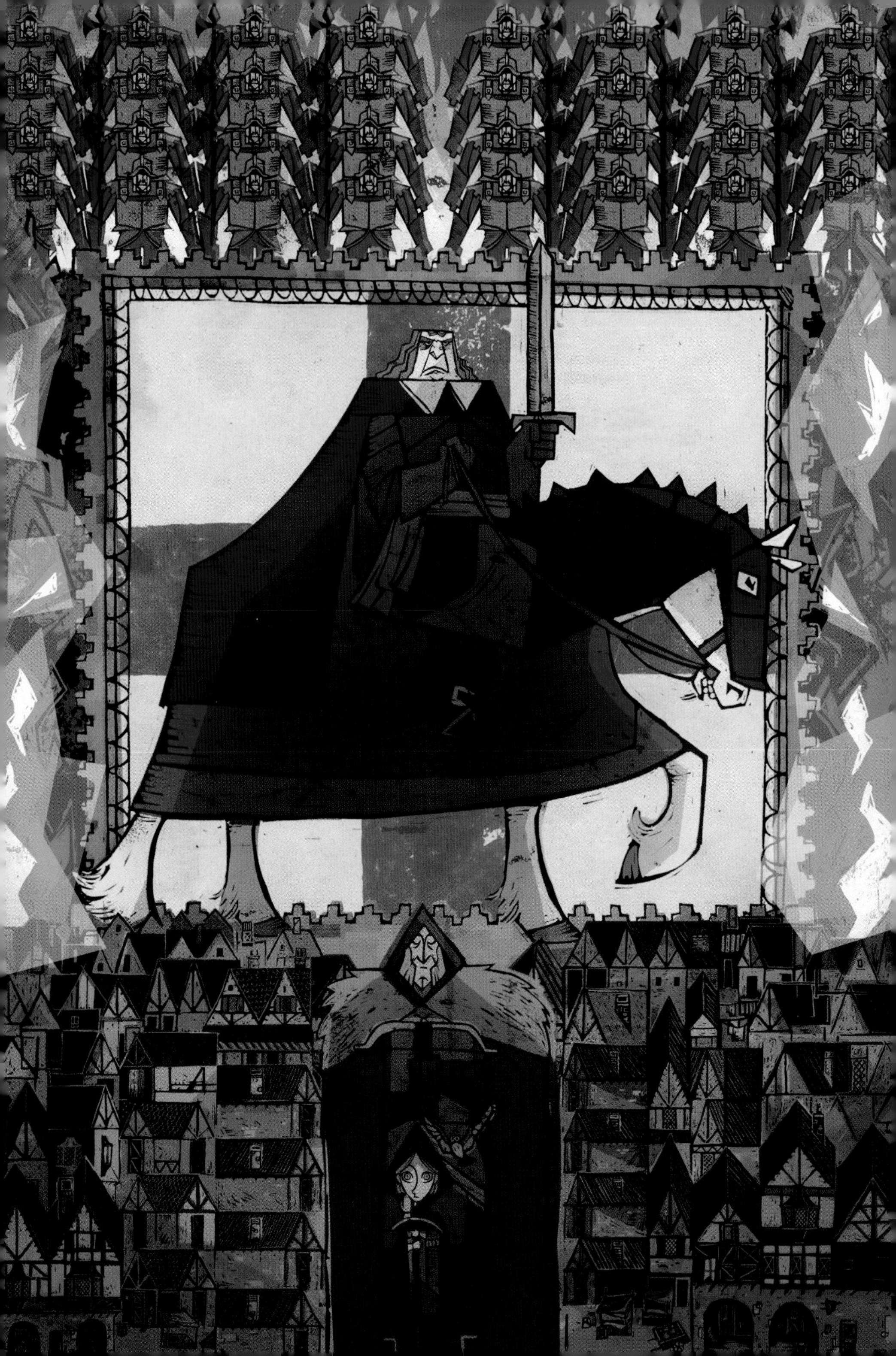

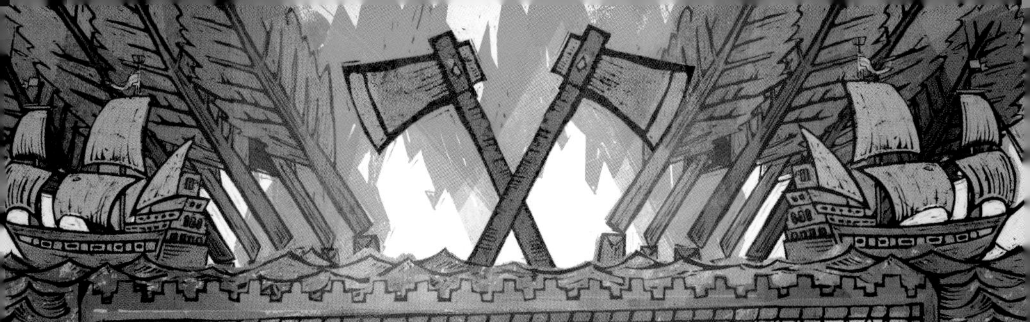

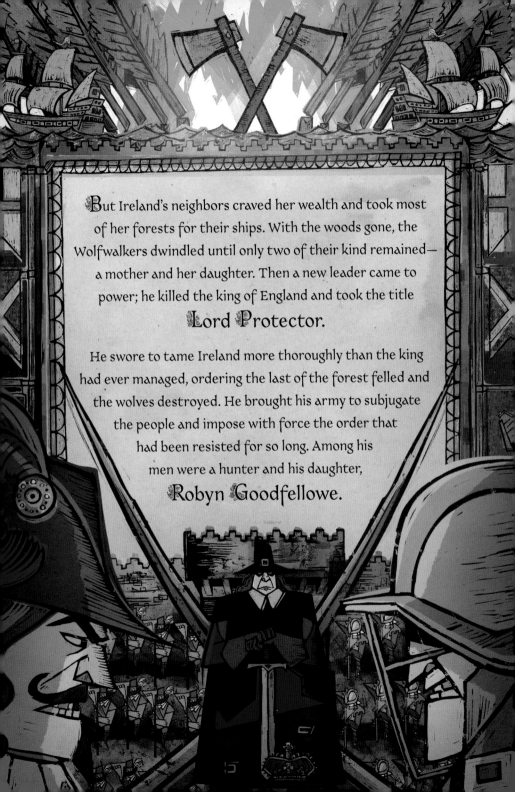

But Ireland's neighbors craved her wealth and took most of her forests for their ships. With the woods gone, the Wolfwalkers dwindled until only two of their kind remained—a mother and her daughter. Then a new leader came to power; he killed the king of England and took the title

Lord Protector.

He swore to tame Ireland more thoroughly than the king had ever managed, ordering the last of the forest felled and the wolves destroyed. He brought his army to subjugate the people and impose with force the order that had been resisted for so long. Among his men were a hunter and his daughter,

Robyn Goodfellowe.

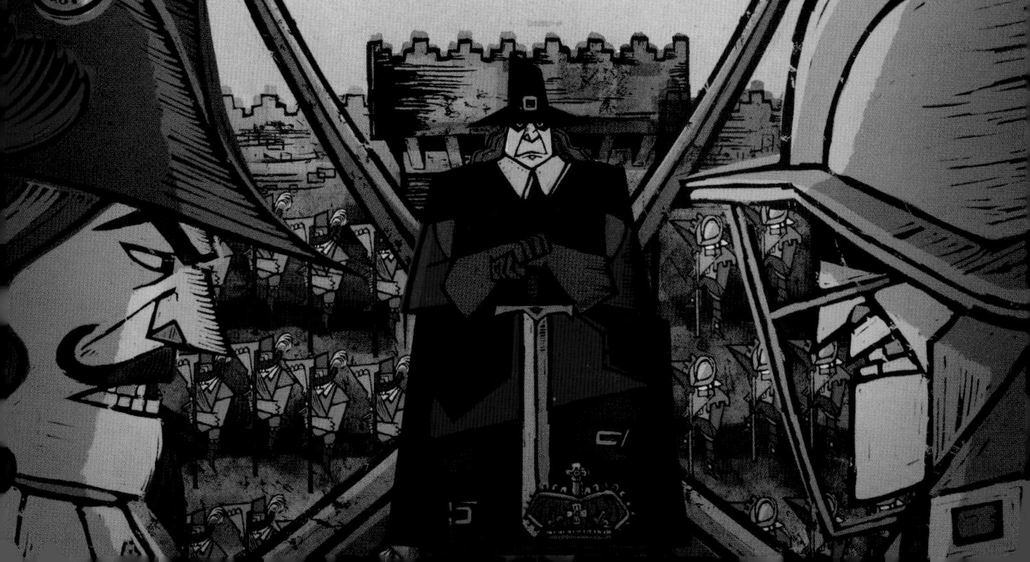

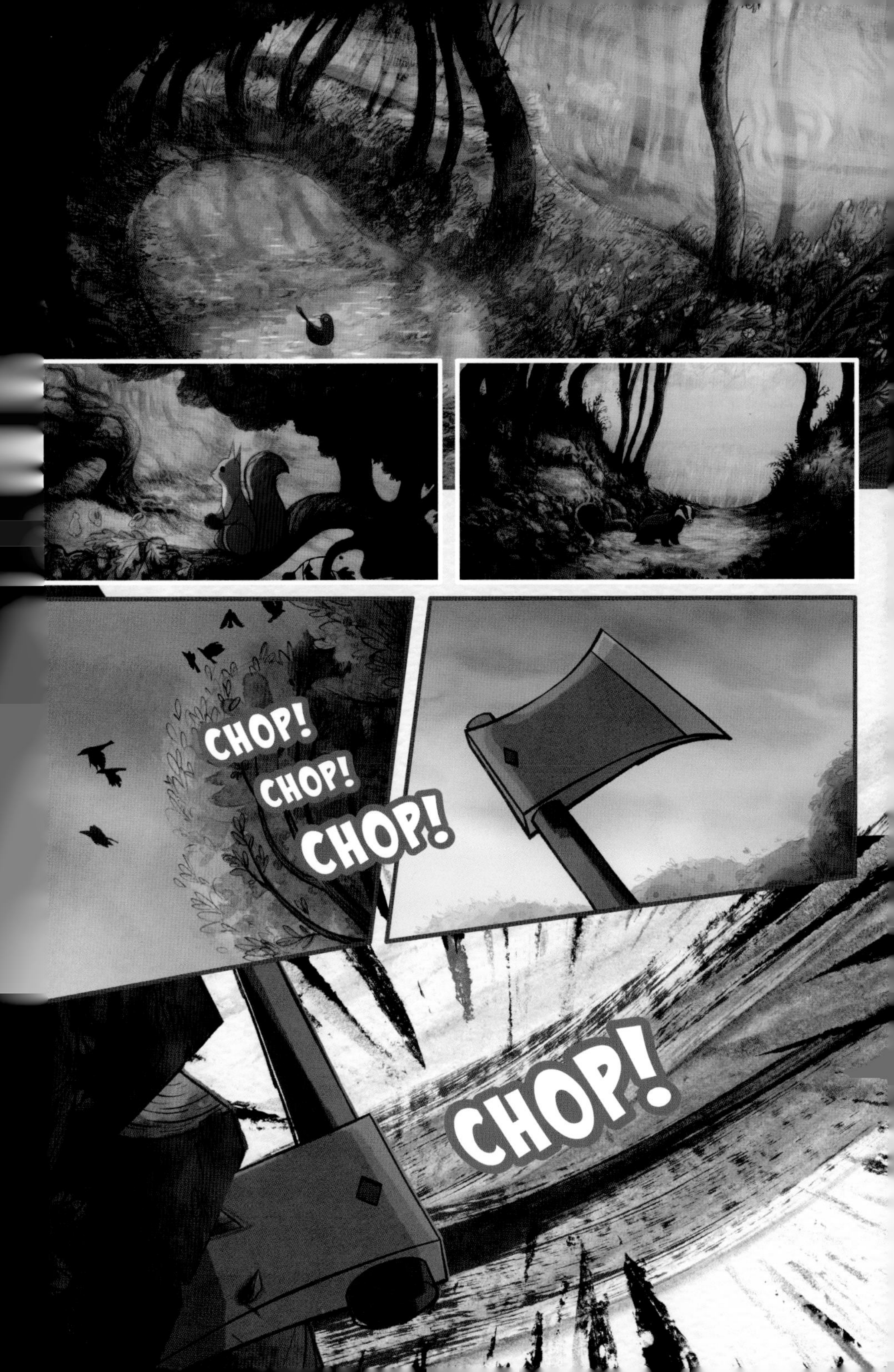
CHOP!
CHOP!
CHOP!
CHOP!

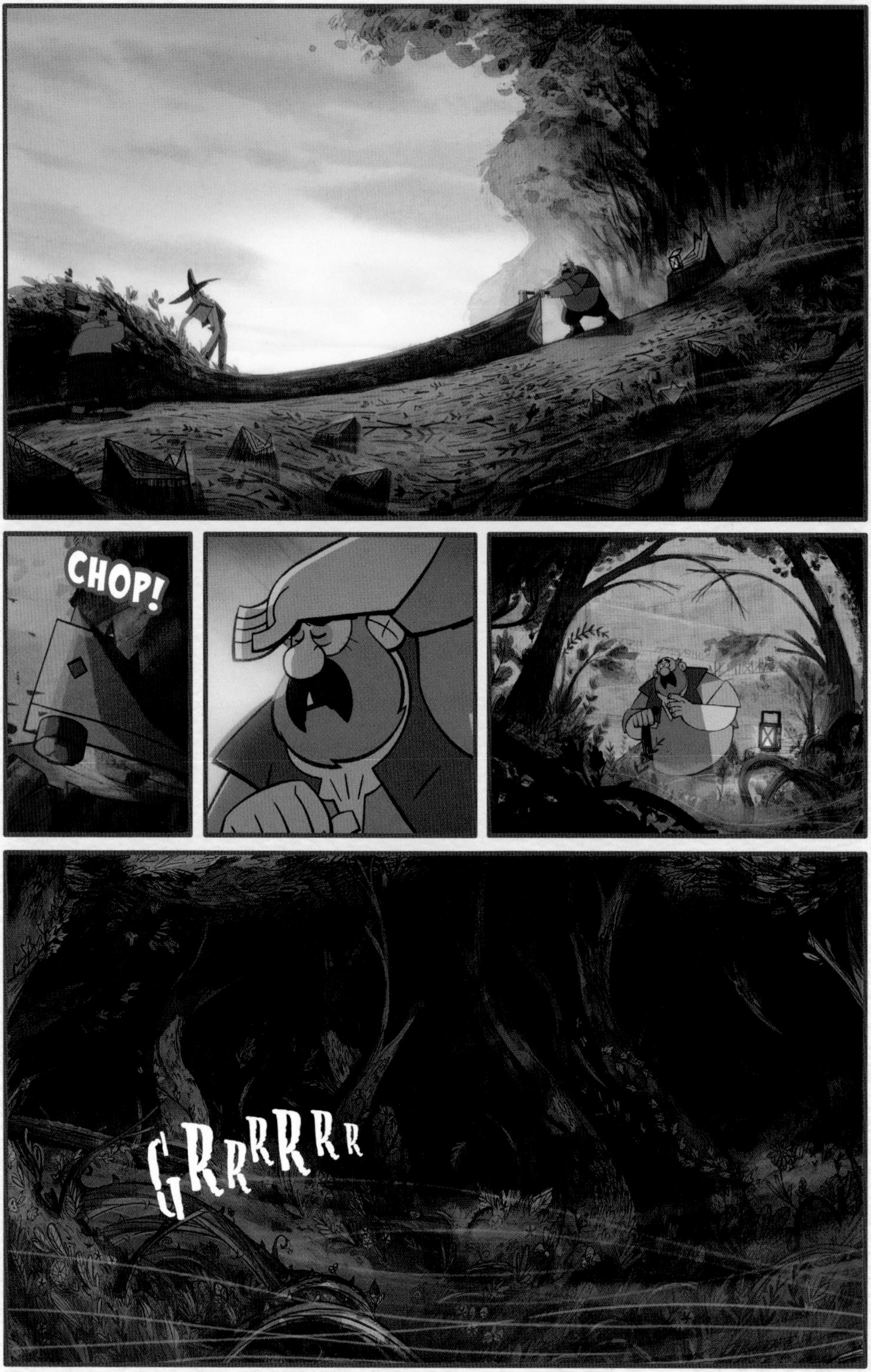
CHOP!
GRRRRRR

Huh?

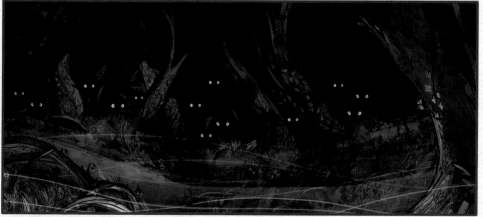

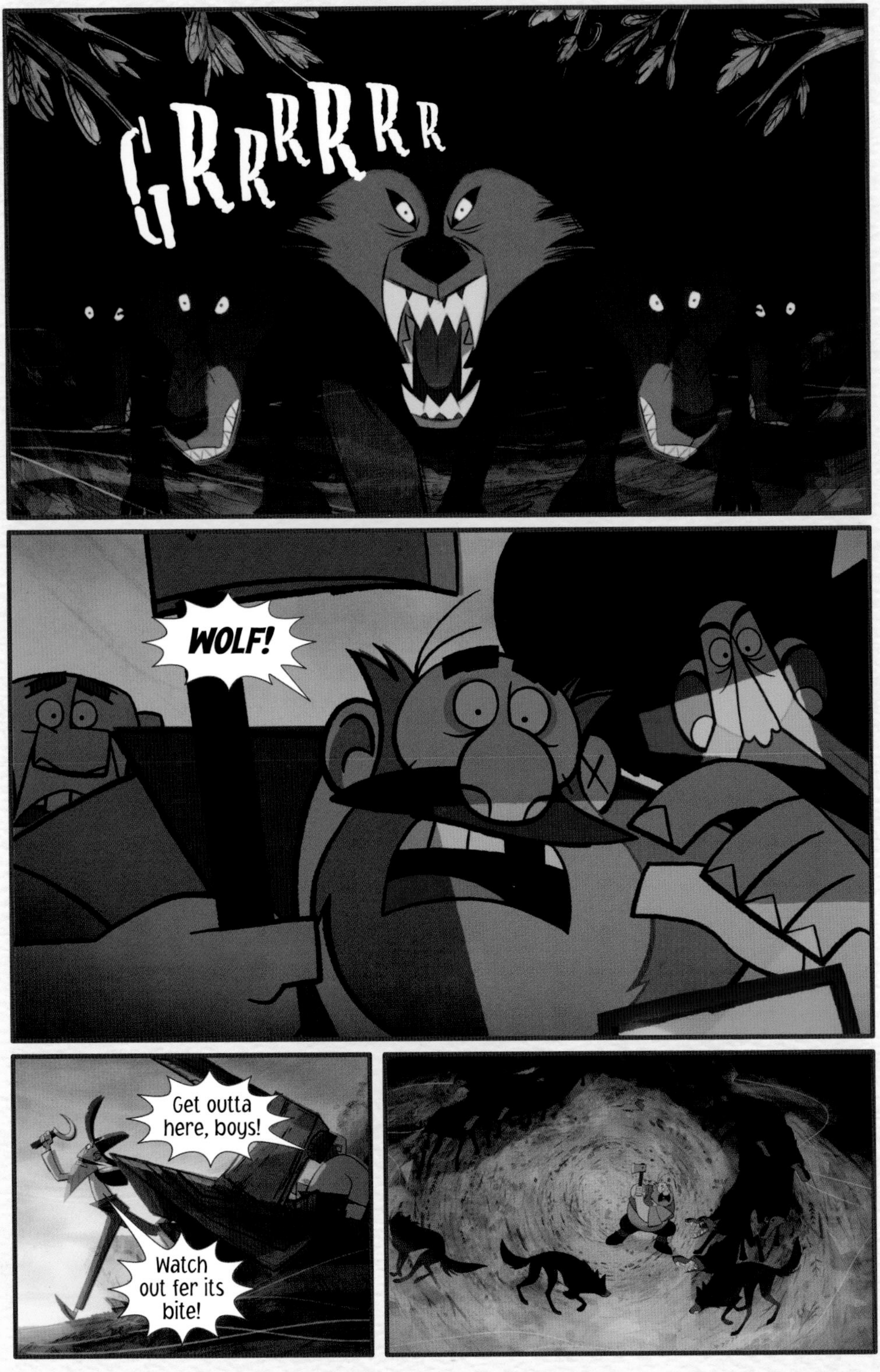
GRRRRRRR
WOLF!
Get outta here, boys!
Watch out fer its bite!

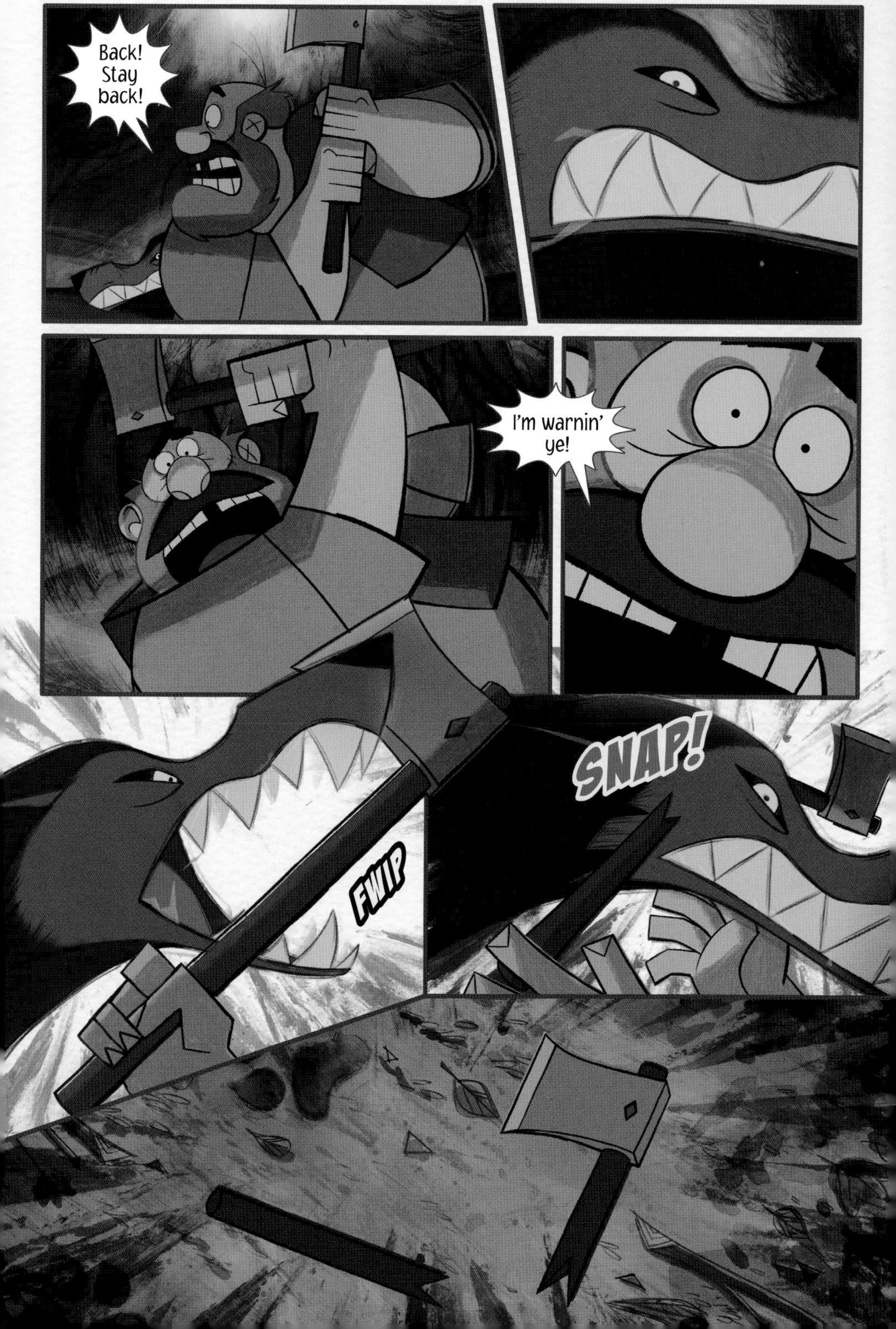
Back! Stay back!
I'm warnin' ye!
FWIP
SNAP!

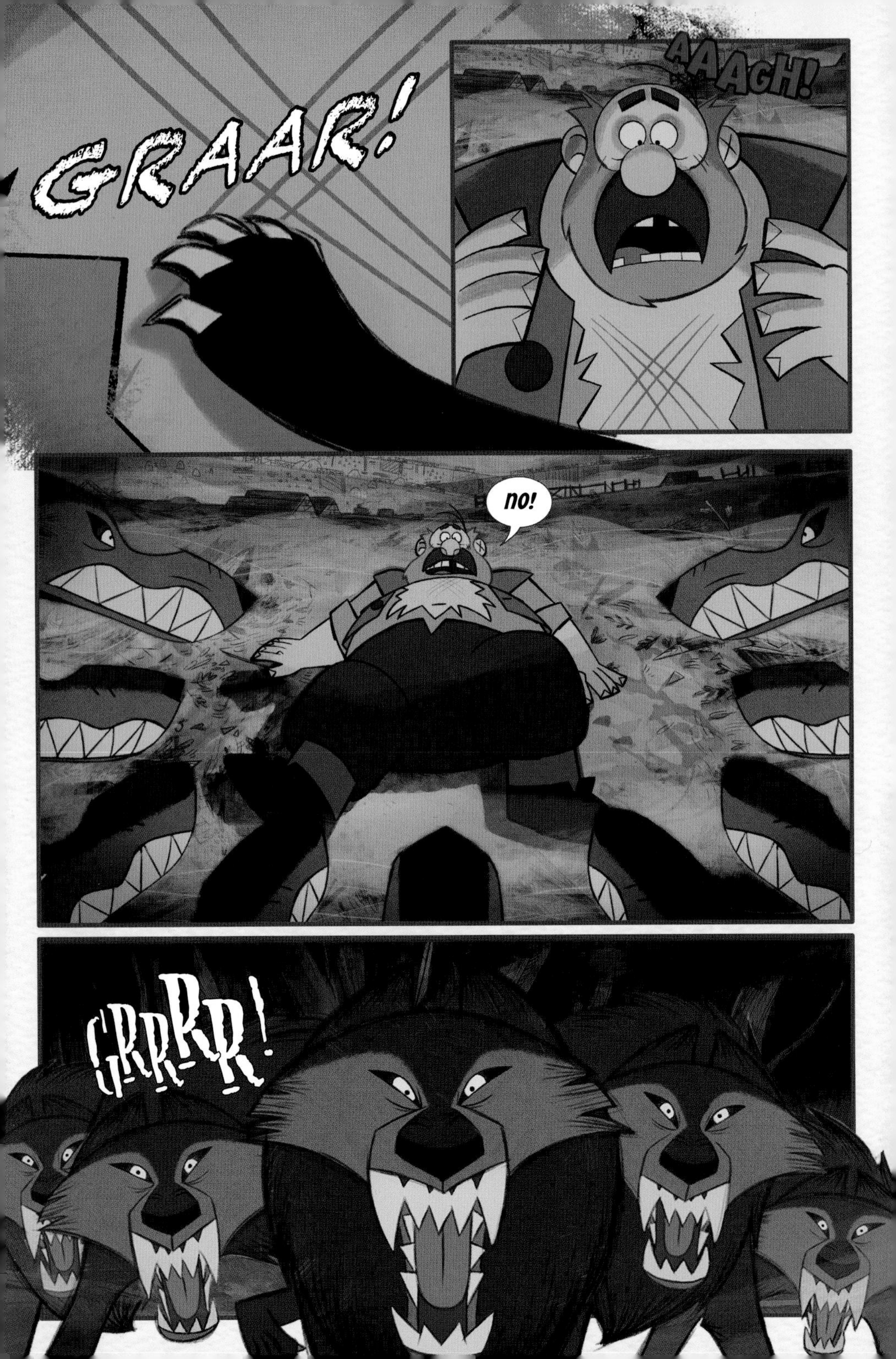
GRAAR!
AAAGH!
no!
GRRRR!

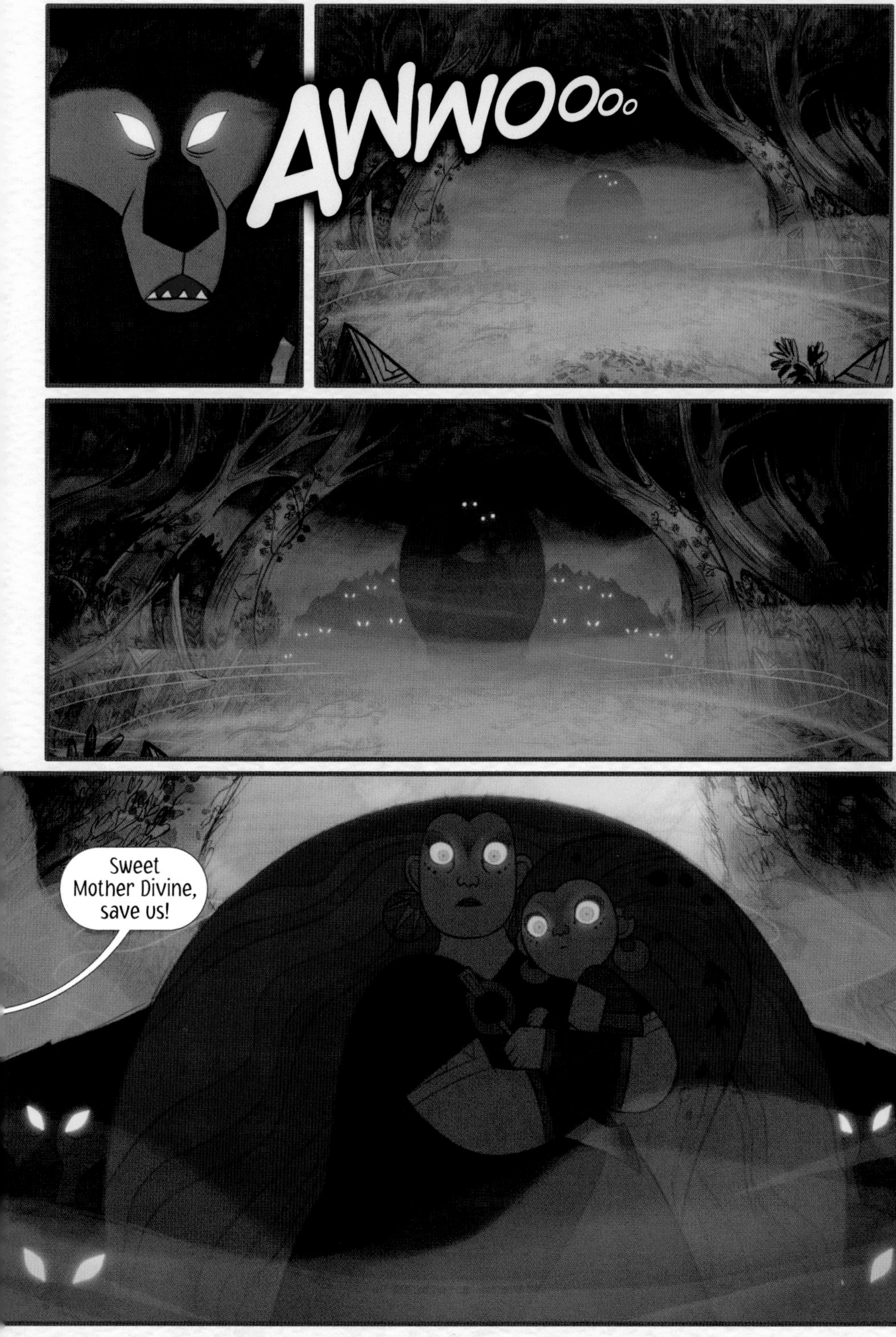
AWWOooo
Sweet Mother Divine, save us!

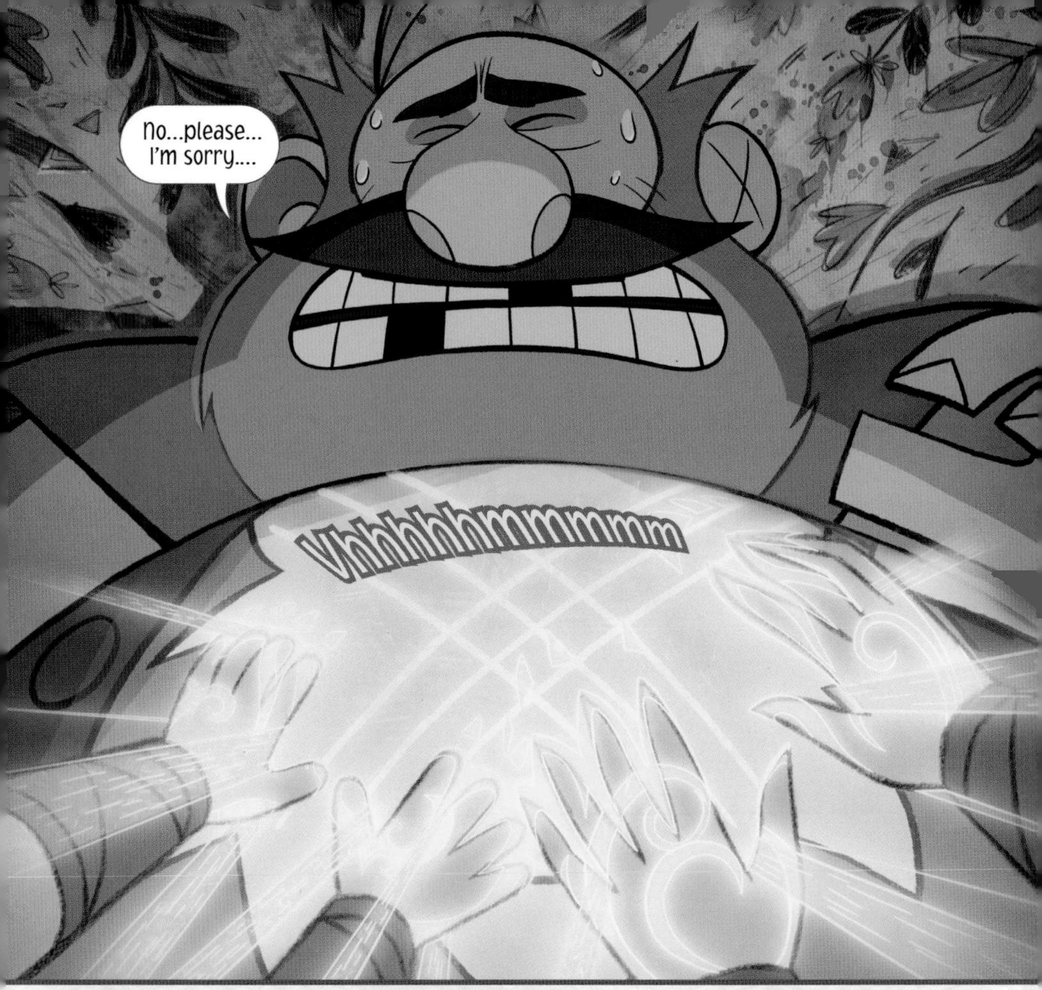
No...please...
I'm sorry....
VHHHHMMMMMM
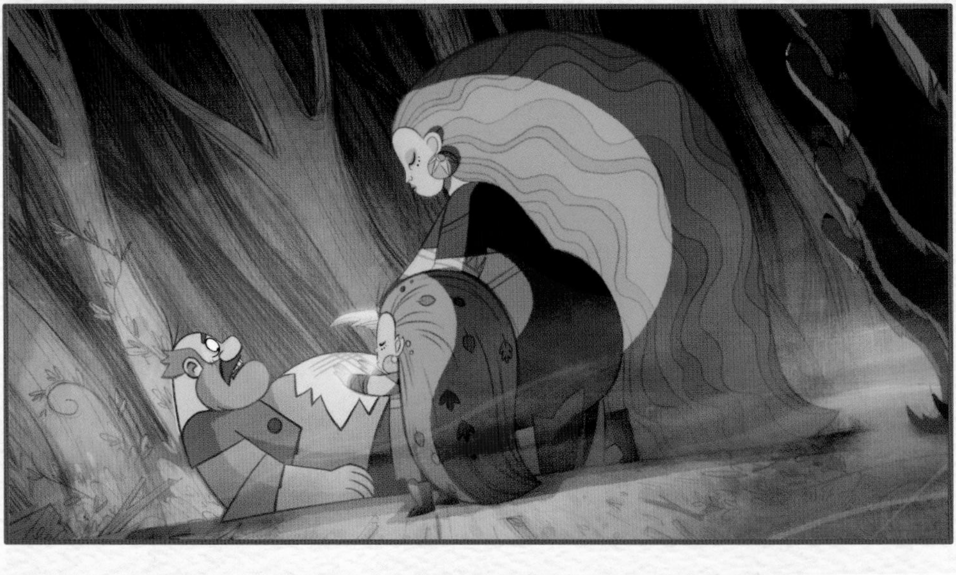

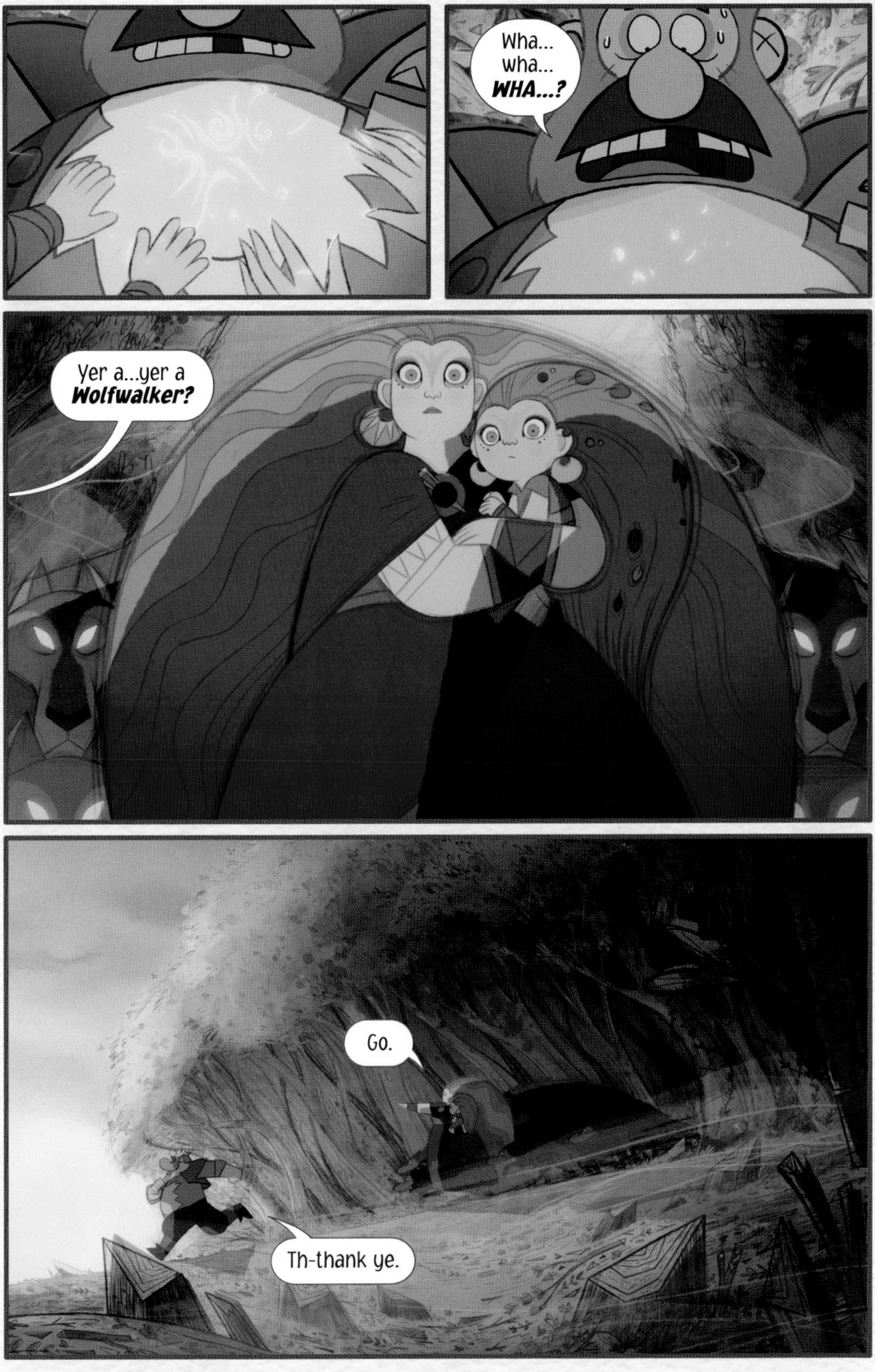
Wha...
wha...
WHA...?
Yer a...yer a **Wolfwalker?**
Go.
Th-thank ye.

BA-BONG!

BA-BONG!

They won't stop, love...these new invaders.

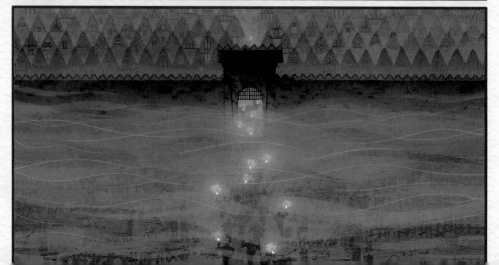

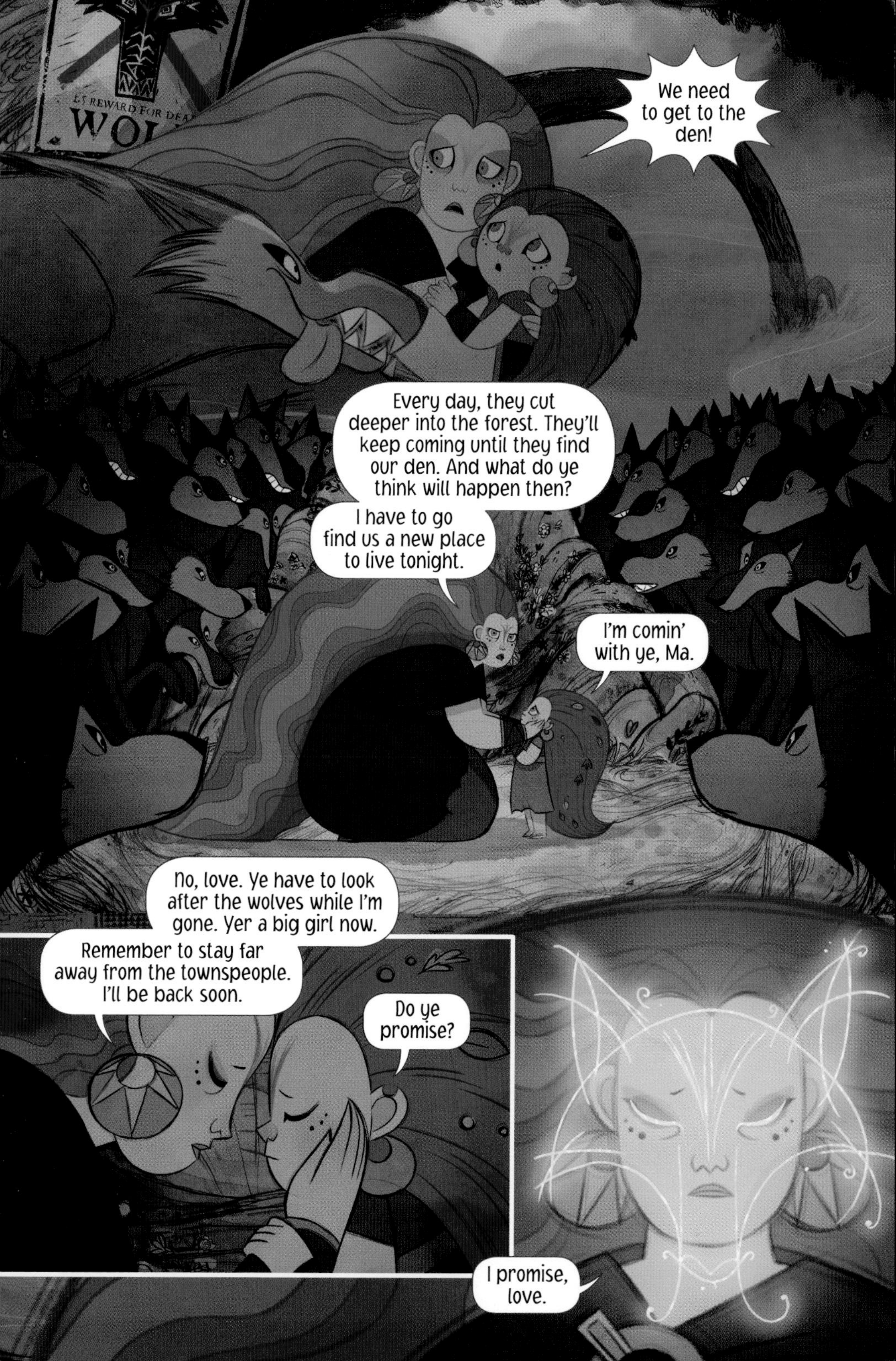
£5 REWARD FOR DEA
WOL
We need to get to the den!
Every day, they cut deeper into the forest. They'll keep coming until they find our den. And what do ye think will happen then?
I have to go find us a new place to live tonight.
I'm comin' with ye, Ma.
No, love. Ye have to look after the wolves while I'm gone. Yer a big girl now.
Remember to stay far away from the townspeople. I'll be back soon.
Do ye promise?
I promise, love.

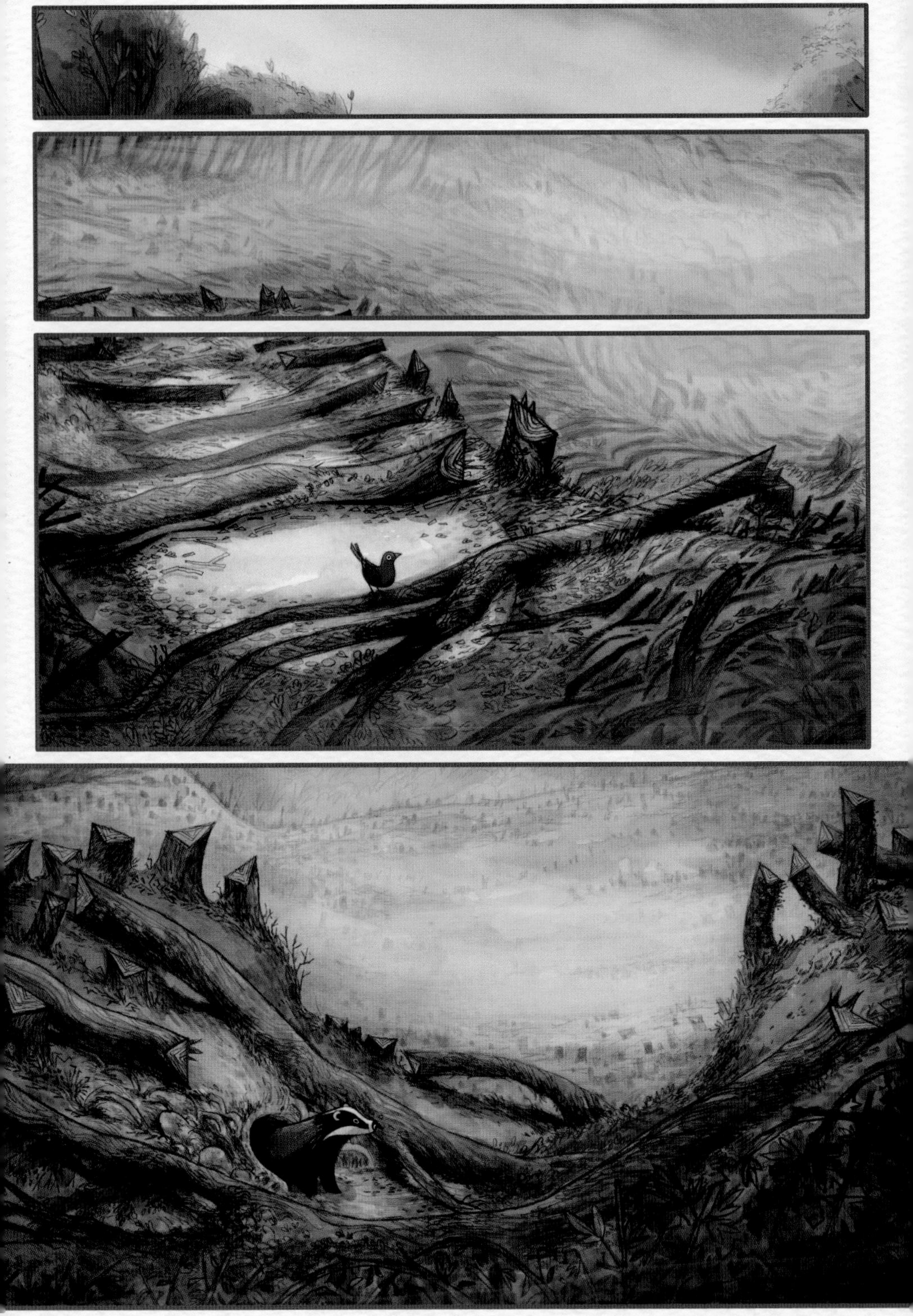

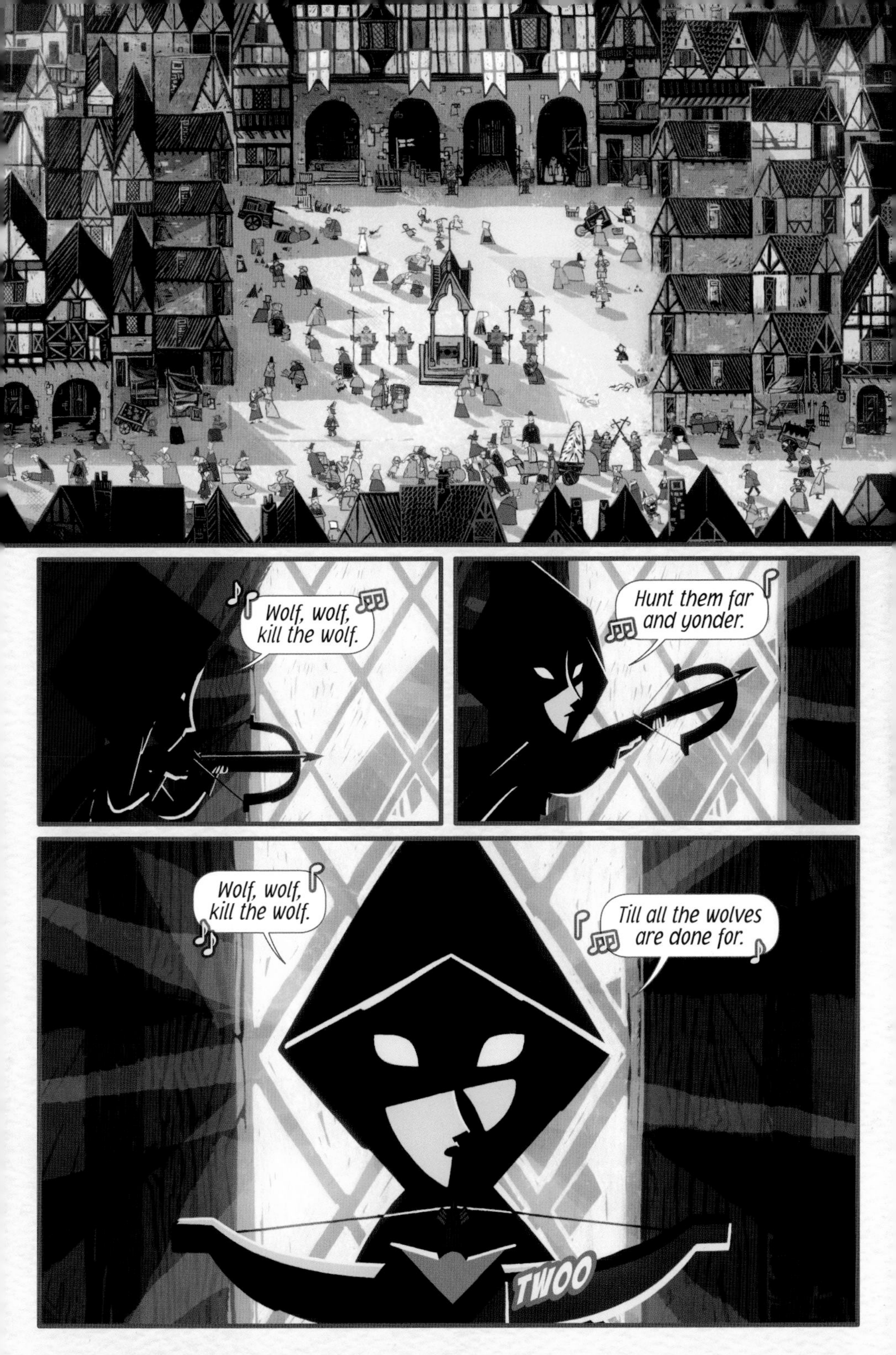
Wolf, wolf, kill the wolf.
Hunt them far and yonder.
Wolf, wolf, kill the wolf.
Till all the wolves are done for.
TWOO

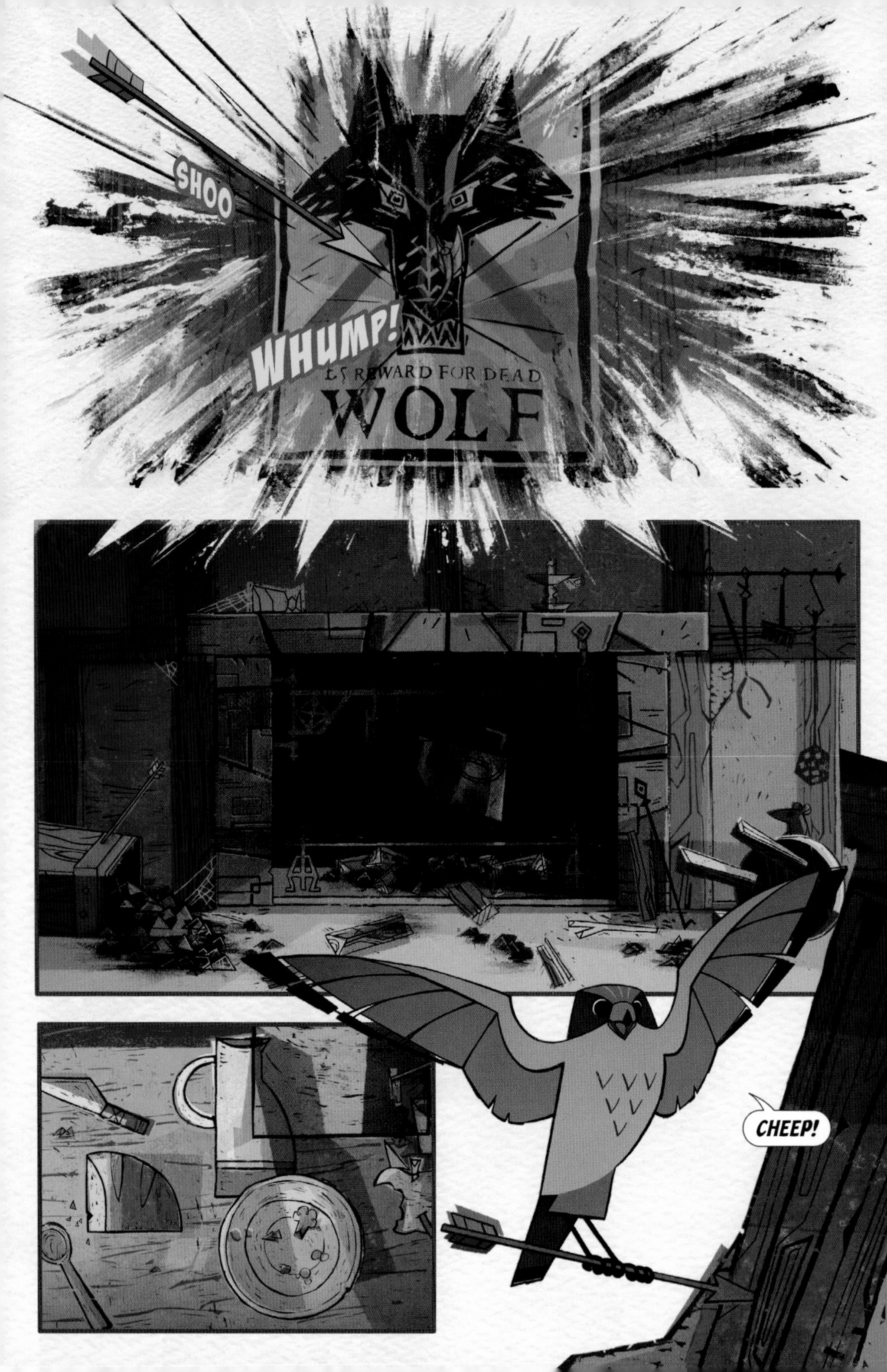
SHOO
WHUMP!
£5 REWARD FOR DEAD
WOLF
CHEEP!

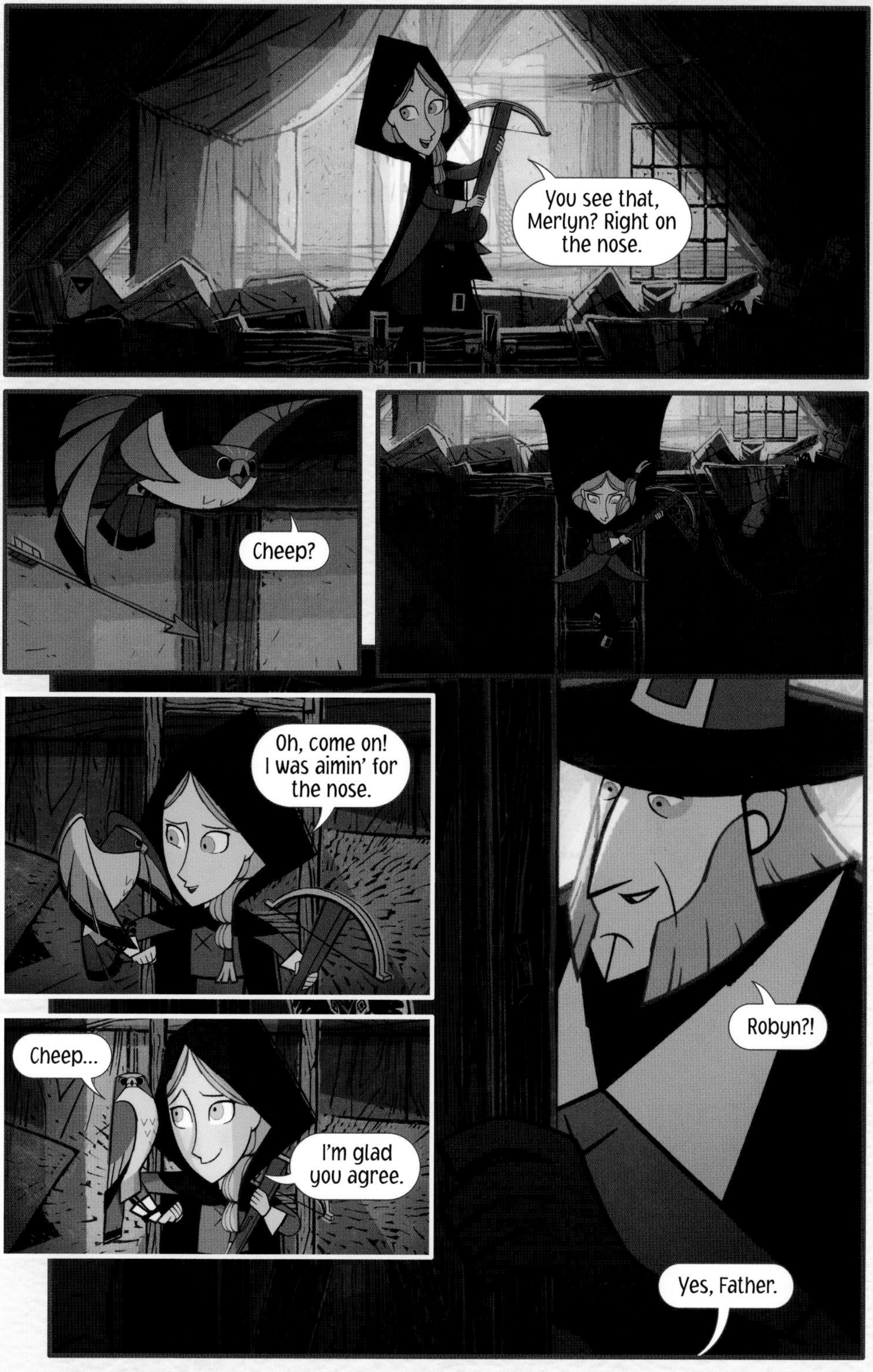
You see that, Merlyn? Right on the nose.
Cheep?
Oh, come on! I was aimin' for the nose.
Cheep...
I'm glad you agree.
Robyn?!
Yes, Father.

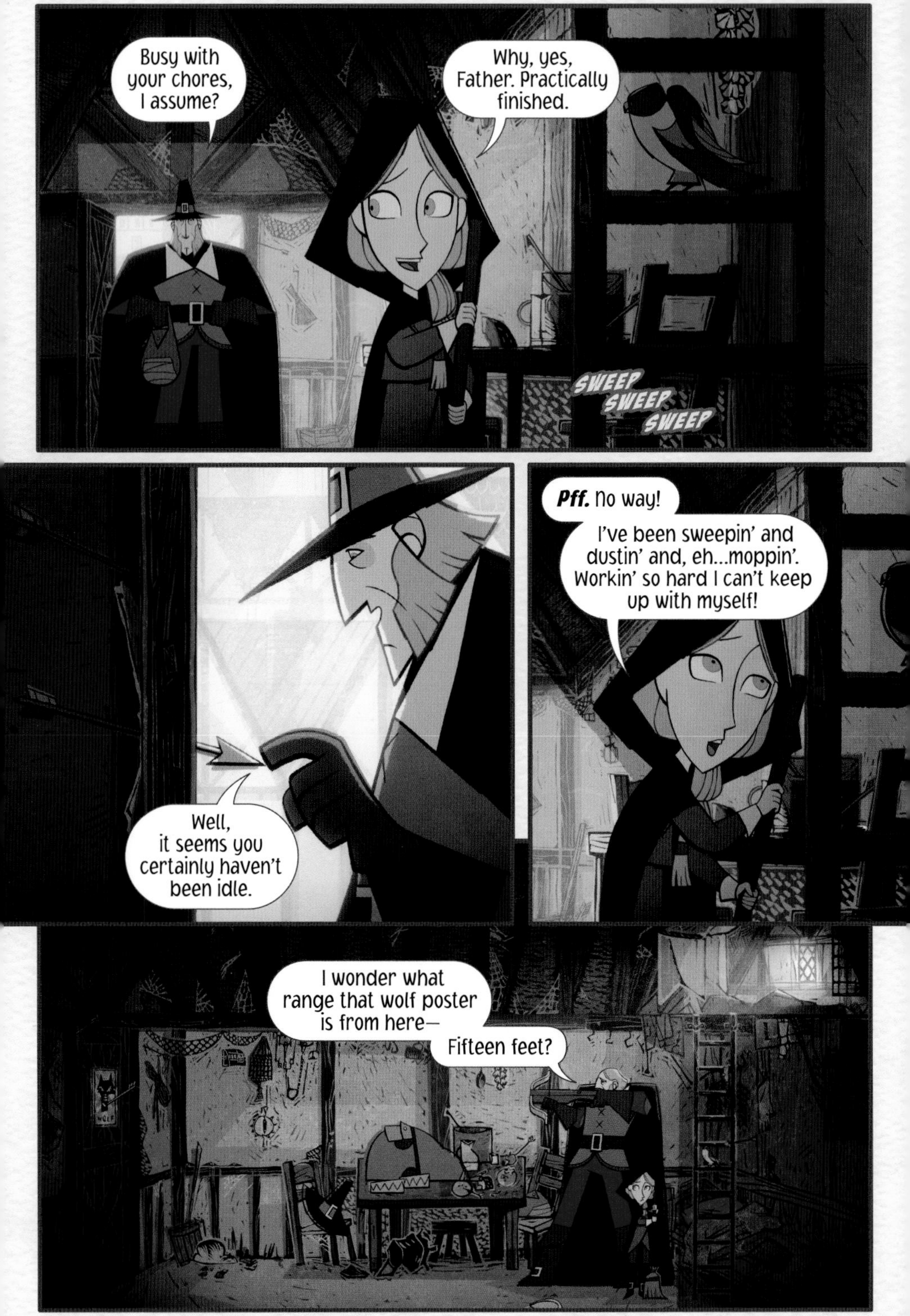
Busy with your chores, I assume?
Why, yes, Father. Practically finished.
SWEEP SWEEP SWEEP
Pff. No way!
I've been sweepin' and dustin' and, eh...moppin'. Workin' so hard I can't keep up with myself!
Well, it seems you certainly haven't been idle.
I wonder what range that wolf poster is from here—
Fifteen feet?
WOLF

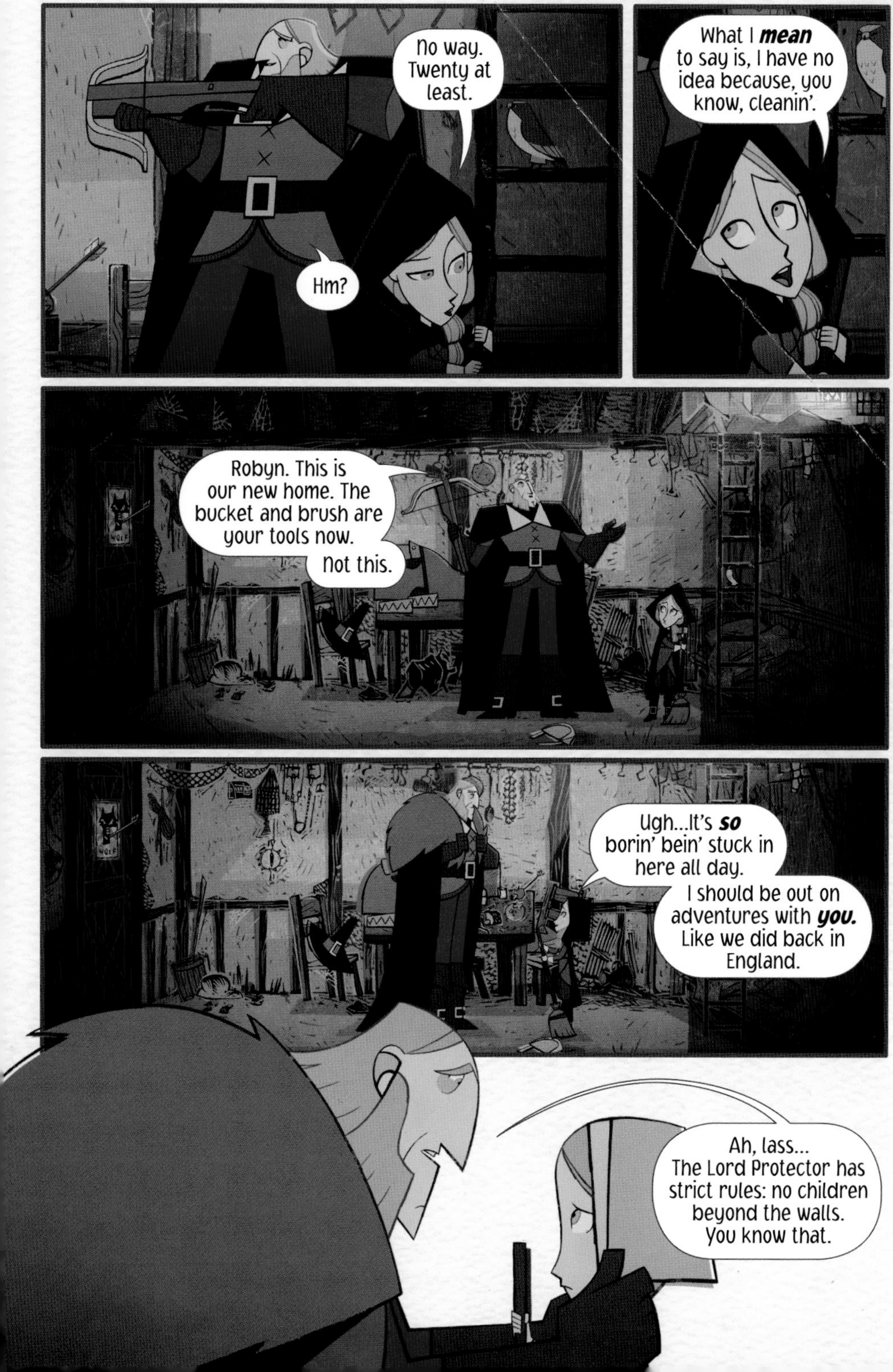
No way. Twenty at least.
Hm?
What I ***mean*** to say is, I have no idea because, you know, cleanin'.
Robyn. This is our new home. The bucket and brush are your tools now.
Not this.
WOLF
Ugh...It's ***so*** borin' bein' stuck in here all day.
I should be out on adventures with ***you.*** Like we did back in England.
Ah, lass... The Lord Protector has strict rules: no children beyond the walls. You know that.

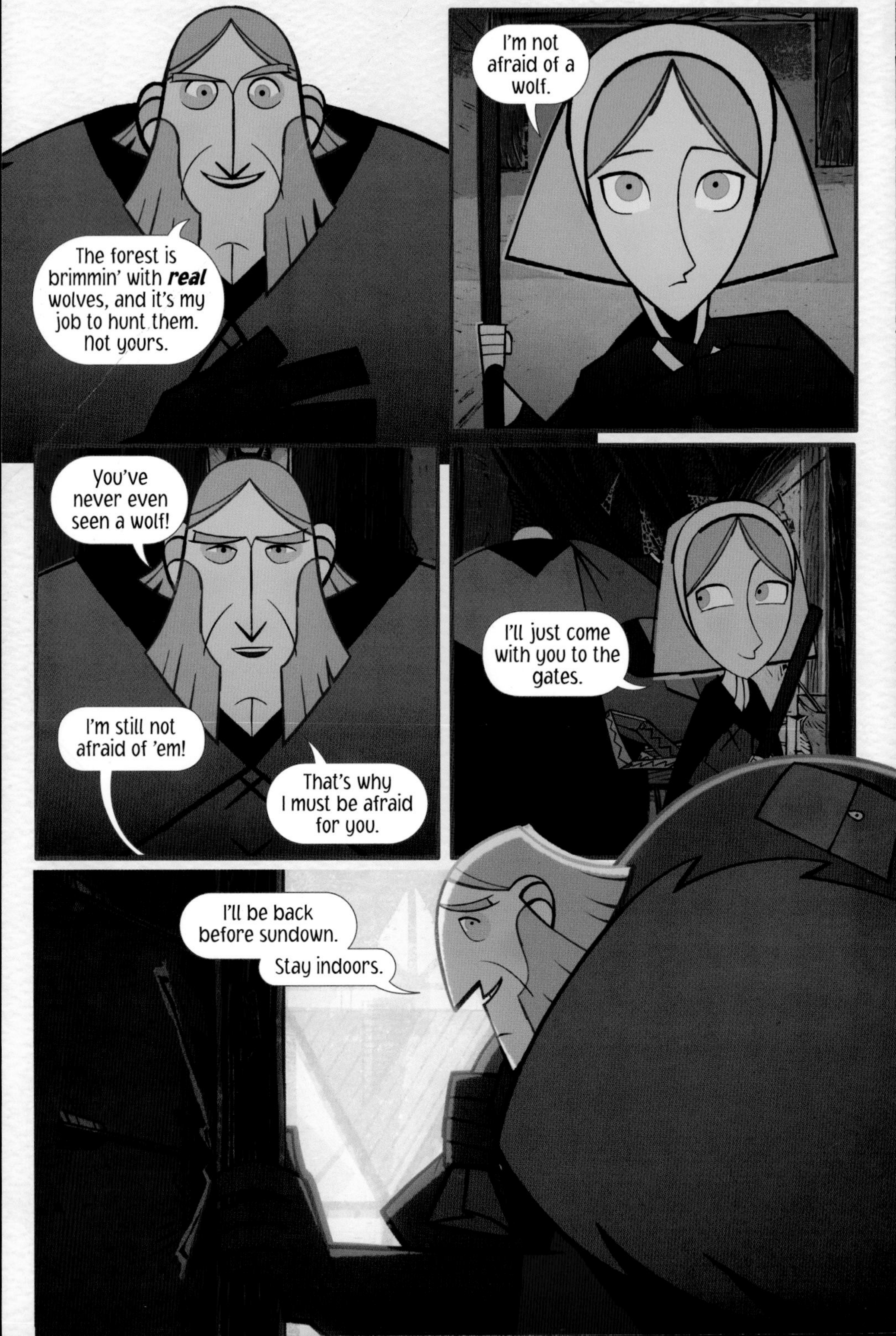
The forest is brimmin' with ***real*** wolves, and it's my job to hunt them. Not yours.
I'm not afraid of a wolf.
You've never even seen a wolf!
I'm still not afraid of 'em!
That's why I must be afraid for you.
I'll just come with you to the gates.
I'll be back before sundown.
Stay indoors.

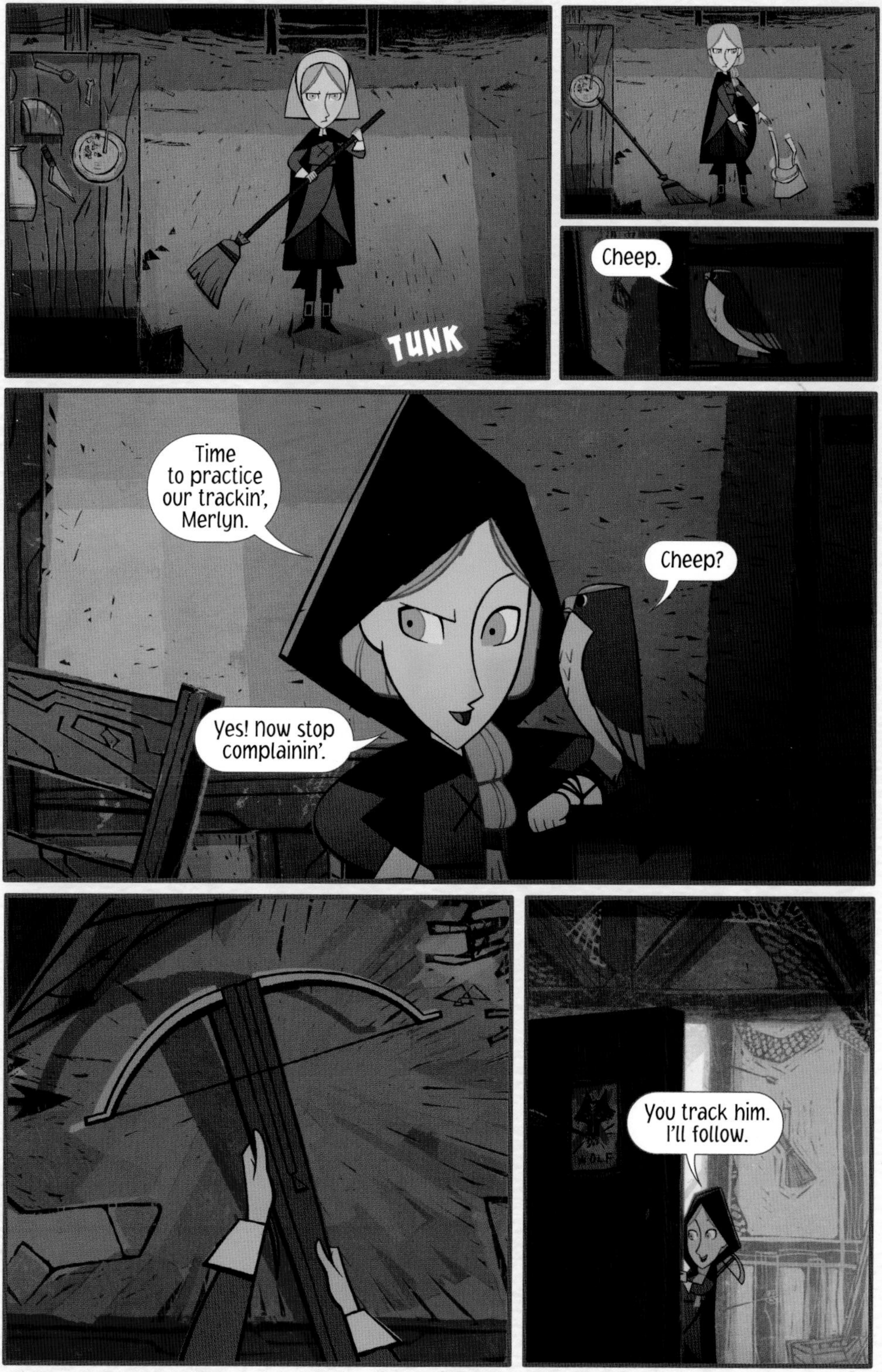
TUNK
Cheep.
Time to practice our trackin', Merlyn.
Cheep?
Yes! Now stop complainin'.
You track him. I'll follow.

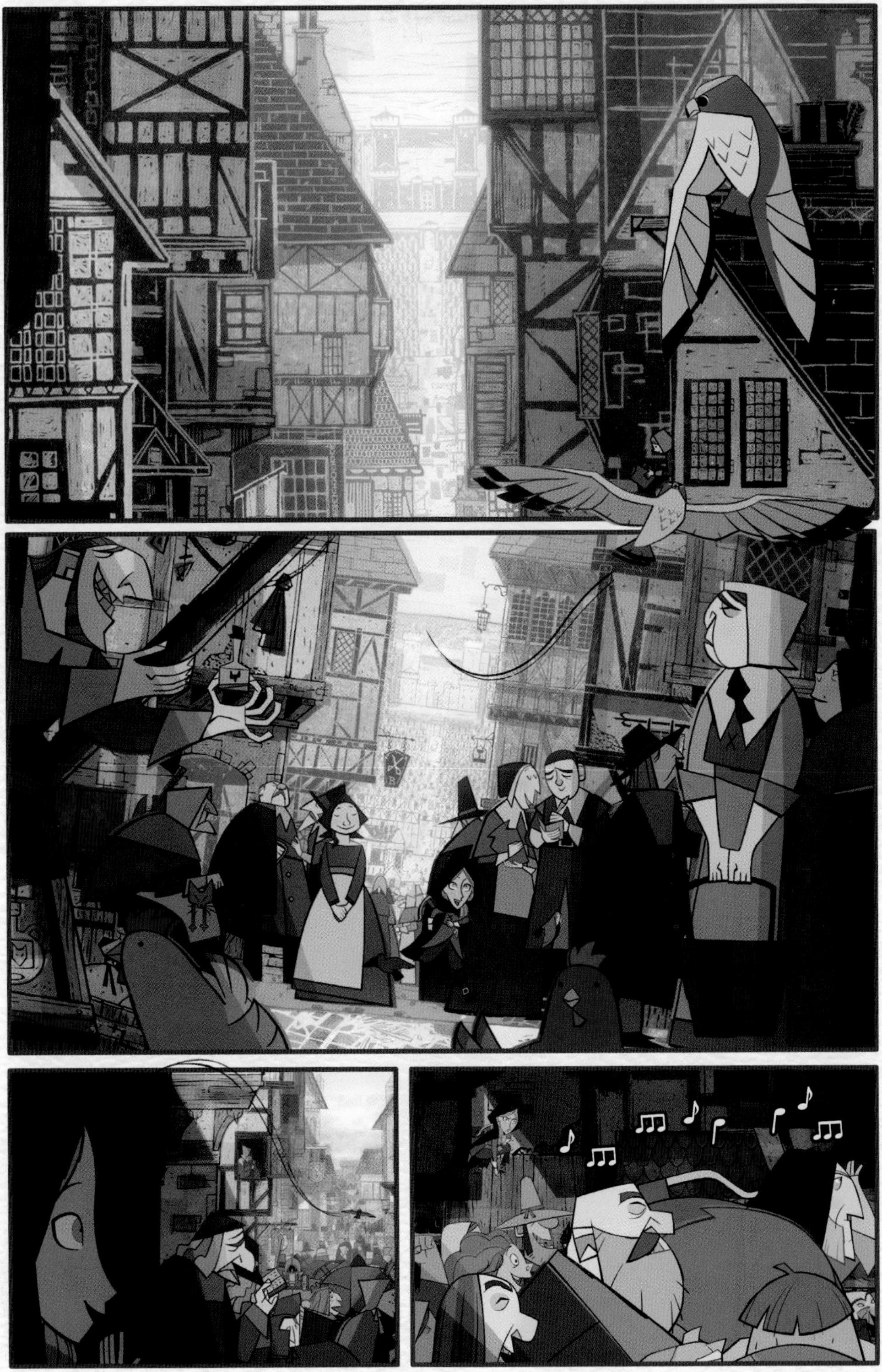

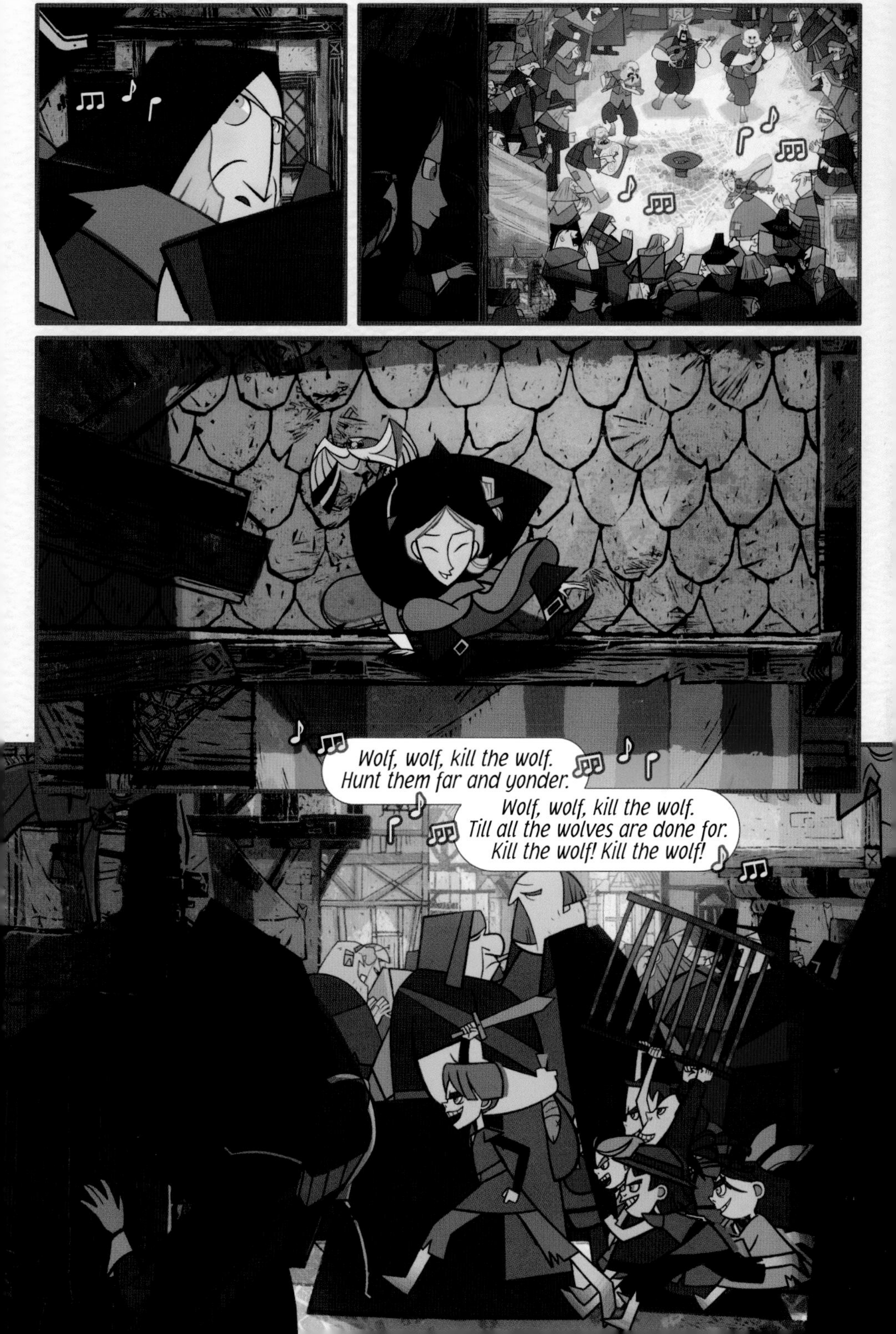
Wolf, wolf, kill the wolf.
Hunt them far and yonder.
Wolf, wolf, kill the wolf.
Till all the wolves are done for.
Kill the wolf! Kill the wolf!

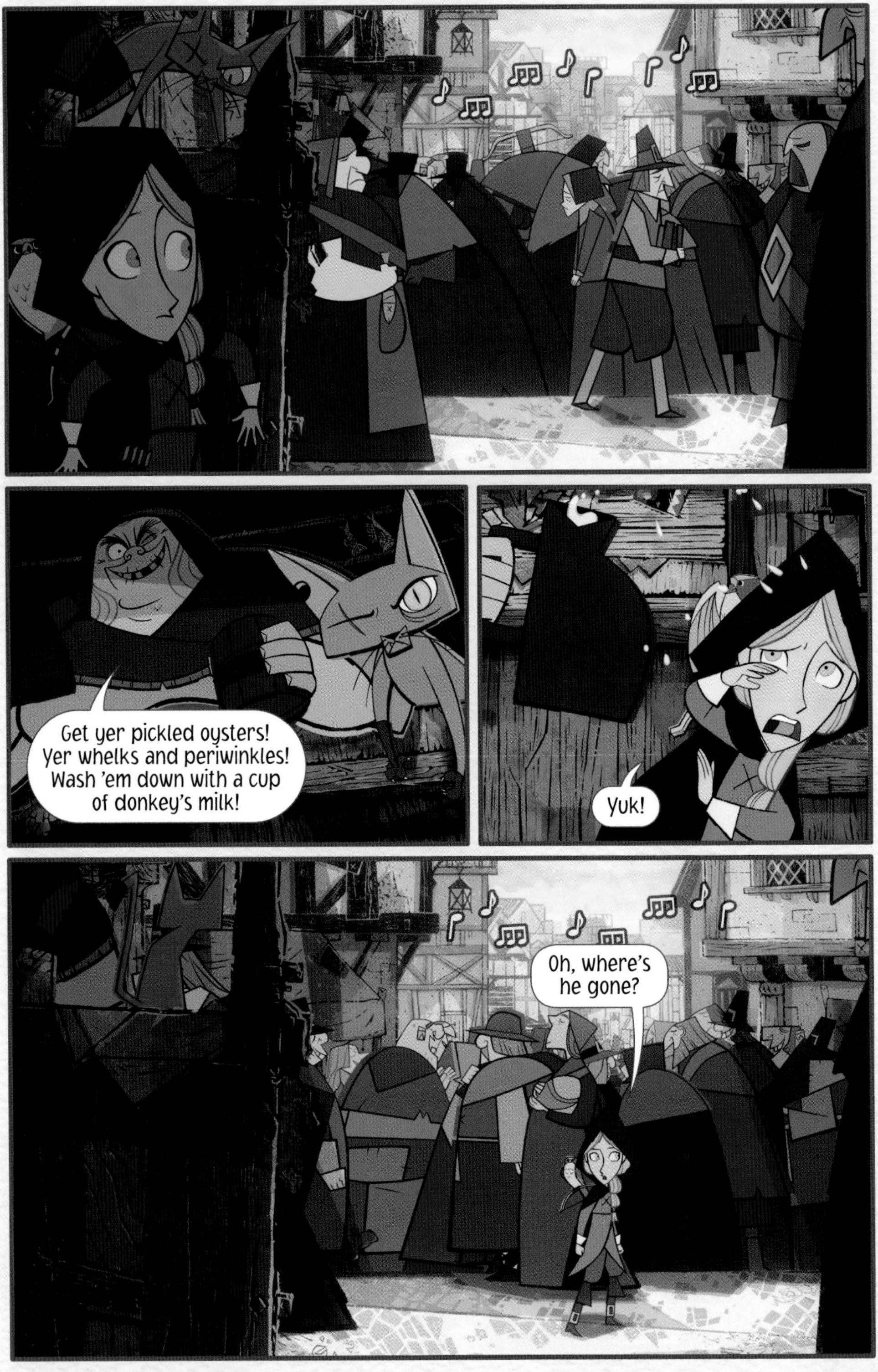
Get yer pickled oysters! Yer whelks and periwinkles! Wash 'em down with a cup of donkey's milk!
Yuk!
Oh, where's he gone?

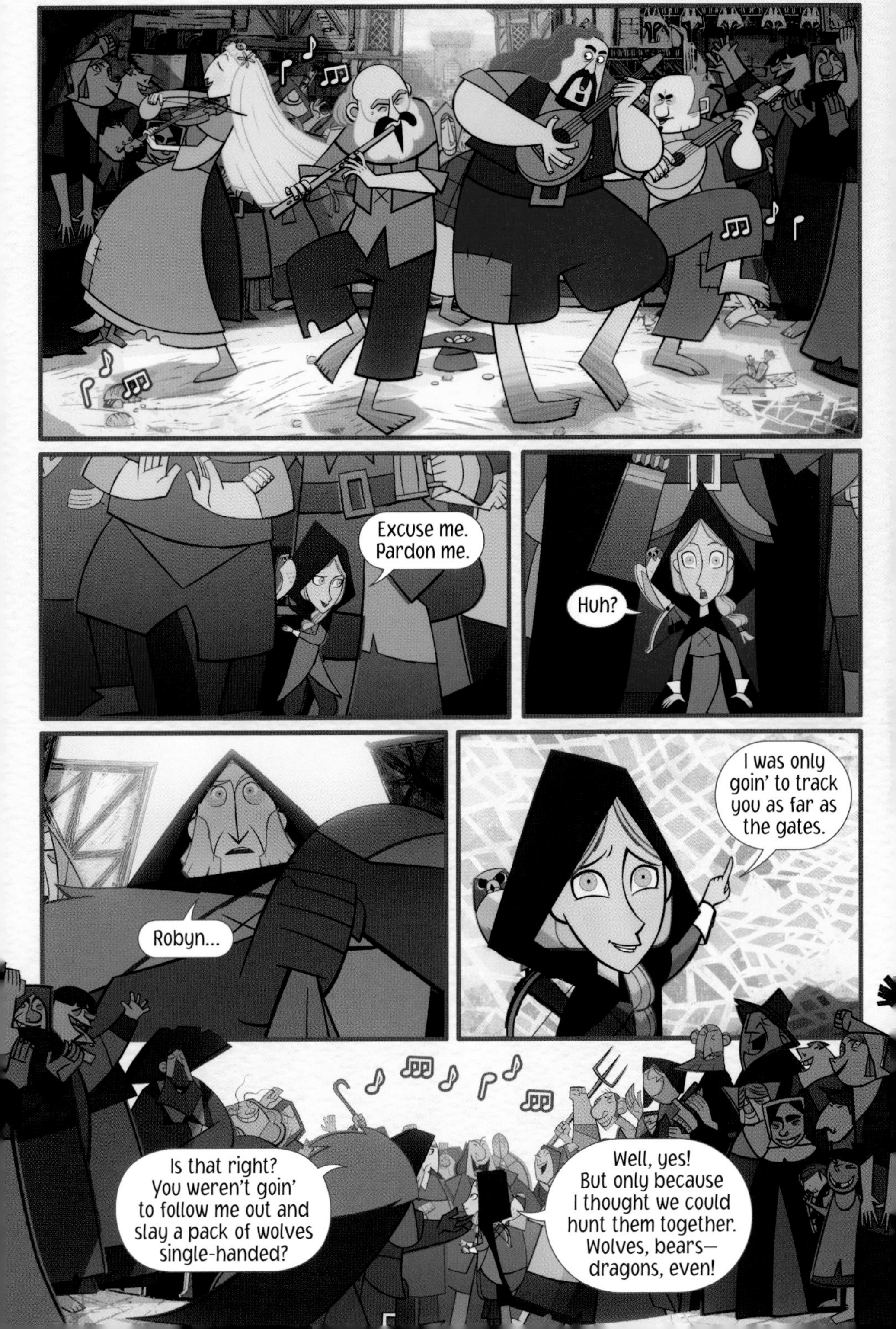
Excuse me. Pardon me.
Huh?
Robyn...
I was only goin' to track you as far as the gates.
Is that right? You weren't goin' to follow me out and slay a pack of wolves single-handed?
Well, yes! But only because I thought we could hunt them together. Wolves, bears—dragons, even!

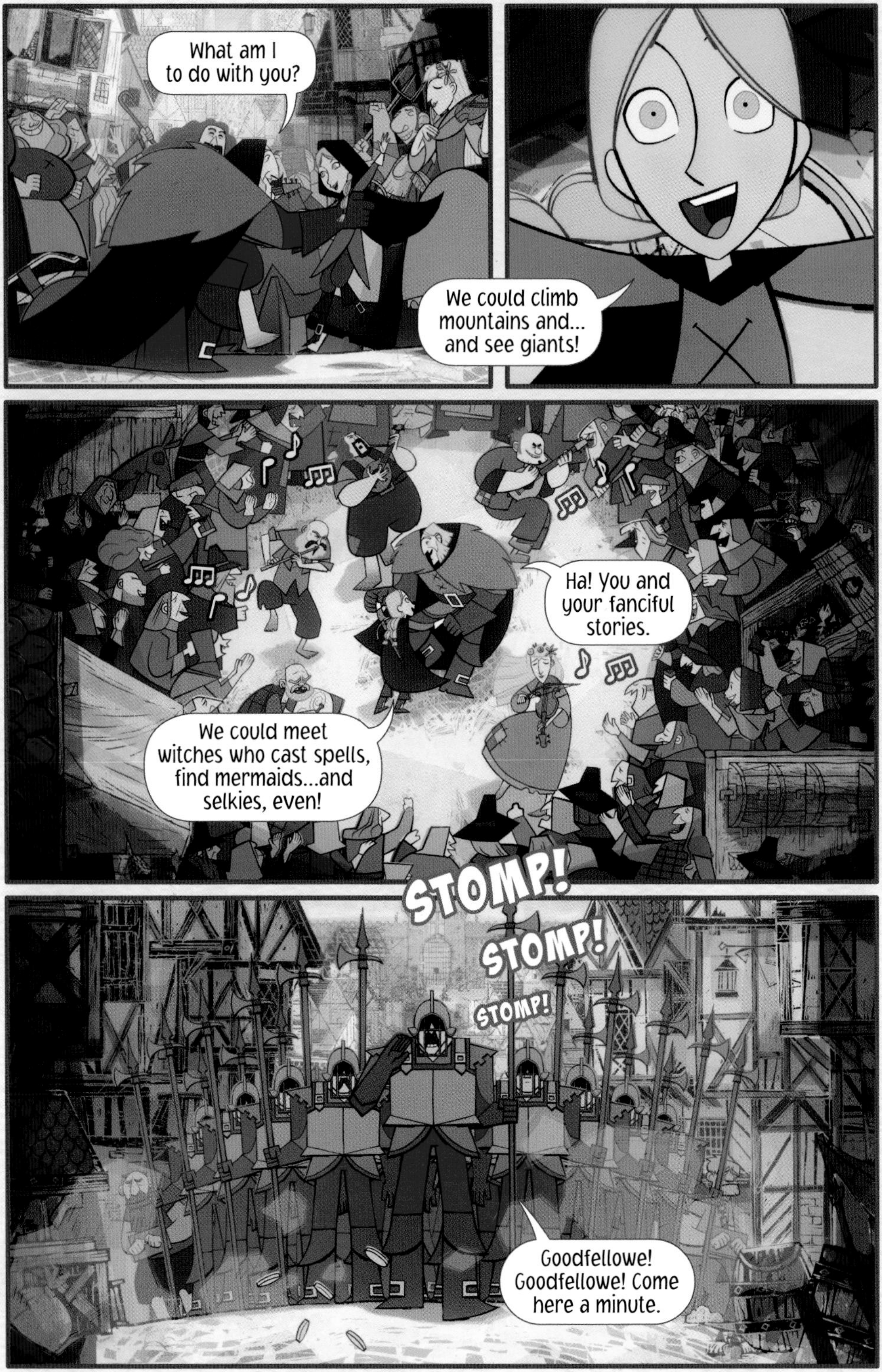
What am I to do with you?
We could climb mountains and... and see giants!
Ha! You and your fanciful stories.
We could meet witches who cast spells, find mermaids...and selkies, even!
STOMP!
STOMP!
STOMP!
Goodfellowe! Goodfellowe! Come here a minute.

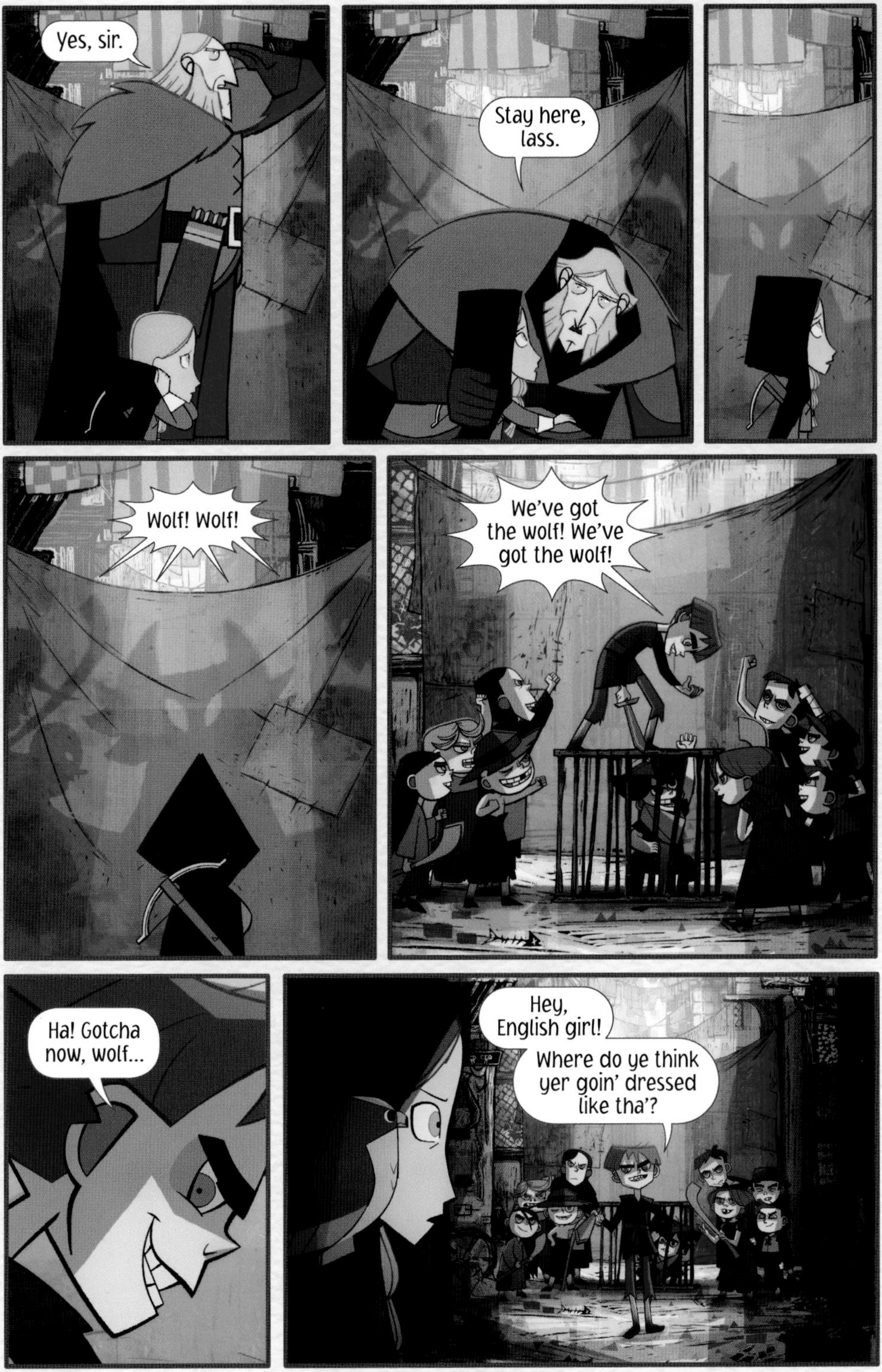
Yes, sir.
Stay here, lass.
Wolf! Wolf!
We've got the wolf! We've got the wolf!
Ha! Gotcha now, wolf...
Hey, English girl!
Where do ye think yer goin' dressed like tha'?

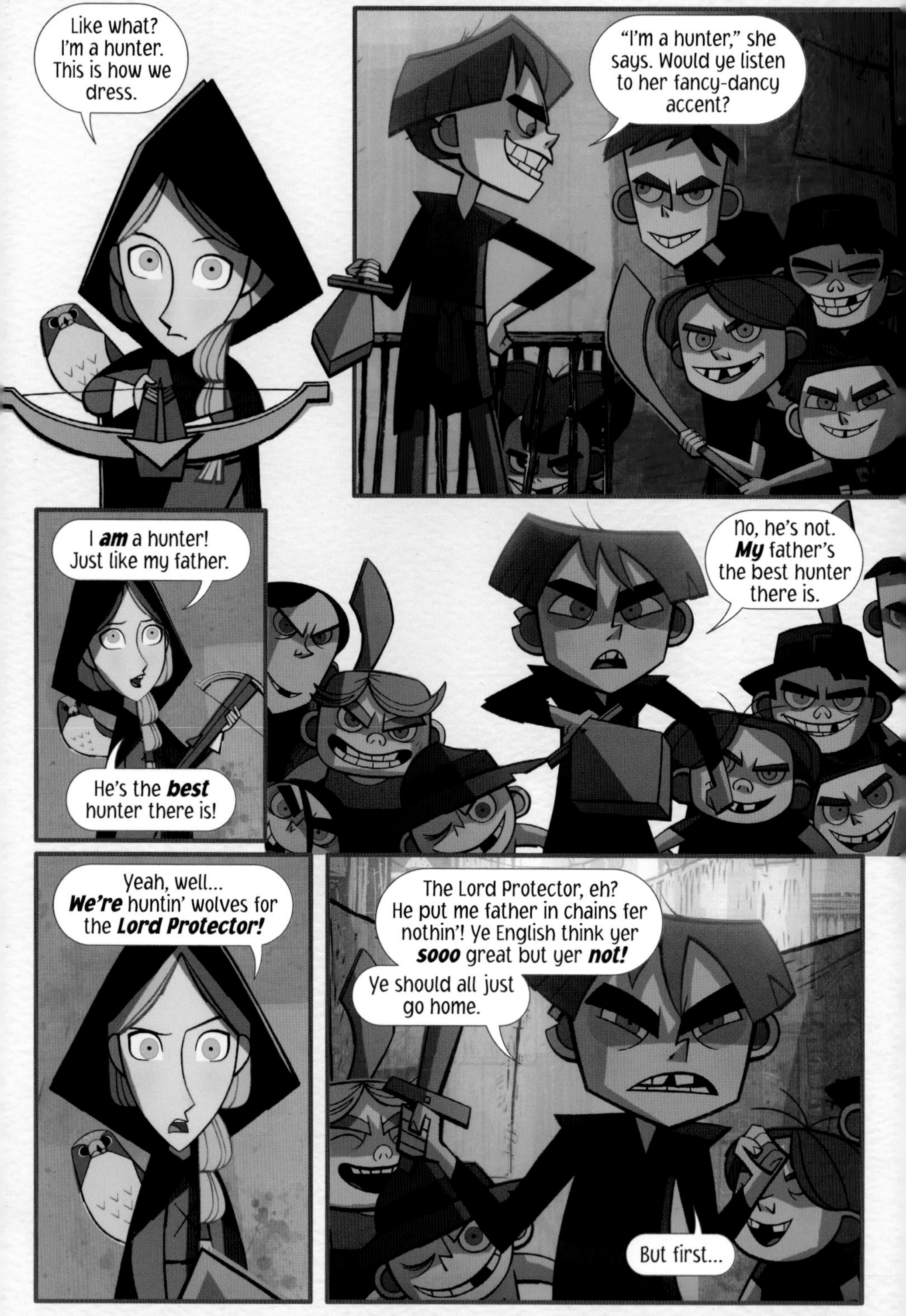

Like what? I'm a hunter. This is how we dress.
"I'm a hunter," she says. Would ye listen to her fancy-dancy accent?
I **am** a hunter! Just like my father.
He's the **best** hunter there is!
No, he's not. **My** father's the best hunter there is.
Yeah, well... **We're** huntin' wolves for the **Lord Protector!**
The Lord Protector, eh? He put me father in chains fer nothin'! Ye English think yer **sooo** great but yer **not!**
Ye should all just go home.
But first...

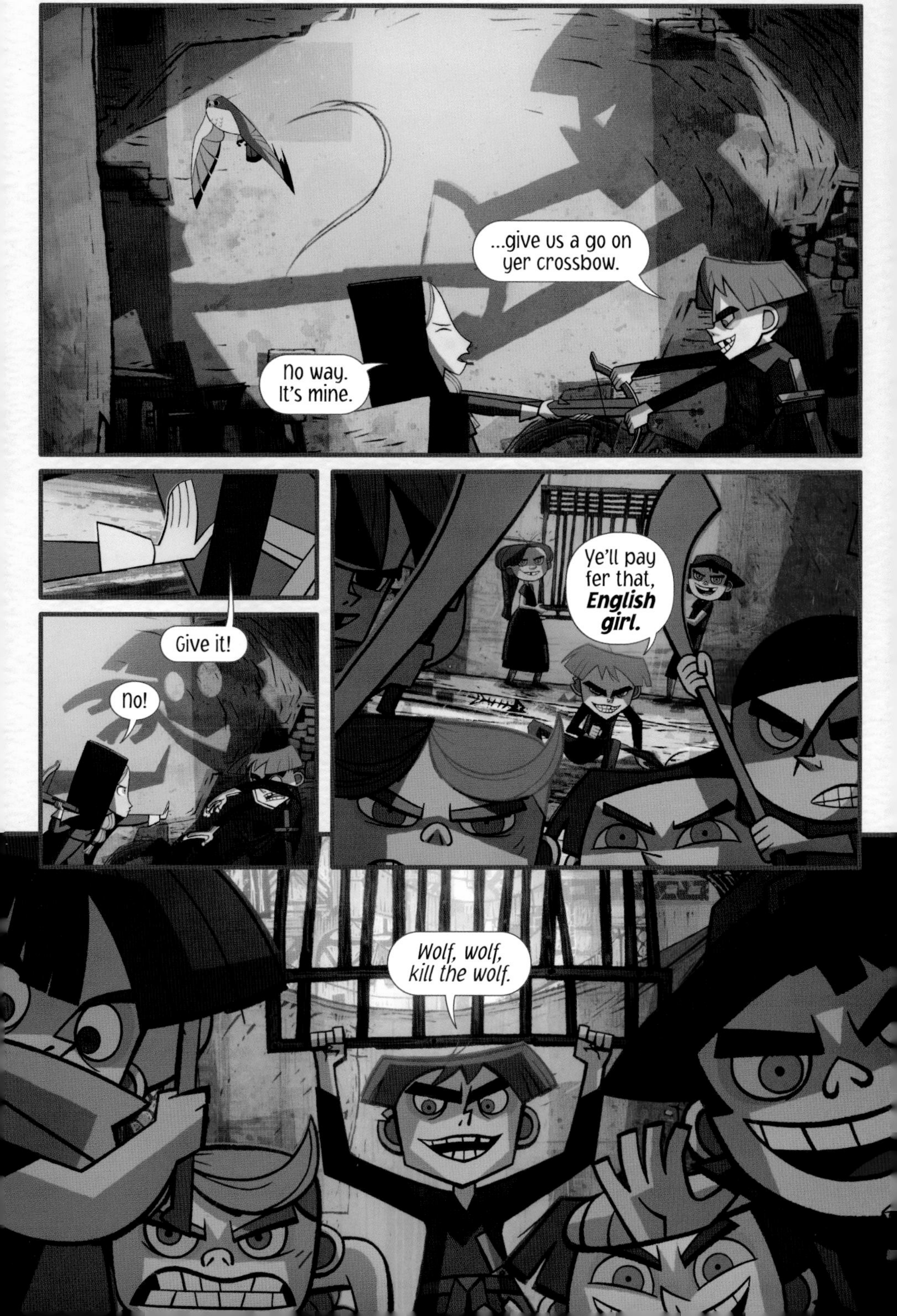
...give us a go on yer crossbow.
No way. It's mine.
Give it!
No!
Ye'll pay fer that, **English girl.**
Wolf, wolf, kill the wolf.

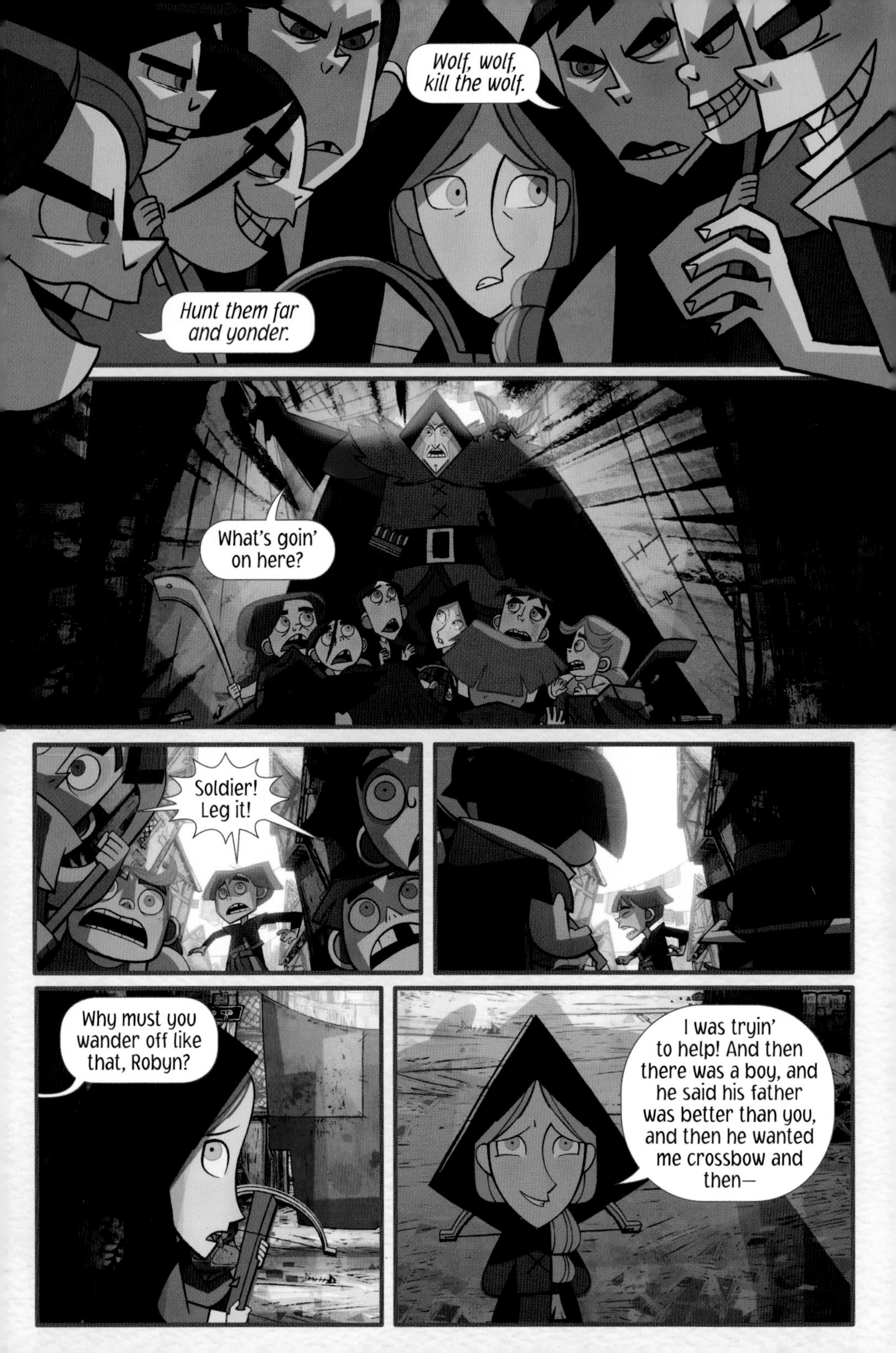

Wolf, wolf, kill the wolf.
Hunt them far and yonder.
What's goin' on here?
Soldier! Leg it!
Why must you wander off like that, Robyn?
I was tryin' to help! And then there was a boy, and he said his father was better than you, and then he wanted me crossbow and then—

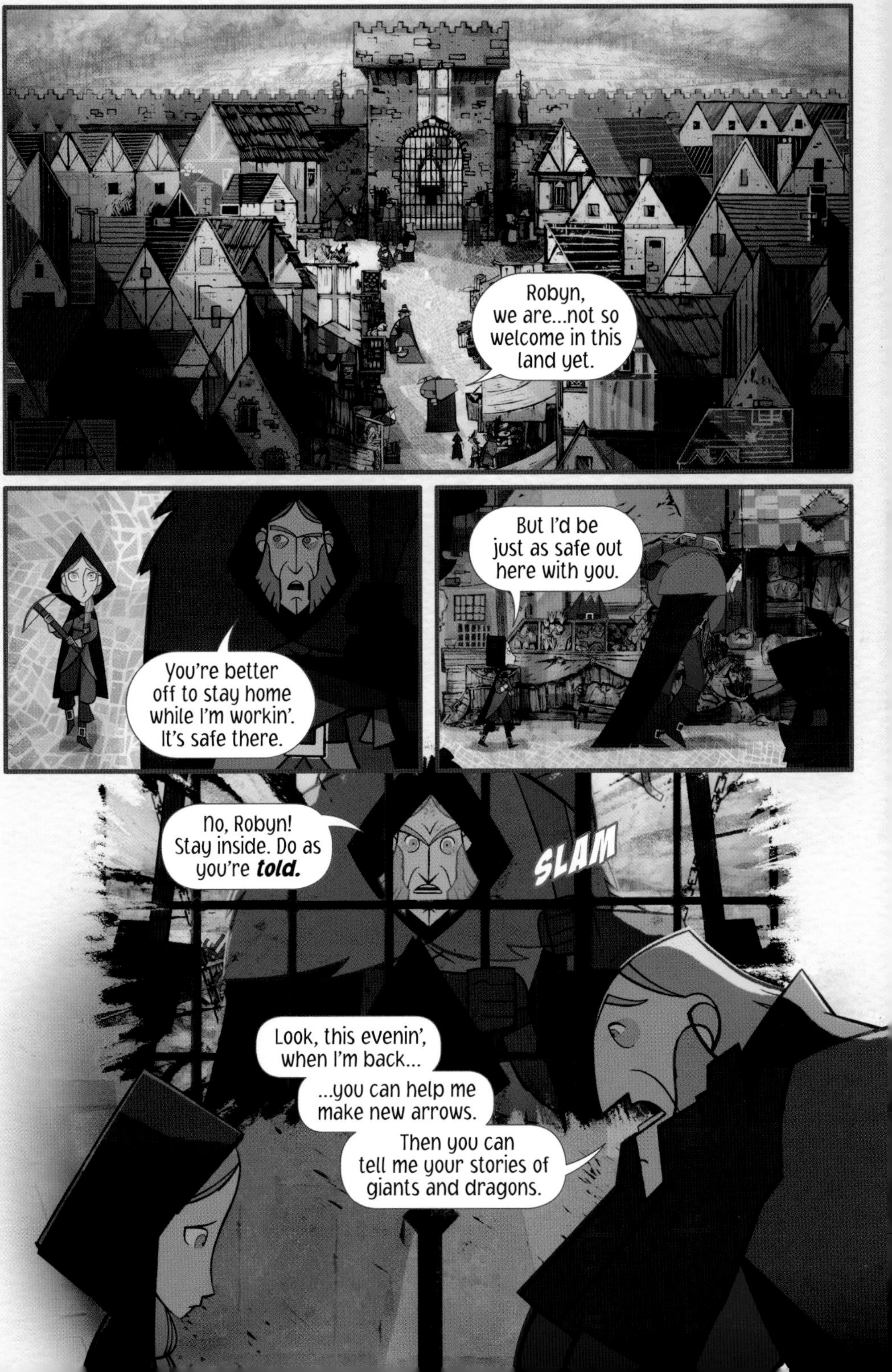
Robyn, we are...not so welcome in this land yet.
You're better off to stay home while I'm workin'. It's safe there.
But I'd be just as safe out here with you.
No, Robyn! Stay inside. Do as you're ***told.***
SLAM
Look, this evenin', when I'm back...
...you can help me make new arrows.
Then you can tell me your stories of giants and dragons.

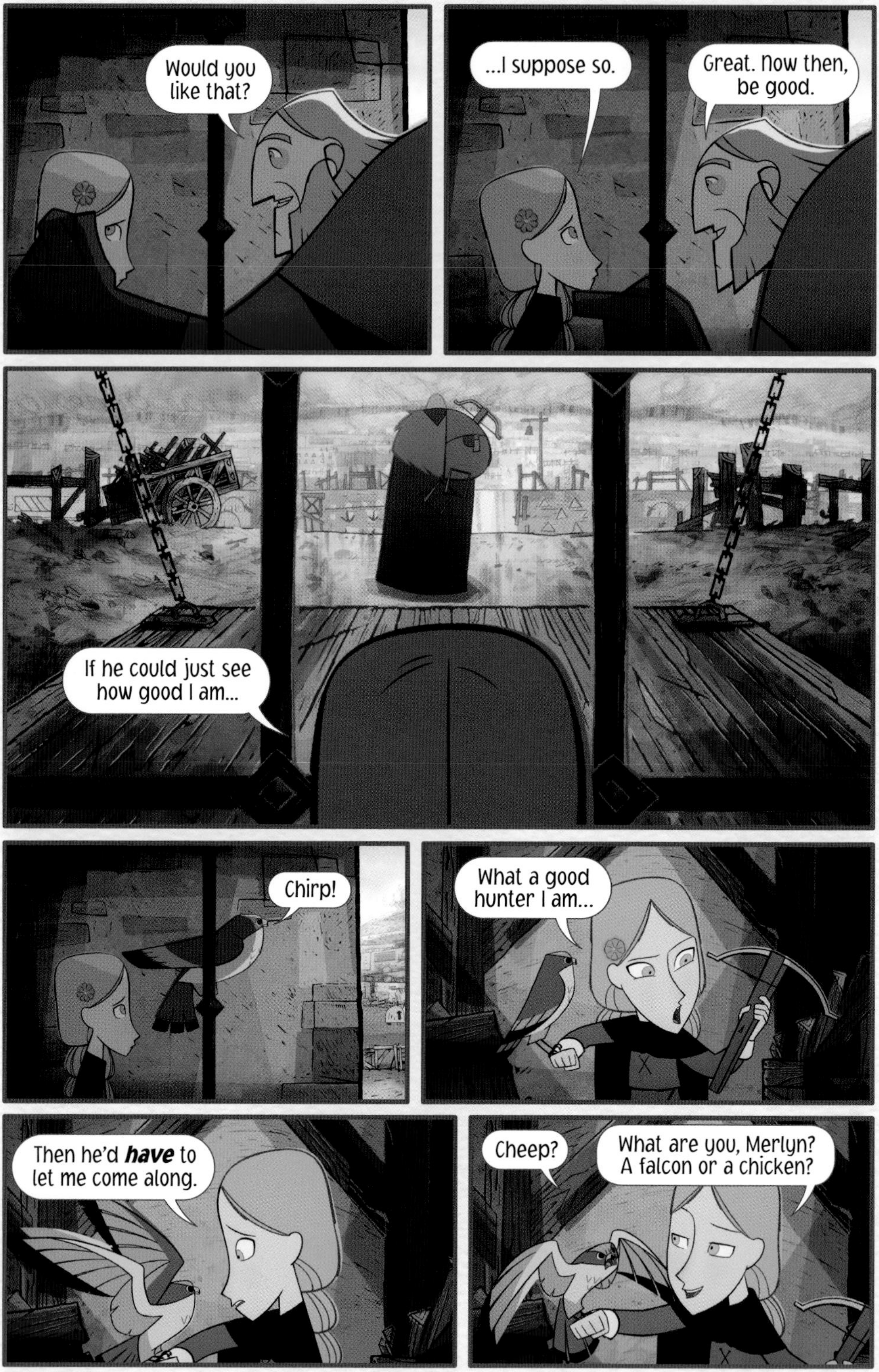
Would you like that?
...I suppose so.
Great. Now then, be good.
If he could just see how good I am...
Chirp!
What a good hunter I am...
Then he'd ***have*** to let me come along.
Cheep?
What are you, Merlyn? A falcon or a chicken?

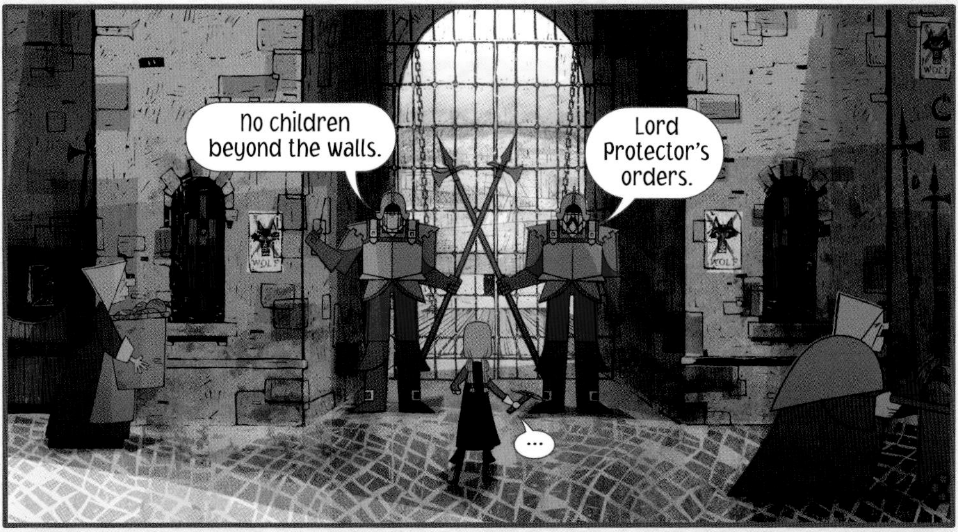
No children beyond the walls.
Lord Protector's orders.
...

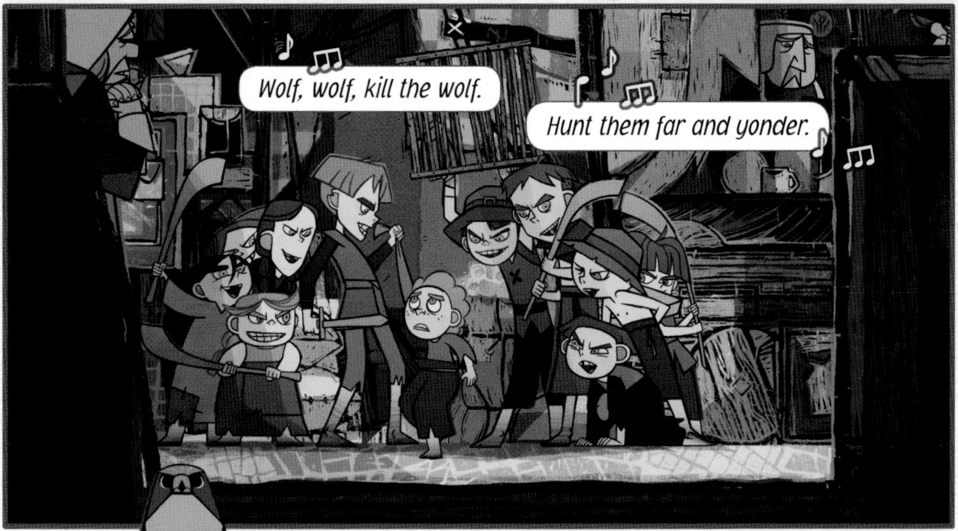
Wolf, wolf, kill the wolf.
Hunt them far and yonder.

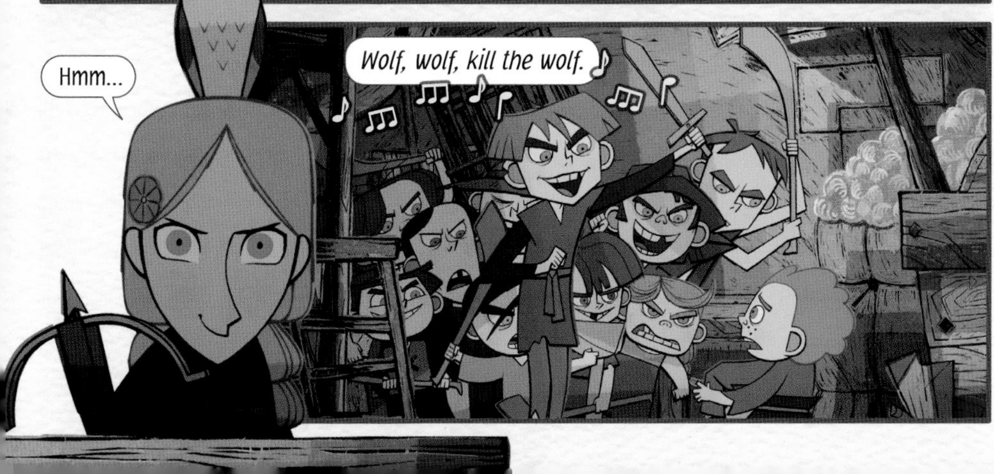
Hmm...
Wolf, wolf, kill the wolf.

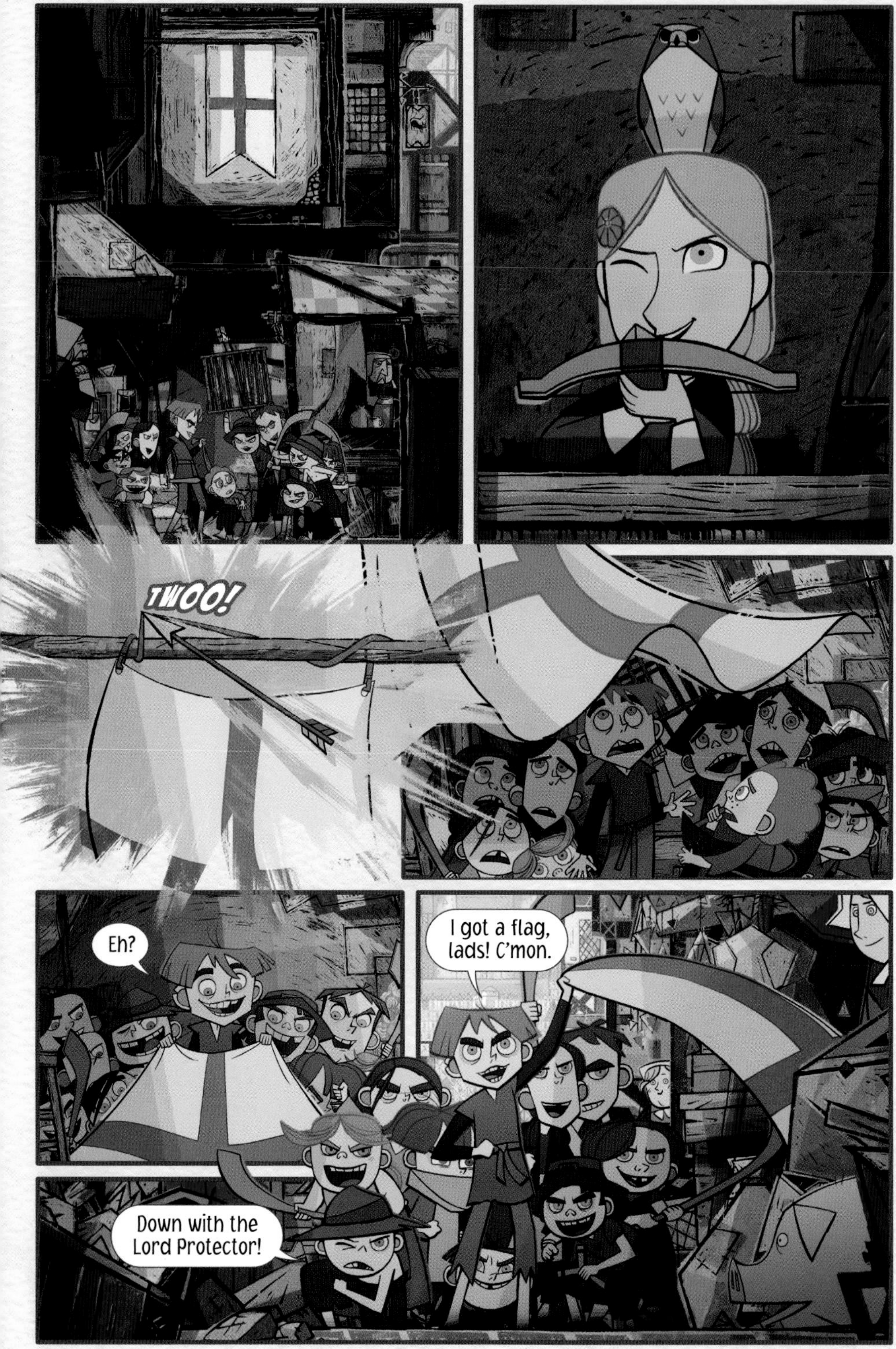
TWOO!
Eh?
I got a flag, lads! C'mon.
Down with the Lord Protector!

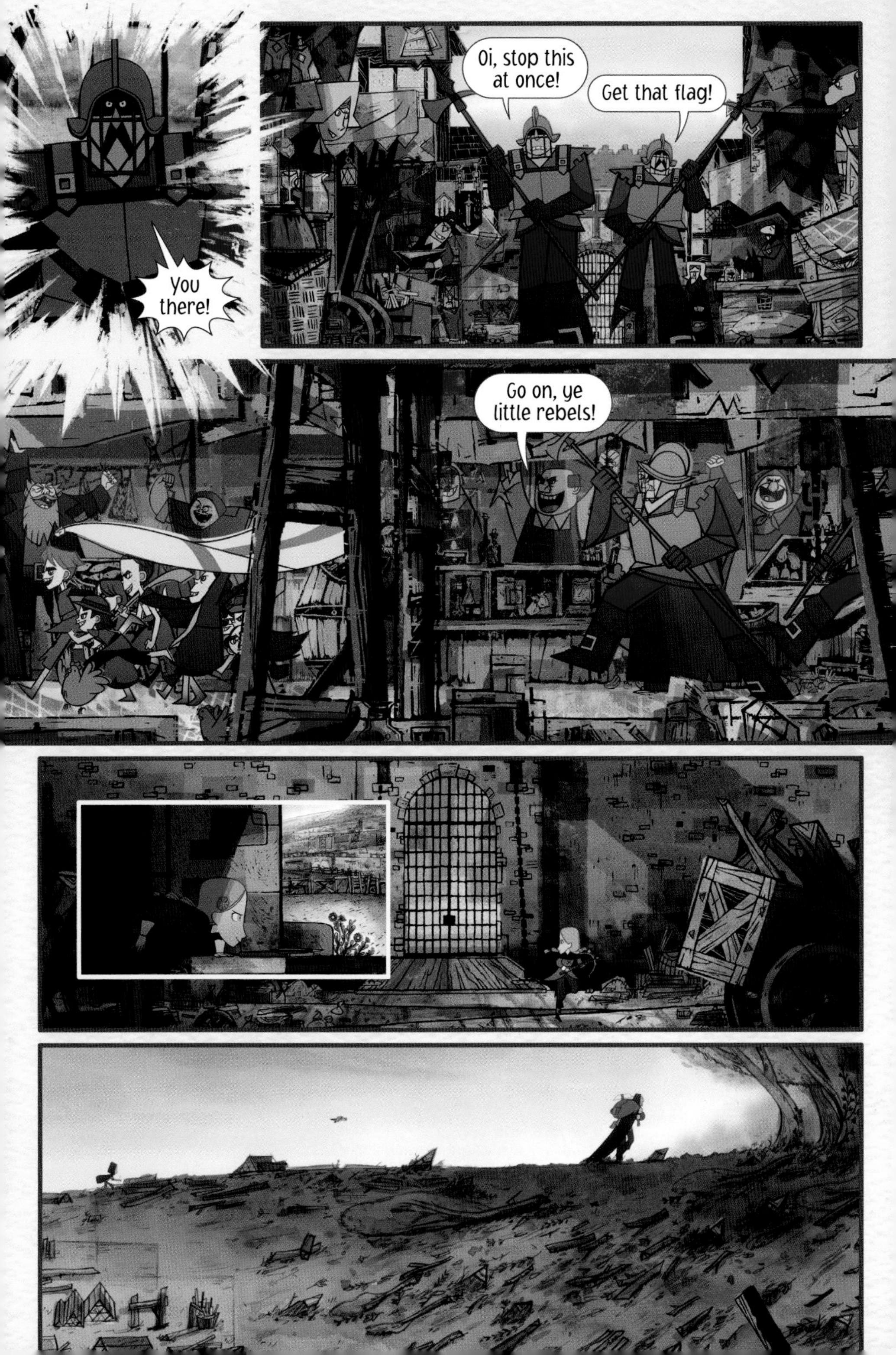
You there!
Oi, stop this at once!
Get that flag!
Go on, ye little rebels!

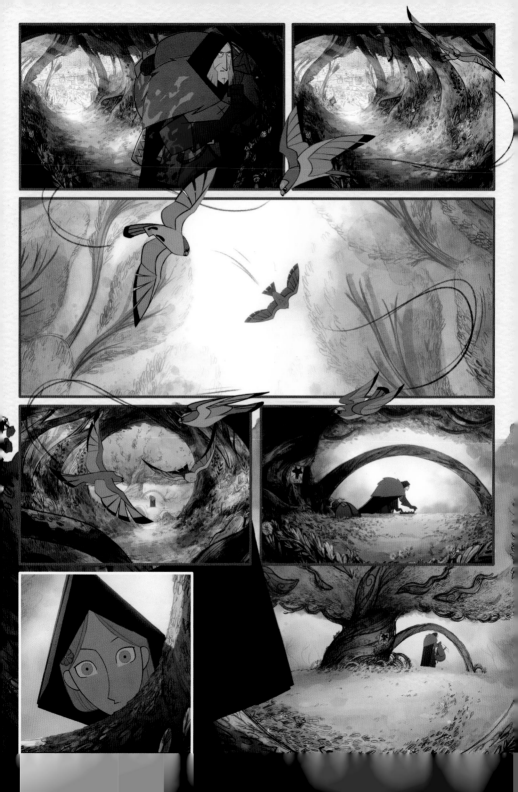

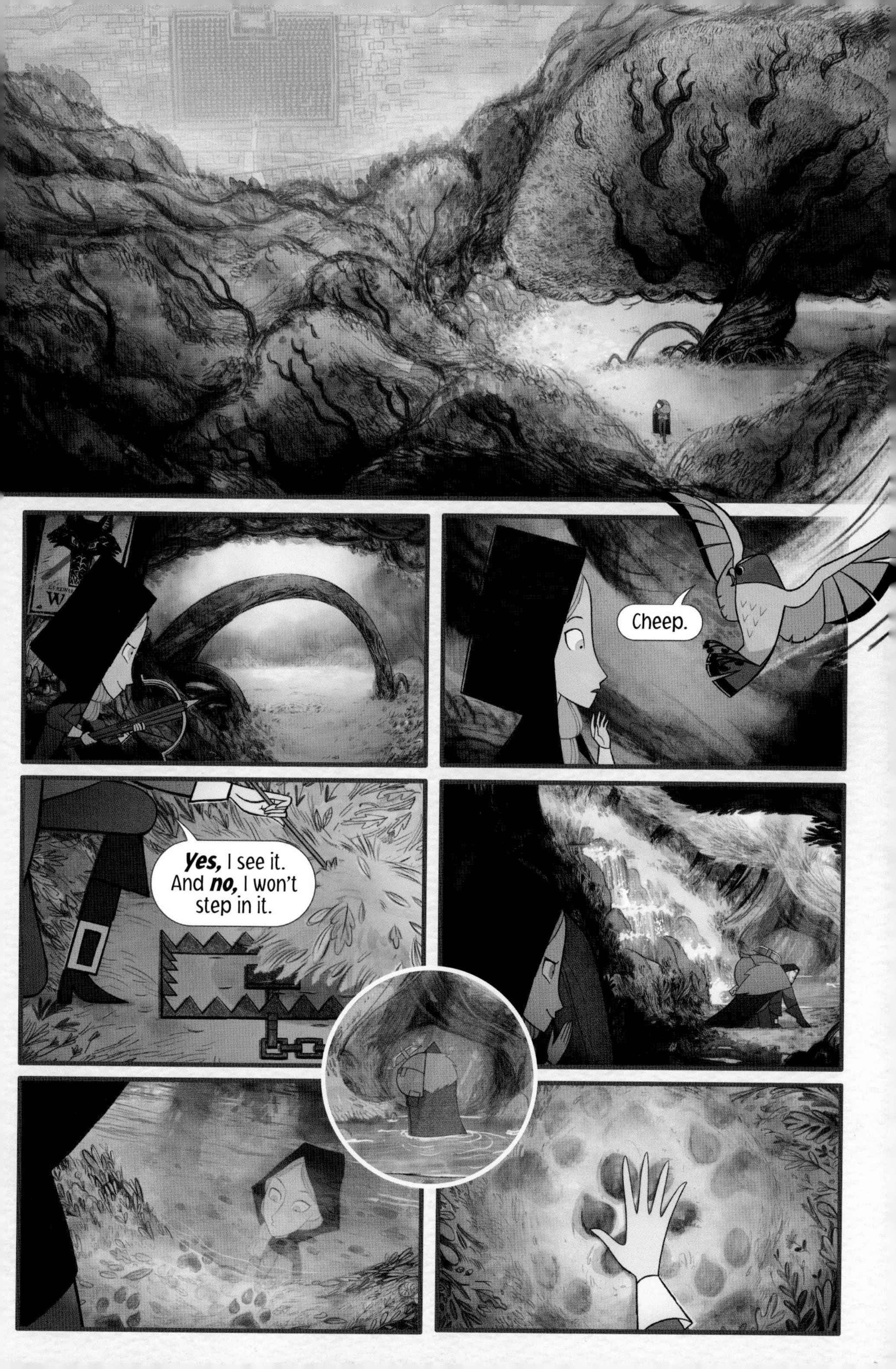
Cheep.
Yes, I see it. And **no,** I won't step in it.

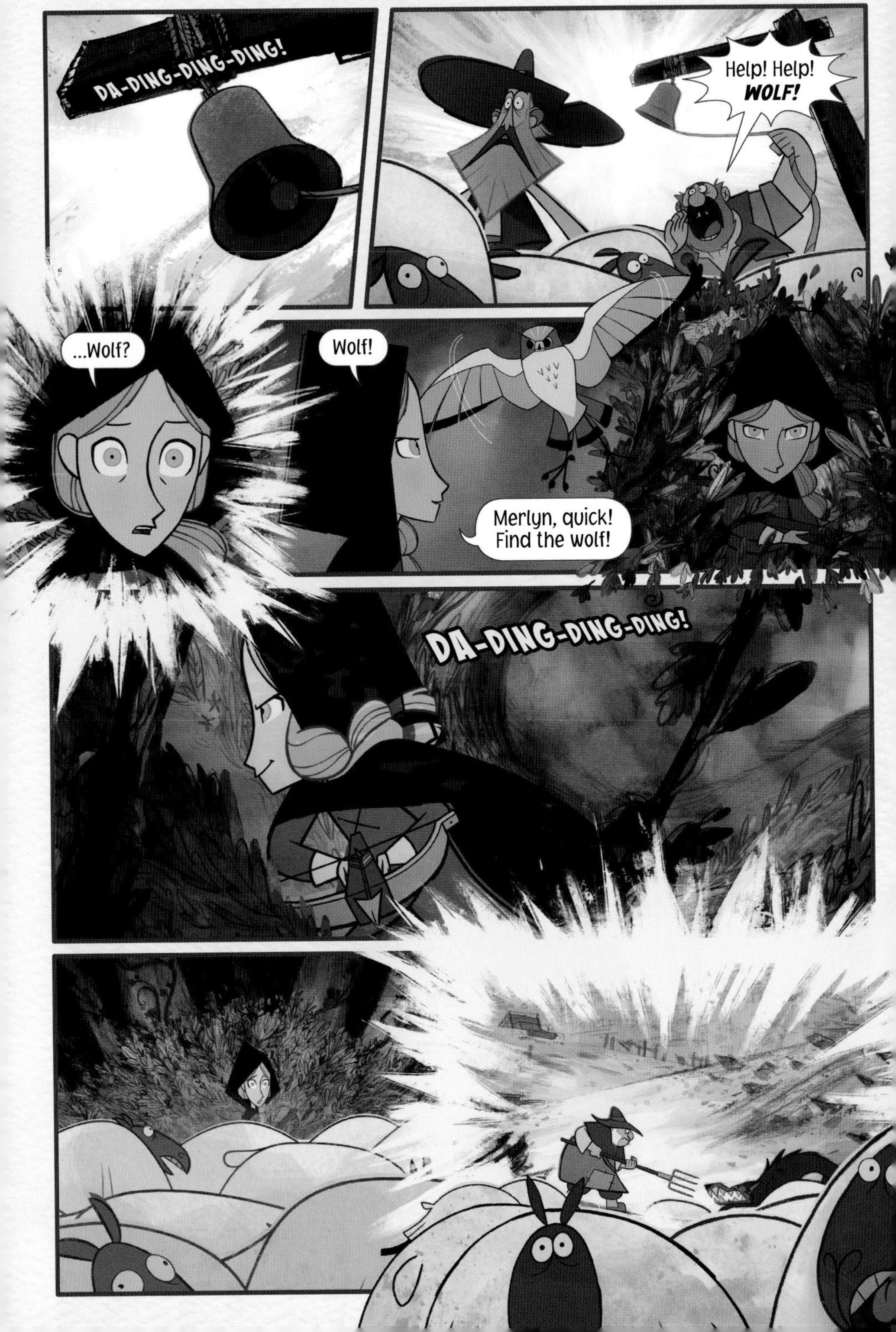
DA-DING-DING-DING!
Help! Help! WOLF!
...Wolf?
Wolf!
Merlyn, quick! Find the wolf!
DA-DING-DING-DING!

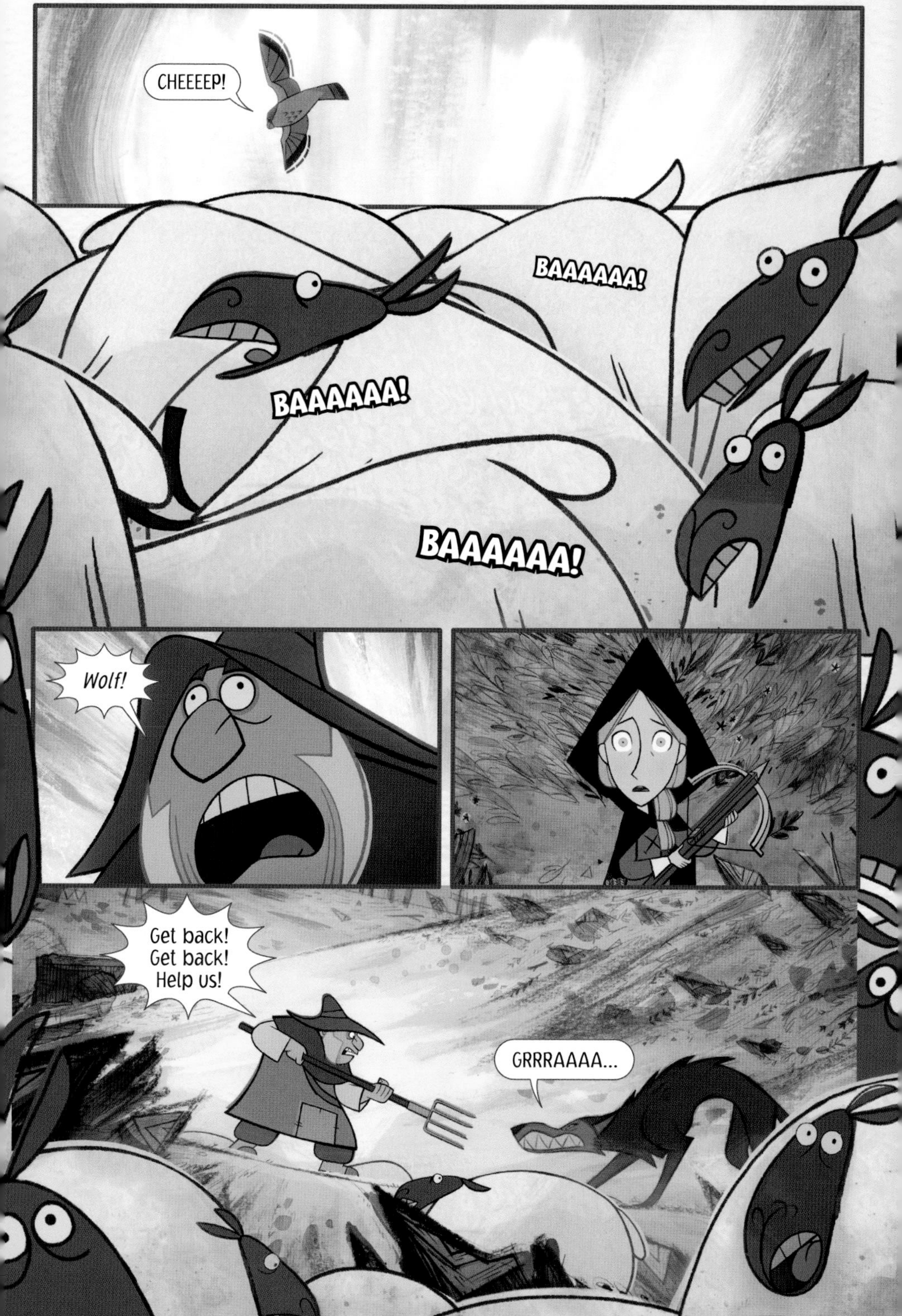
CHEEEEP!
BAAAAAA!
BAAAAAA!
BAAAAAA!
Wolf!
Get back! Get back! Help us!
GRRRAAAA...

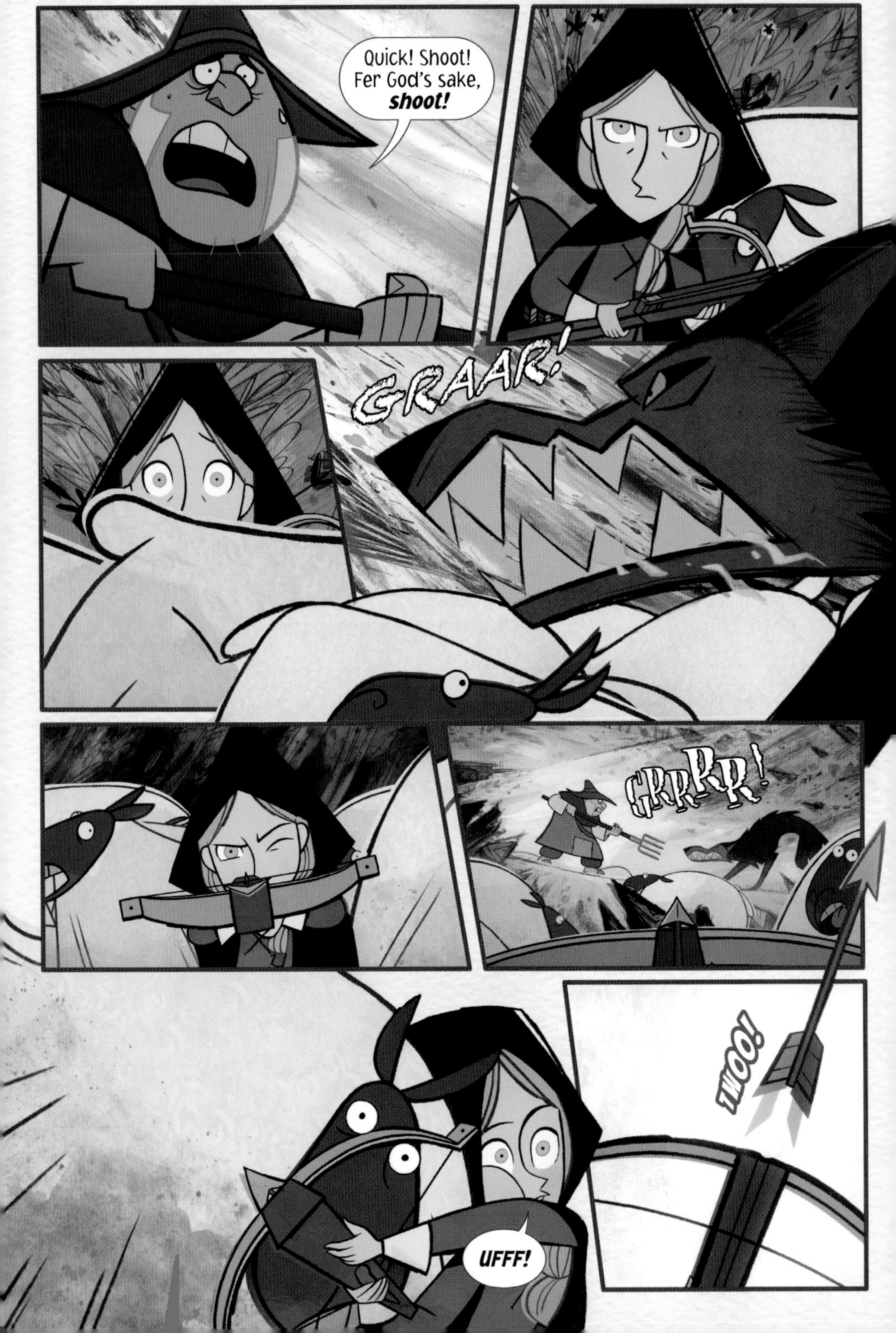
Quick! Shoot! Fer God's sake, shoot!
GRAAR!
GRRRRR!
TWOO!
UFFF!

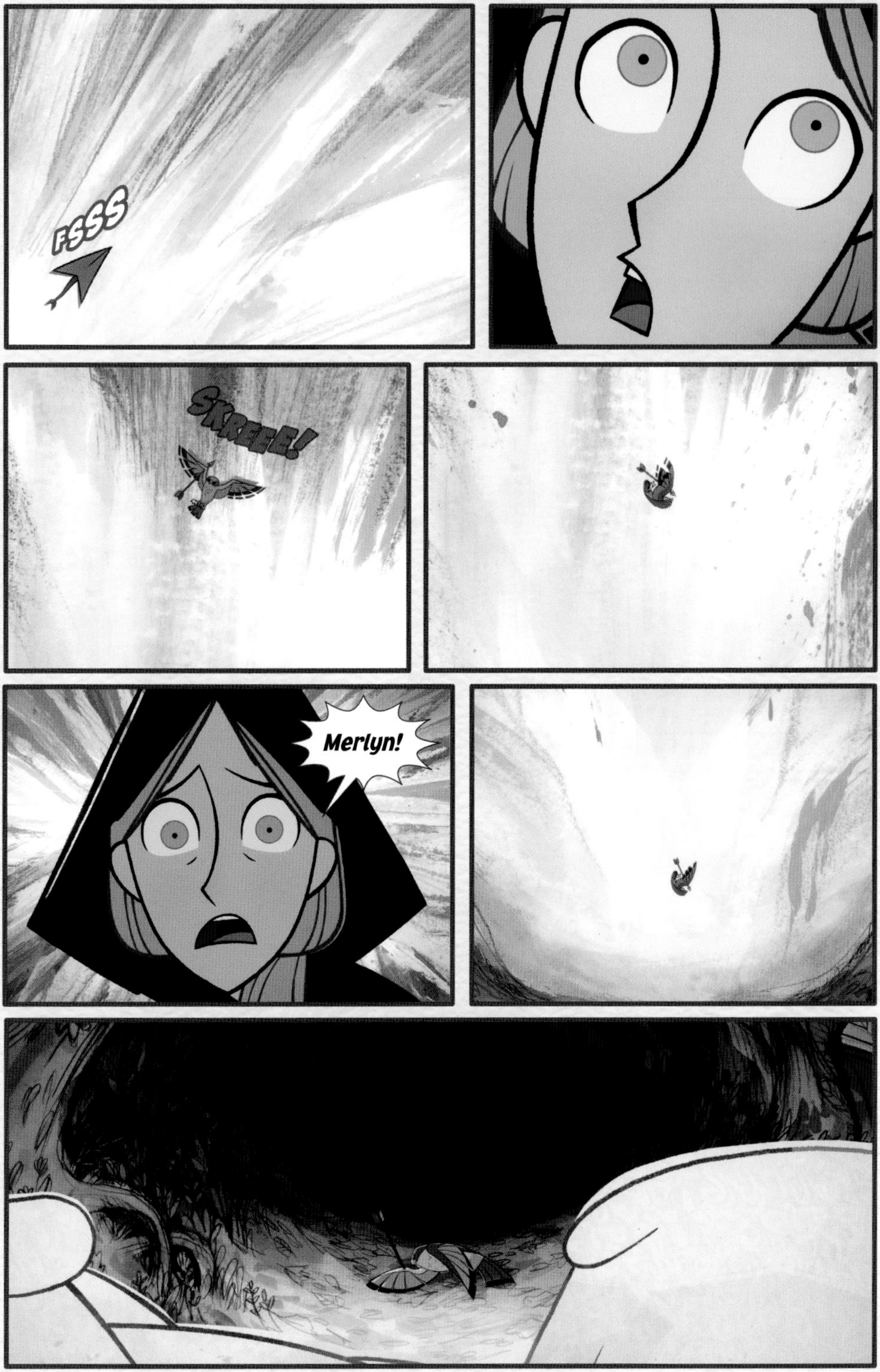
FSSS
SKREEEE!
Merlyn!

AWWOoₒₒ

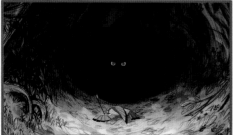

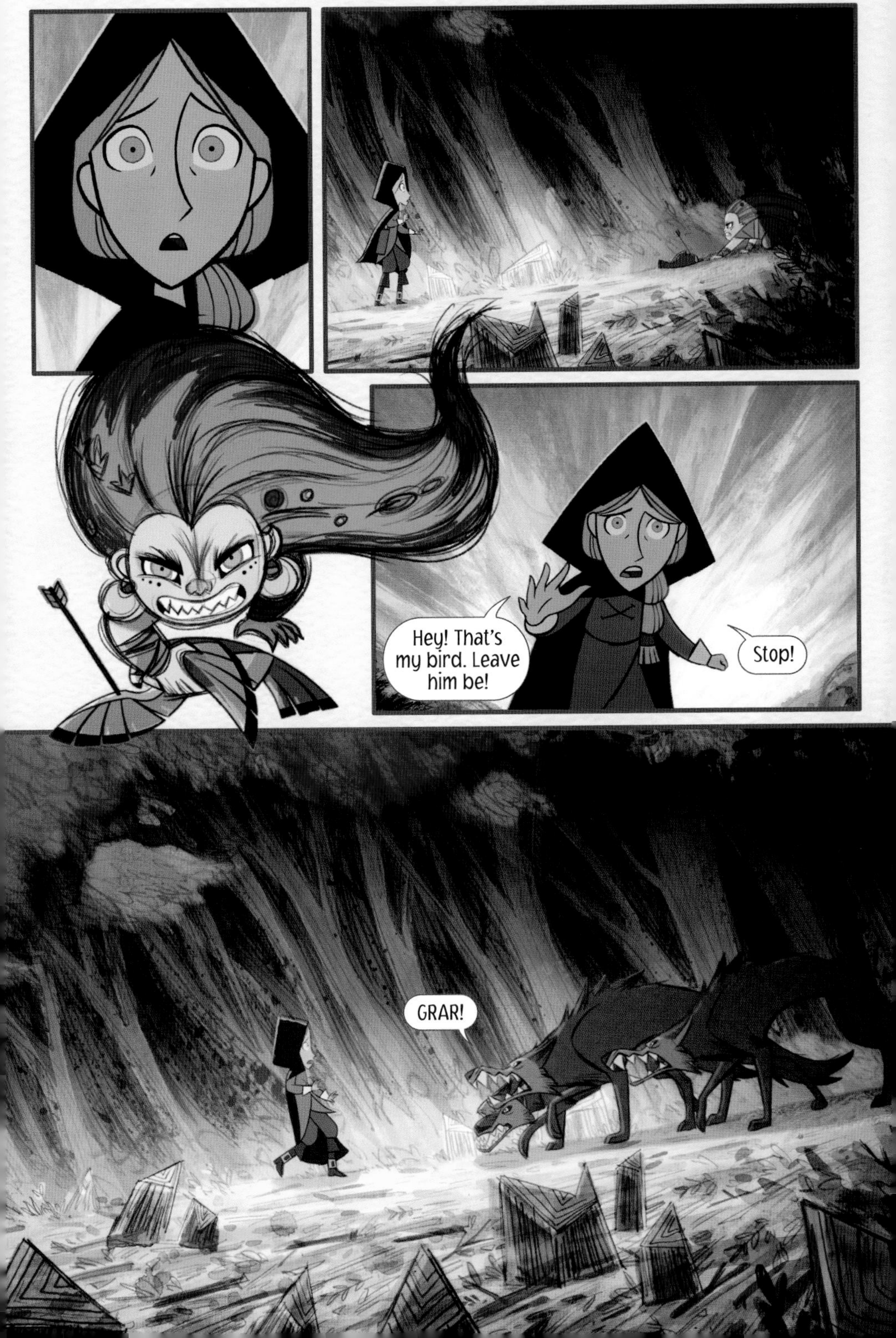
Hey! That's my bird. Leave him be!
Stop!
GRAR!

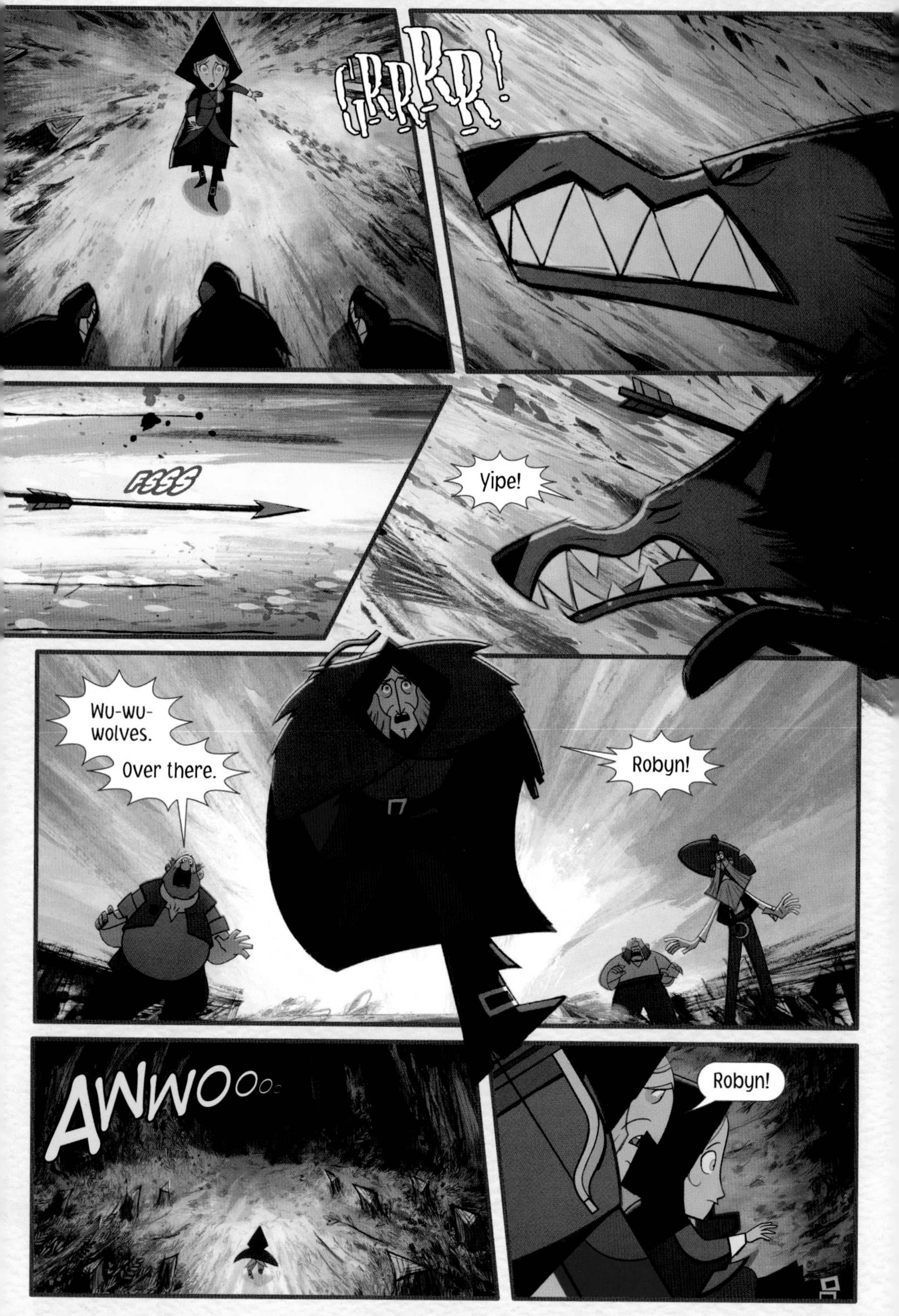
GRRRR!
FSSS
Yipe!
Wu-wu-wolves.
Over there.
Robyn!
AWWOooo
Robyn!

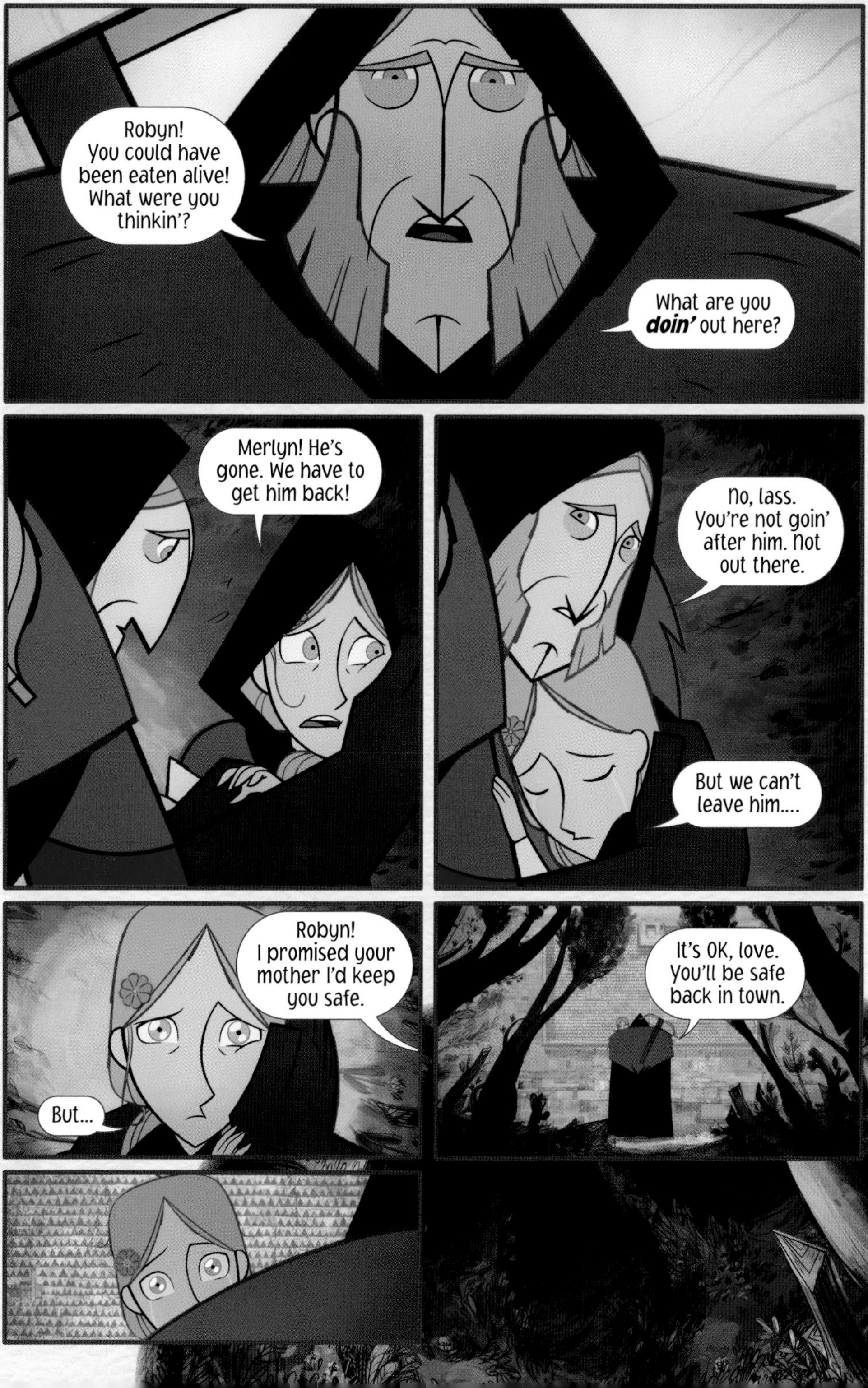
Robyn! You could have been eaten alive! What were you thinkin'?
What are you **doin'** out here?
Merlyn! He's gone. We have to get him back!
No, lass. You're not goin' after him. Not out there.
But we can't leave him....
Robyn! I promised your mother I'd keep you safe.
But...
It's OK, love. You'll be safe back in town.

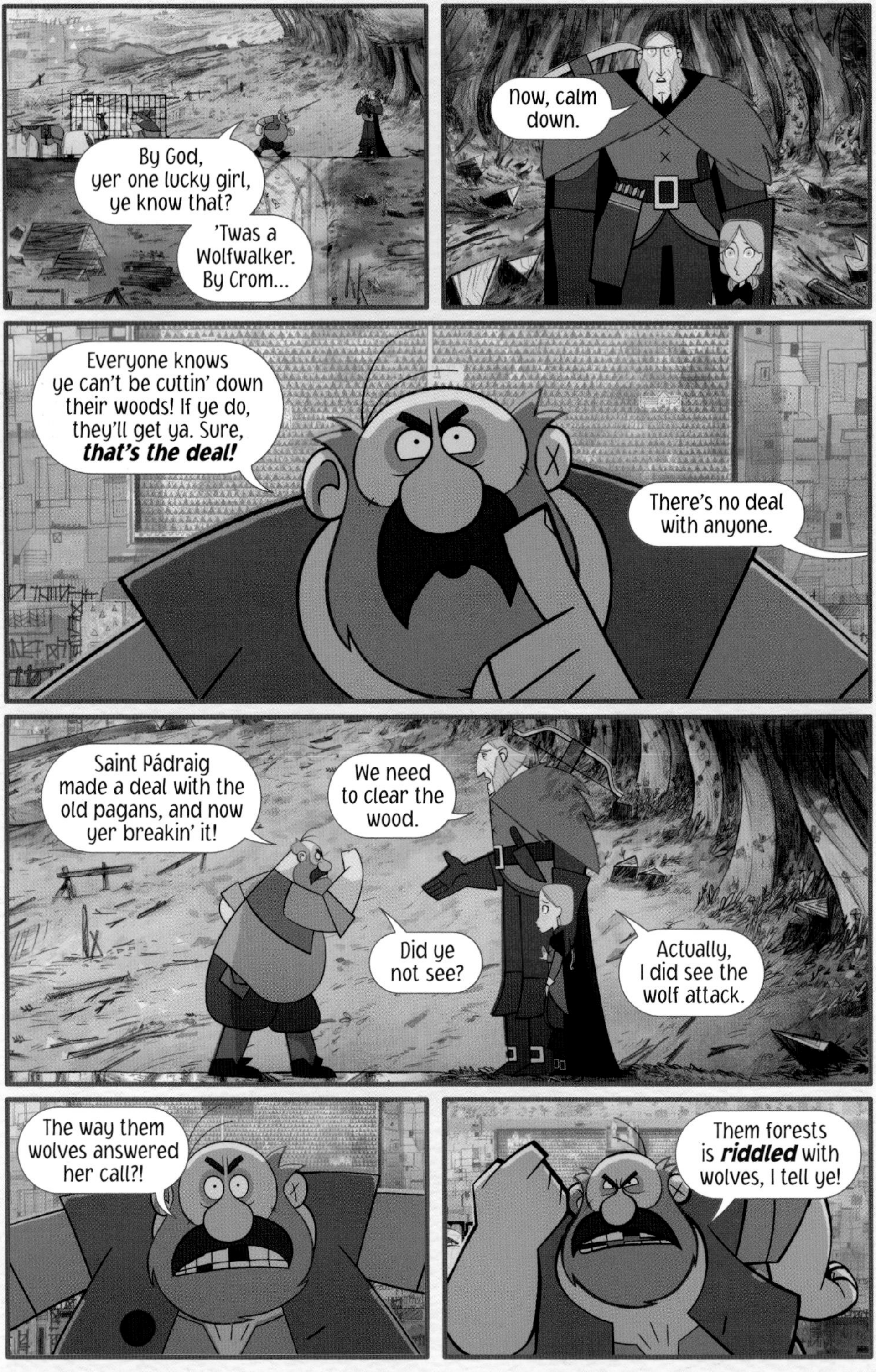
By God, yer one lucky girl, ye know that?
'Twas a Wolfwalker. By Crom…
Now, calm down.
Everyone knows ye can't be cuttin' down their woods! If ye do, they'll get ya. Sure, ***that's the deal!***
There's no deal with anyone.
Saint Pádraig made a deal with the old pagans, and now yer breakin' it!
We need to clear the wood.
Did ye not see?
Actually, I did see the wolf attack.
The way them wolves answered her call?!
Them forests is ***riddled*** with wolves, I tell ye!

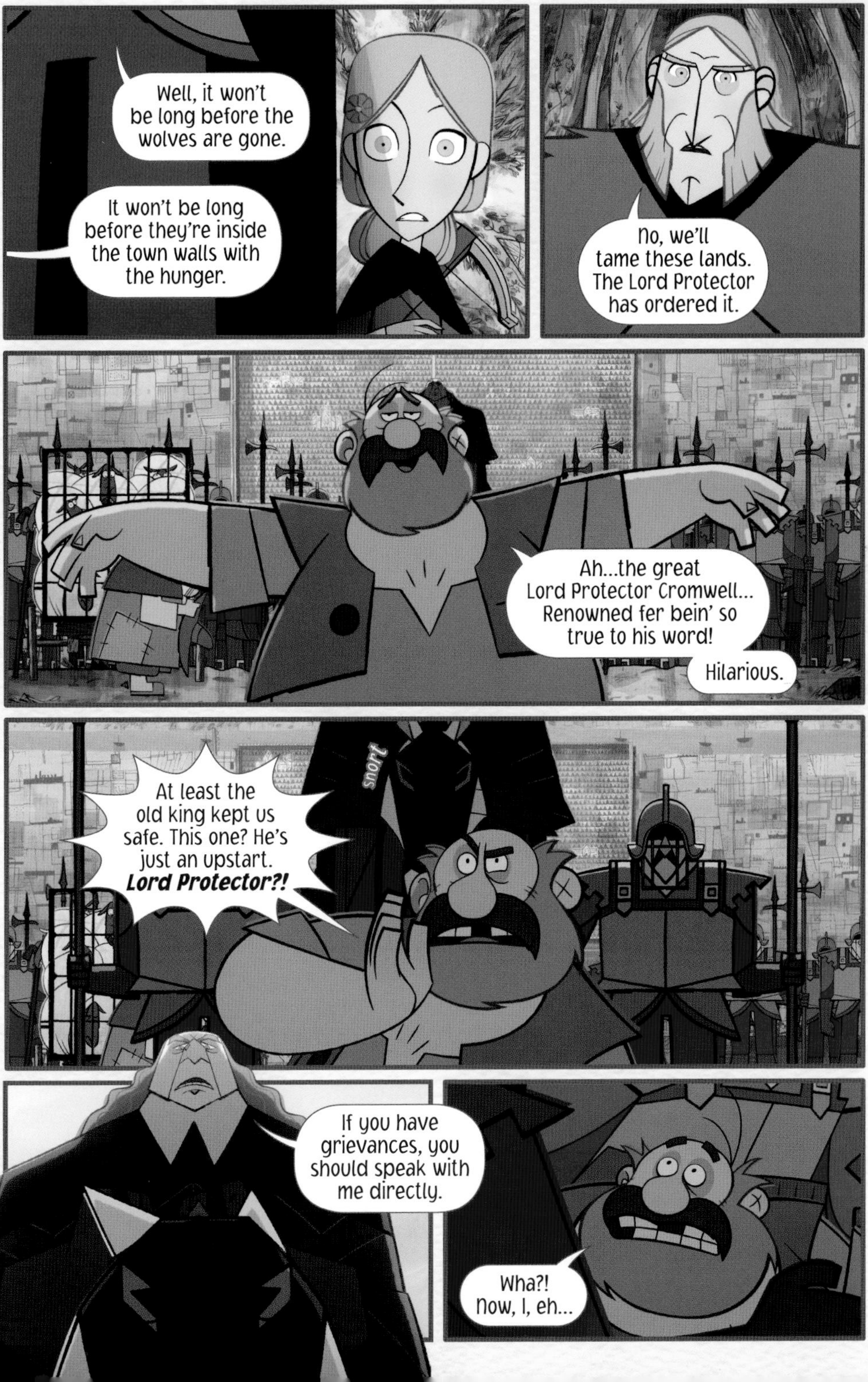
Well, it won't be long before the wolves are gone.
It won't be long before they're inside the town walls with the hunger.
No, we'll tame these lands. The Lord Protector has ordered it.
Ah...the great Lord Protector Cromwell... Renowned fer bein' so true to his word!
Hilarious.
snort
At least the old king kept us safe. This one? He's just an upstart. ***Lord Protector?!***
If you have grievances, you should speak with me directly.
Wha?! Now, I, eh...

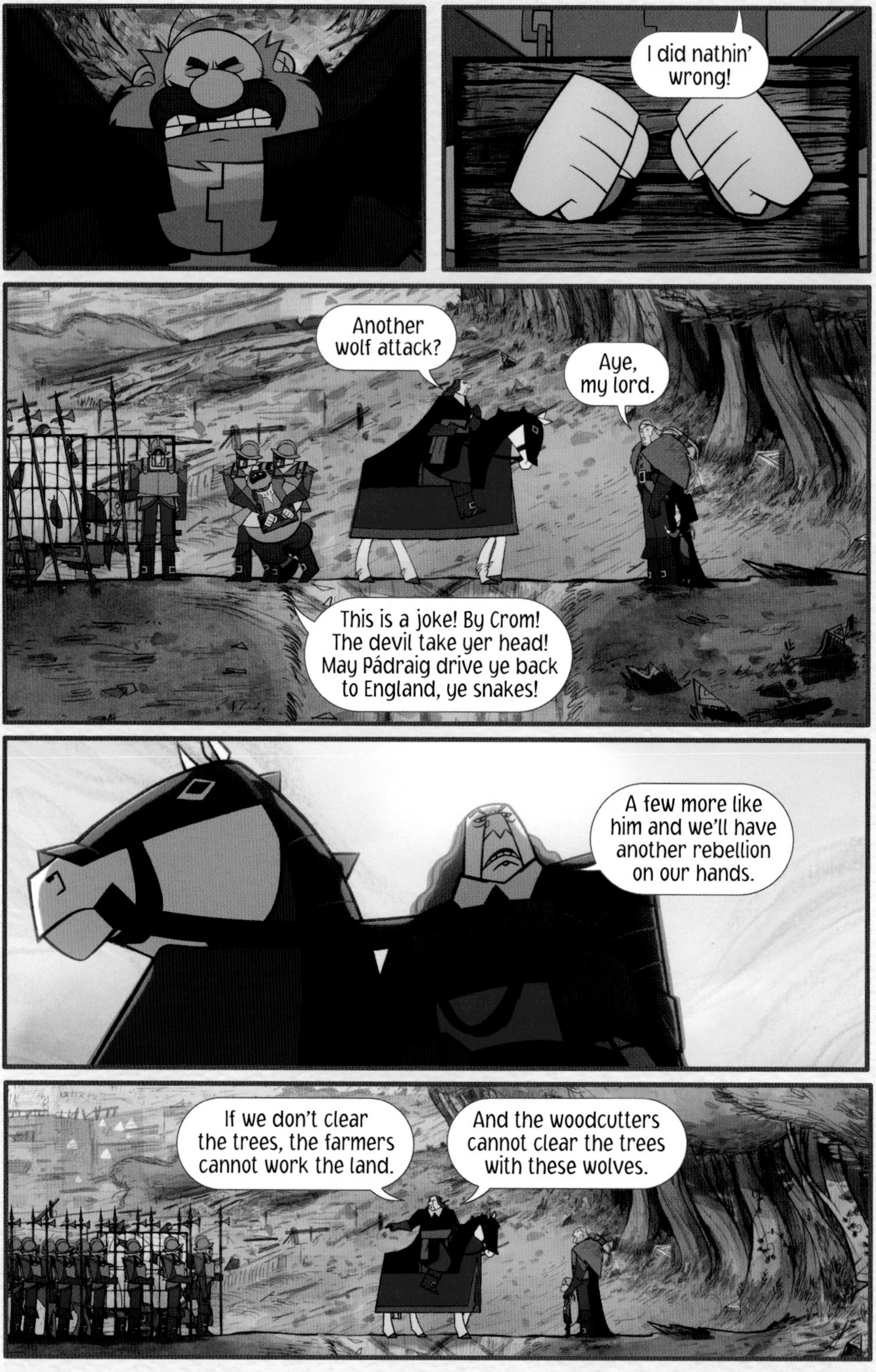
I did nathin' wrong!
Another wolf attack?
Aye, my lord.
This is a joke! By Crom! The devil take yer head! May Pádraig drive ye back to England, ye snakes!
A few more like him and we'll have another rebellion on our hands.
If we don't clear the trees, the farmers cannot work the land.
And the woodcutters cannot clear the trees with these wolves.

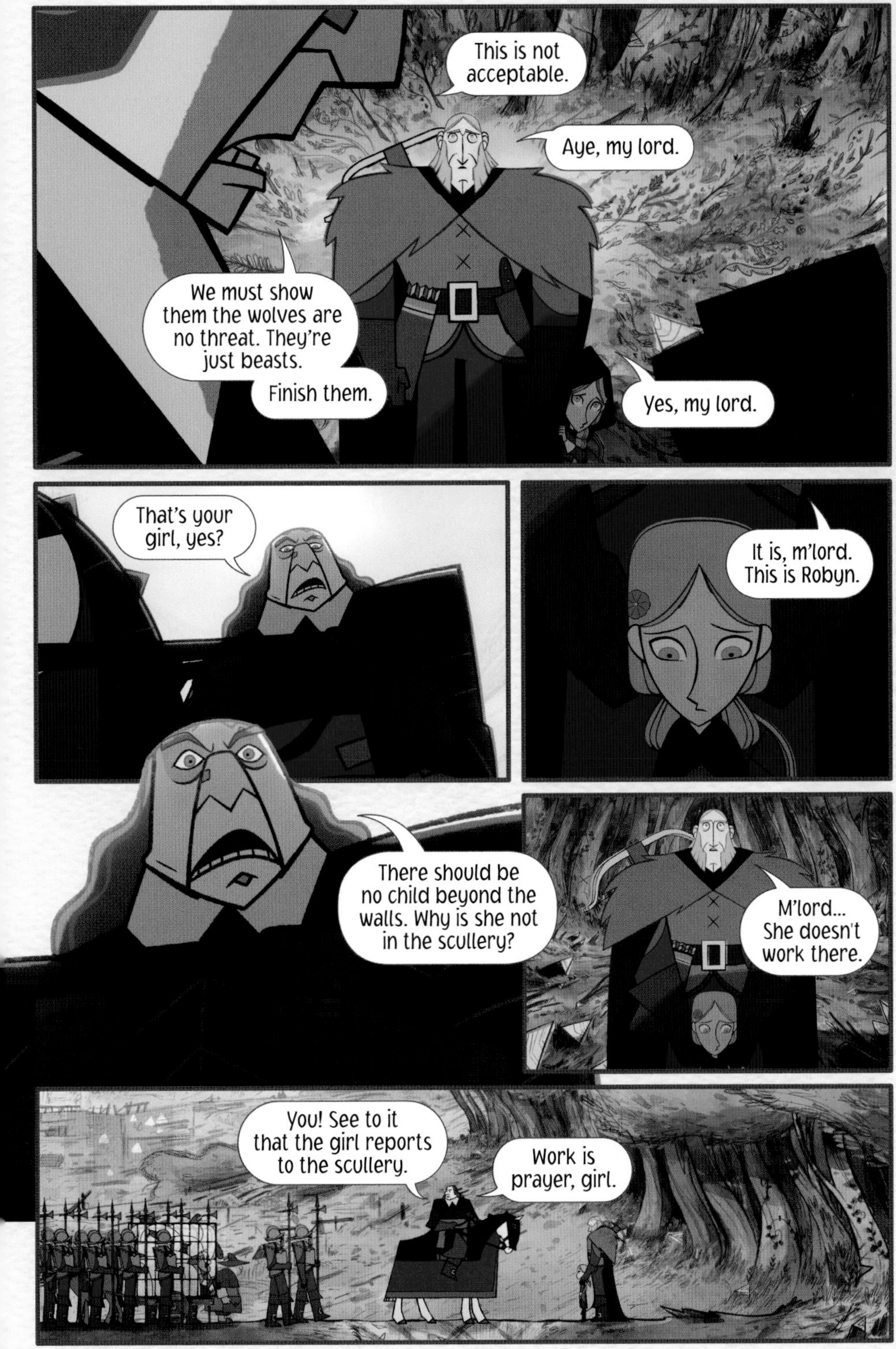
This is not acceptable.
Aye, my lord.
We must show them the wolves are no threat. They're just beasts.
Finish them.
Yes, my lord.
That's your girl, yes?
It is, m'lord. This is Robyn.
There should be no child beyond the walls. Why is she not in the scullery?
M'lord... She doesn't work there.
You! See to it that the girl reports to the scullery.
Work is prayer, girl.

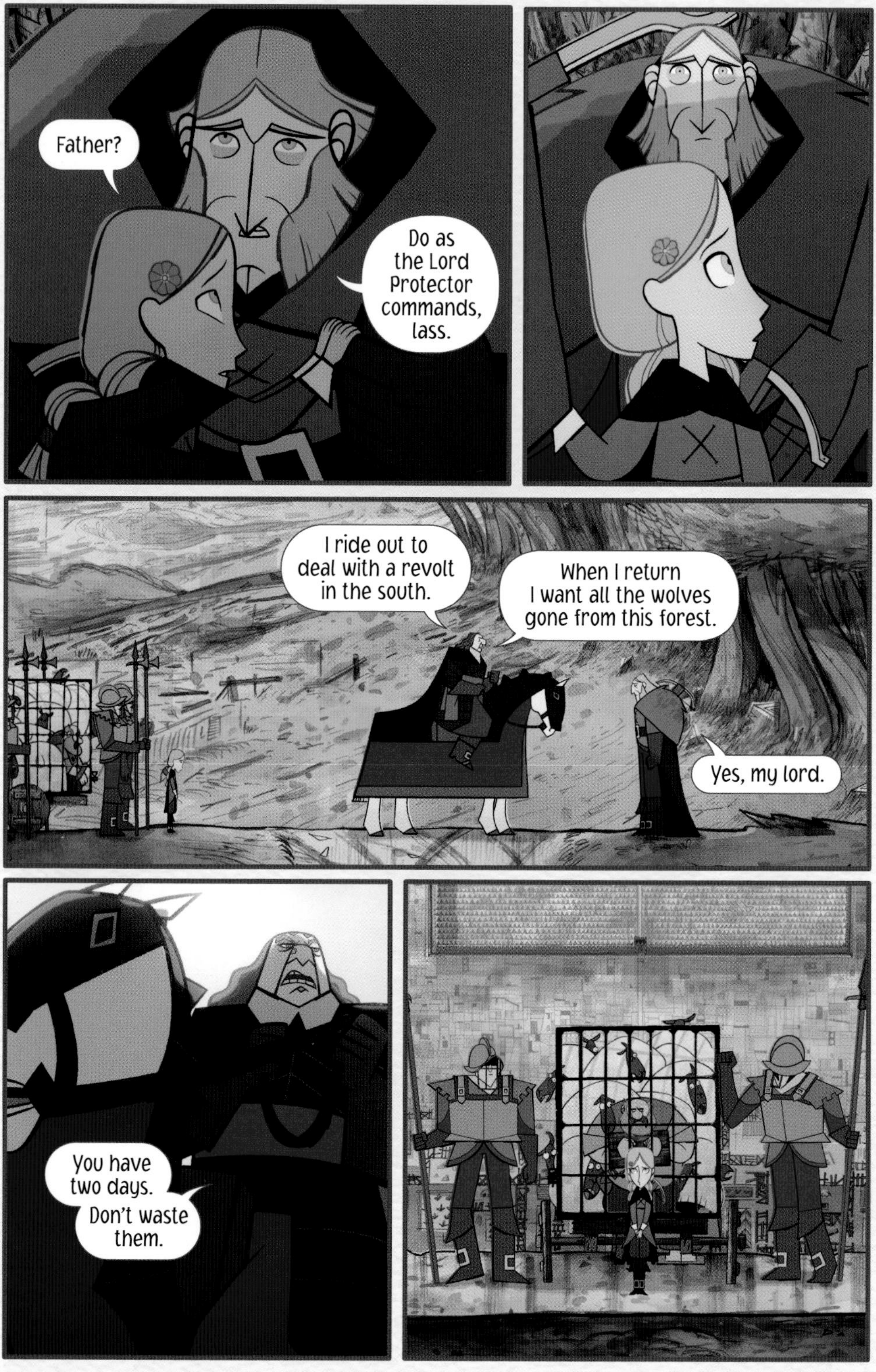
Father?
Do as the Lord Protector commands, lass.
I ride out to deal with a revolt in the south.
When I return I want all the wolves gone from this forest.
Yes, my lord.
You have two days.
Don't waste them.

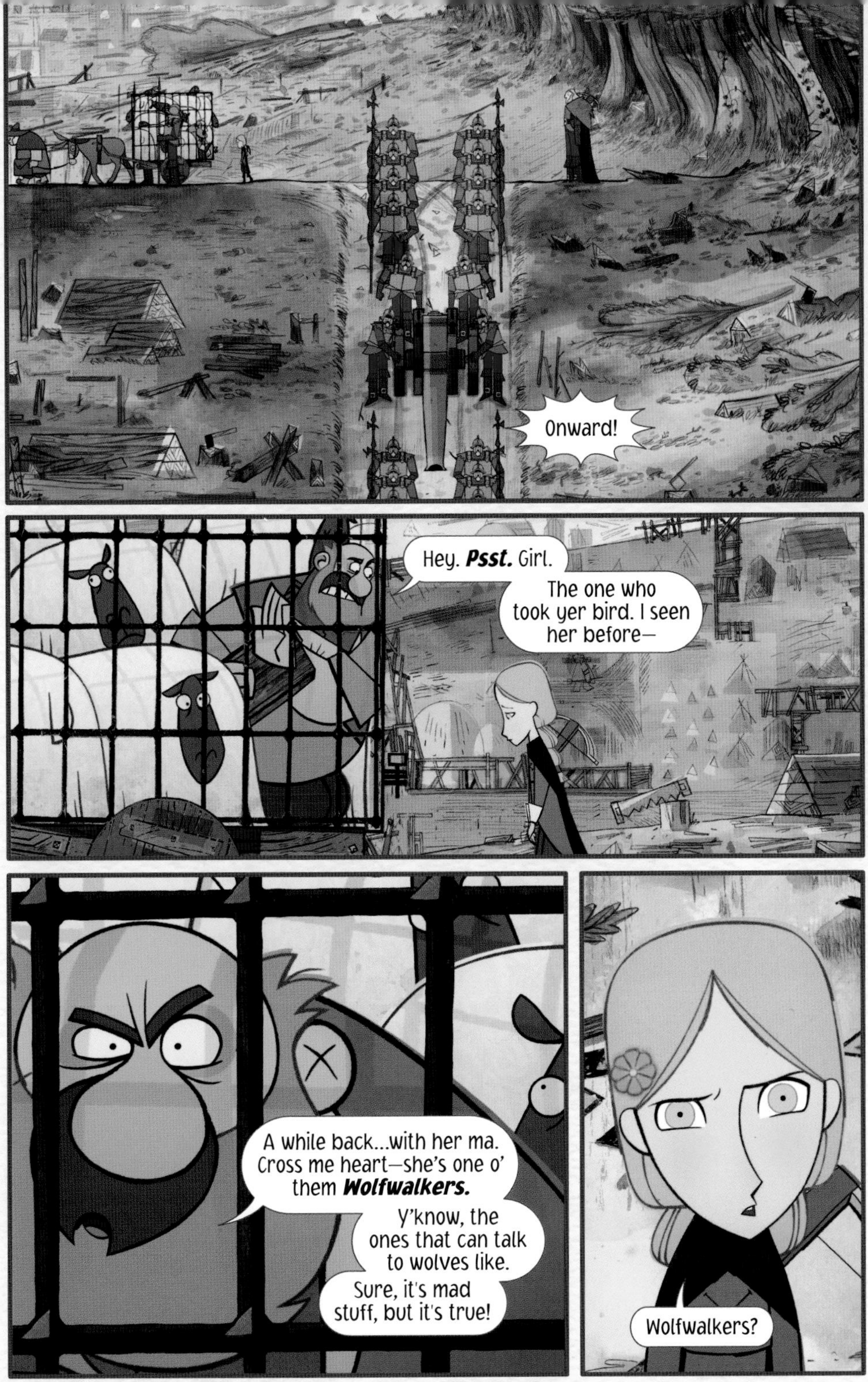

Onward!
Hey. **Psst.** Girl.
The one who took yer bird. I seen her before—
A while back...with her ma. Cross me heart—she's one o' them ***Wolfwalkers.***
Y'know, the ones that can talk to wolves like.
Sure, it's mad stuff, but it's true!
Wolfwalkers?

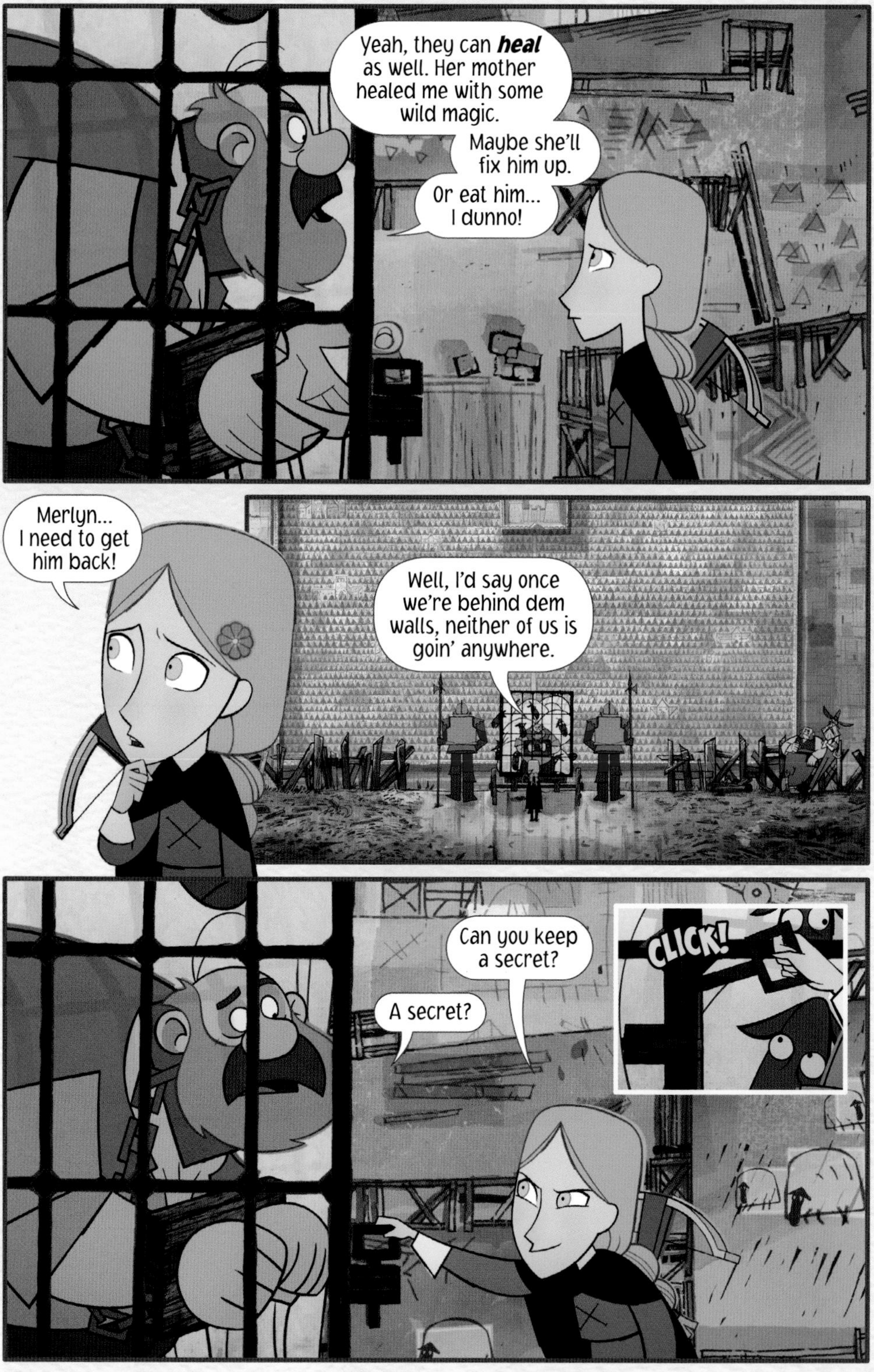
Yeah, they can **heal** as well. Her mother healed me with some wild magic.
Maybe she'll fix him up.
Or eat him... I dunno!
Merlyn... I need to get him back!
Well, I'd say once we're behind dem walls, neither of us is goin' anywhere.
Can you keep a secret?
A secret?
CLICK!

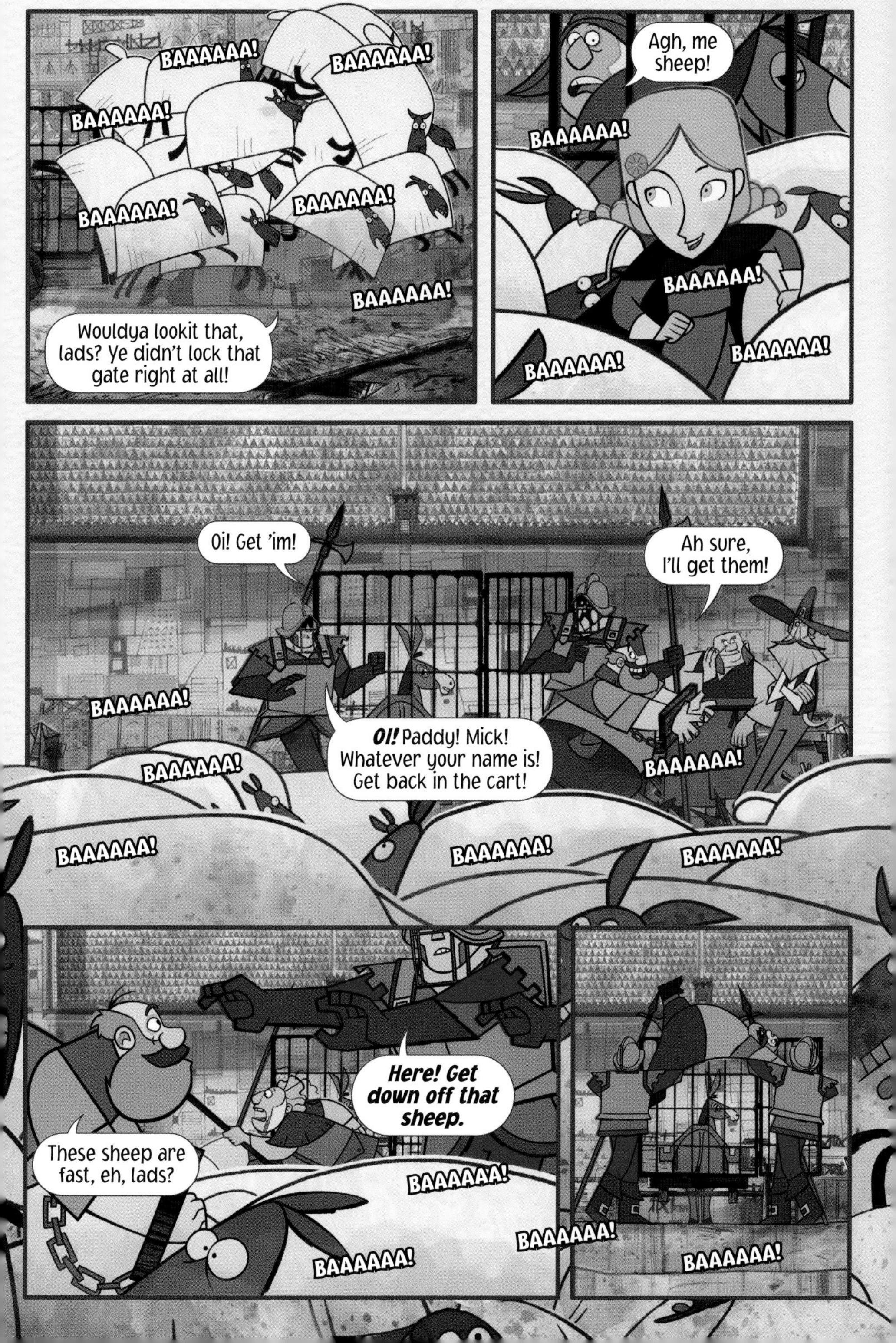
BAAAAAA!
BAAAAAA!
BAAAAAA!
BAAAAAA!
BAAAAAA!
BAAAAAA!
Wouldya lookit that, lads? Ye didn't lock that gate right at all!
Agh, me sheep!
BAAAAAA!
BAAAAAA!
BAAAAAA!
BAAAAAA!
Oi! Get 'im!
Ah sure, I'll get them!
BAAAAAA!
OI! Paddy! Mick! Whatever your name is! Get back in the cart!
BAAAAAA!
BAAAAAA!
BAAAAAA!
BAAAAAA!
BAAAAAA!
Here! Get down off that sheep.
These sheep are fast, eh, lads?
BAAAAAA!
BAAAAAA!
BAAAAAA!
BAAAAAA!

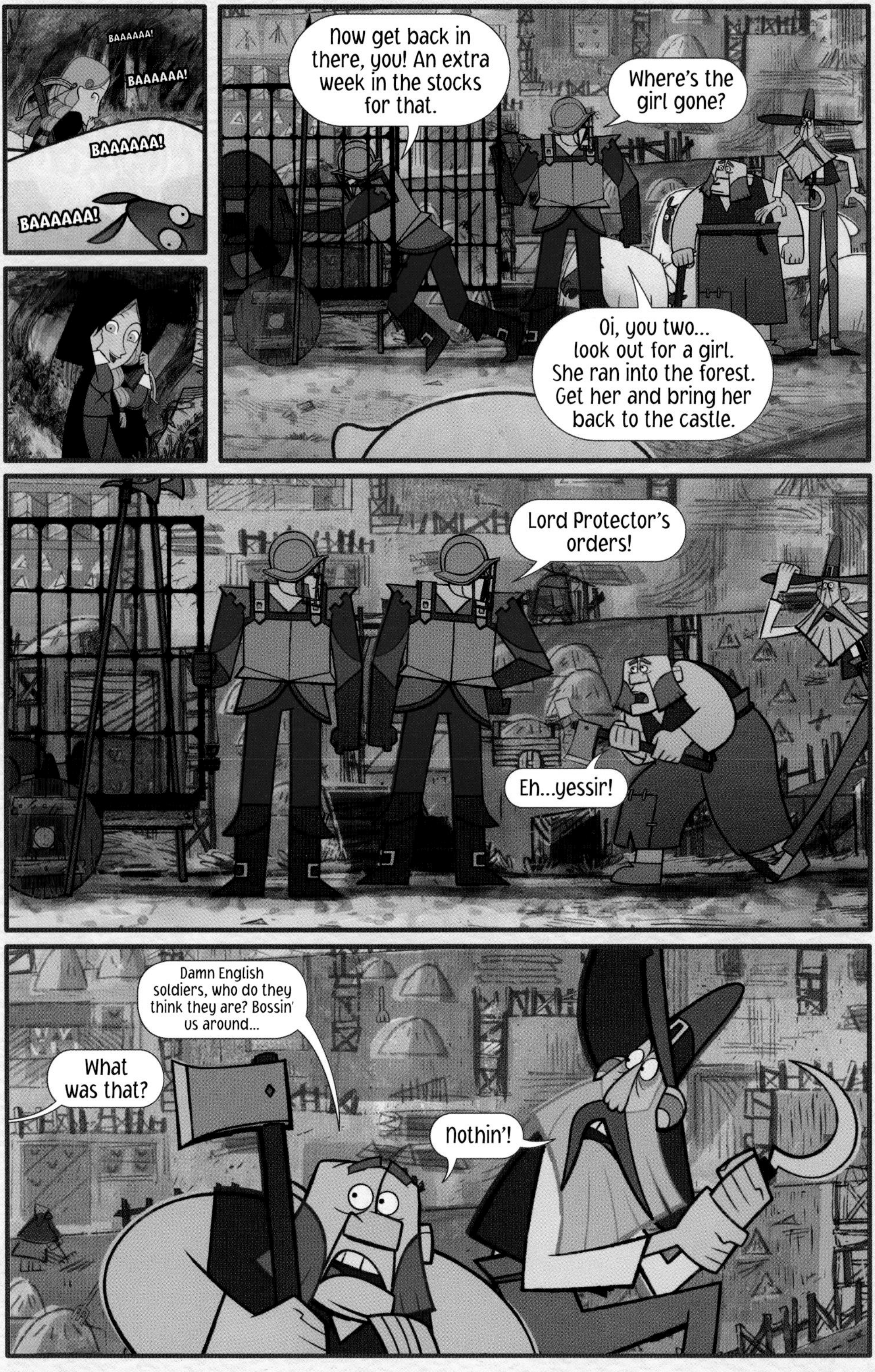
BAAAAAA!
BAAAAAA!
BAAAAAA!
BAAAAAA!
Now get back in there, you! An extra week in the stocks for that.
Where's the girl gone?
Oi, you two... look out for a girl. She ran into the forest. Get her and bring her back to the castle.
Lord Protector's orders!
Eh...yessir!
Damn English soldiers, who do they think they are? Bossin' us around...
What was that?
Nothin'!

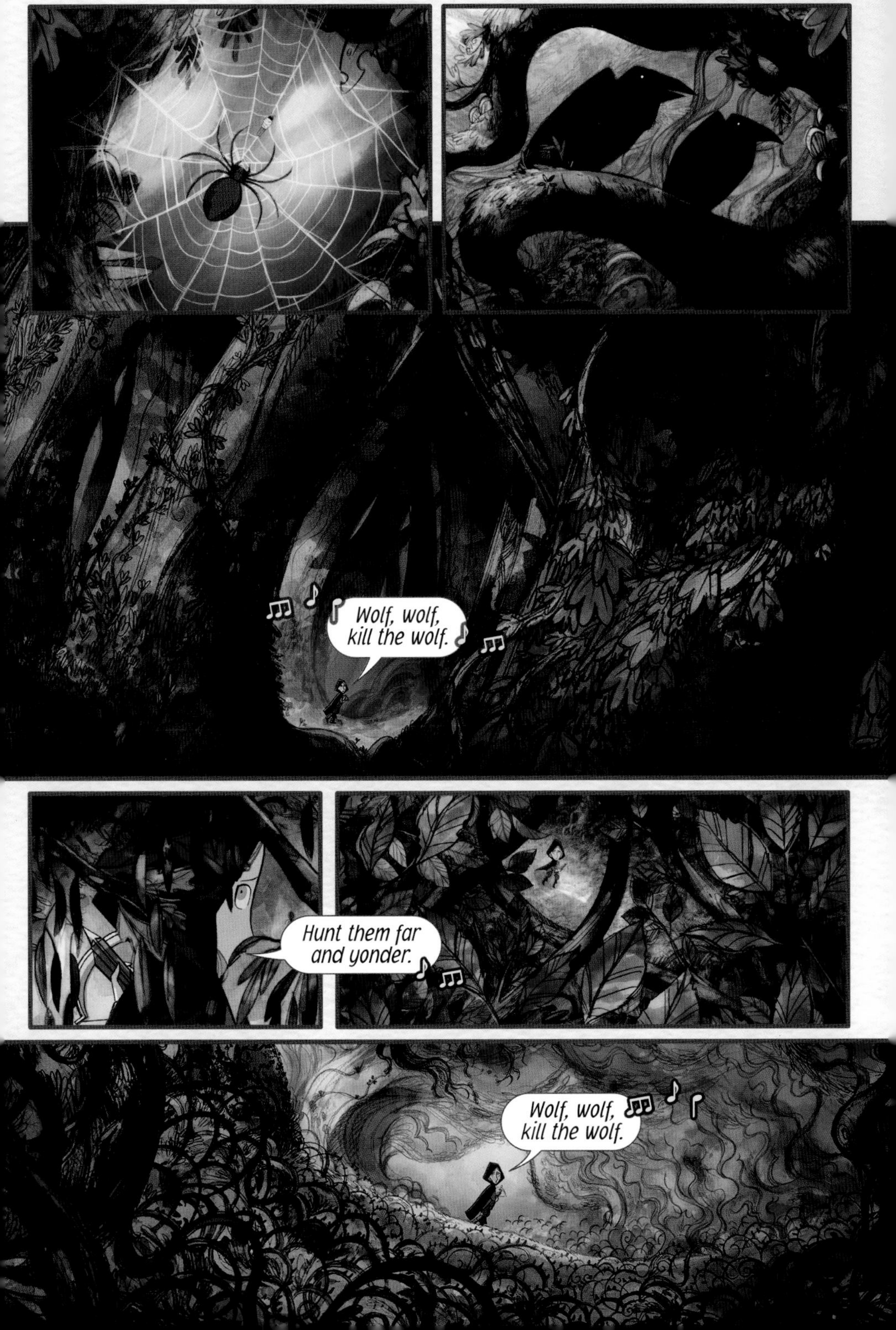
Wolf, wolf, kill the wolf.
Hunt them far and yonder.
Wolf, wolf, kill the wolf.

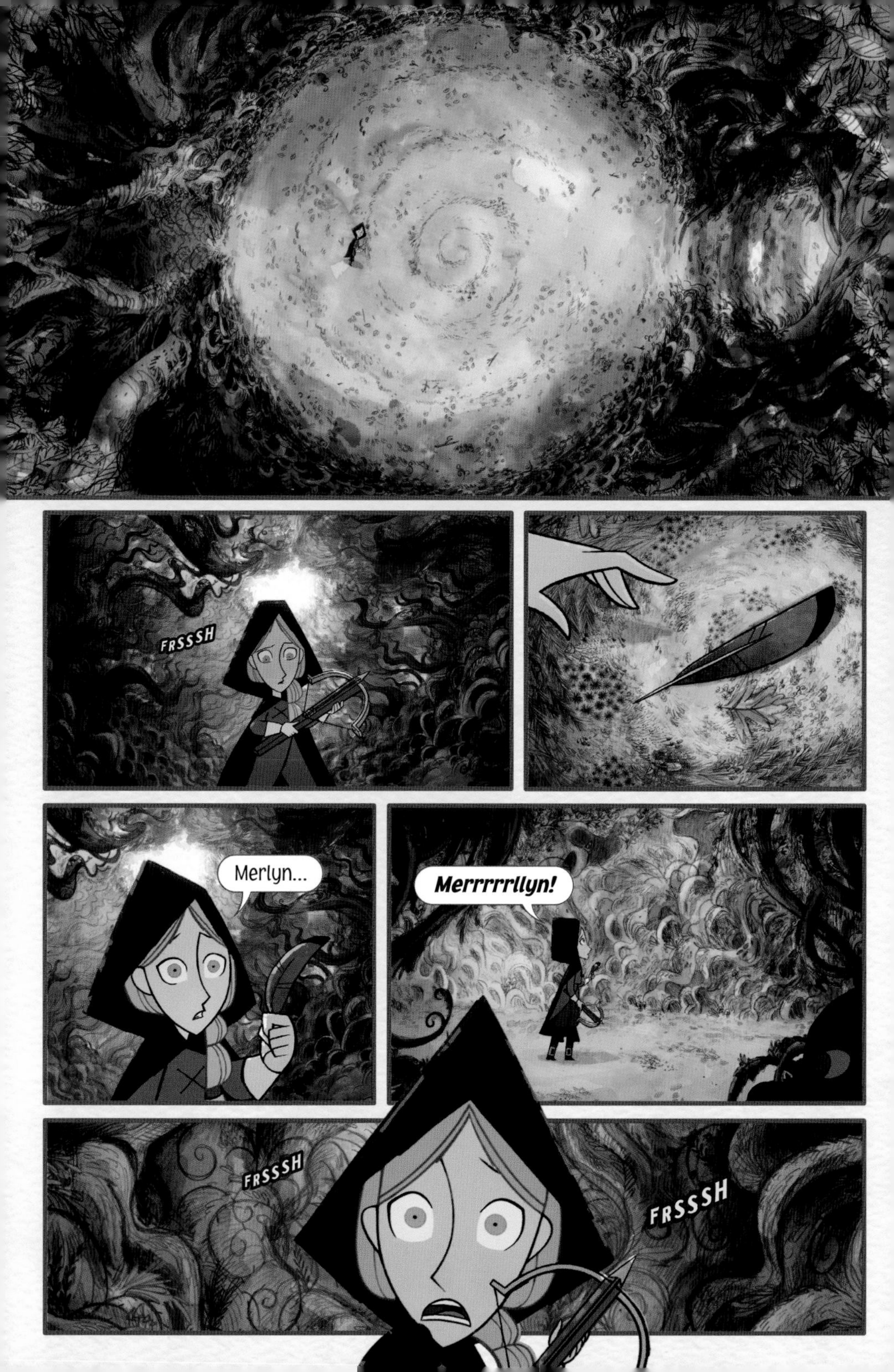
FRSSSH
Merlyn...
Merrrrrrllyn!
FRSSSH
FRSSSH

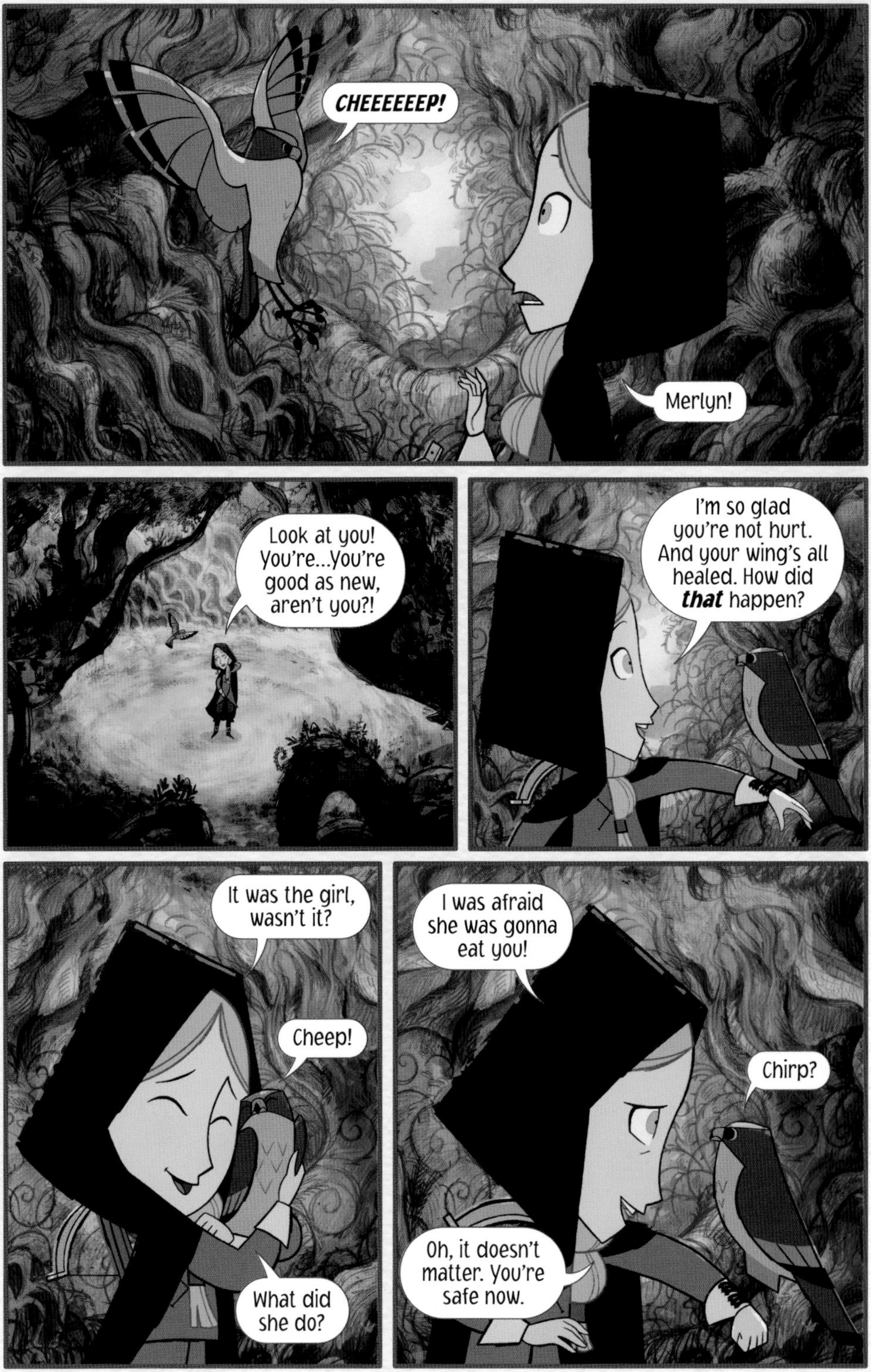
CHEEEEEEP!
Merlyn!
Look at you! You're...You're good as new, aren't you?!
I'm so glad you're not hurt. And your wing's all healed. How did ***that*** happen?
It was the girl, wasn't it?
Cheep!
What did she do?
I was afraid she was gonna eat you!
Chirp?
Oh, it doesn't matter. You're safe now.

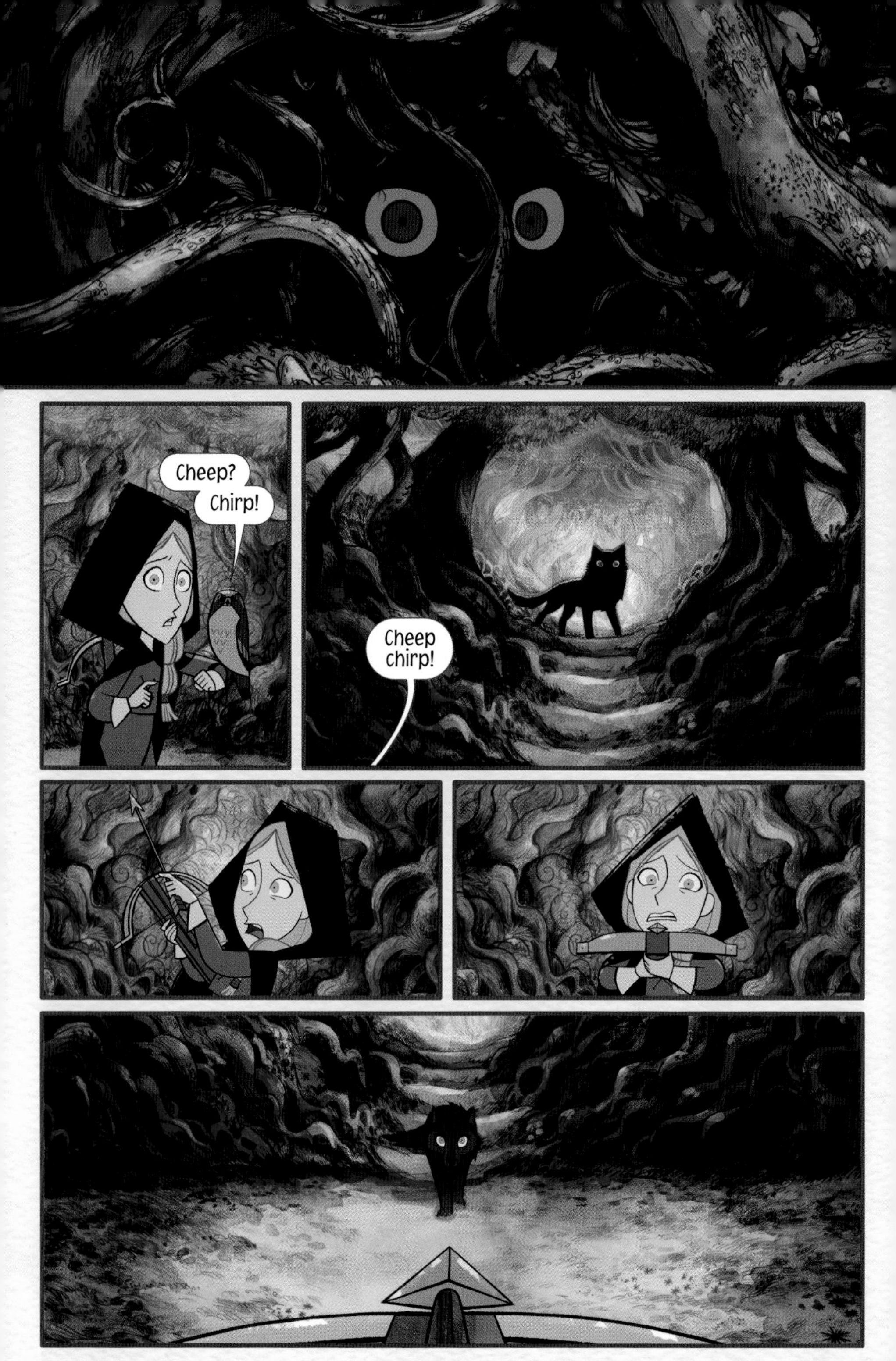
Cheep?
Chirp!
Cheep chirp!

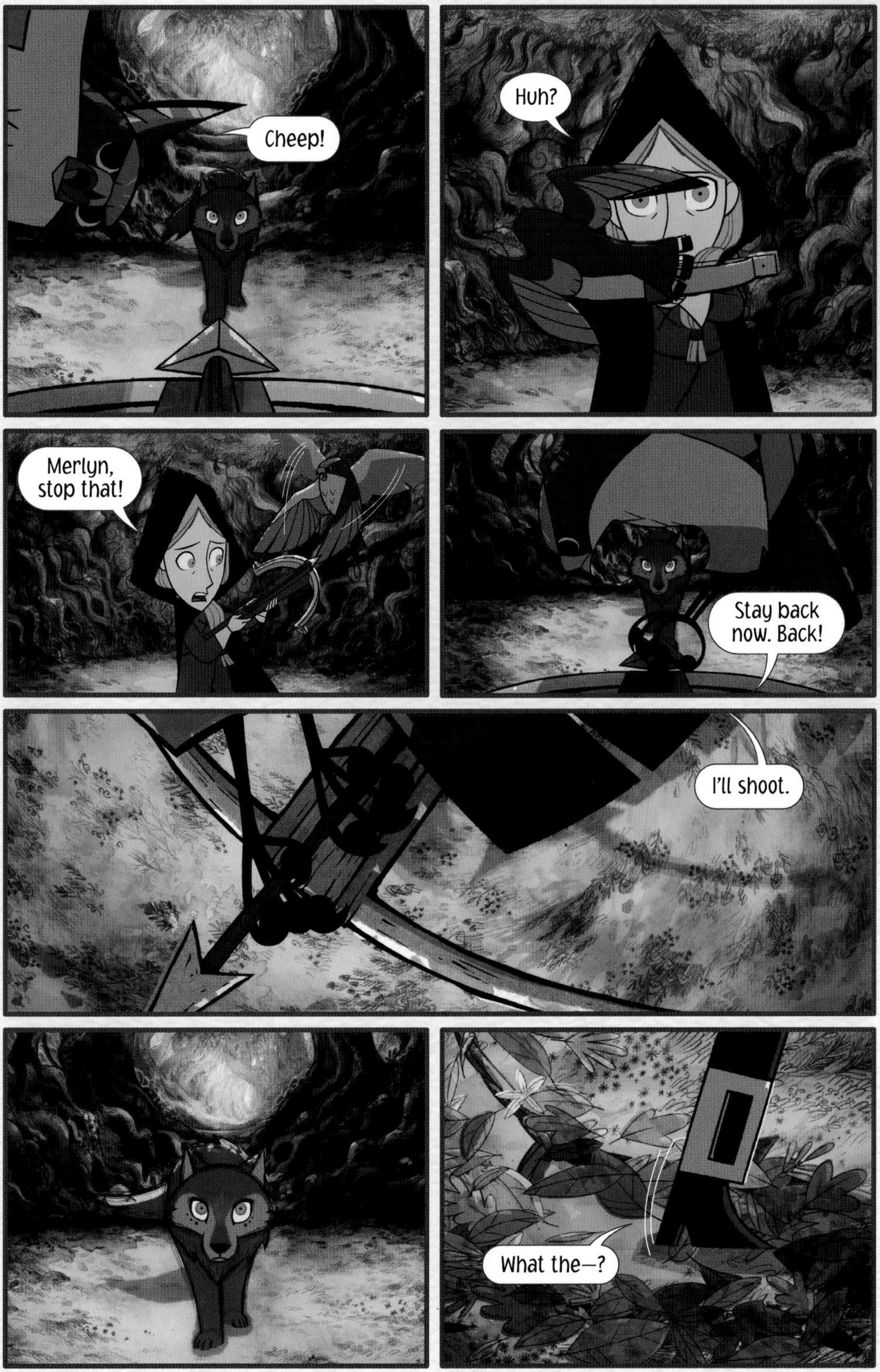
Cheep!
Huh?
Merlyn, stop that!
Stay back now. Back!
I'll shoot.
What the—?

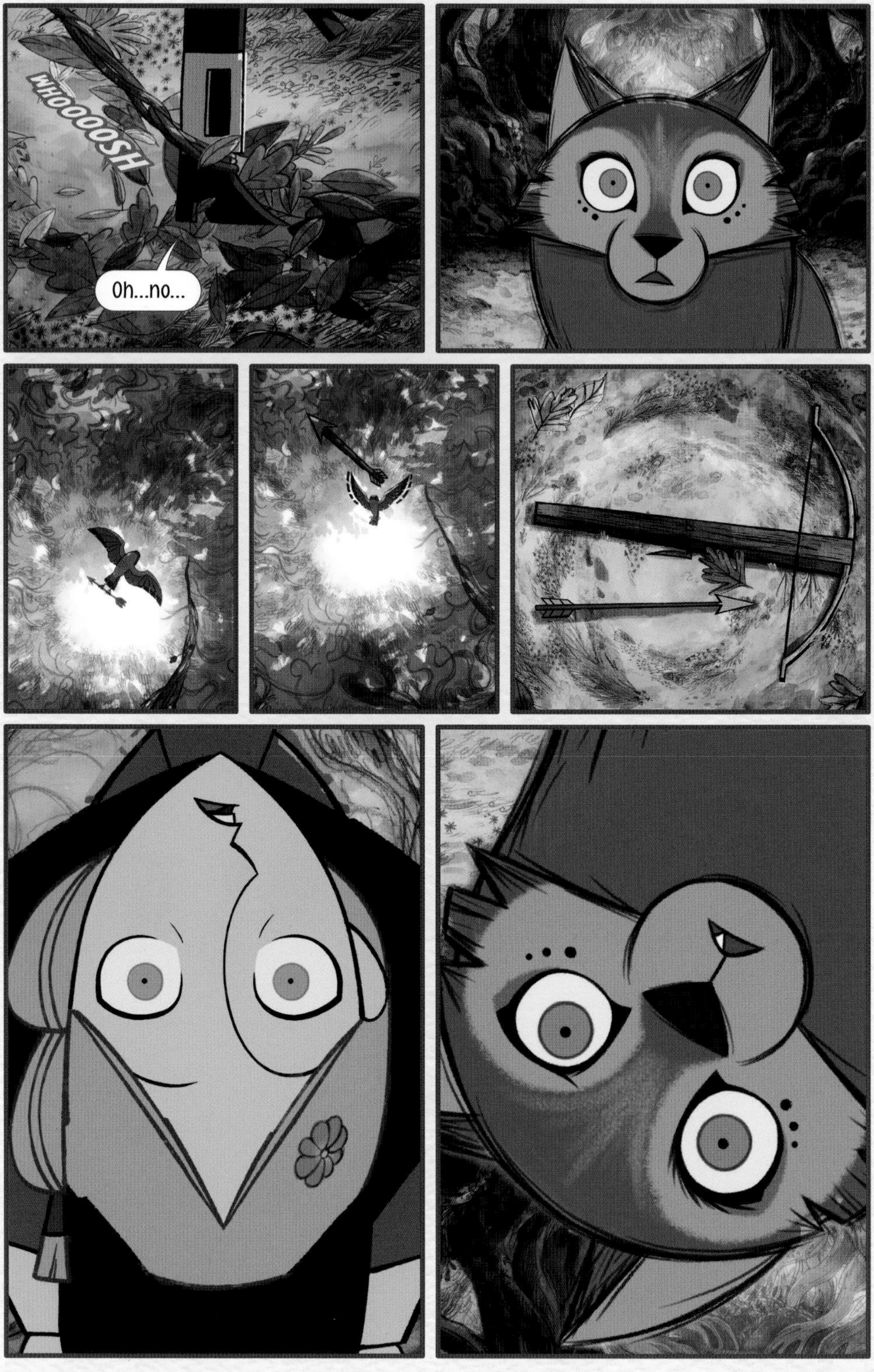
WHOOOOOSH
Oh...no...

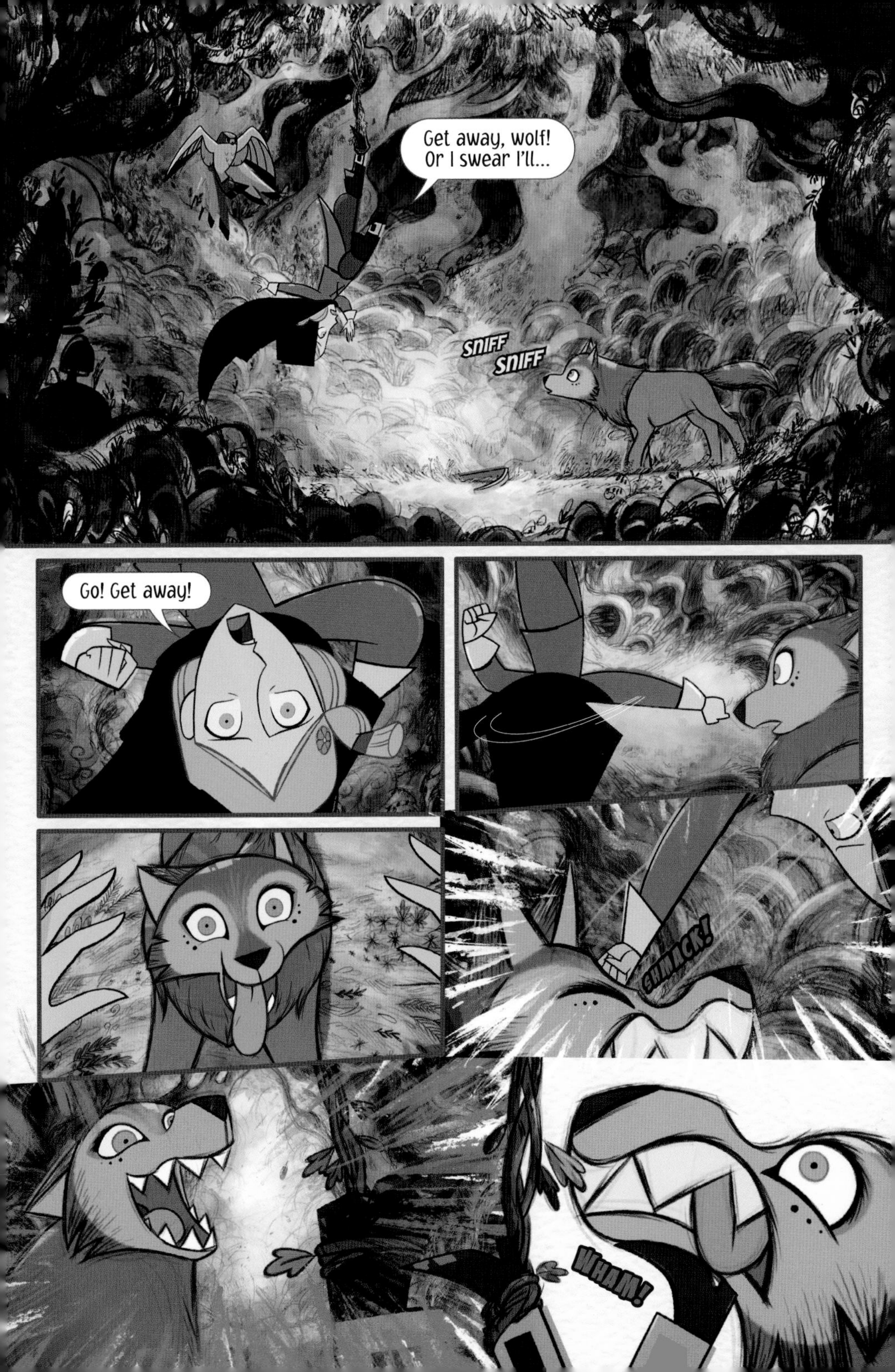
Get away, wolf! Or I swear I'll...
SNIFF
SNIFF
Go! Get away!
SHMACK!
WHAM!

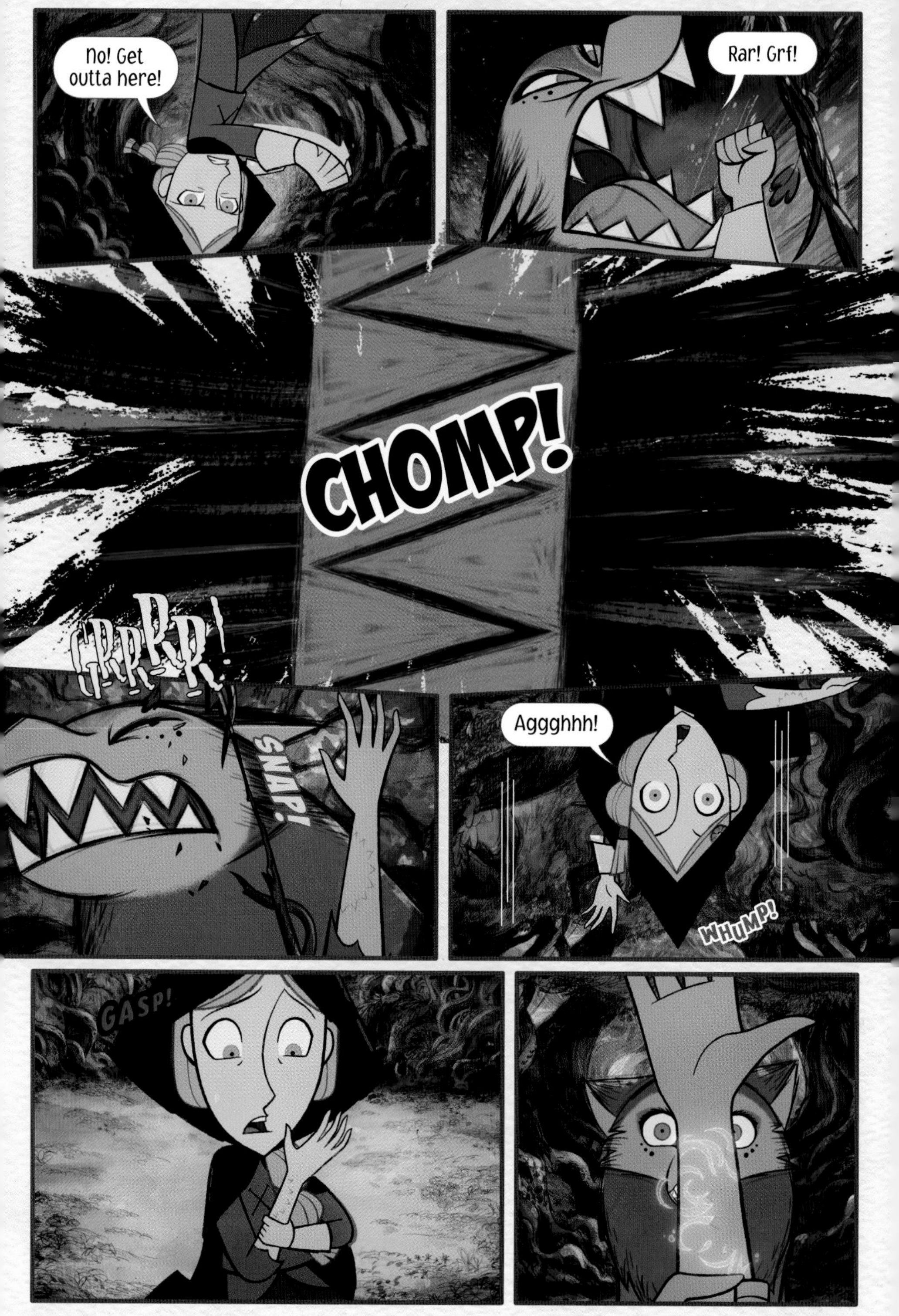
No! Get outta here!
Rar! Grf!
CHOMP!
GRRRRR!
SNAP!
Aggghhh!
WHUMP!
GASP!

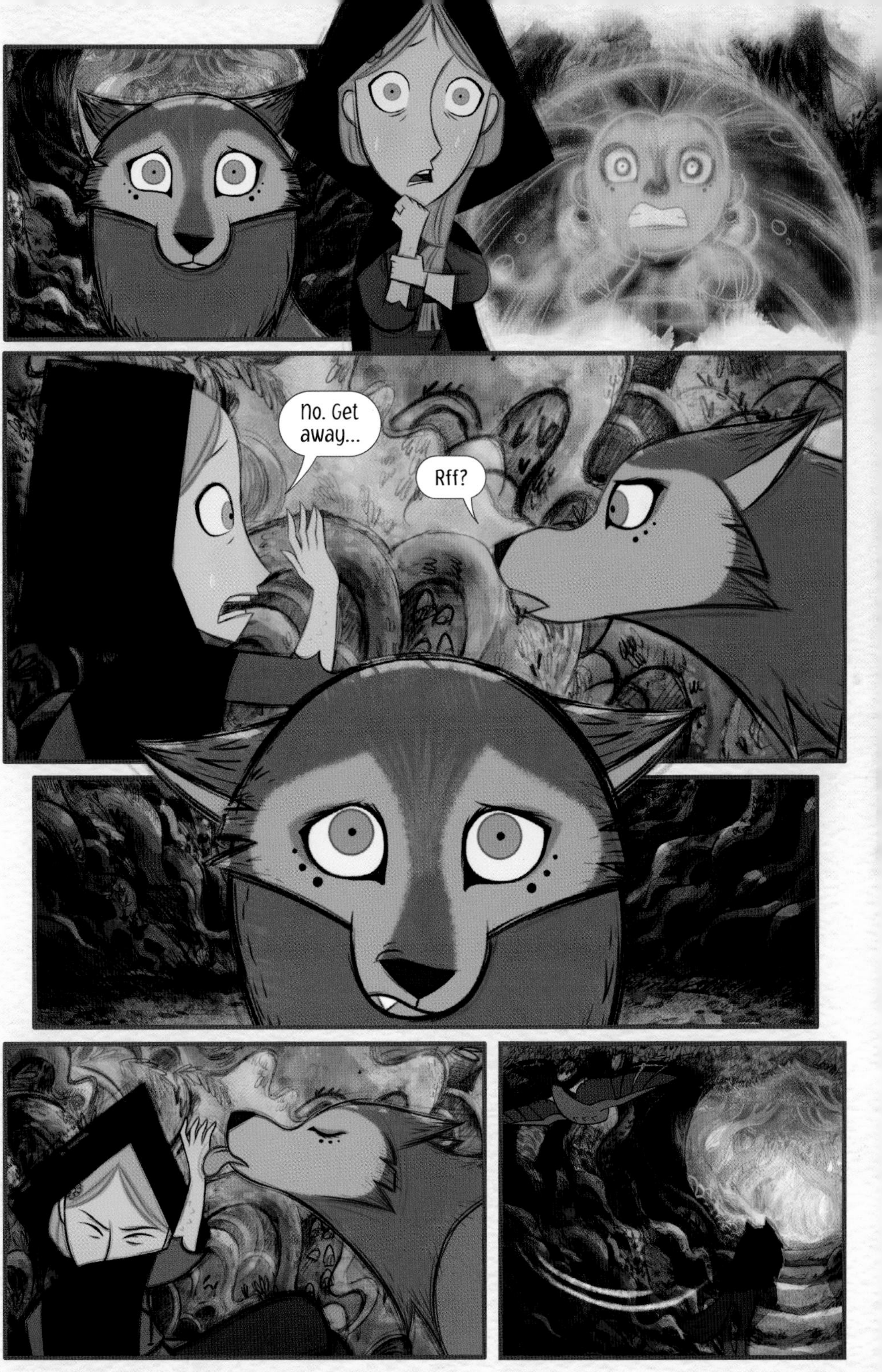
No. Get away...
Rff?

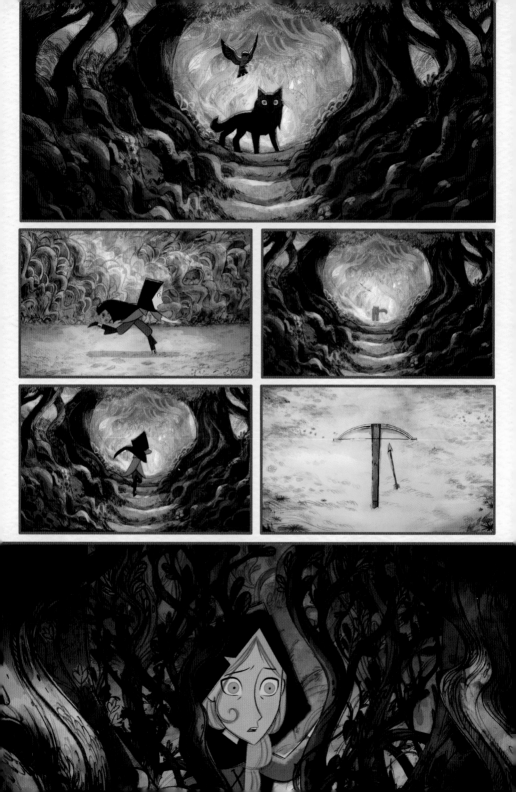

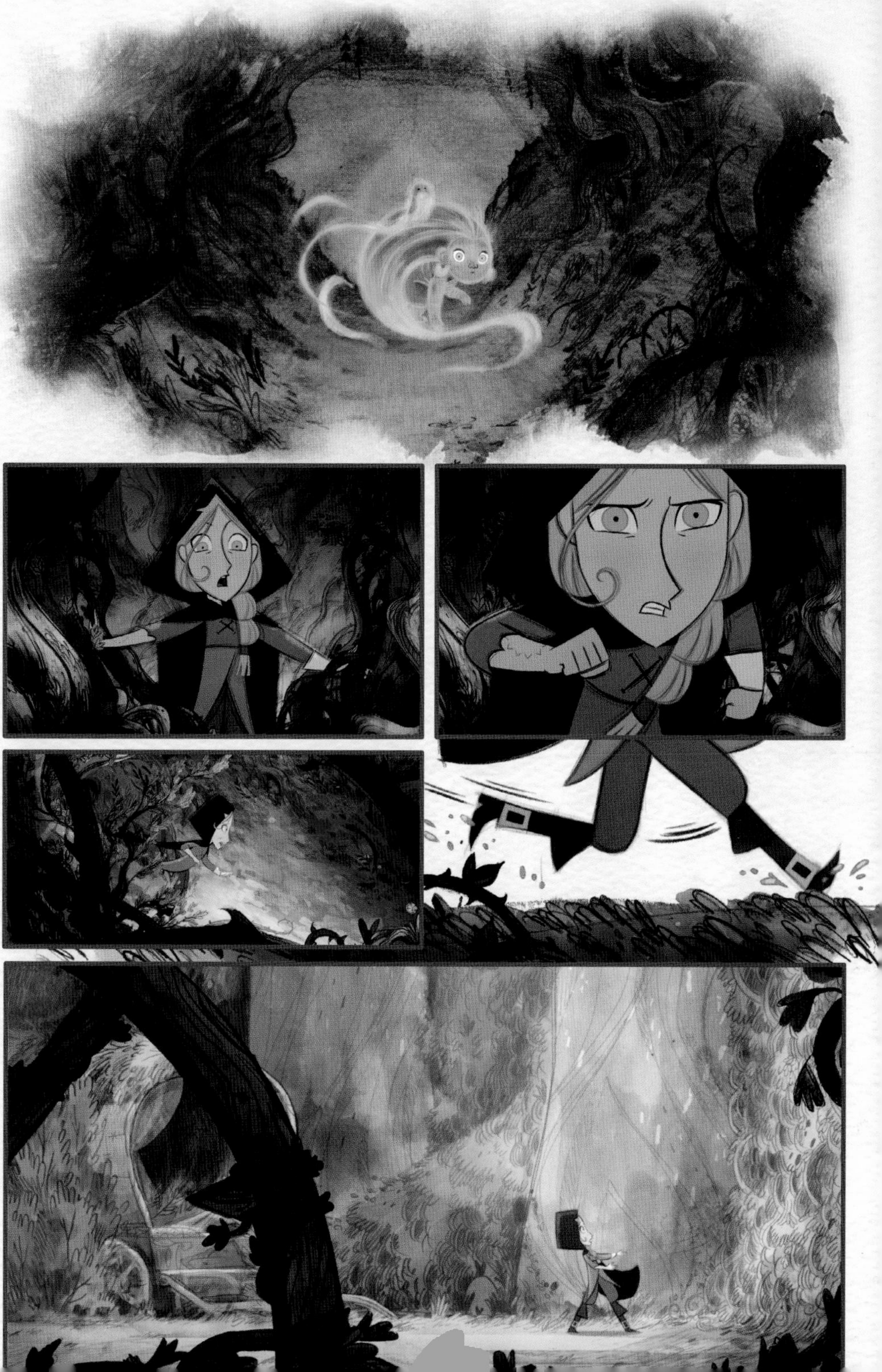

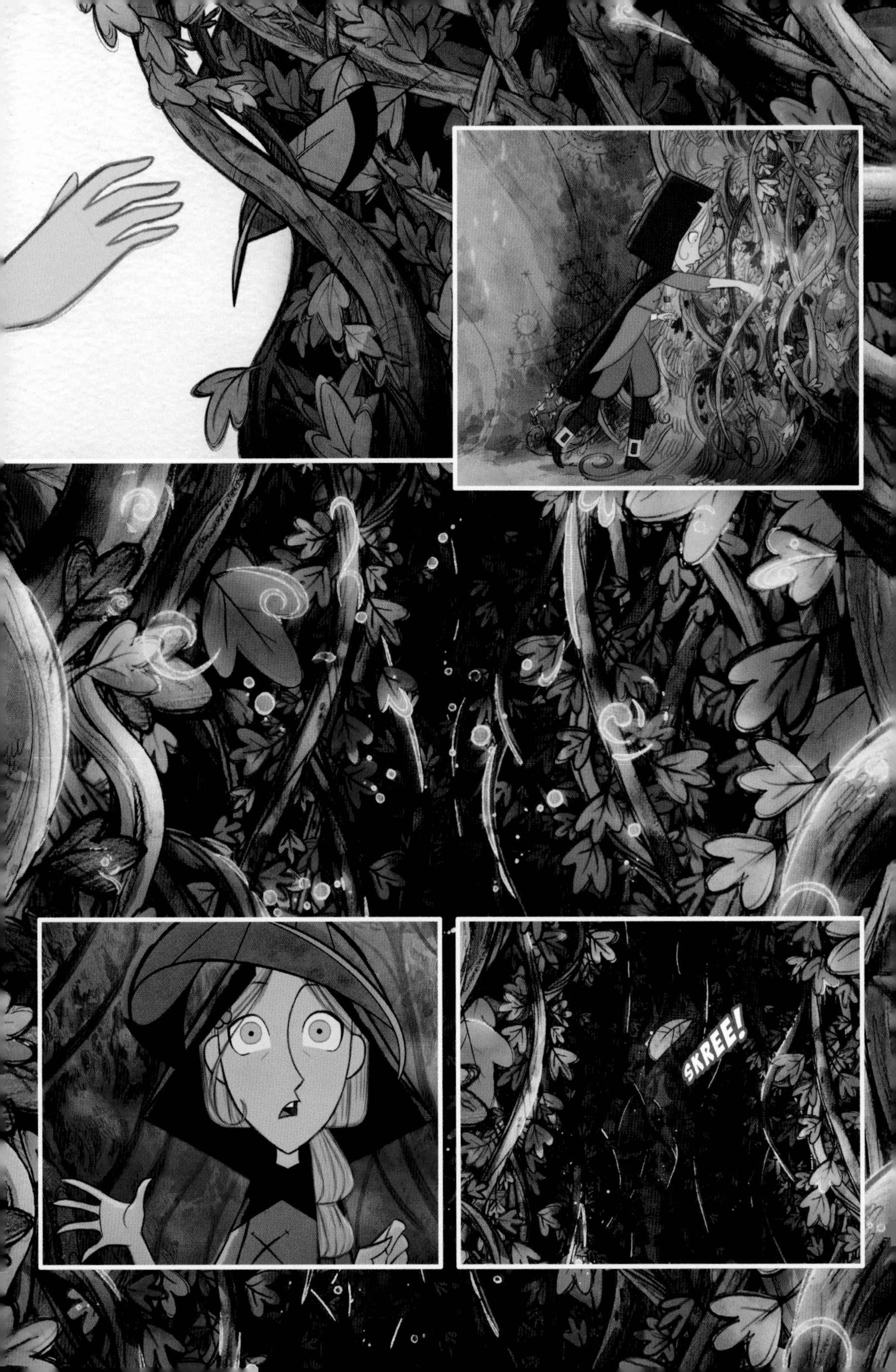
SKREE!

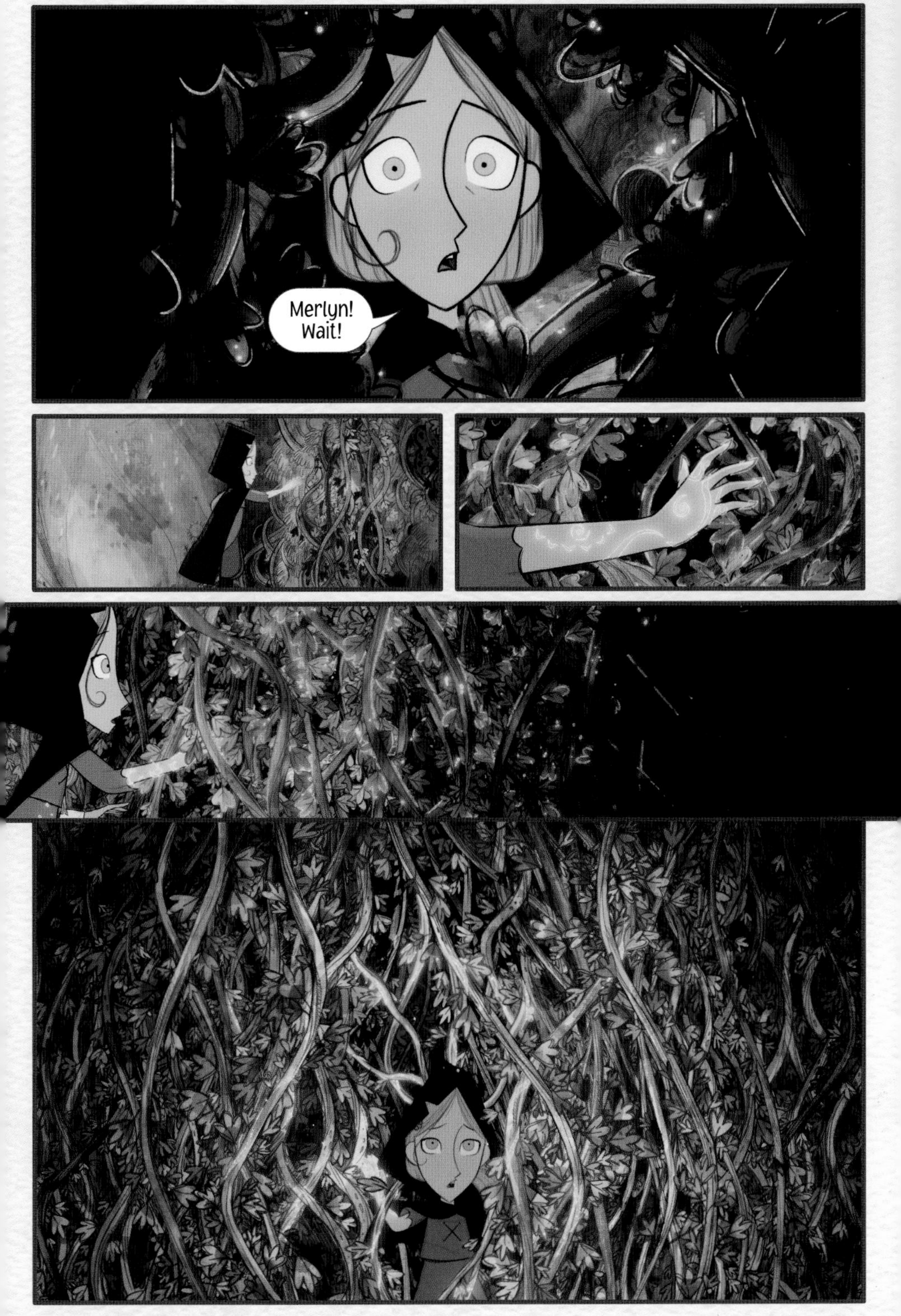
Merlyn! Wait!

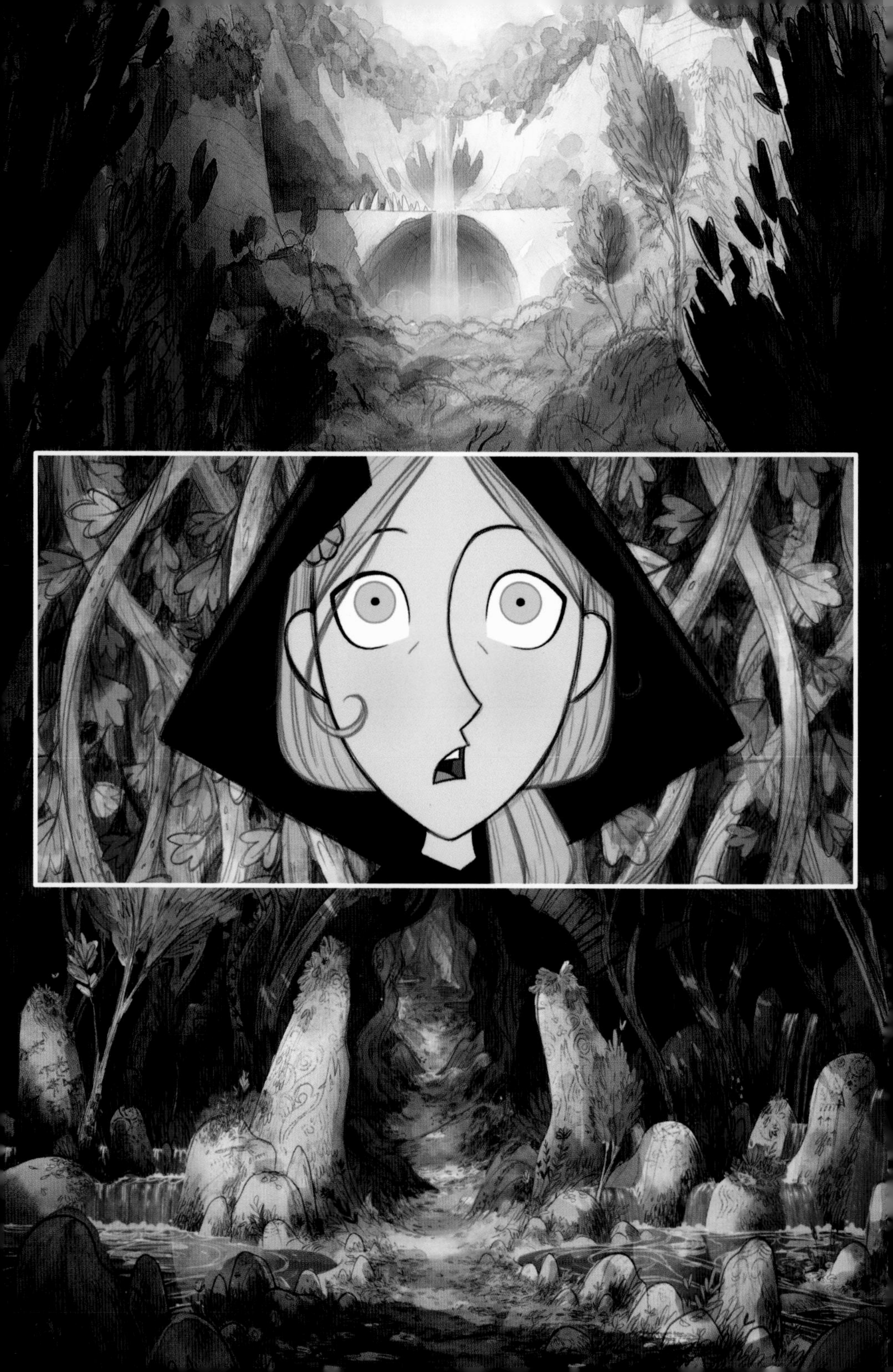

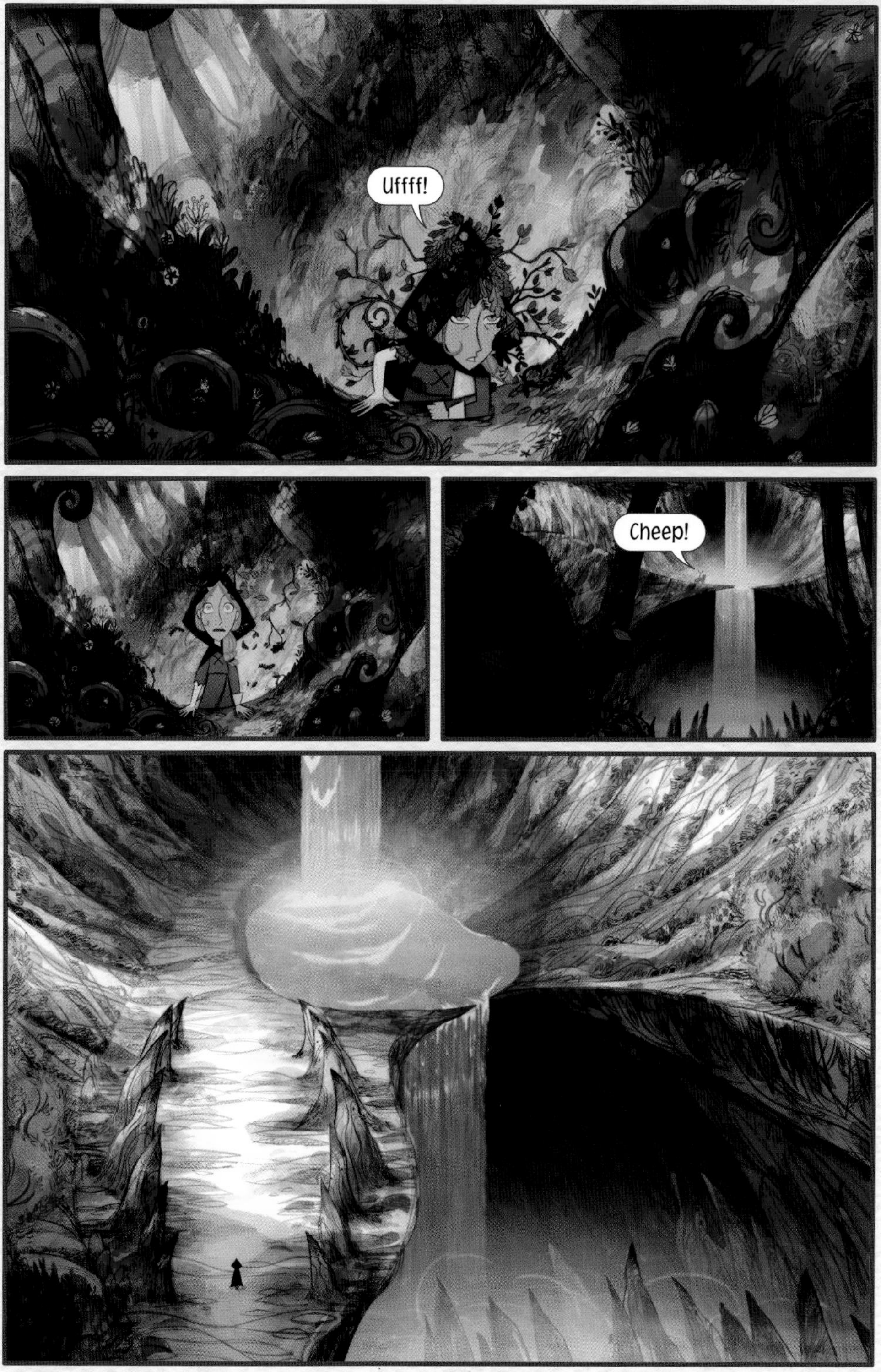
Uffff!
Cheep!

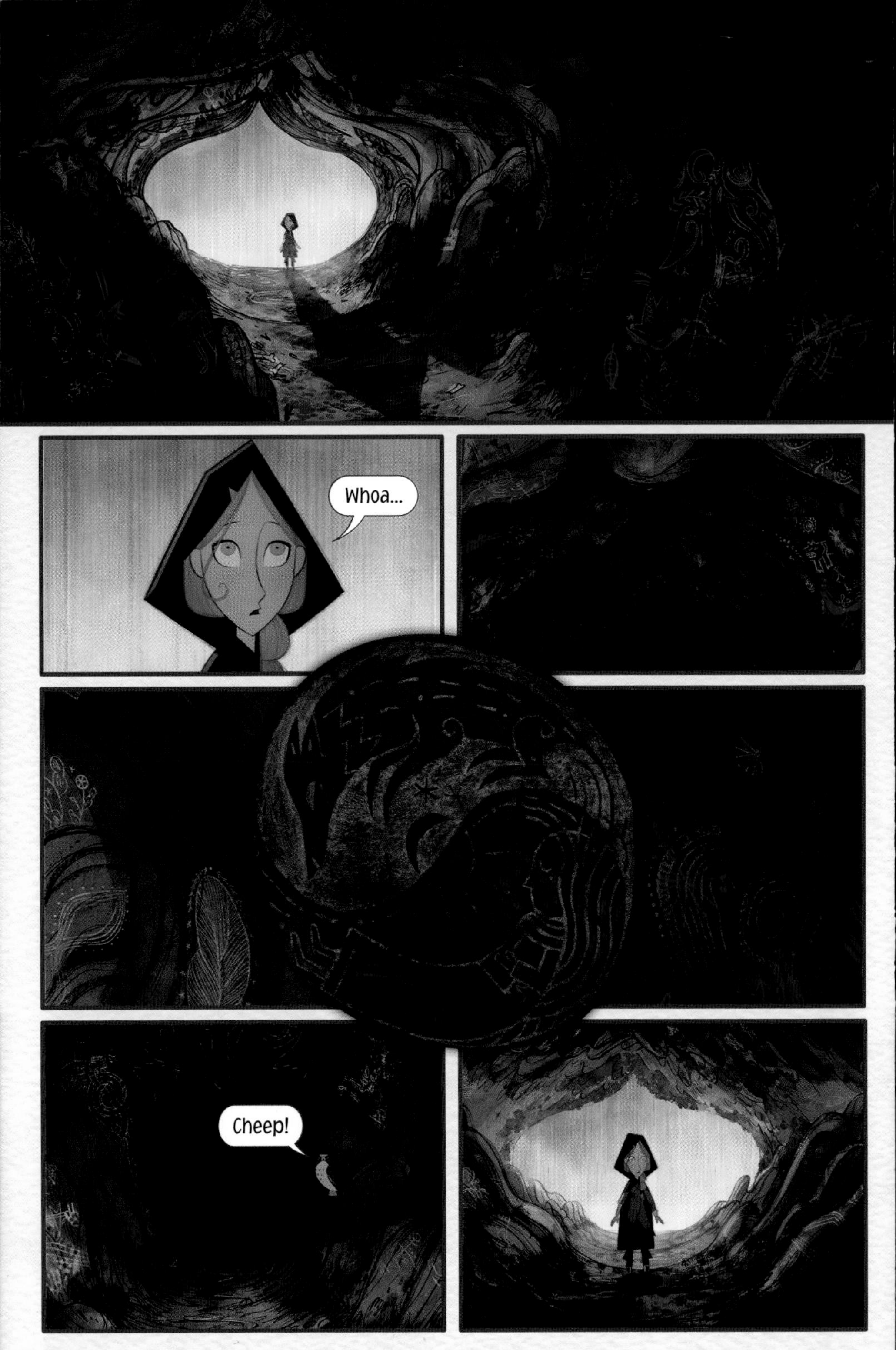
Whoa...
Cheep!

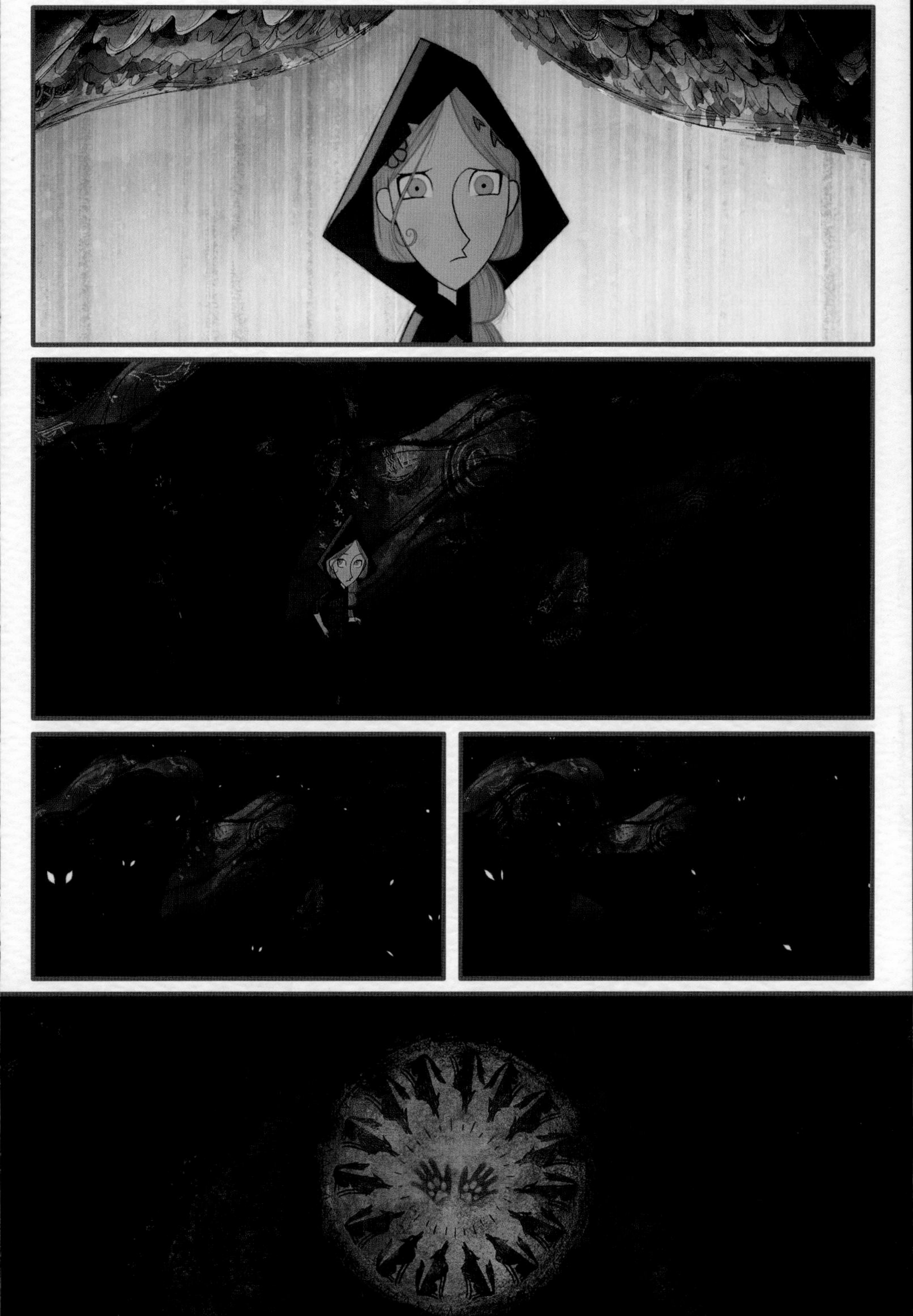

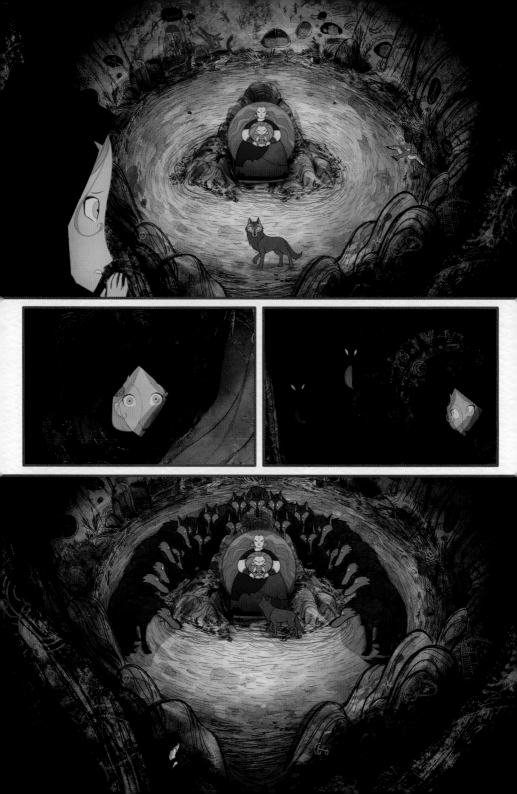

VHMMM

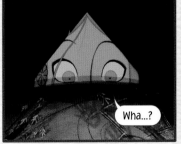

Wha...?

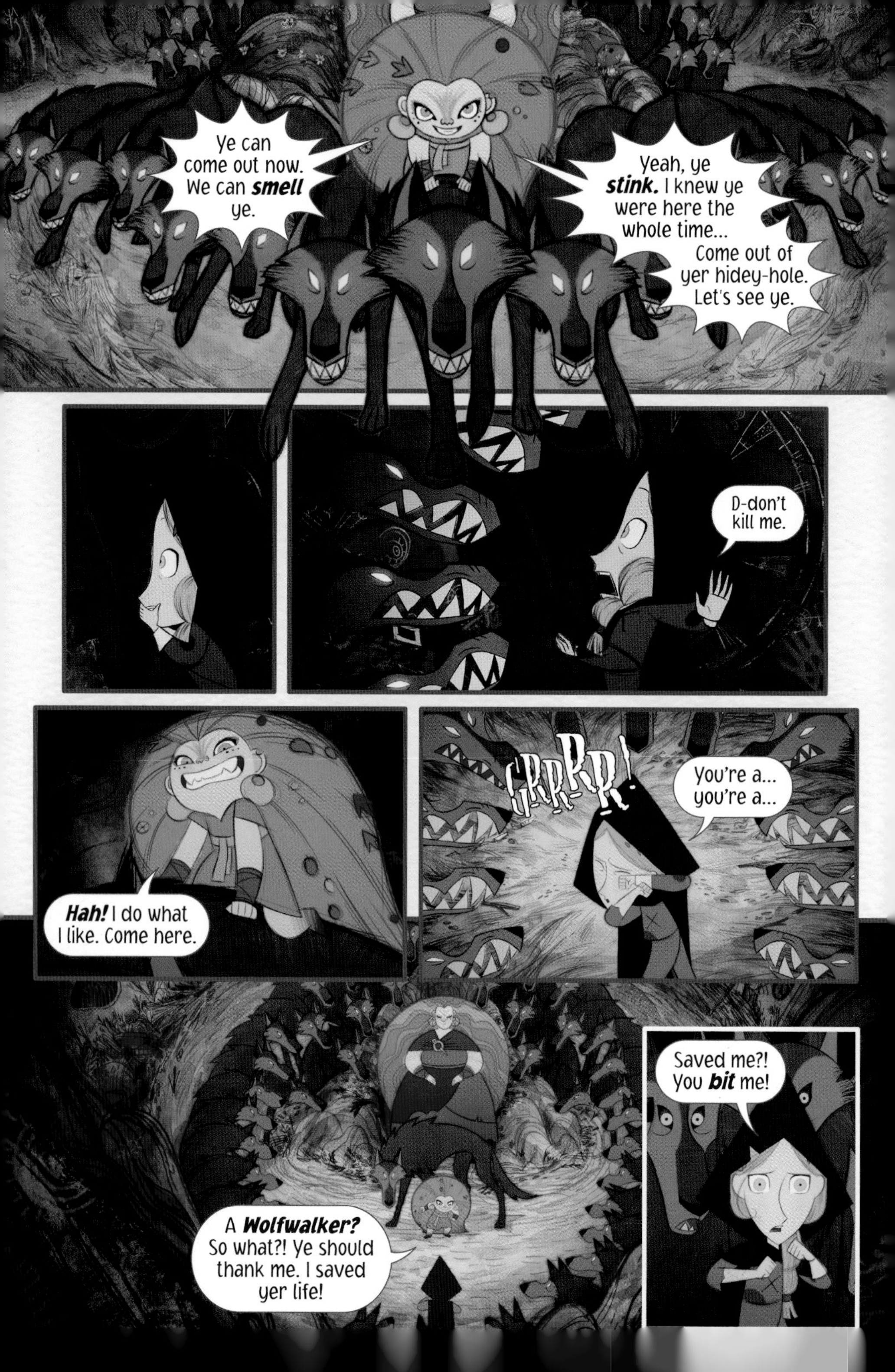
Ye can come out now. We can **smell** ye.
Yeah, ye **stink.** I knew ye were here the whole time...
Come out of yer hidey-hole. Let's see ye.
D-don't kill me.
Hah! I do what I like. Come here.
GRRRR!
You're a... you're a...
A **Wolfwalker?** So what?! Ye should thank me. I saved yer life!
Saved me?! You **bit** me!

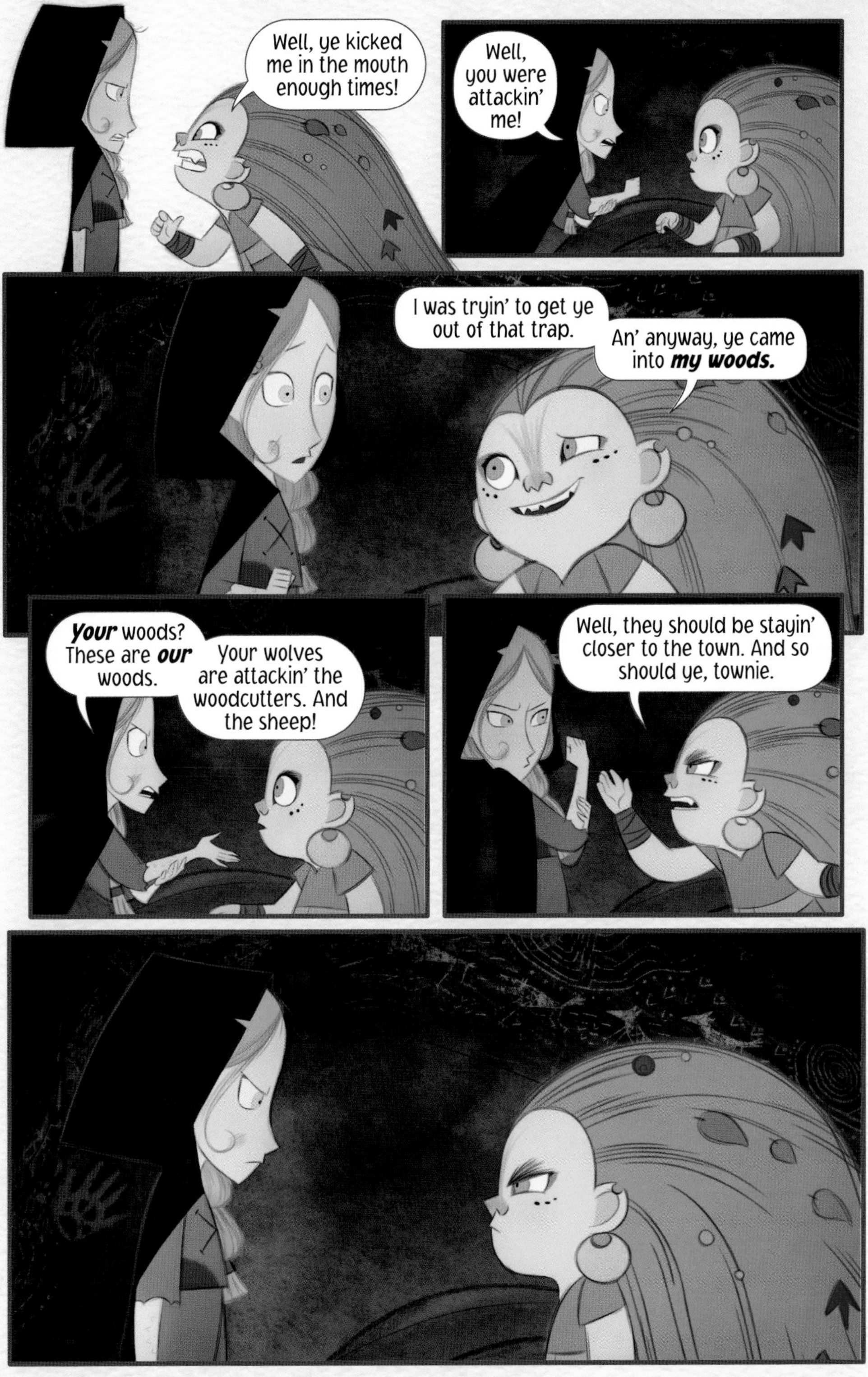
Well, ye kicked me in the mouth enough times!
Well, you were attackin' me!
I was tryin' to get ye out of that trap.
An' anyway, ye came into **my woods.**
Your woods? These are ***our*** woods.
Your wolves are attackin' the woodcutters. And the sheep!
Well, they should be stayin' closer to the town. And so should ye, townie.

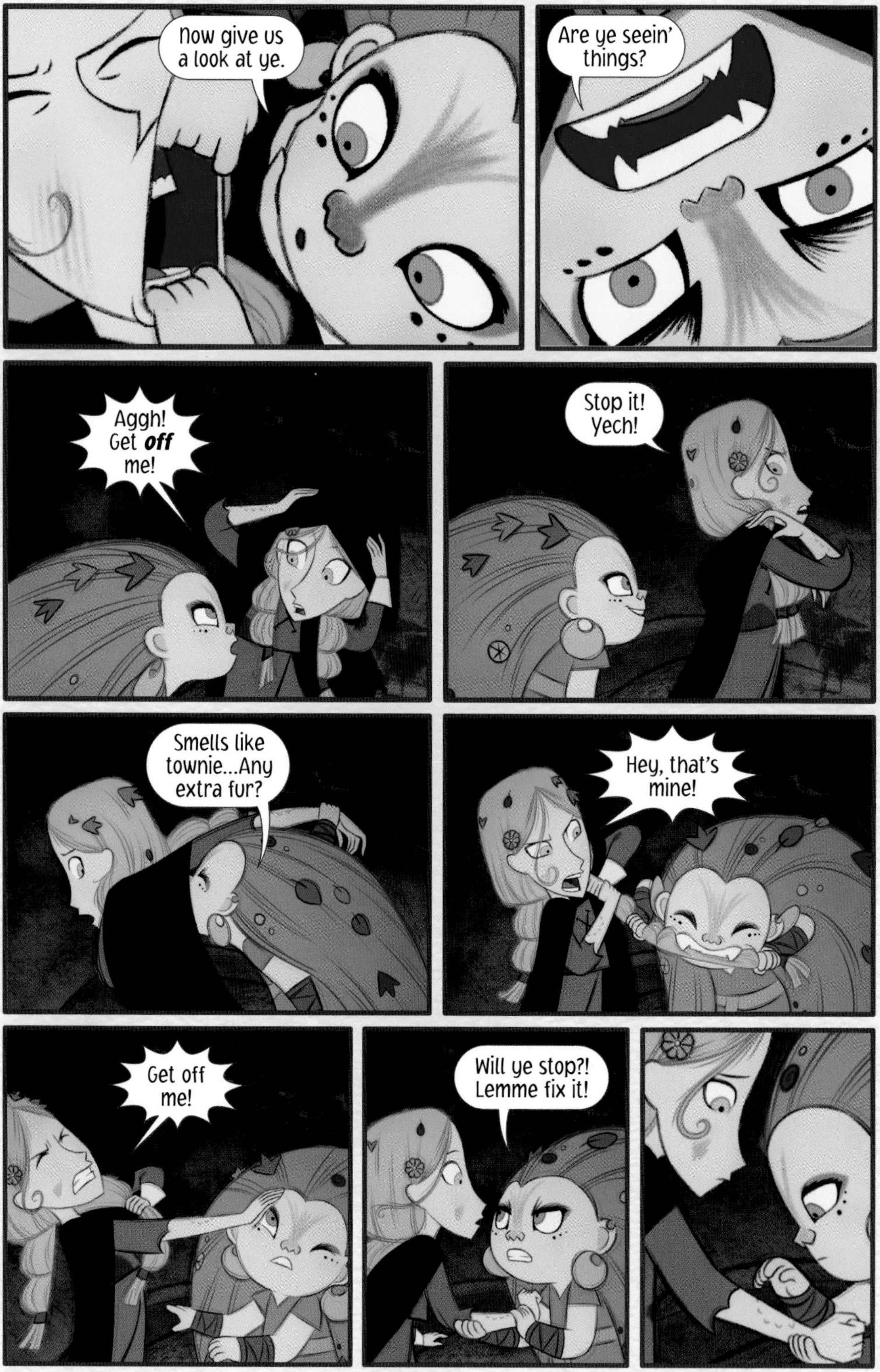
Now give us a look at ye.
Are ye seein' things?
Aggh! Get *off* me!
Stop it! Yech!
Smells like townie...Any extra fur?
Hey, that's mine!
Get off me!
Will ye stop?! Lemme fix it!

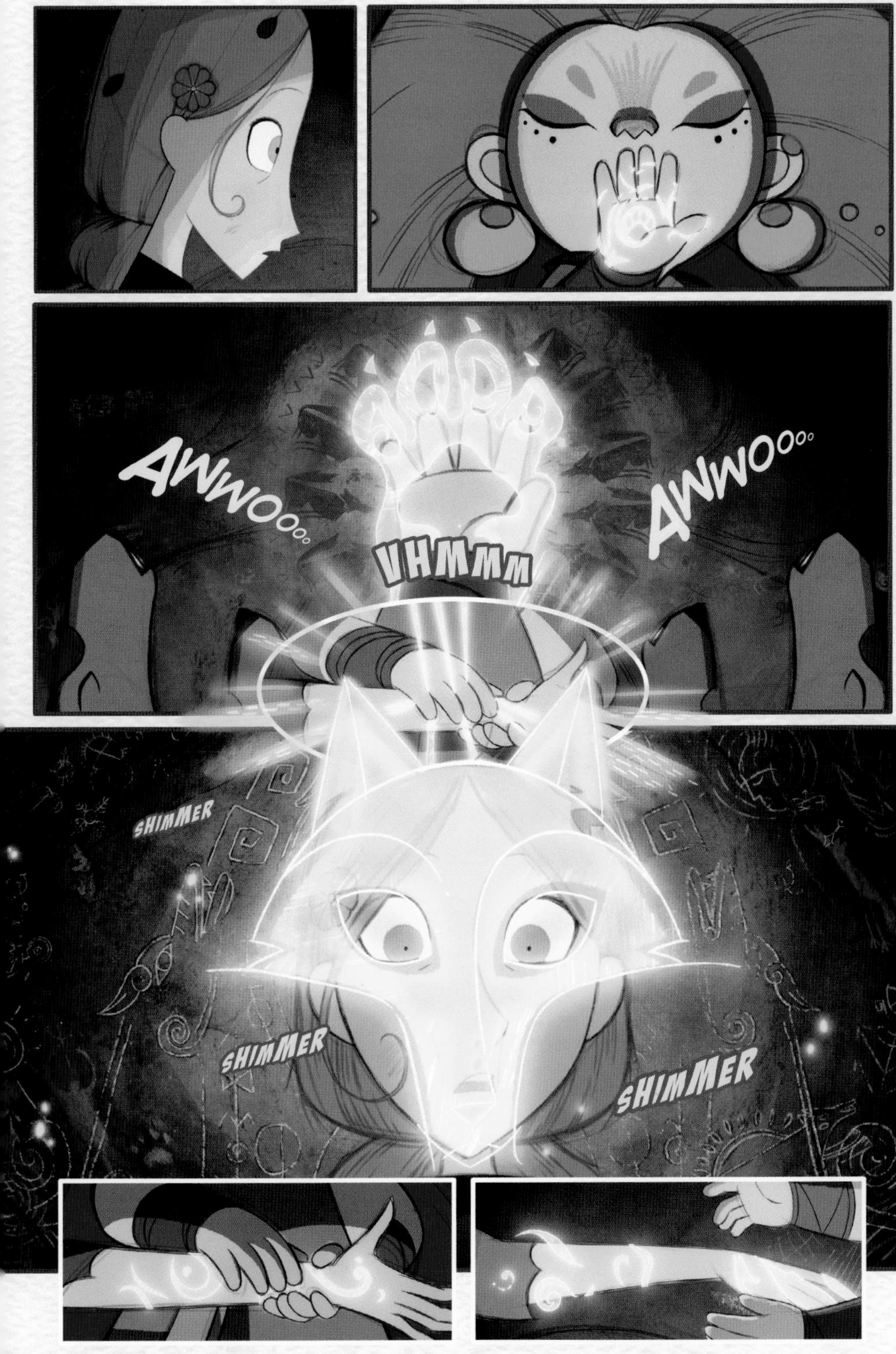
AWWOooo
VHMMM
AWWOooo
SHIMMER
SHIMMER
SHIMMER

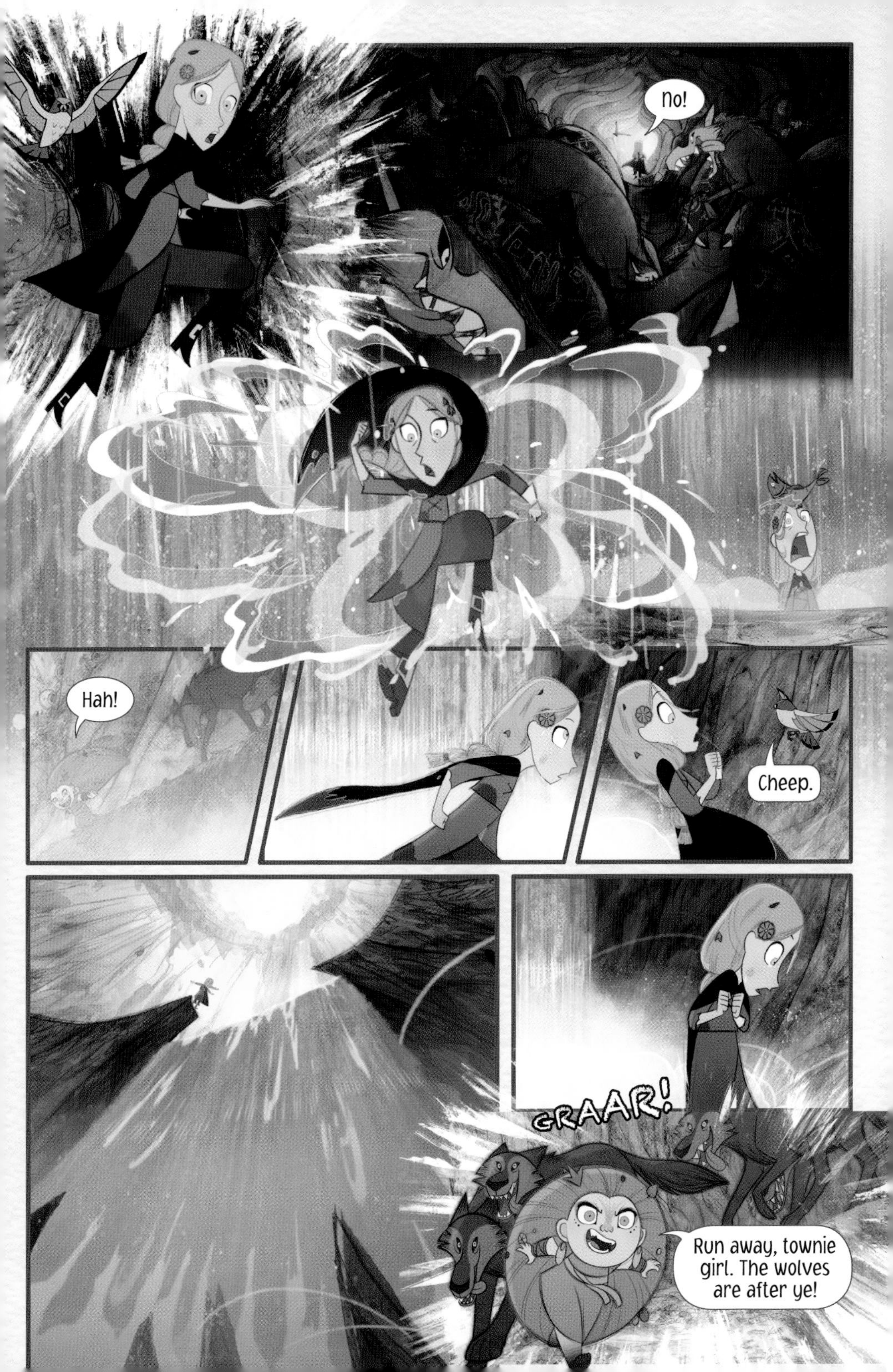
No!
Hah!
Cheep.
GRAAR!
Run away, townie girl. The wolves are after ye!

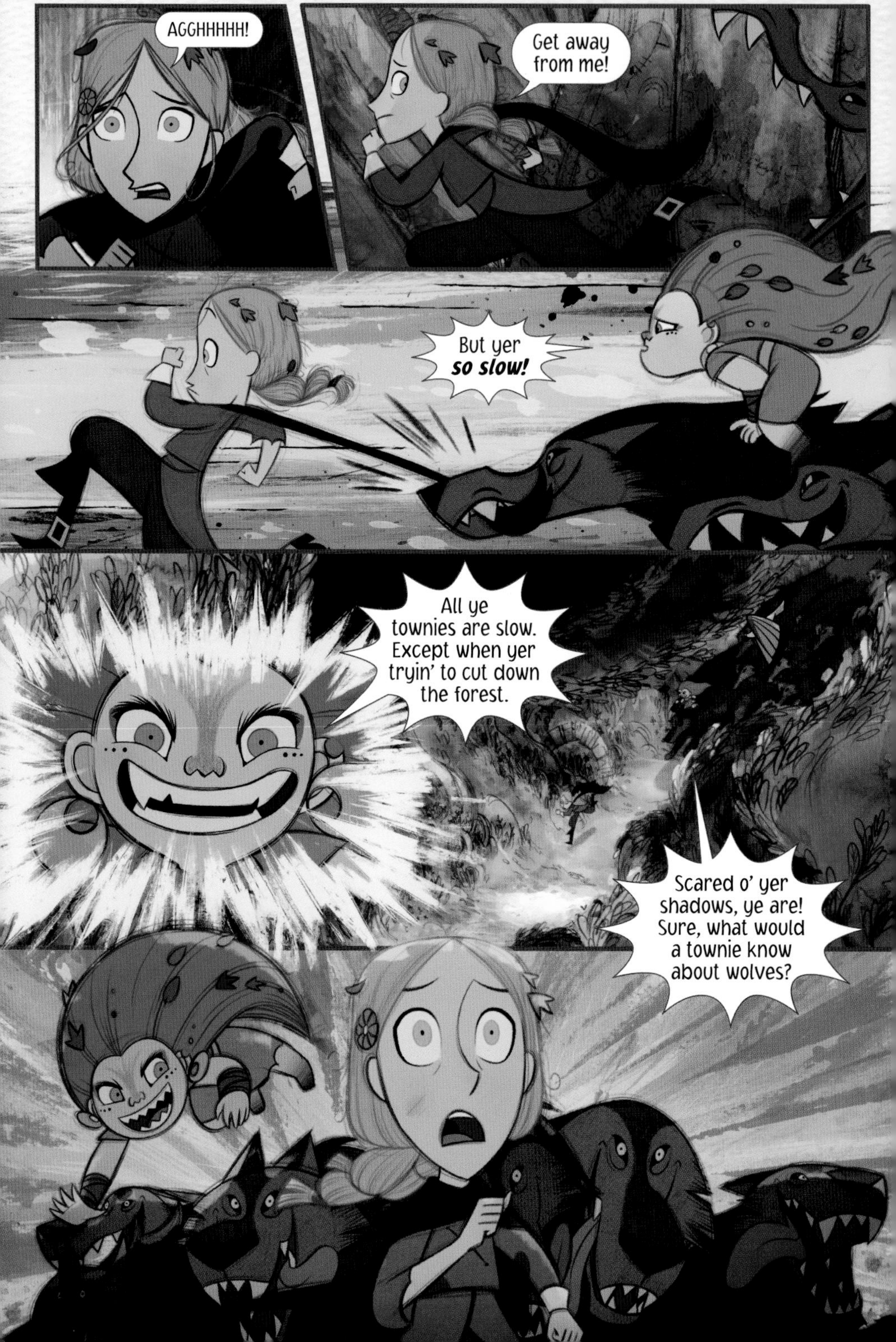
AGGHHHHH!
Get away from me!
But yer **so slow!**
All ye townies are slow. Except when yer tryin' to cut down the forest.
Scared o' yer shadows, ye are! Sure, what would a townie know about wolves?

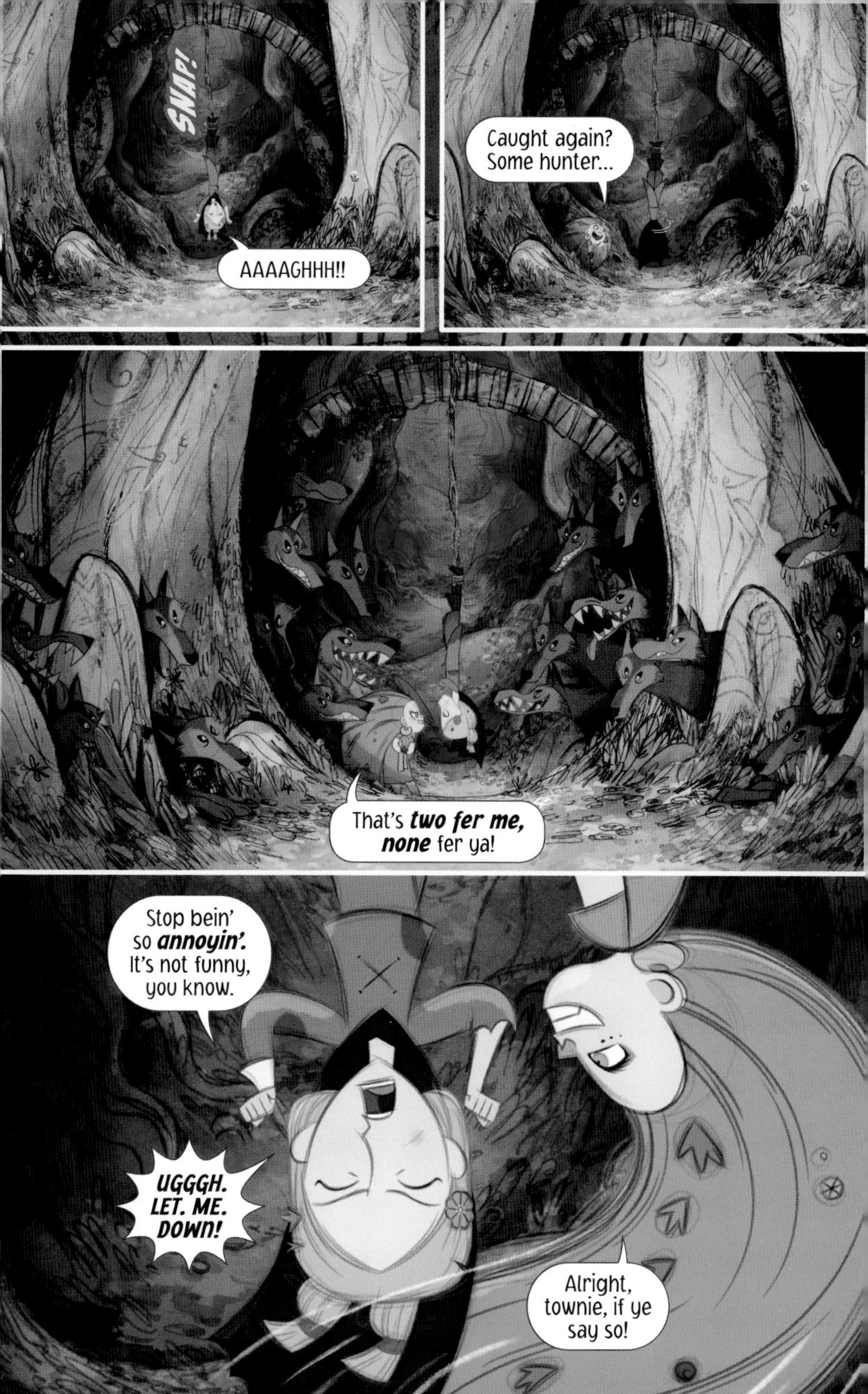
SNAP!
AAAAGHHH!!
Caught again? Some hunter...
That's **two fer me, none** fer ya!
Stop bein' so **annoyin'.** It's not funny, you know.
UGGGH. LET. ME. DOWN!
Alright, townie, if ye say so!

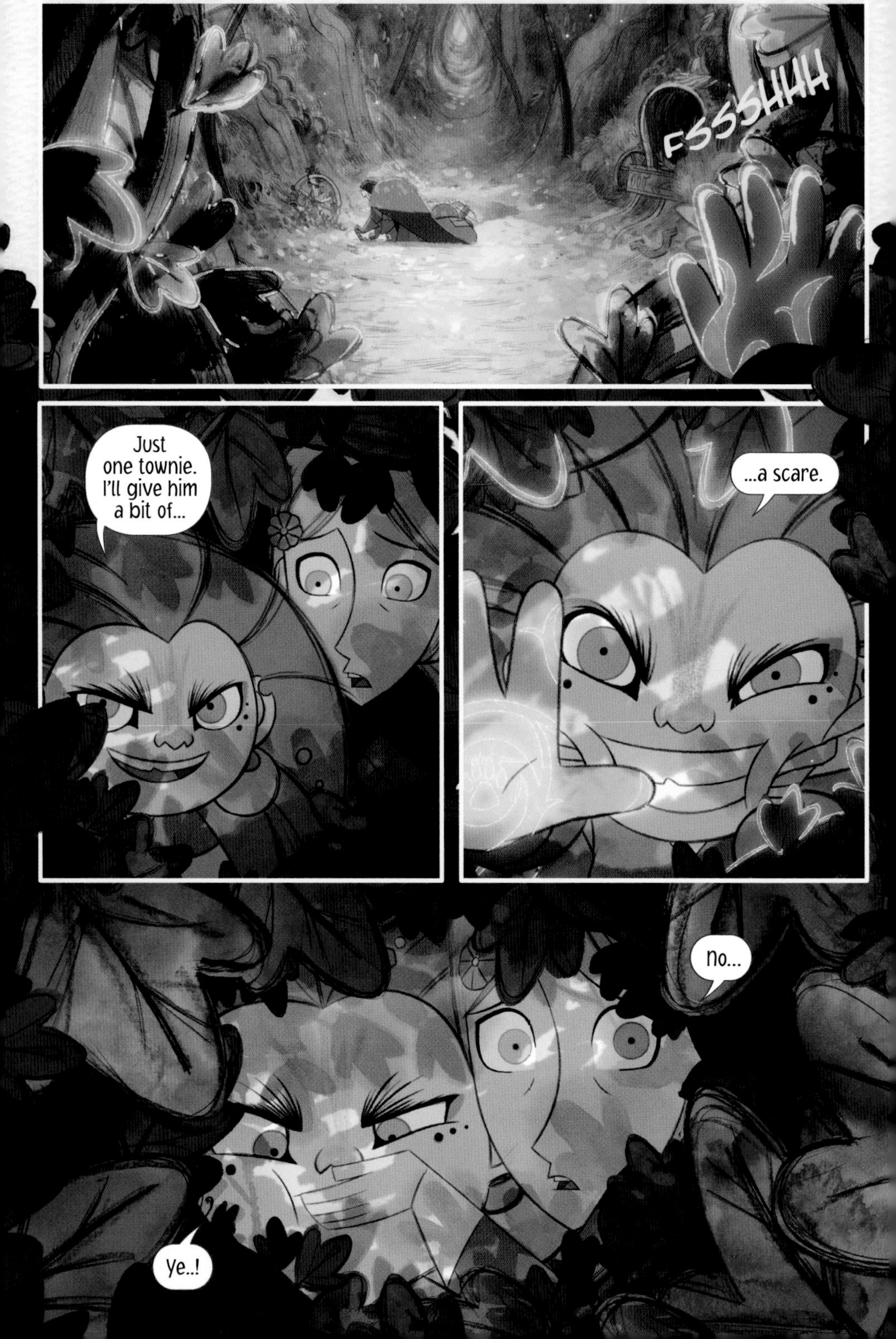
FSSSHHH
Just one townie. I'll give him a bit of...
...a scare.
no...
ye..!

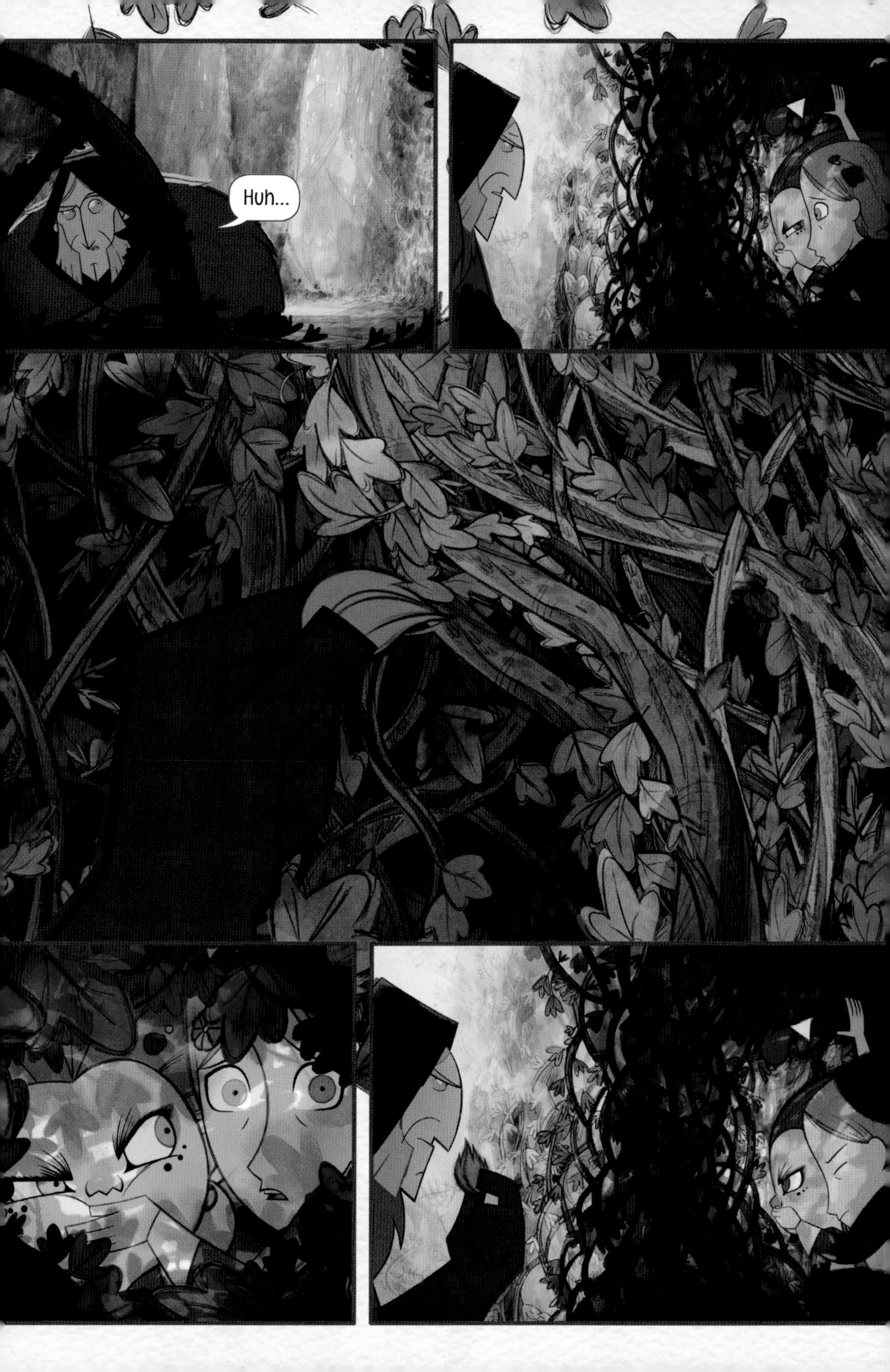
Huh...

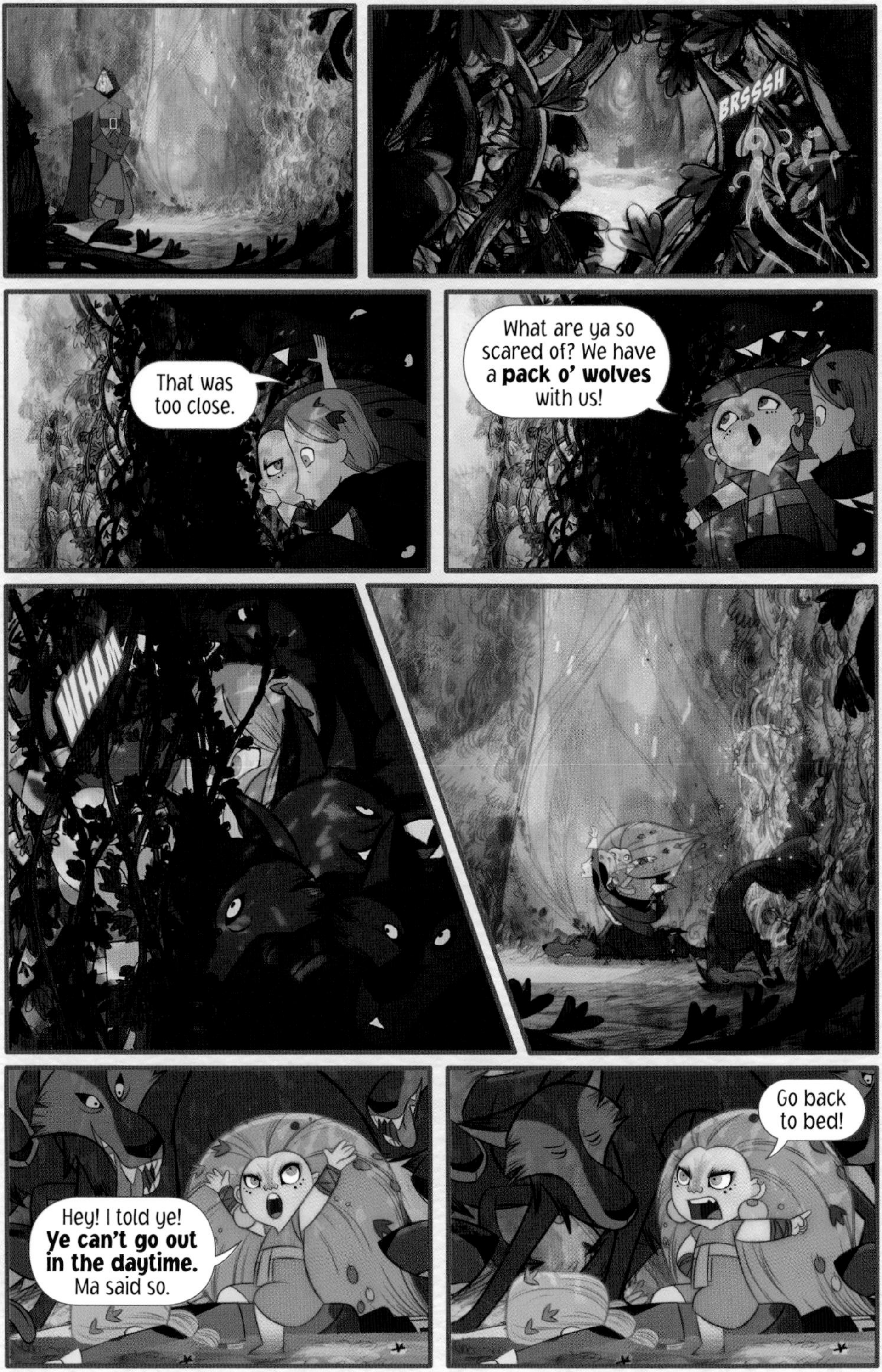
BRSSSH
That was too close.
What are ya so scared of? We have a **pack o' wolves** with us!
WHAM
Hey! I told ye! **Ye can't go out in the daytime.** Ma said so.
Go back to bed!

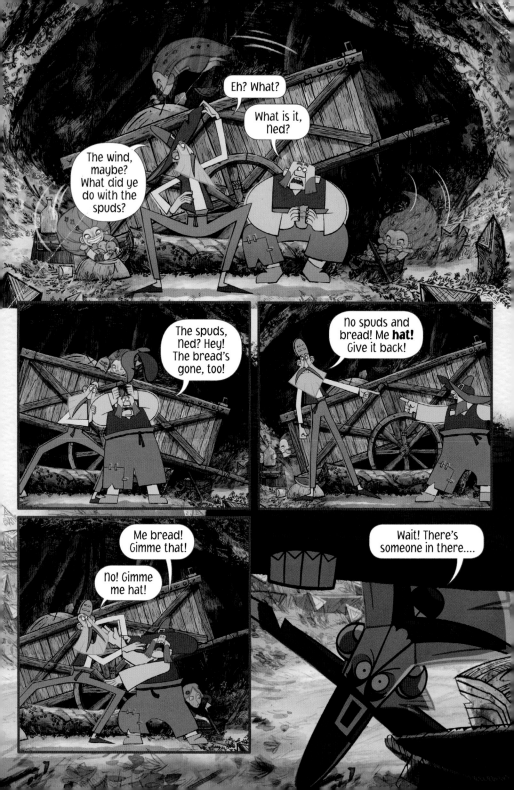

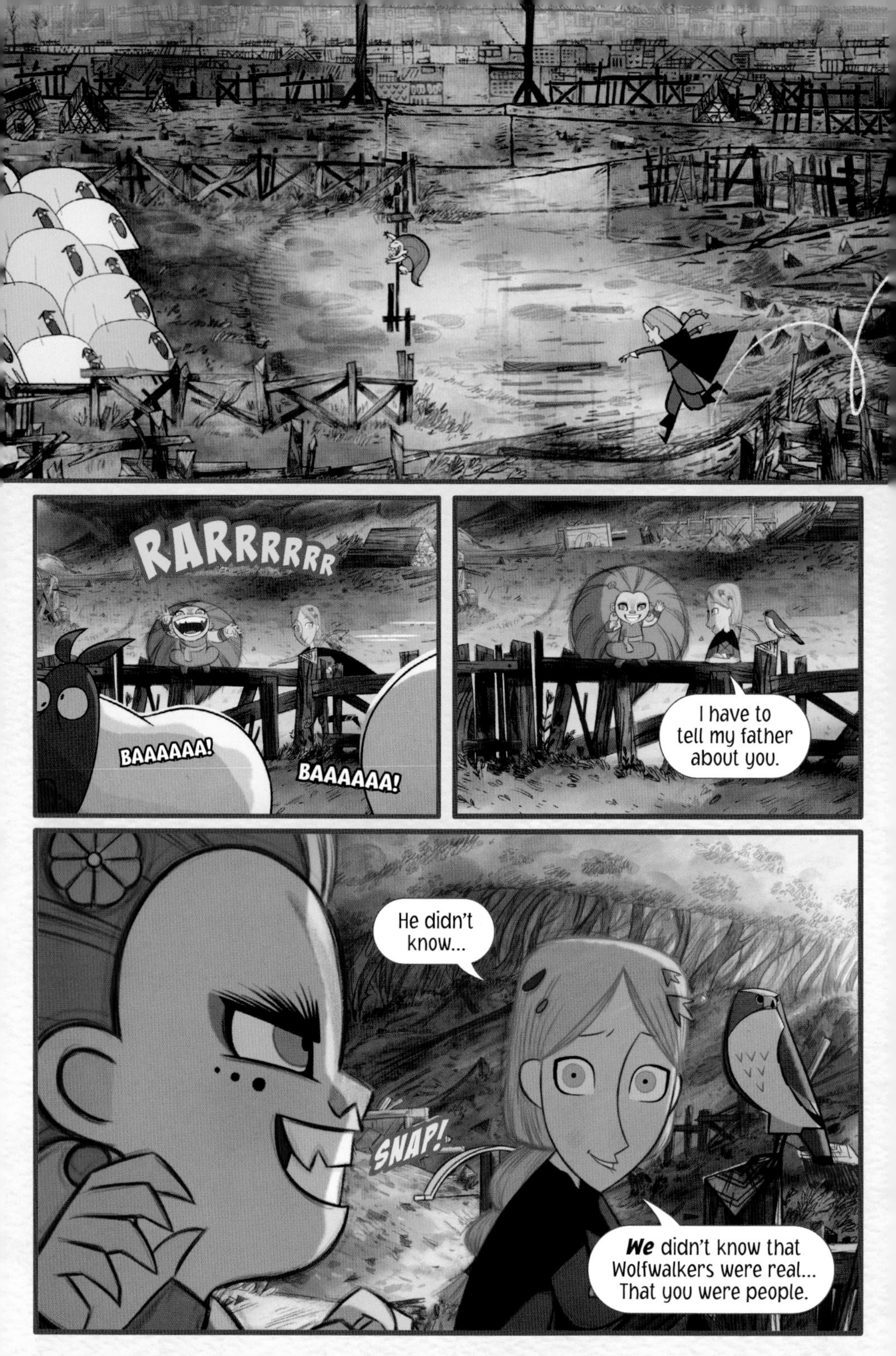
RARRRRRR
BAAAAAA!
BAAAAAAA!
I have to tell my father about you.
He didn't know...
SNAP!
We didn't know that Wolfwalkers were real... That you were people.

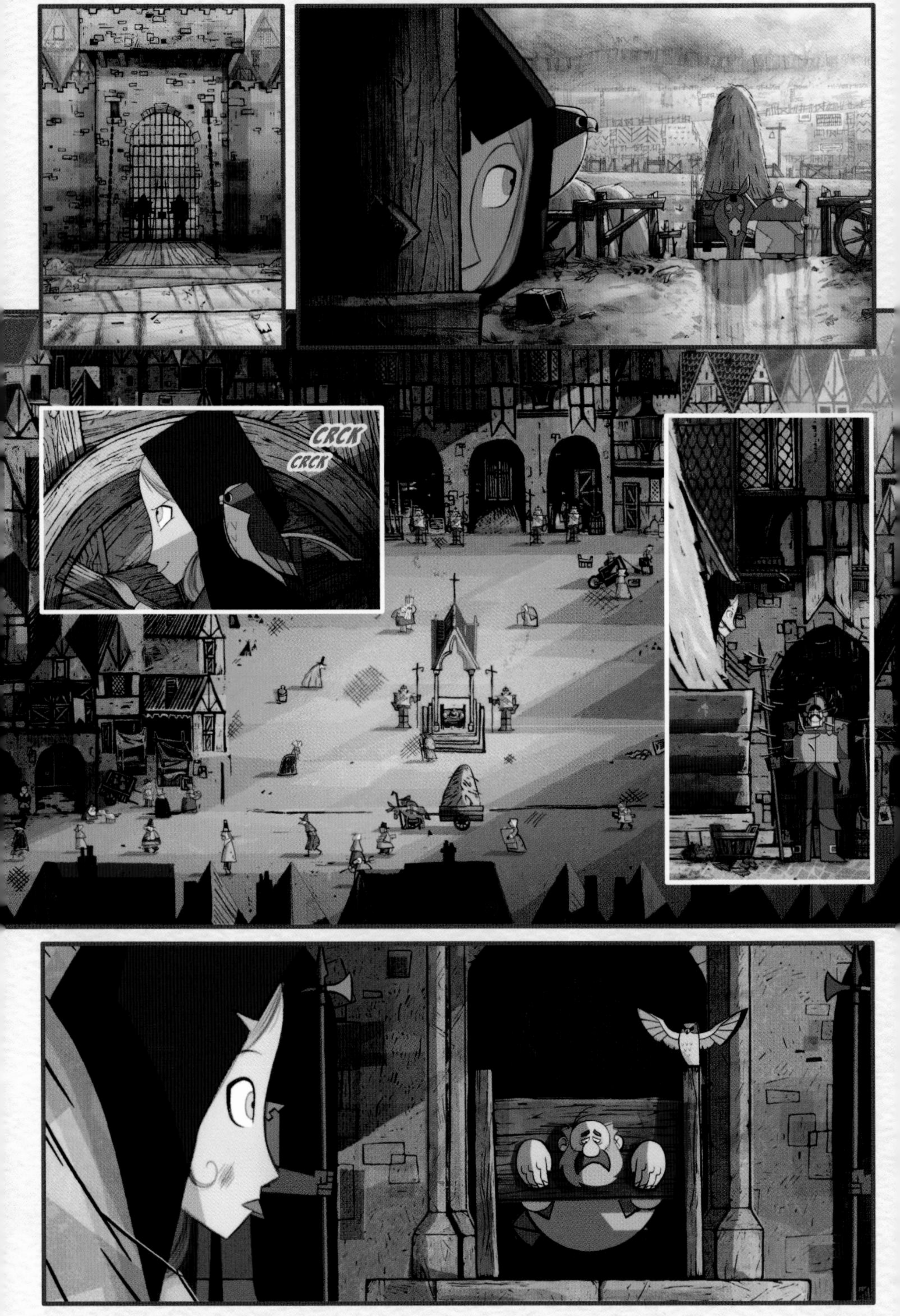
CRCK
CRCK

Father?
Father?

We need to tidy this place up before he gets back.

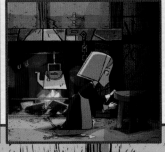

"My, Robyn.
This place is
sparklin'."

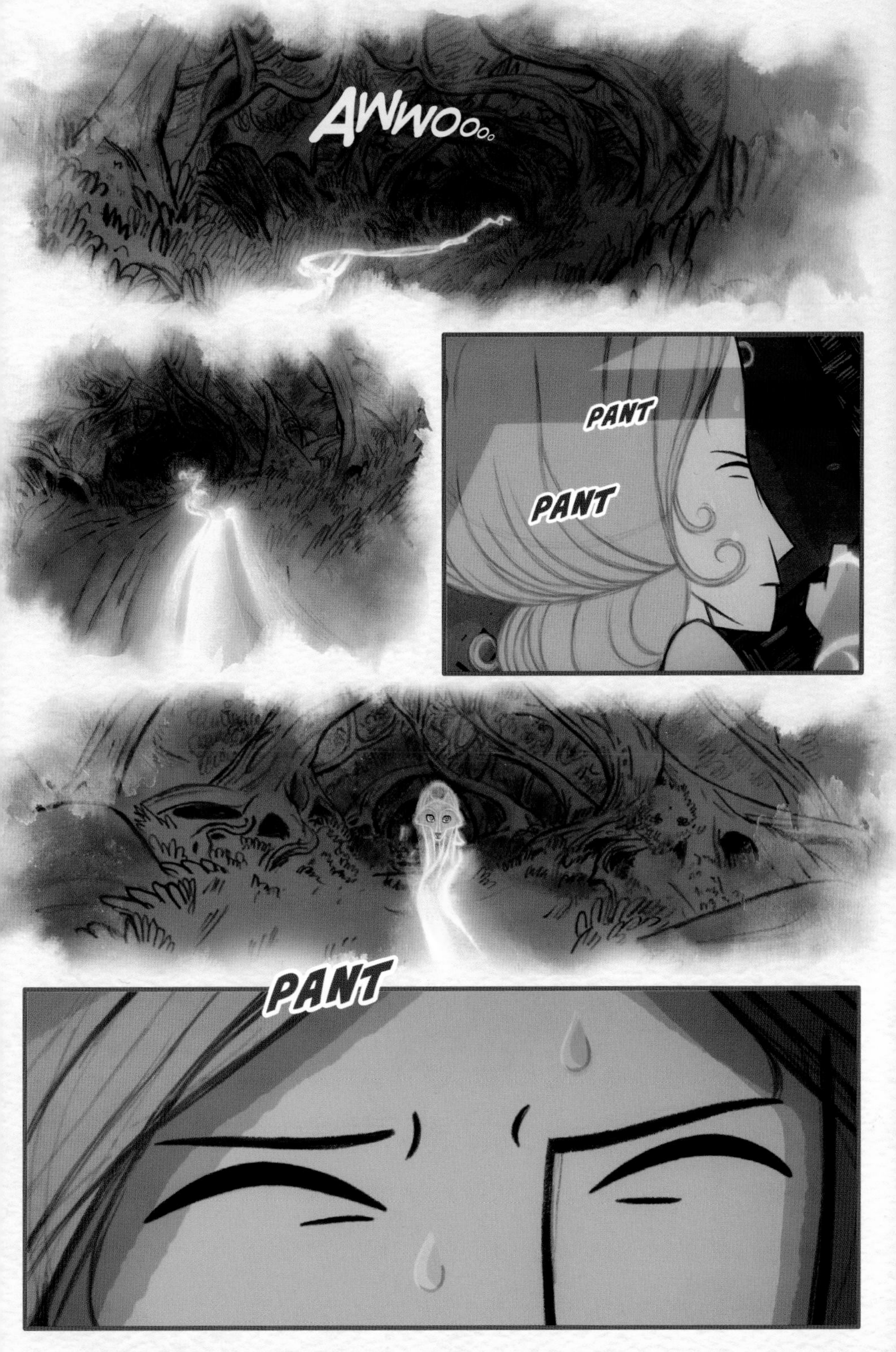
AWWOooo
PANT
PANT
PANT

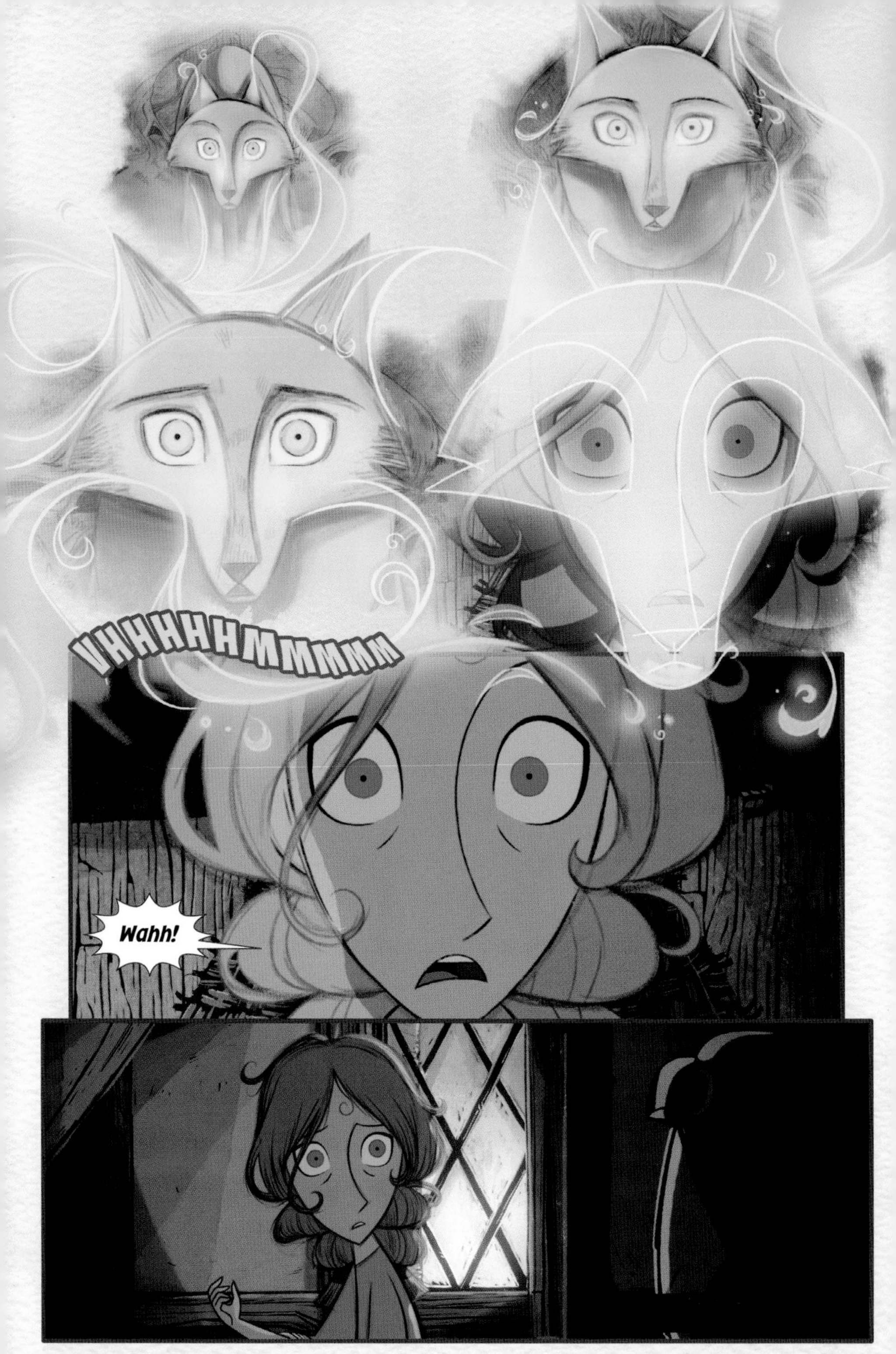

VHHHHHMMMMMM
Wahh!

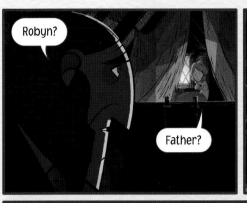

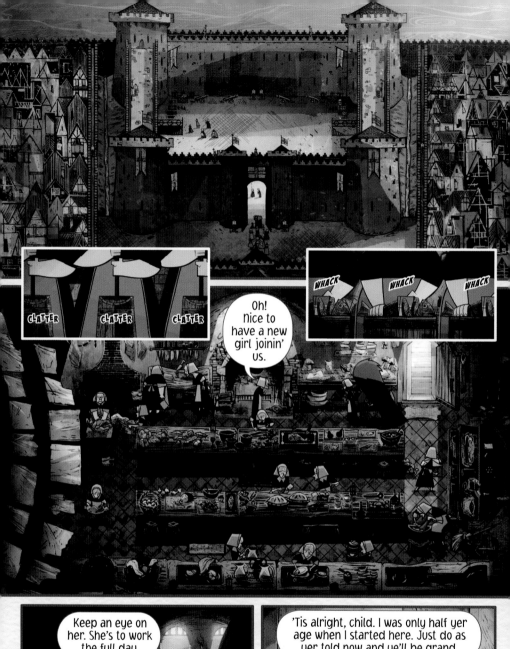

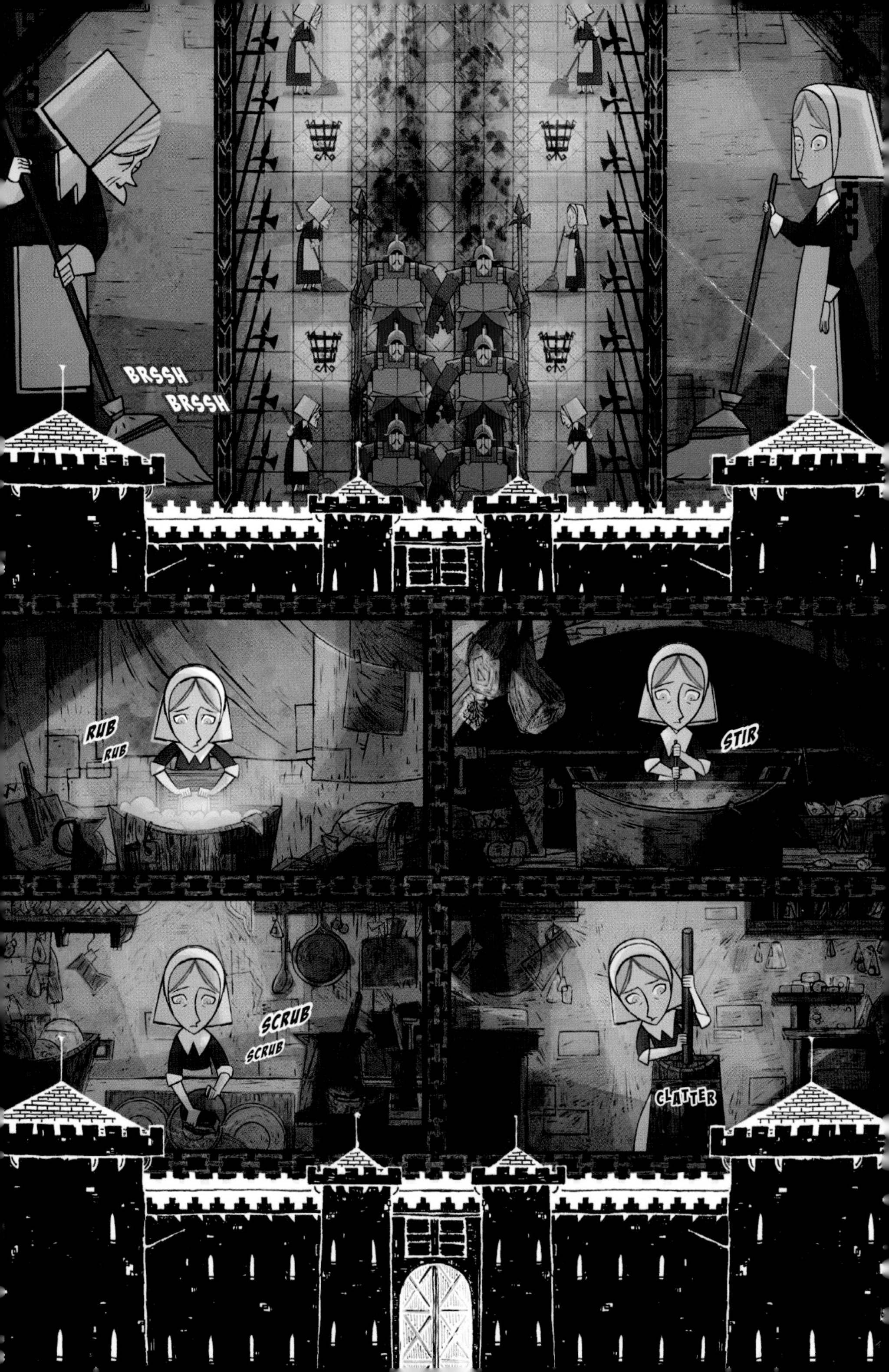
BRSSH
BRSSH
RUB
RUB
STIR
SCRUB
SCRUB
CLATTER

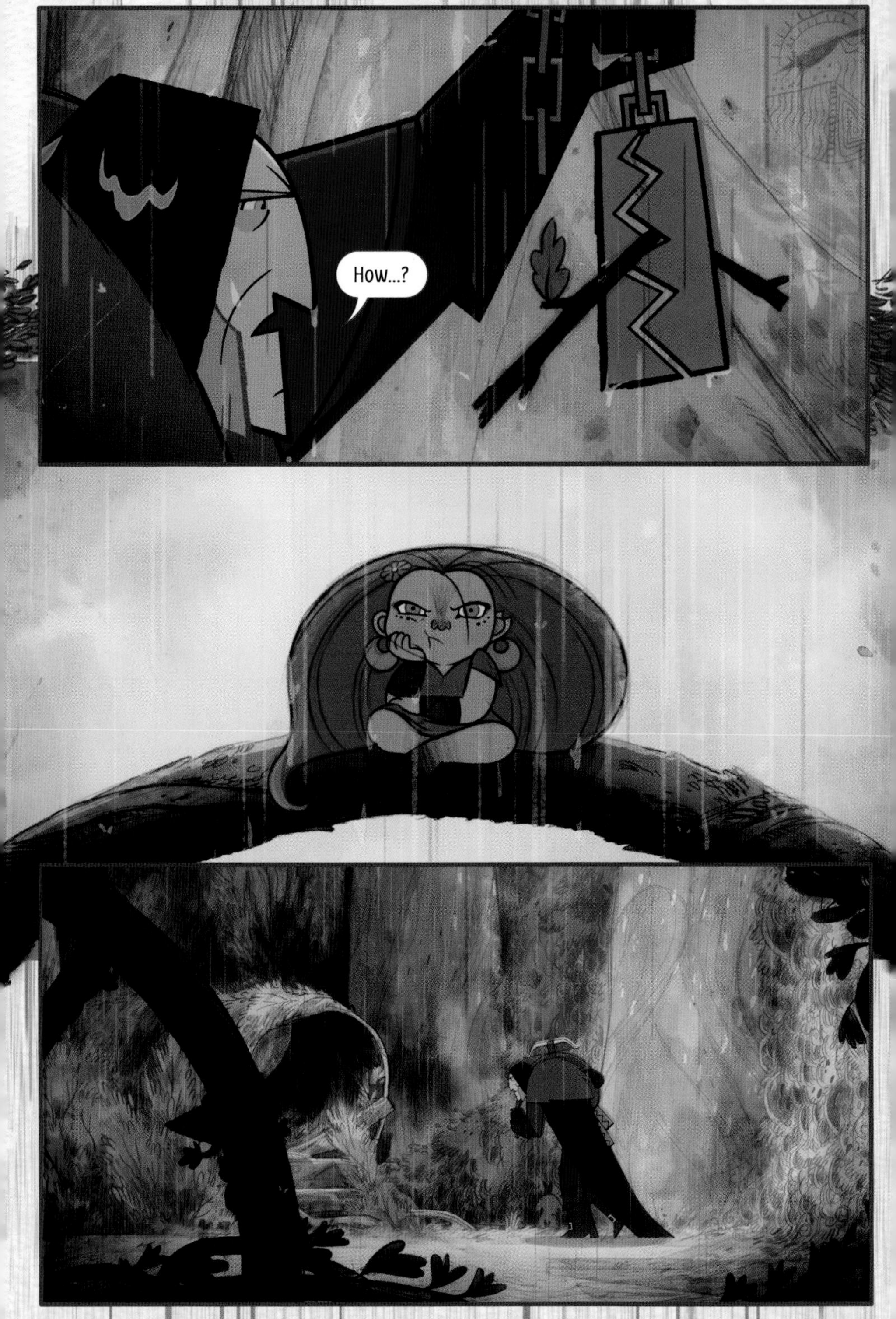
How...?

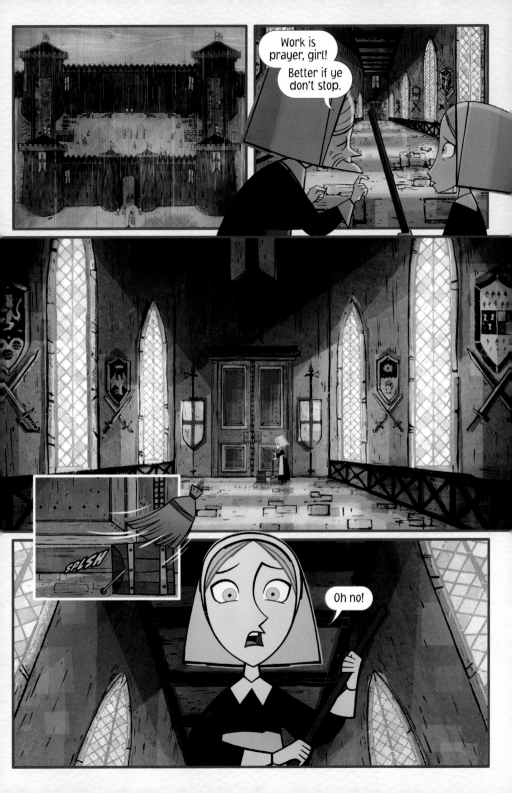

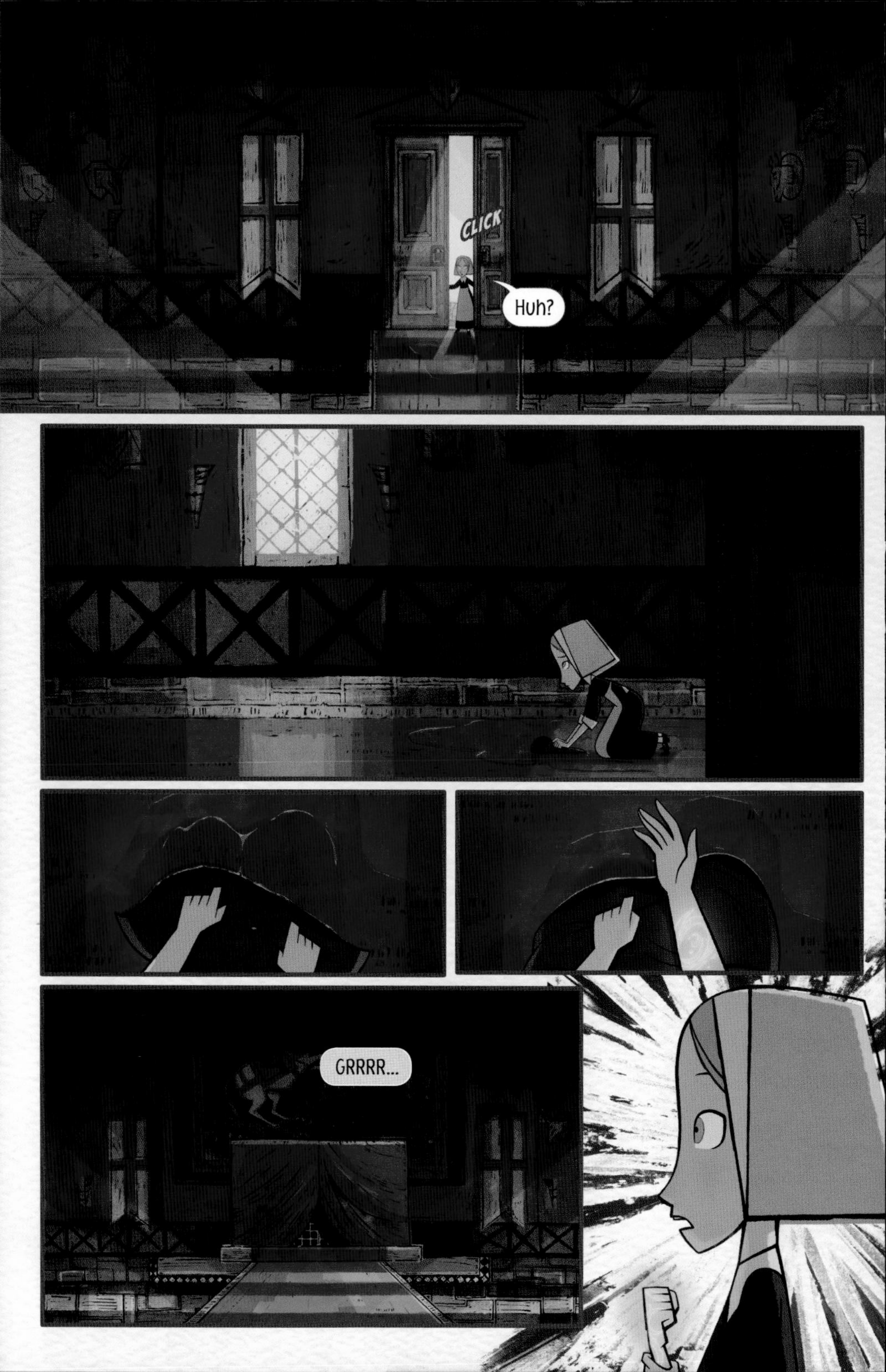
CLICK
Huh?
GRRRR...

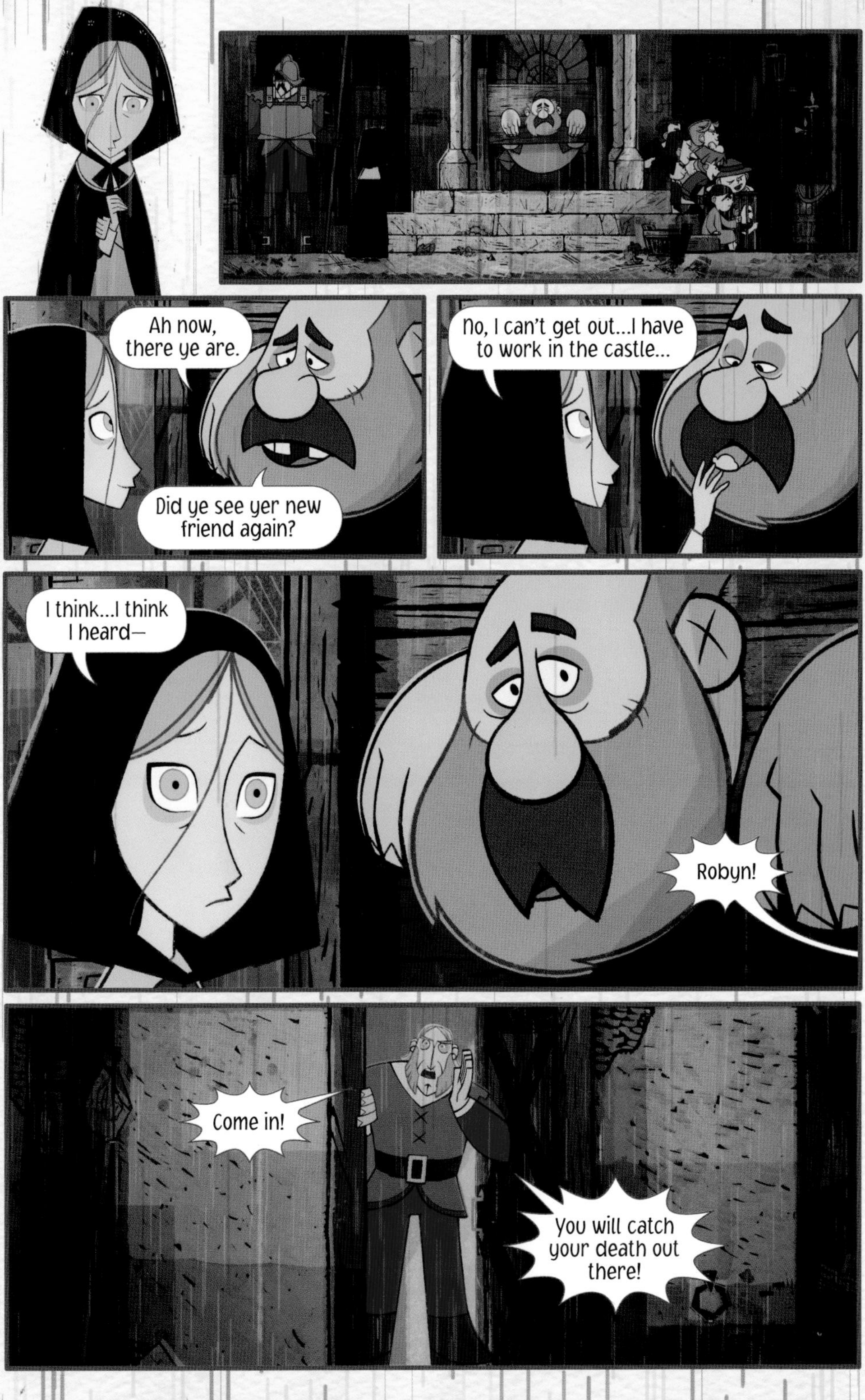
Ah now, there ye are.
Did ye see yer new friend again?
No, I can't get out...I have to work in the castle...
I think...I think I heard—
Robyn!
Come in!
You will catch your death out there!

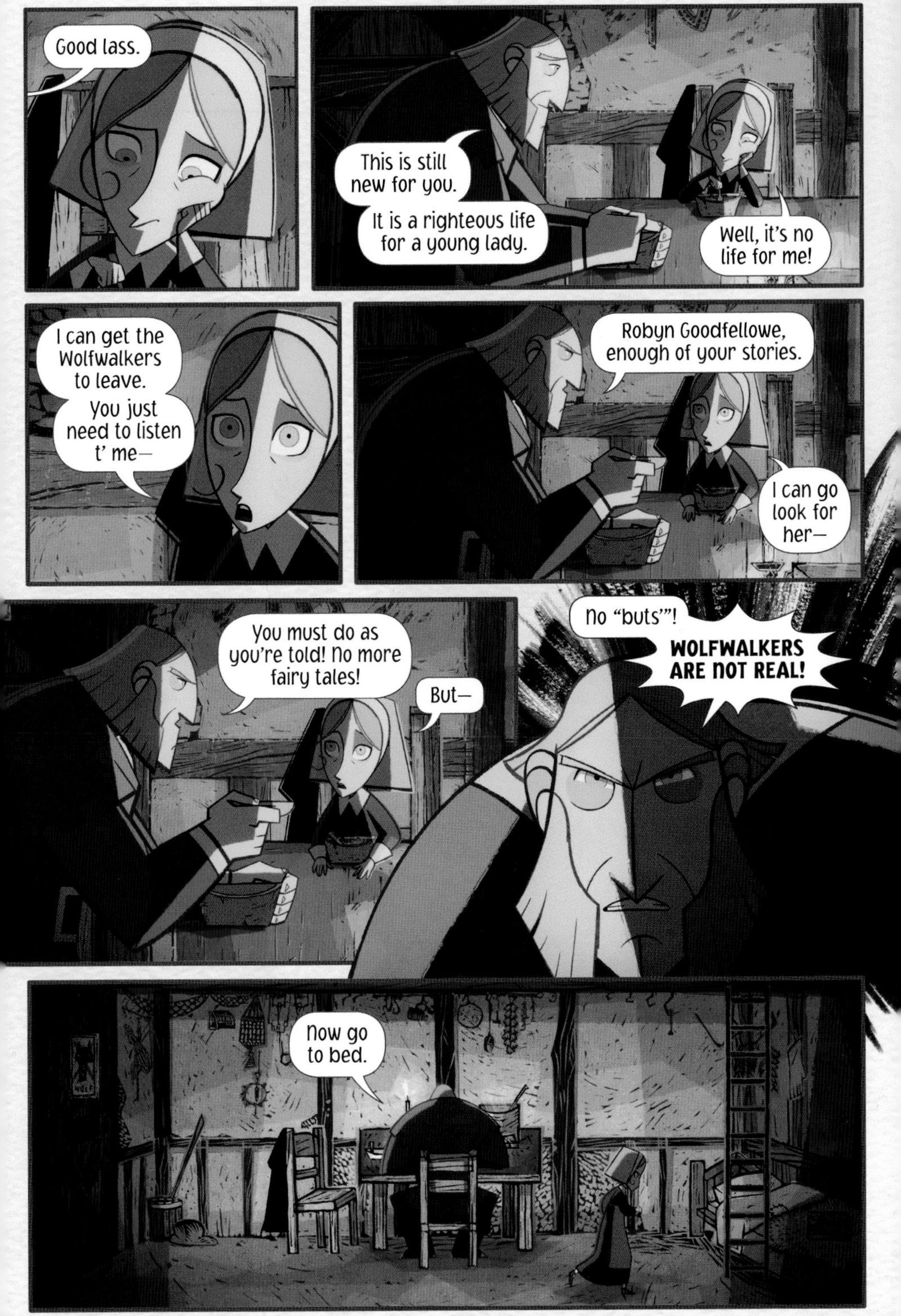
Good lass.
This is still new for you.
It is a righteous life for a young lady.
Well, it's no life for me!
I can get the Wolfwalkers to leave.
You just need to listen t' me—
Robyn Goodfellowe, enough of your stories.
I can go look for her—
You must do as you're told! No more fairy tales!
But—
No "buts"!
WOLFWALKERS ARE NOT REAL!
Now go to bed.
WOLF

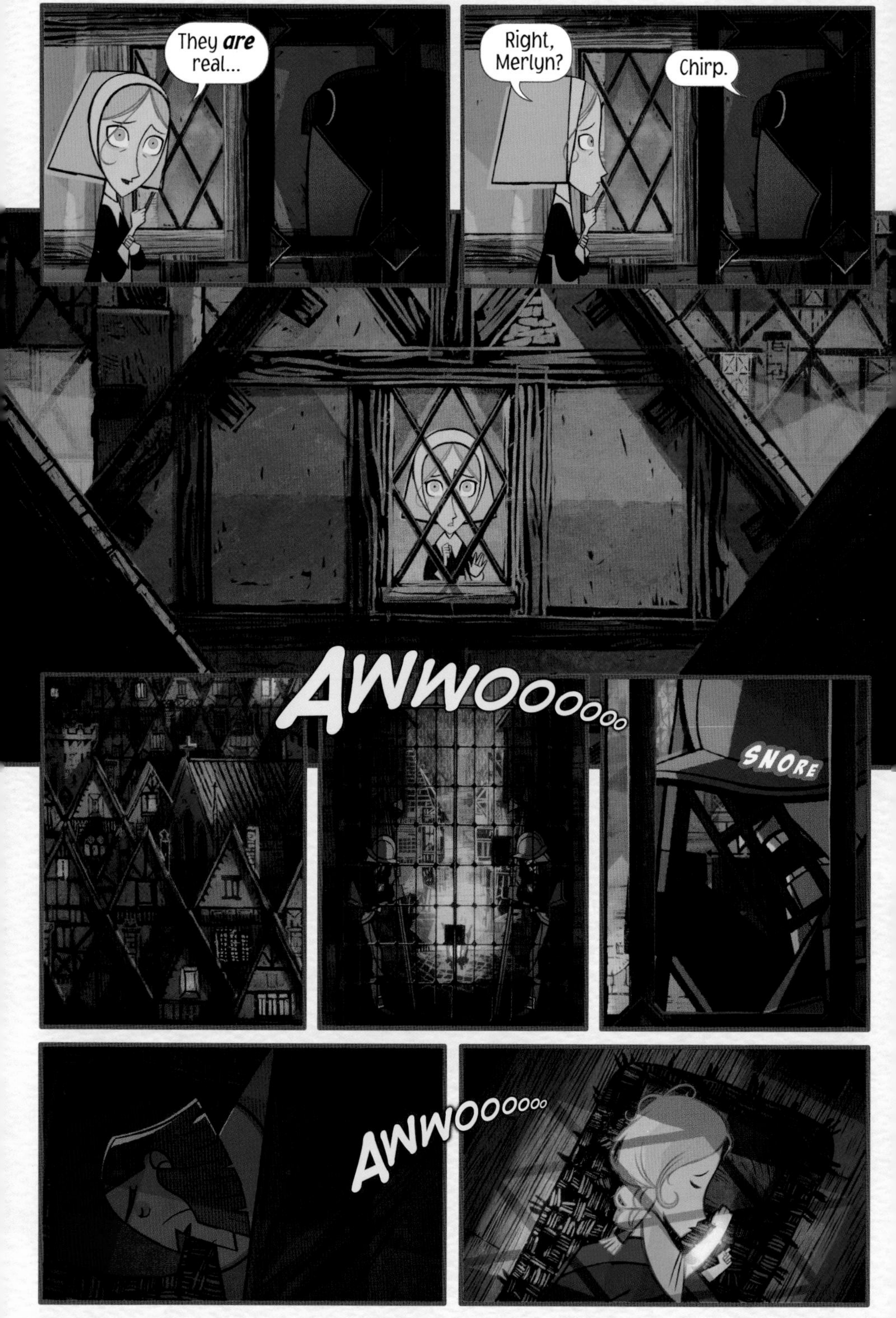
They *are* real...
Right, Merlyn?
Chirp.
AWWOOOOOOO
SNORE
AWWOOOOOO

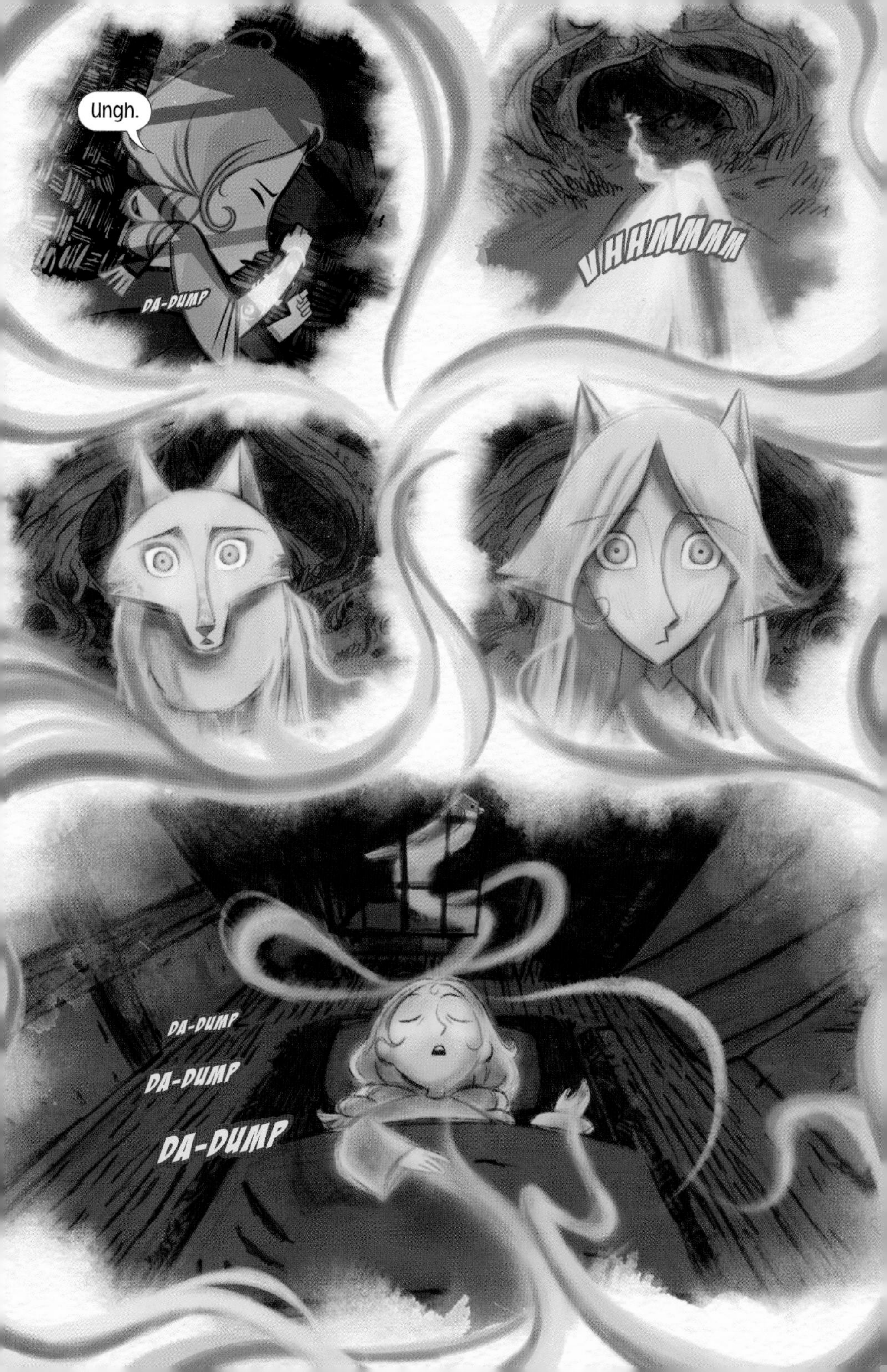
Ungh.
DA-DUMP
VHMMMM
DA-DUMP
DA-DUMP
DA-DUMP

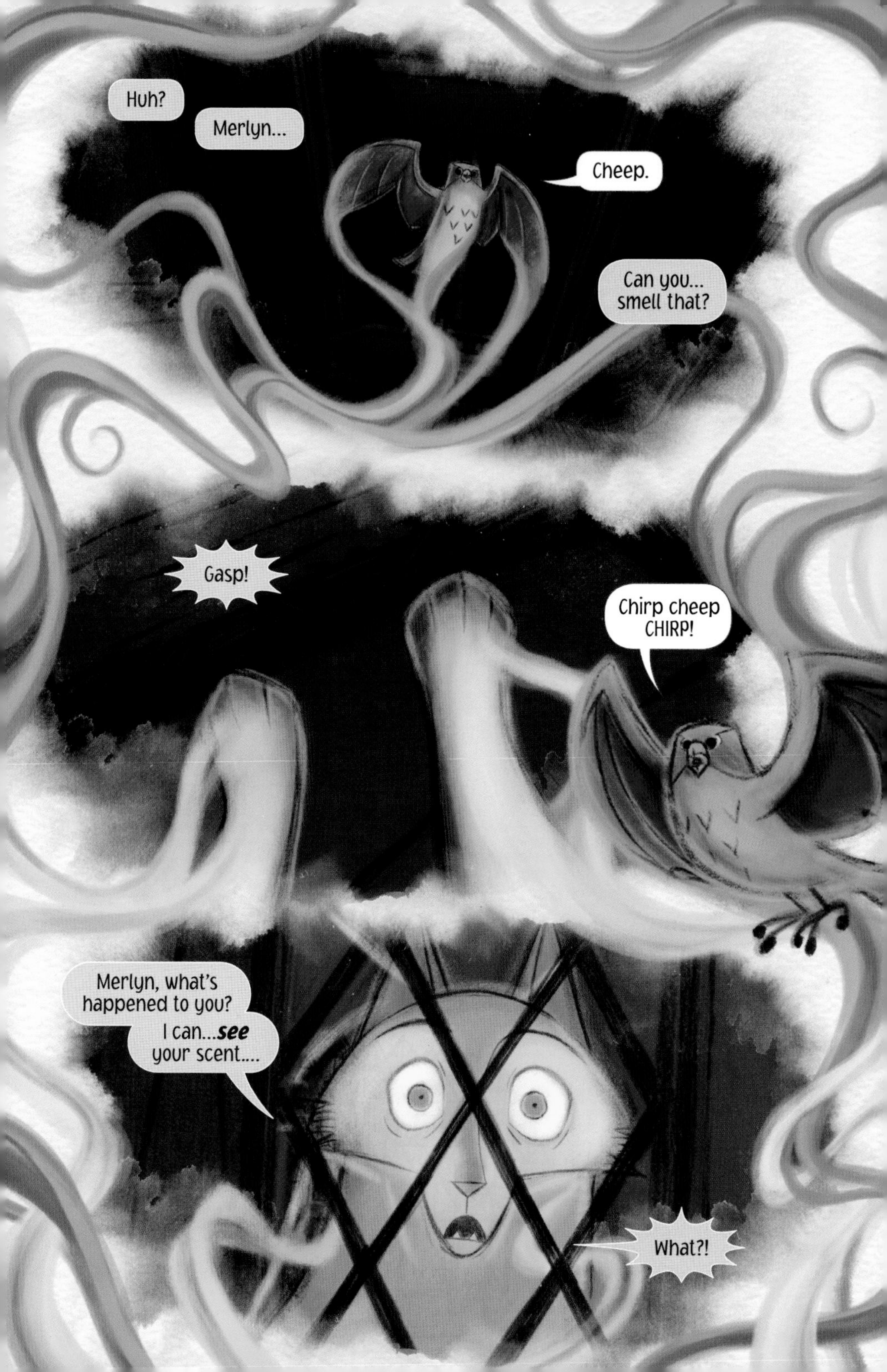
Huh?
Merlyn...
Cheep.
Can you... smell that?
Gasp!
Chirp cheep CHIRP!
Merlyn, what's happened to you?
I can...***see*** your scent....
What?!

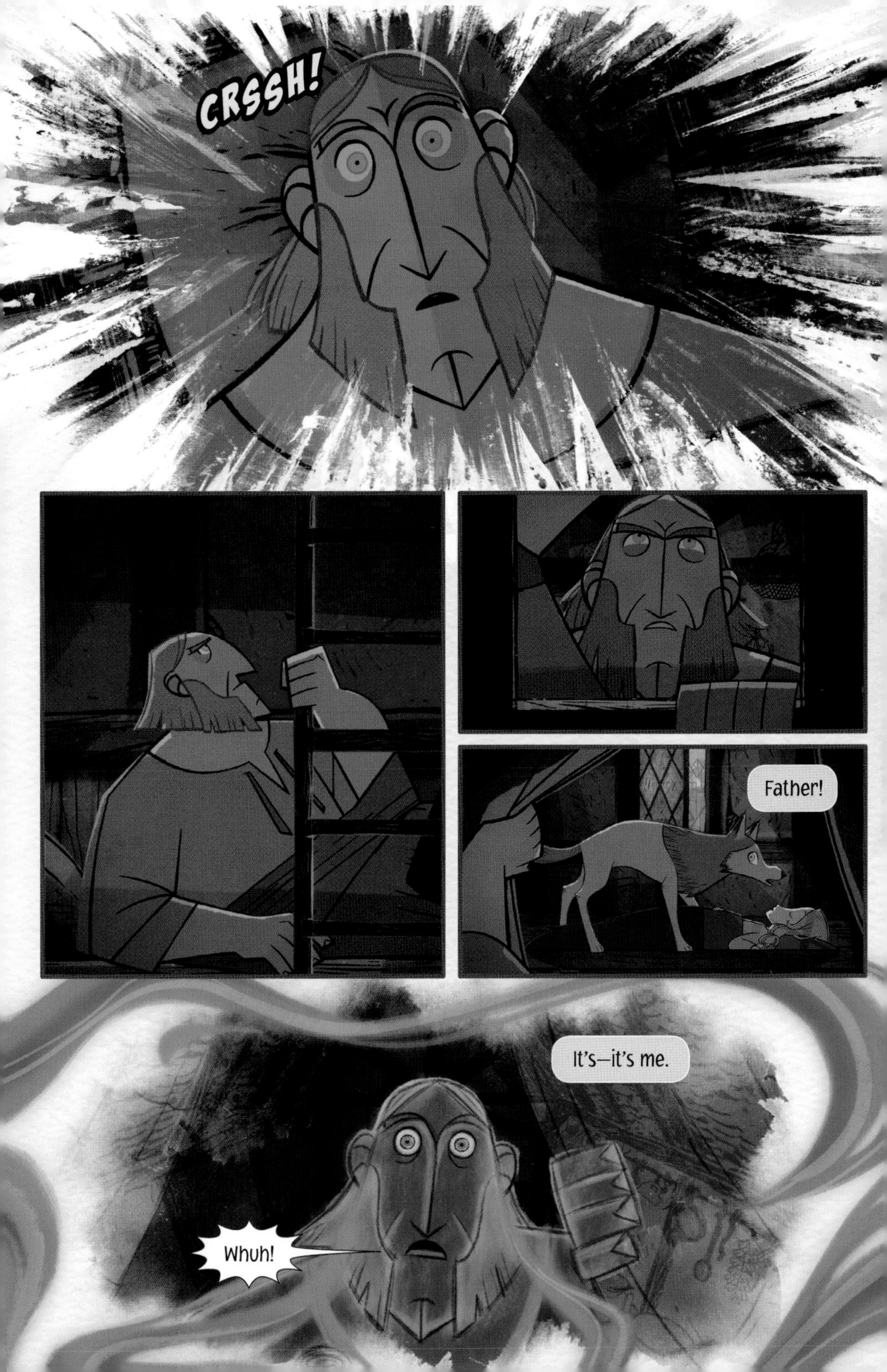
CRSSH!
Father!
It's—it's me.
Whuh!

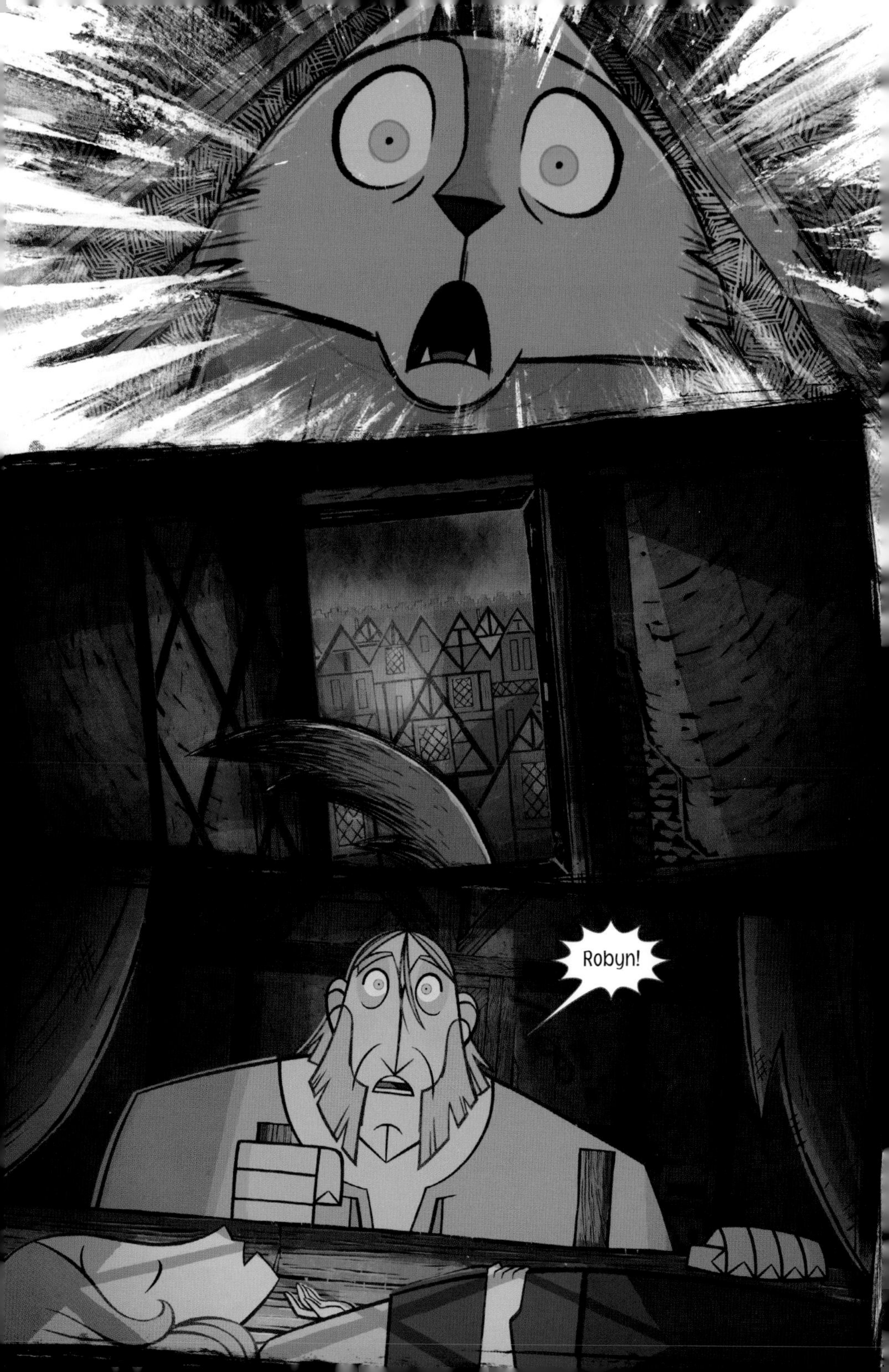
Robyn!

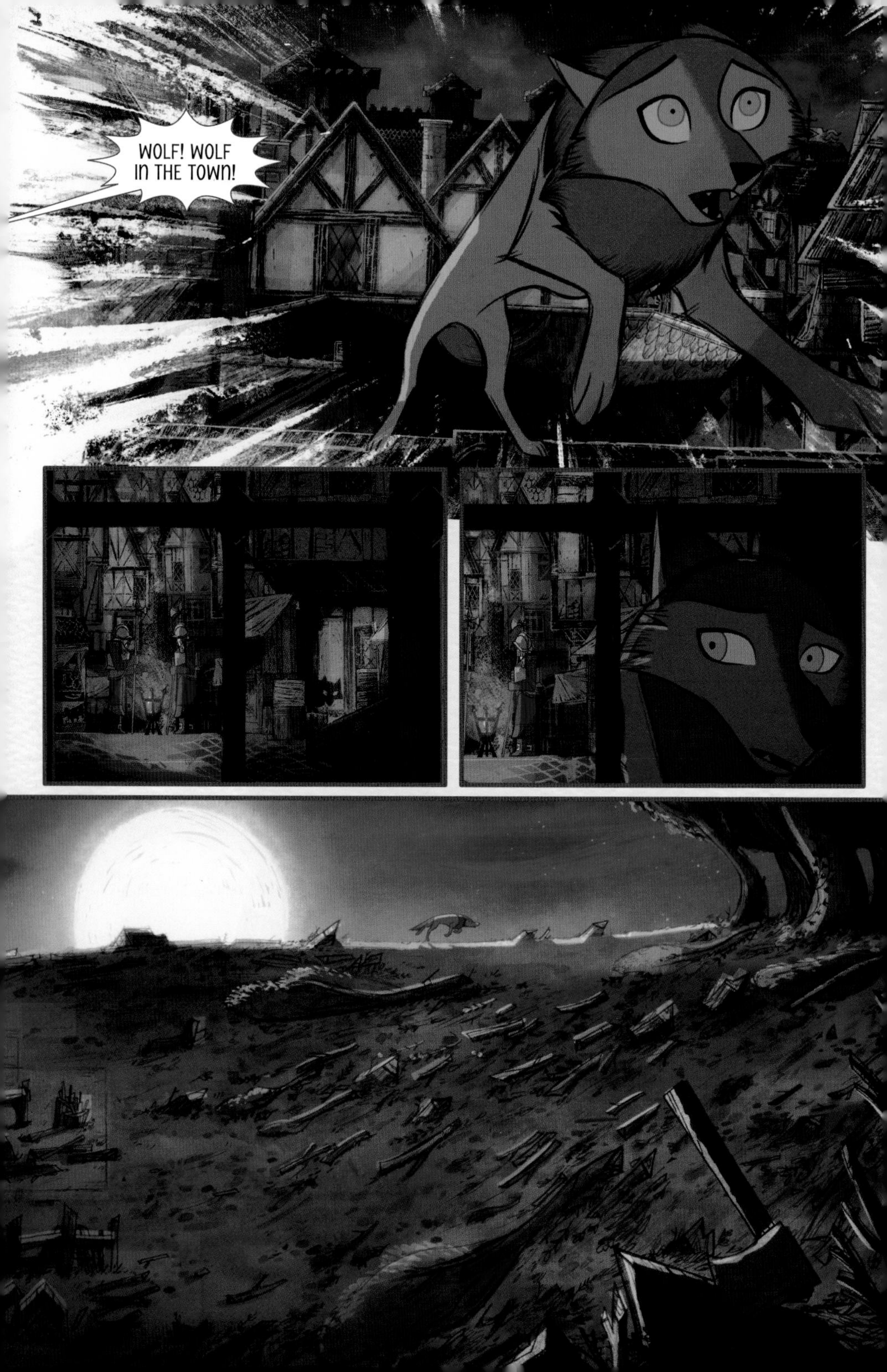
WOLF! WOLF
IN THE TOWN!

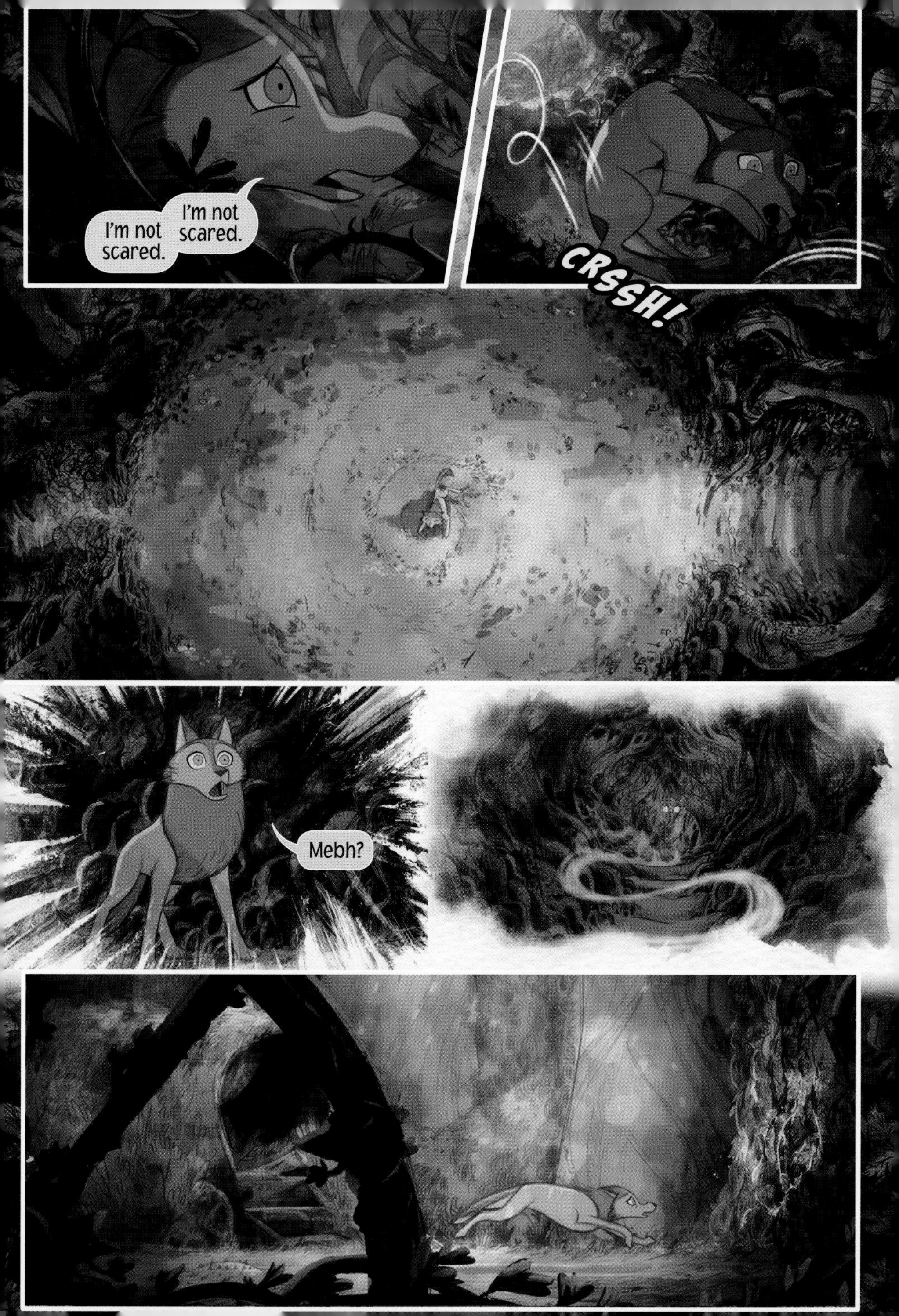
I'm not scared.
I'm not scared.
CRSSH!
Mebh?

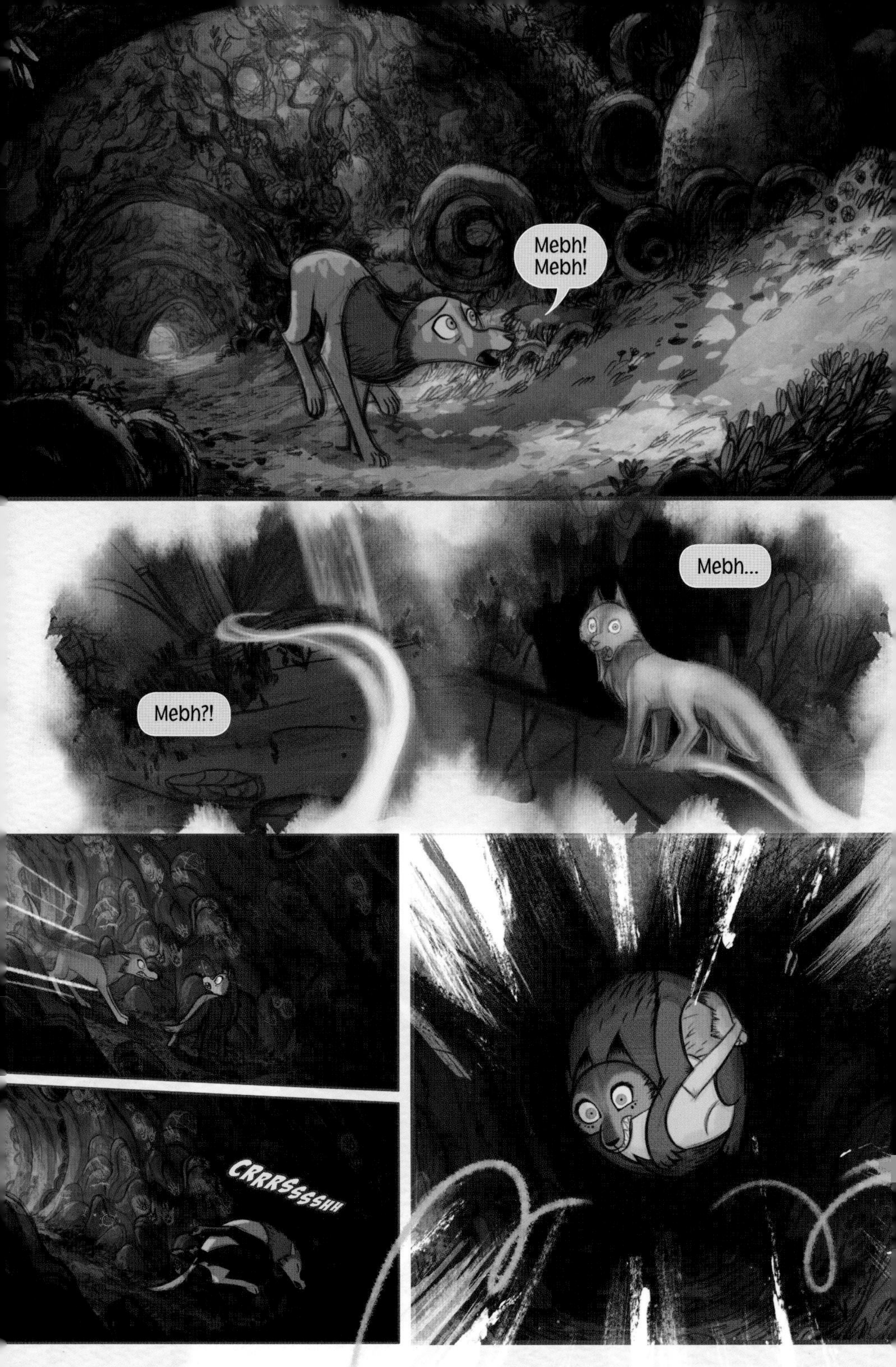
Mebh! Mebh!
Mebh...
Mebh?!
CRRRSSSSHH

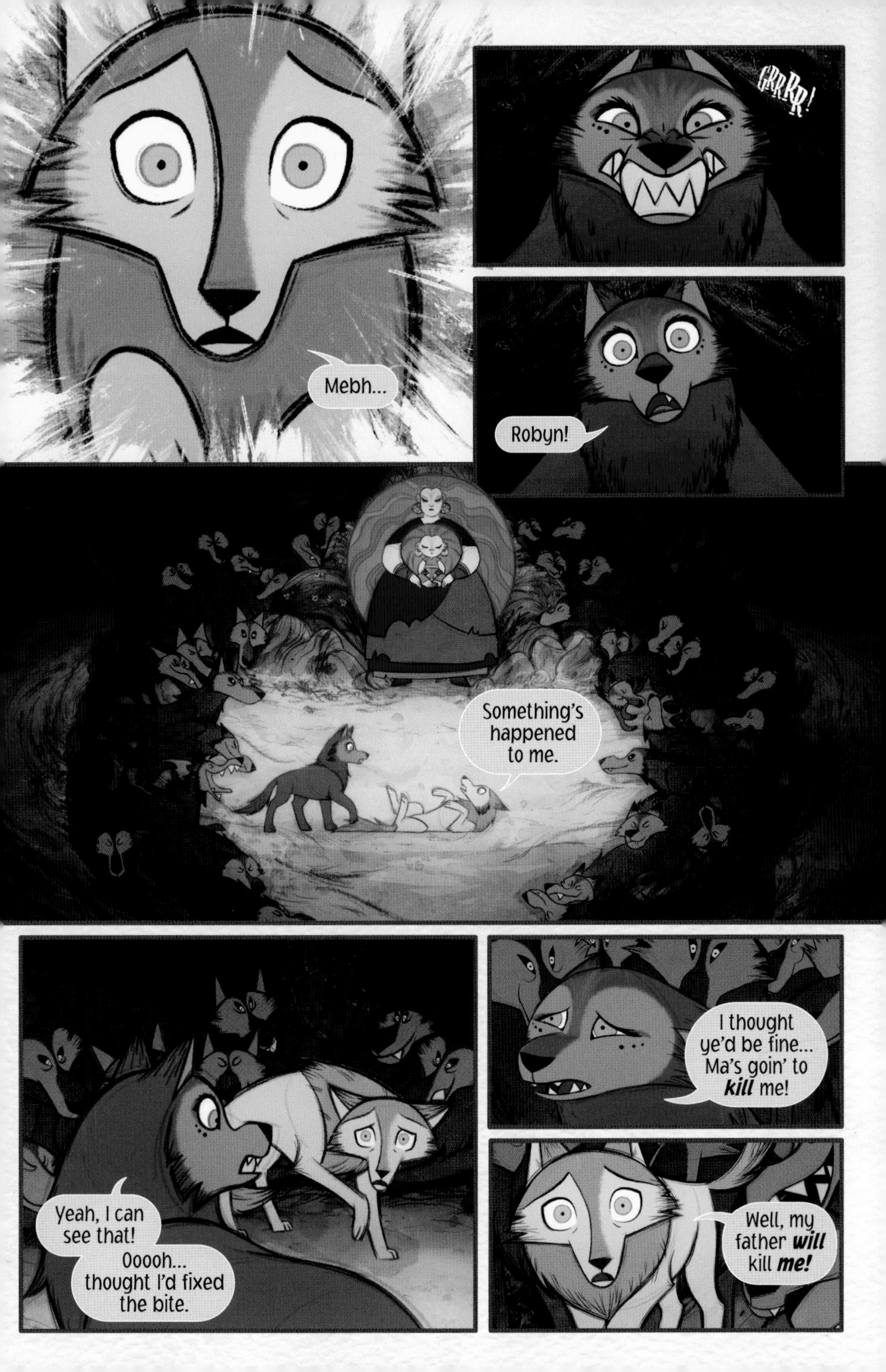
GRRRR!
Mebh...
Robyn!
Something's happened to me.
Yeah, I can see that!
Ooooh... thought I'd fixed the bite.
I thought ye'd be fine... Ma's goin' to **kill** me!
Well, my father **will** kill **me!**

Hey! Calm down and give her room.

SNF SNF

WHIMPER

Go back to bed!

WHIMPER

Now I see ye like this, it's flippin' great.

I thought we were the last ones.

It's *great?!* I'm a **Wolfwalker!**

I know! Ma said this would be bad.

Like, never to bite anyone...but...I *love* it! It's smashin'!

This is bad. I'll get killed like this. What about my body?

It's asleep, nice and cozy. Look...

...yer a wolf when ye sleep. A girl when yer awake.

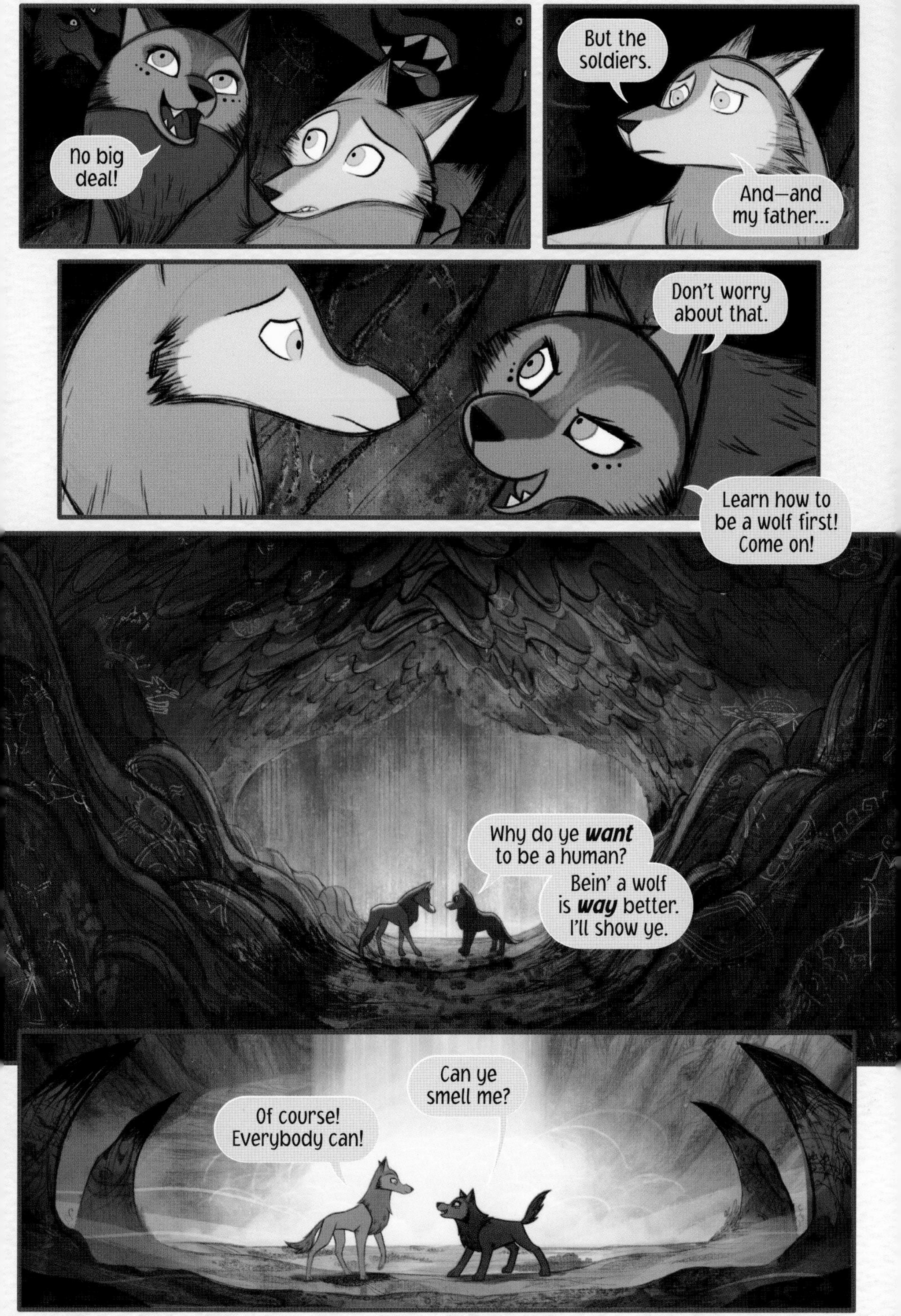
No big deal!
But the soldiers.
And—and my father...
Don't worry about that.
Learn how to be a wolf first! Come on!
Why do ye **want** to be a human?
Bein' a wolf is **way** better. I'll show ye.
Can ye smell me?
Of course! Everybody can!

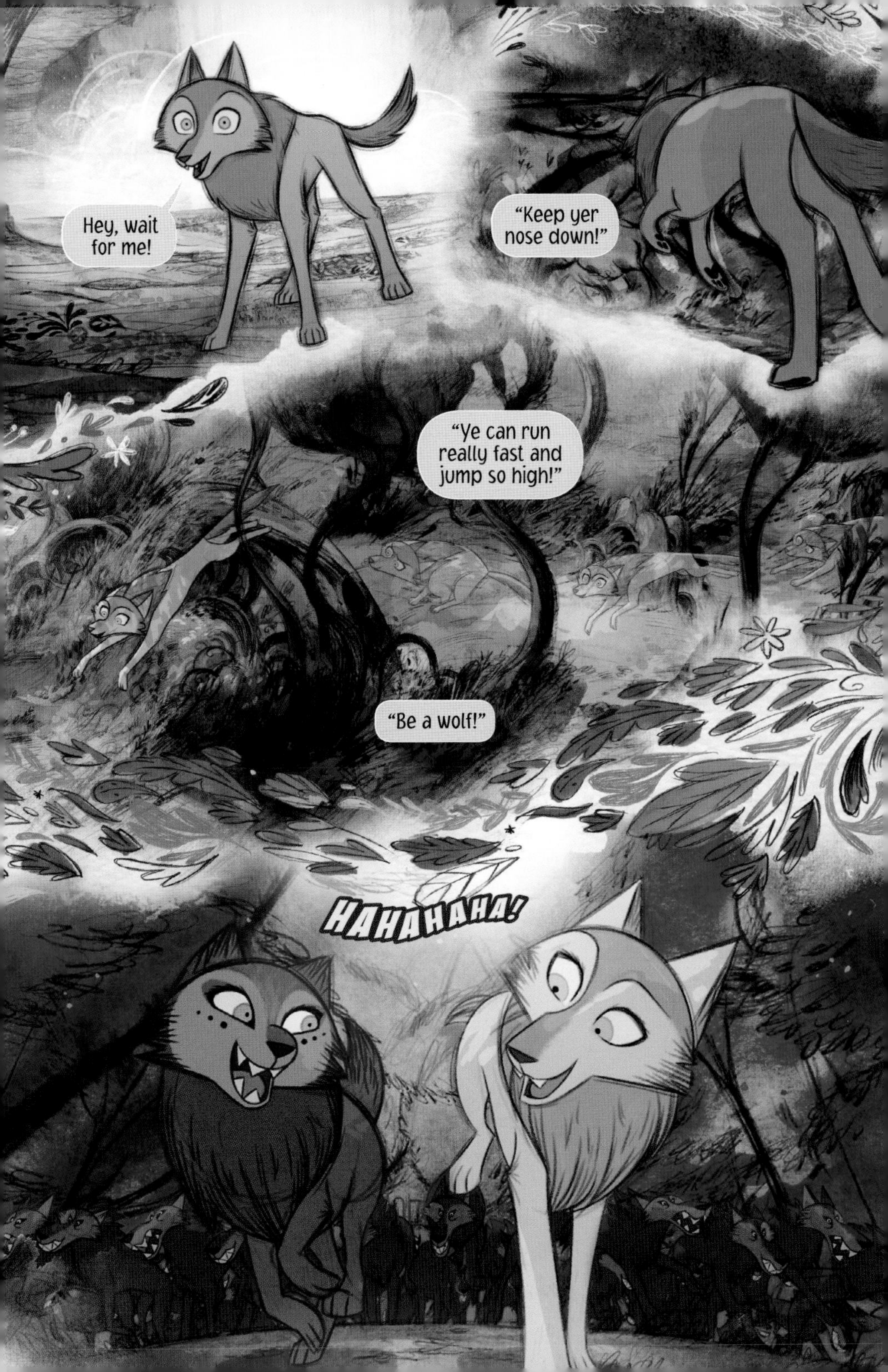
Hey, wait for me!
"Keep yer nose down!"
"Ye can run really fast and jump so high!"
"Be a wolf!"
HAHAHAHA!

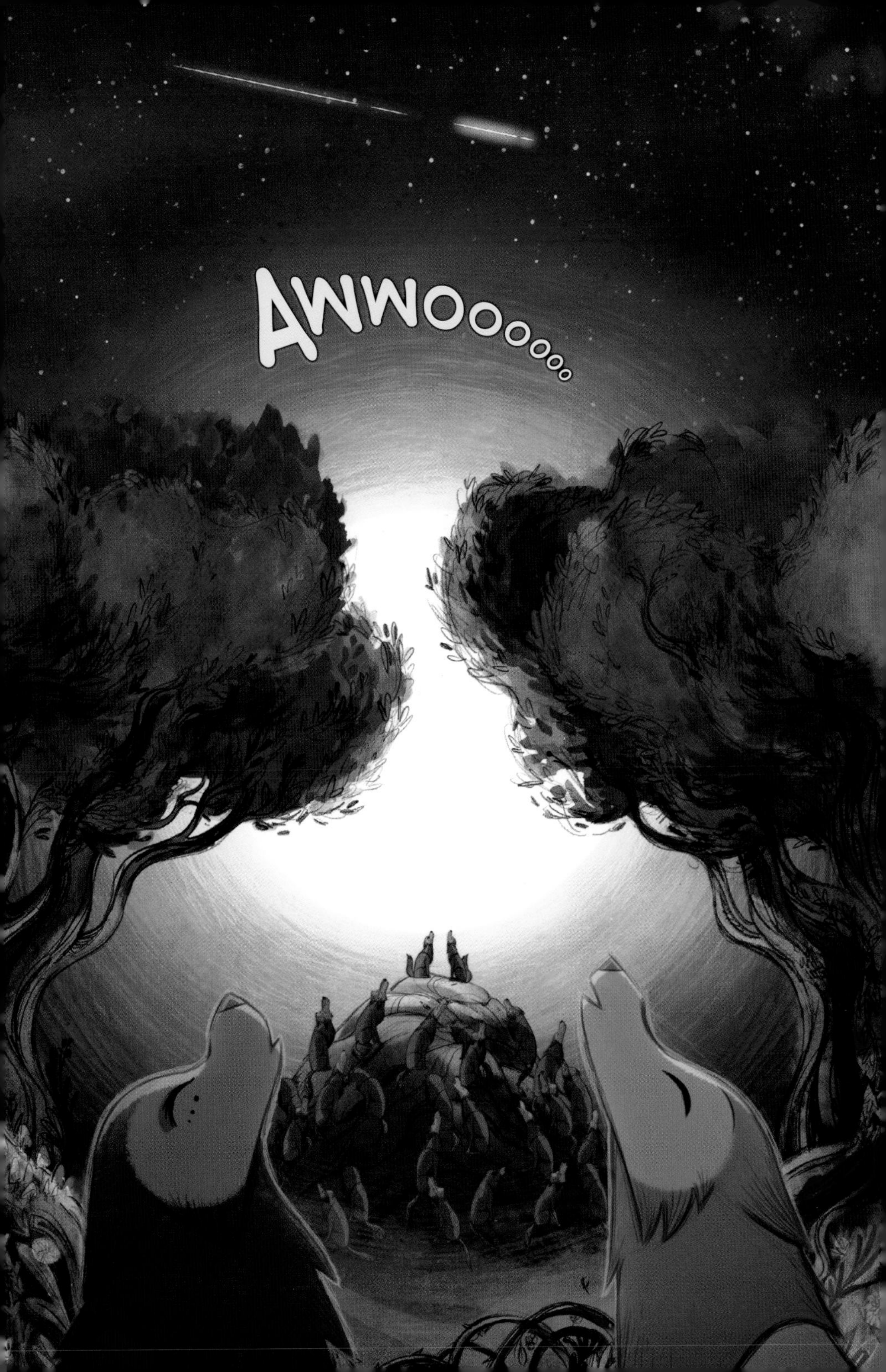
AWWOOOOOO

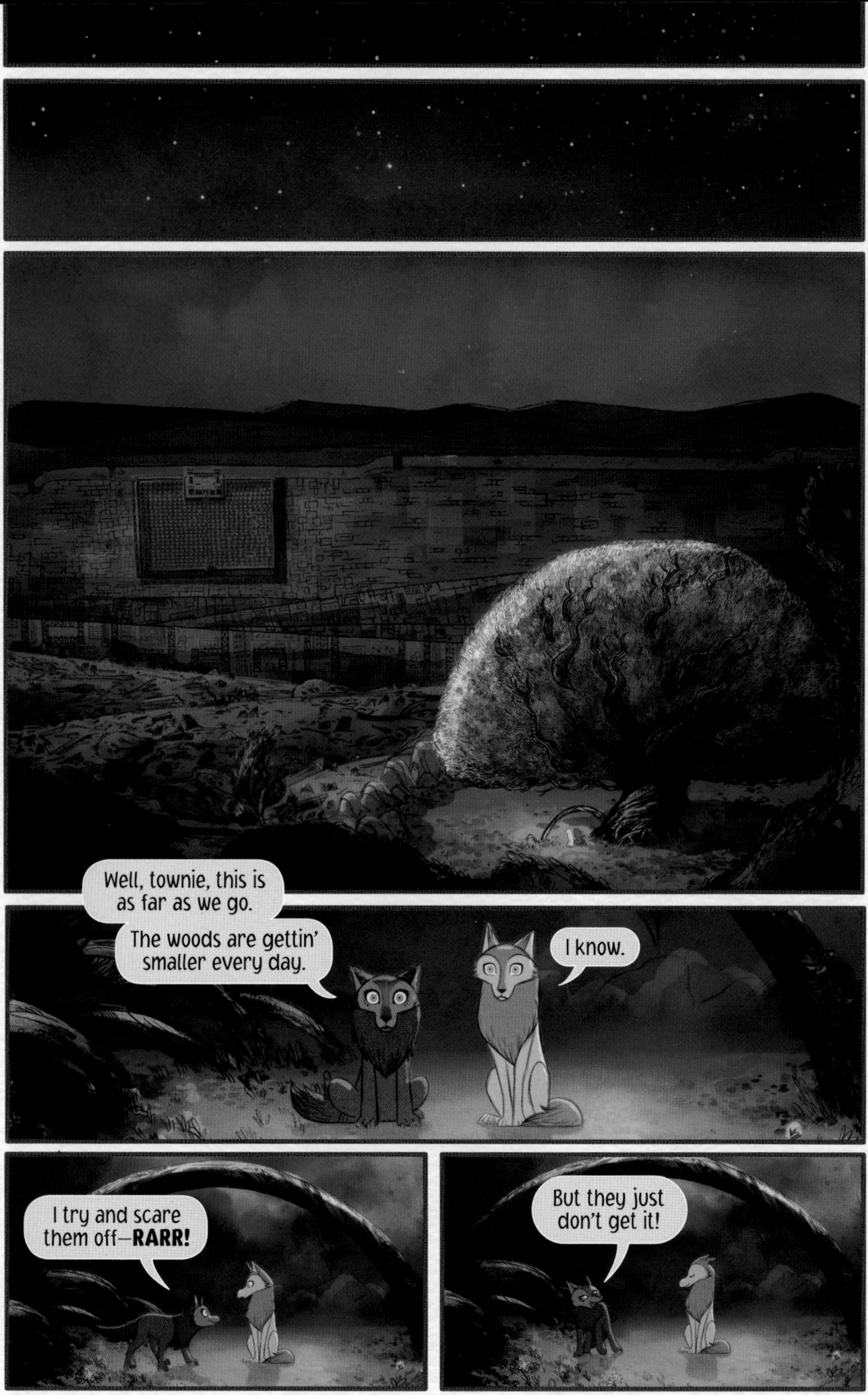
Well, townie, this is as far as we go.
The woods are gettin' smaller every day.
I know.
I try and scare them off—**RARR!**
But they just don't get it!

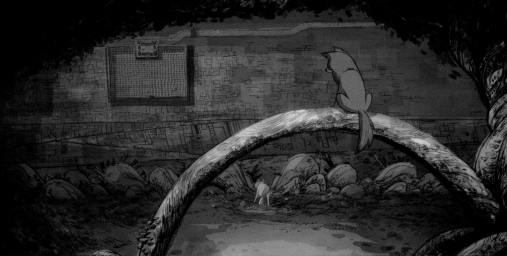

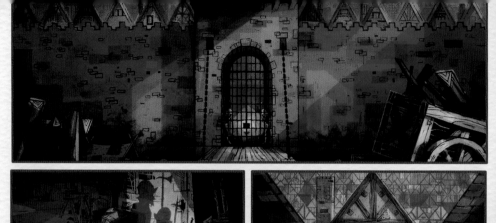

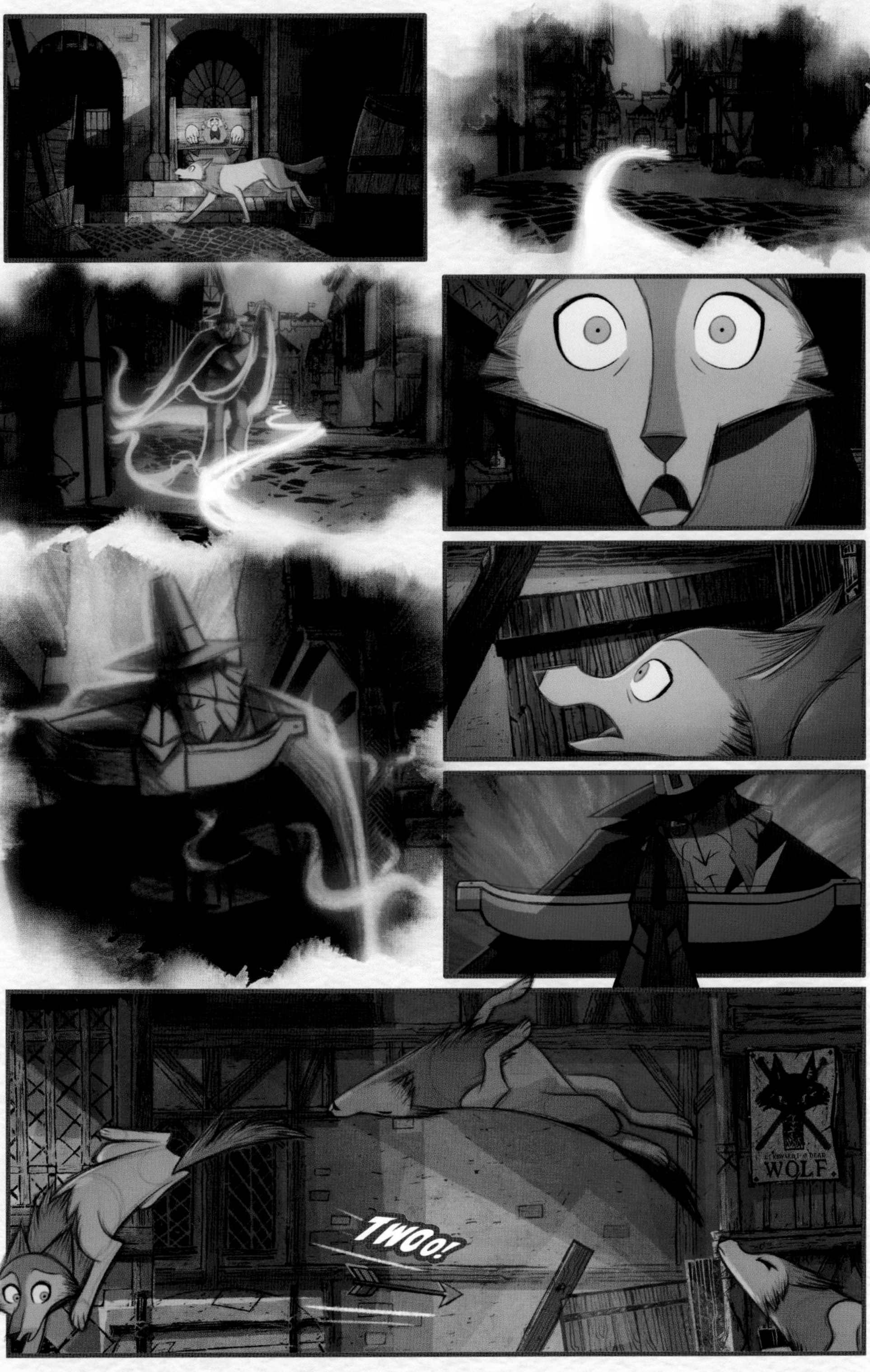
WOLF
TWOo!

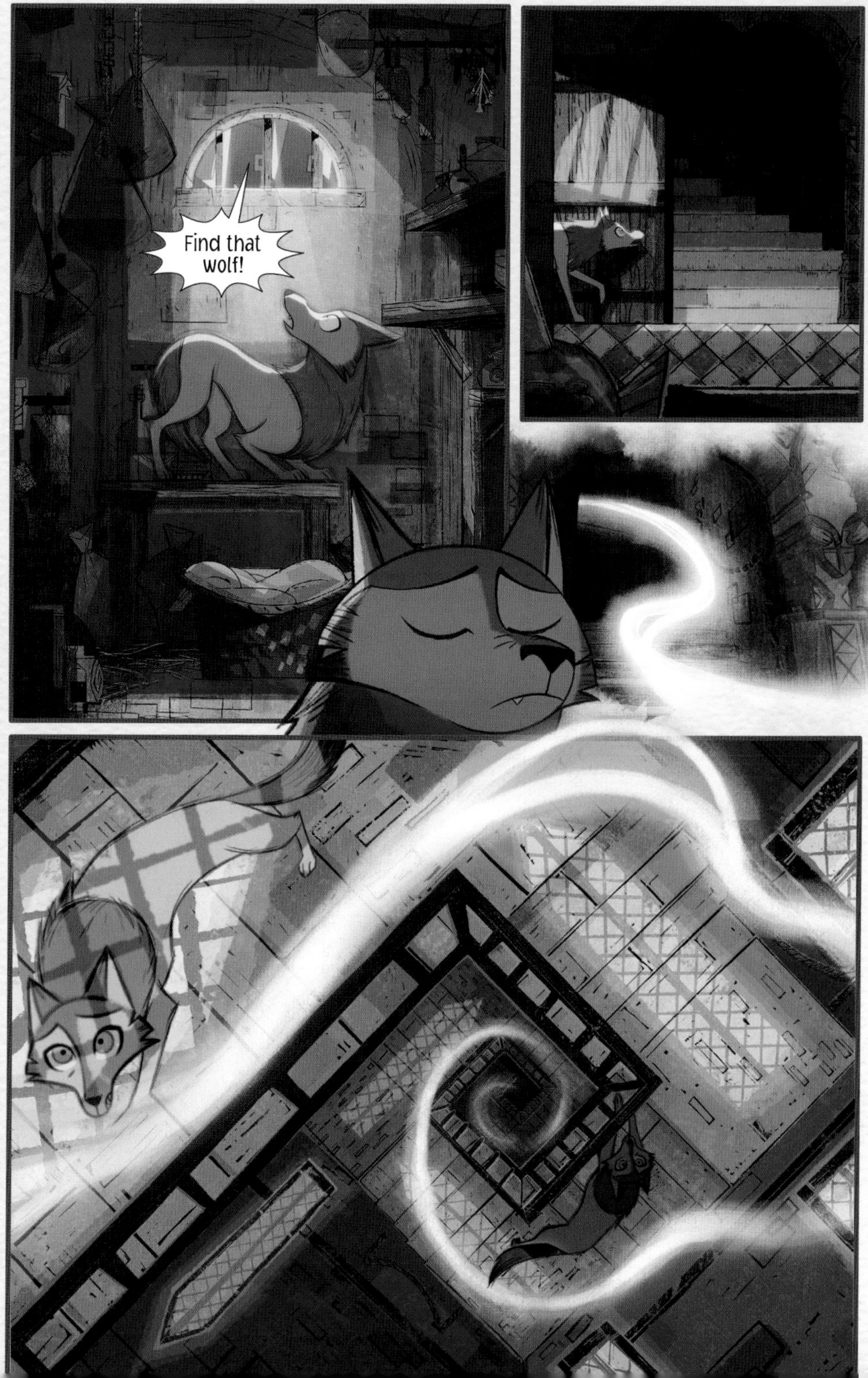
Find that wolf!

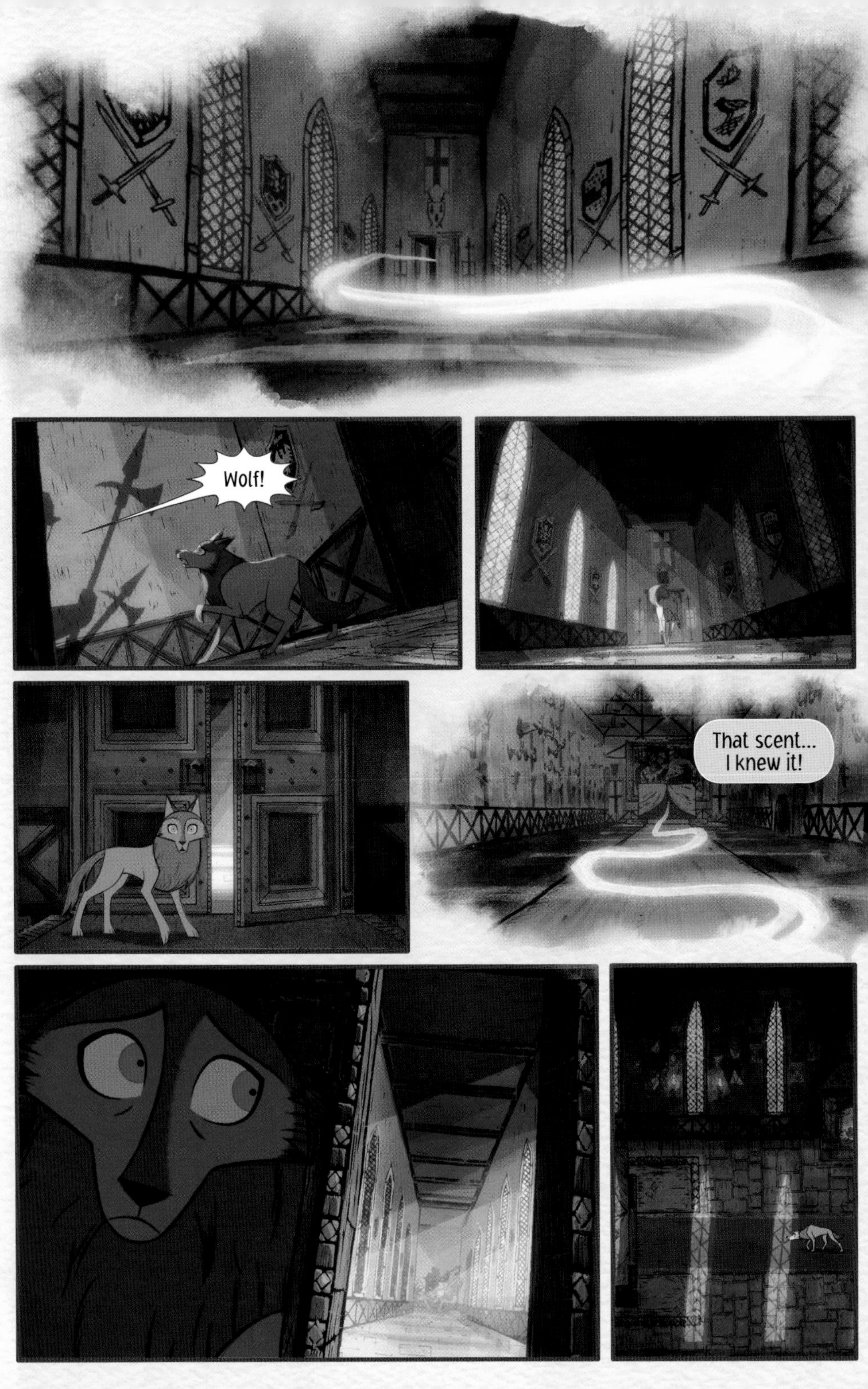
Wolf!
That scent...
I knew it!

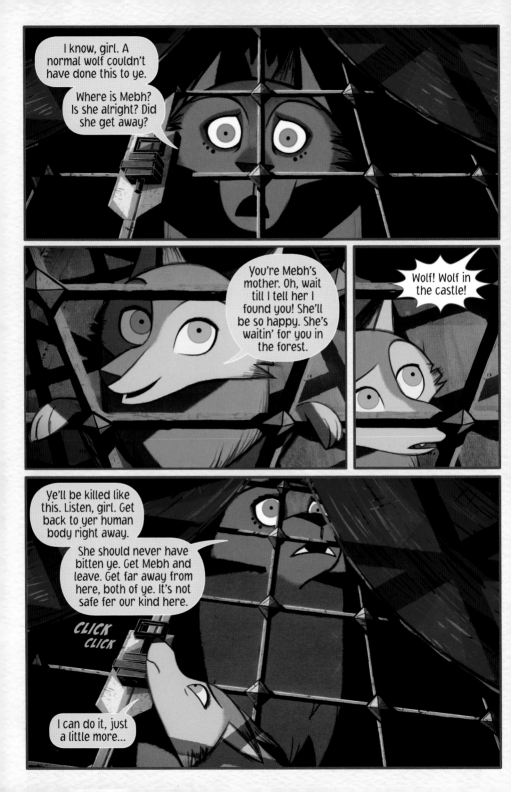

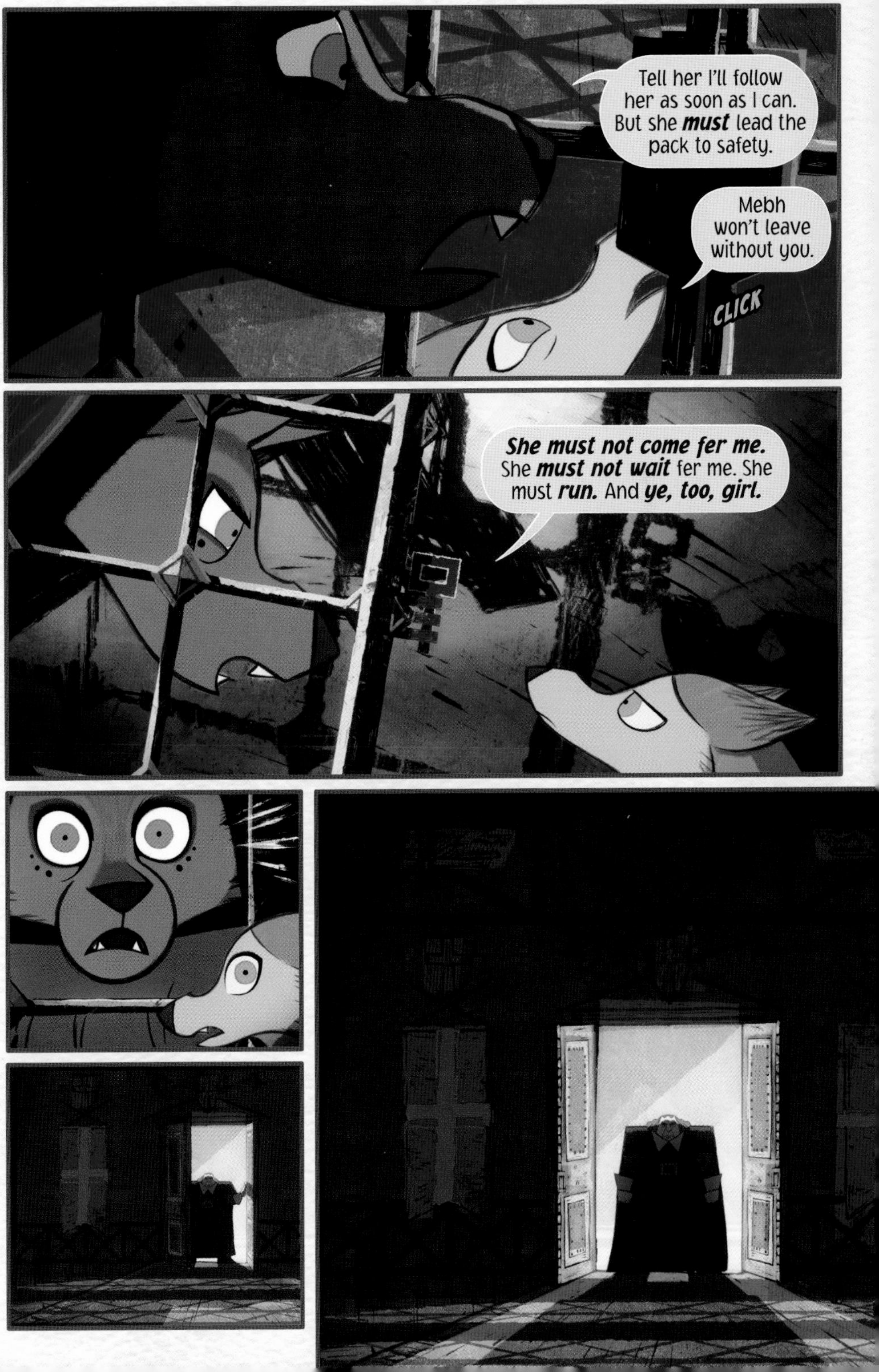
Tell her I'll follow her as soon as I can. But she ***must*** lead the pack to safety.
Mebh won't leave without you.
CLICK
She must not come fer me. She ***must not wait*** fer me. She must ***run.*** And ***ye, too, girl.***

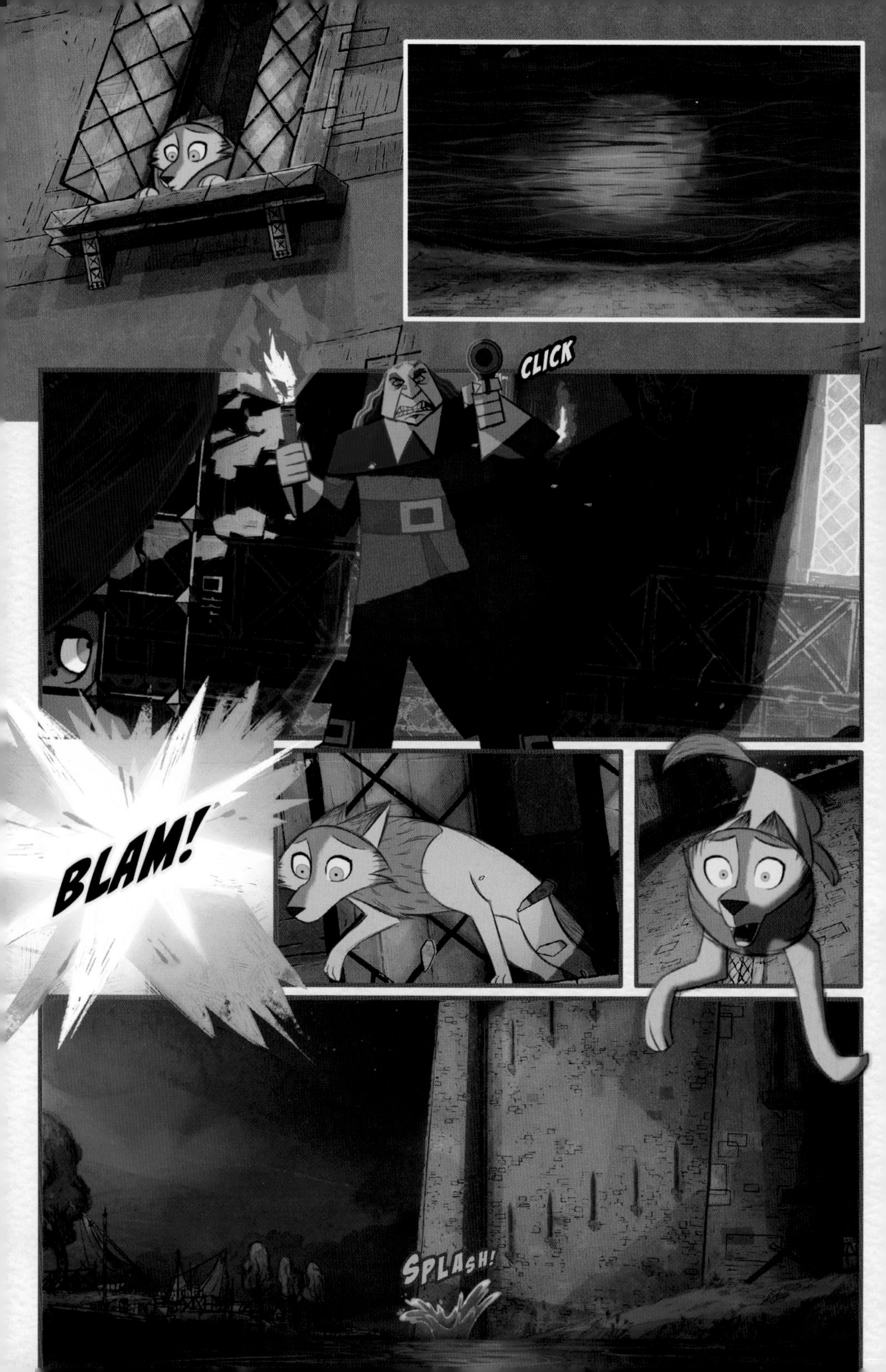
CLICK
BLAM!
SPLASH!

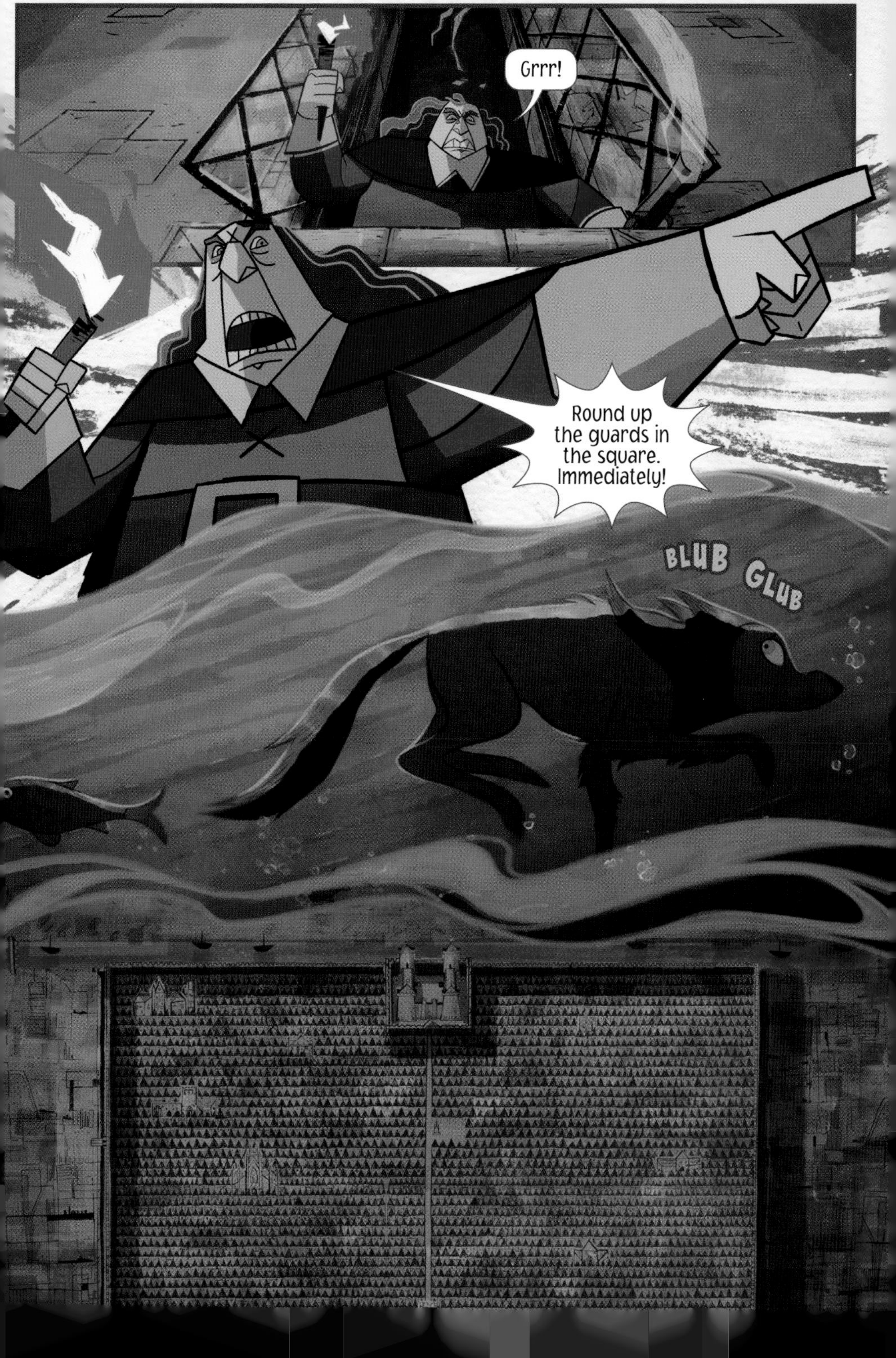
Grrr!
Round up the guards in the square. Immediately!
BLUB GLUB

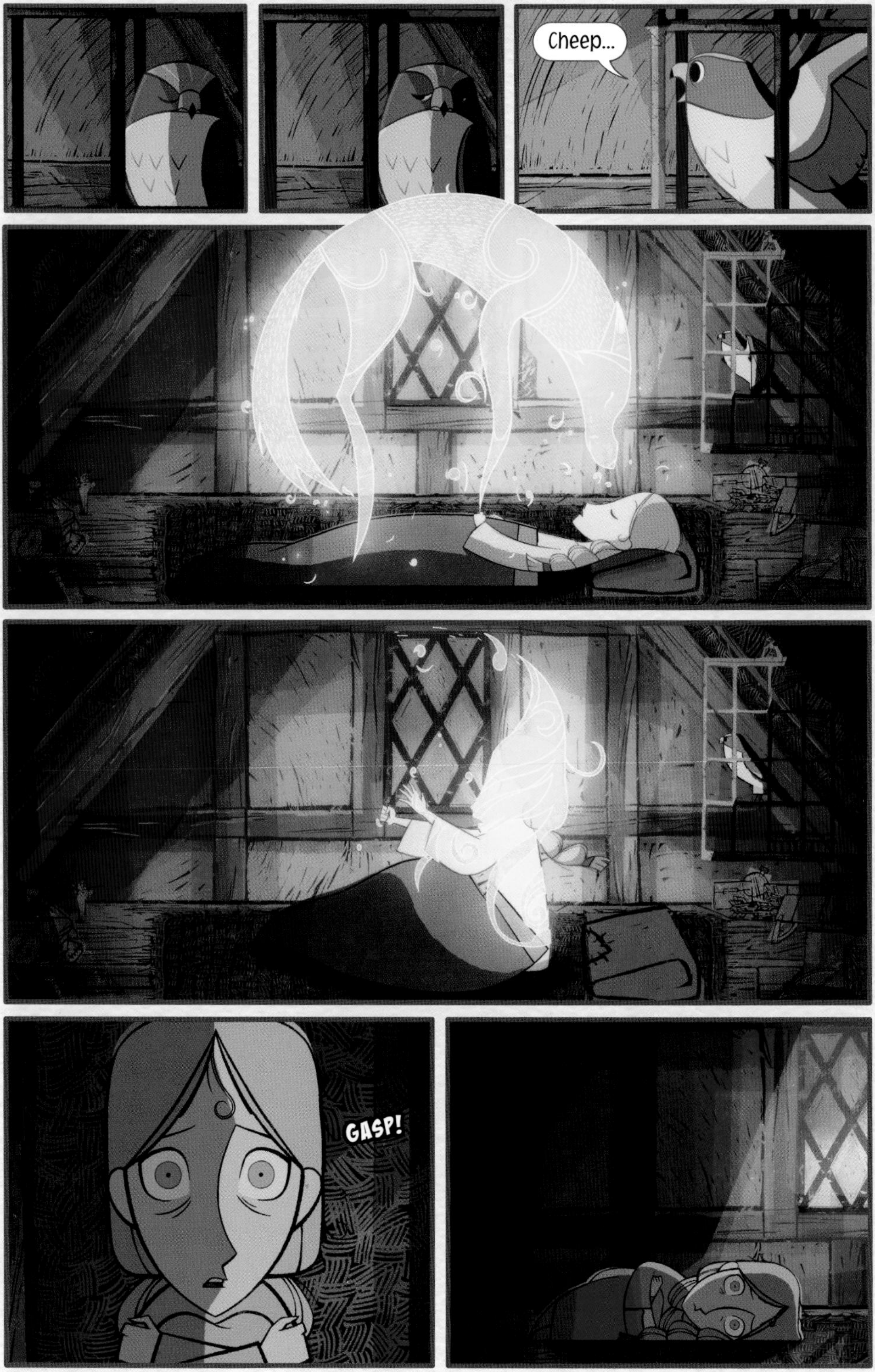
Cheep...
GASP!

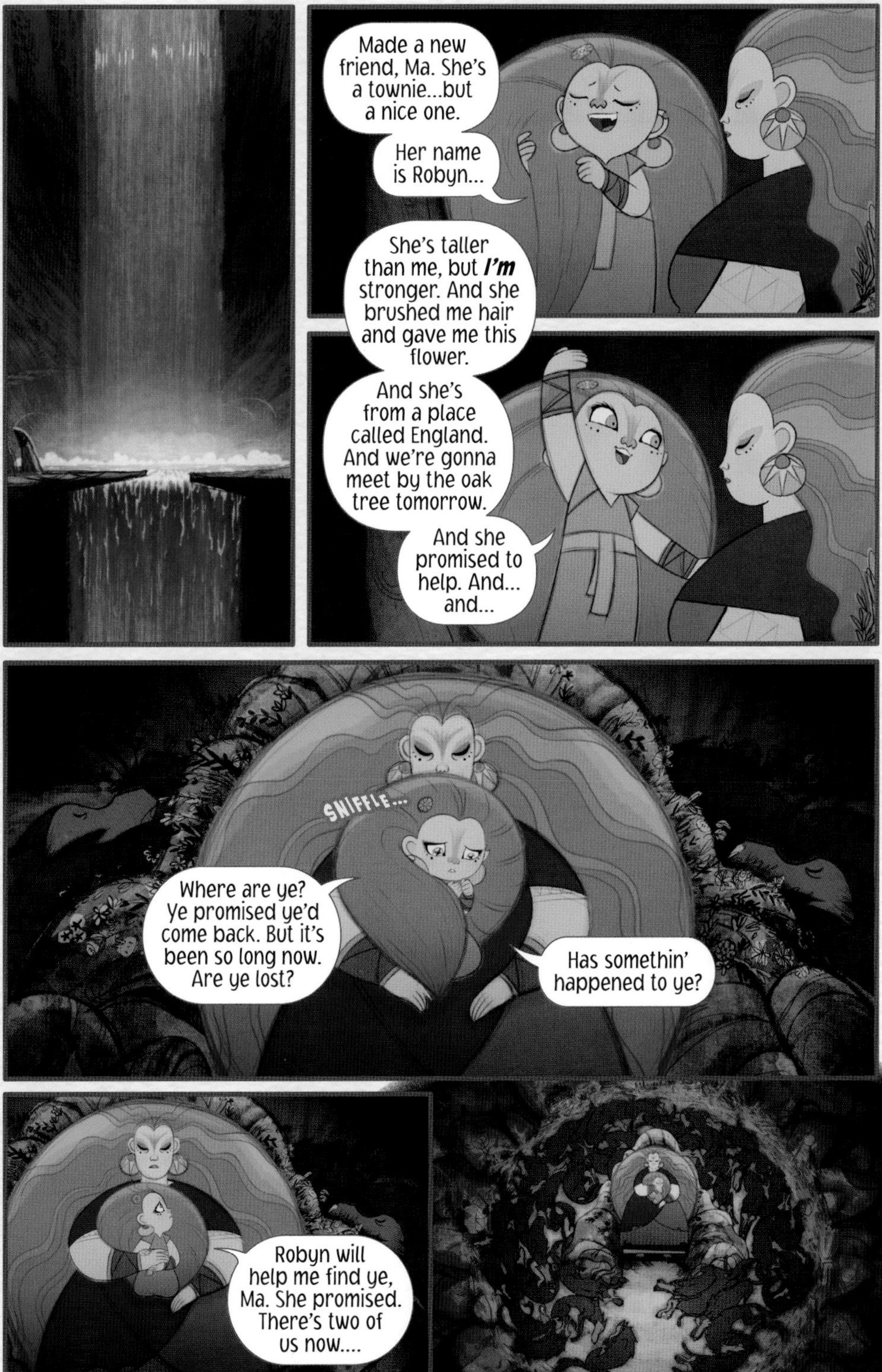
Made a new friend, Ma. She's a townie...but a nice one.
Her name is Robyn...
She's taller than me, but ***I'm*** stronger. And she brushed me hair and gave me this flower.
And she's from a place called England. And we're gonna meet by the oak tree tomorrow.
And she promised to help. And... and...
SNIFFLE...
Where are ye? Ye promised ye'd come back. But it's been so long now. Are ye lost?
Has somethin' happened to ye?
Robyn will help me find ye, Ma. She promised. There's two of us now....

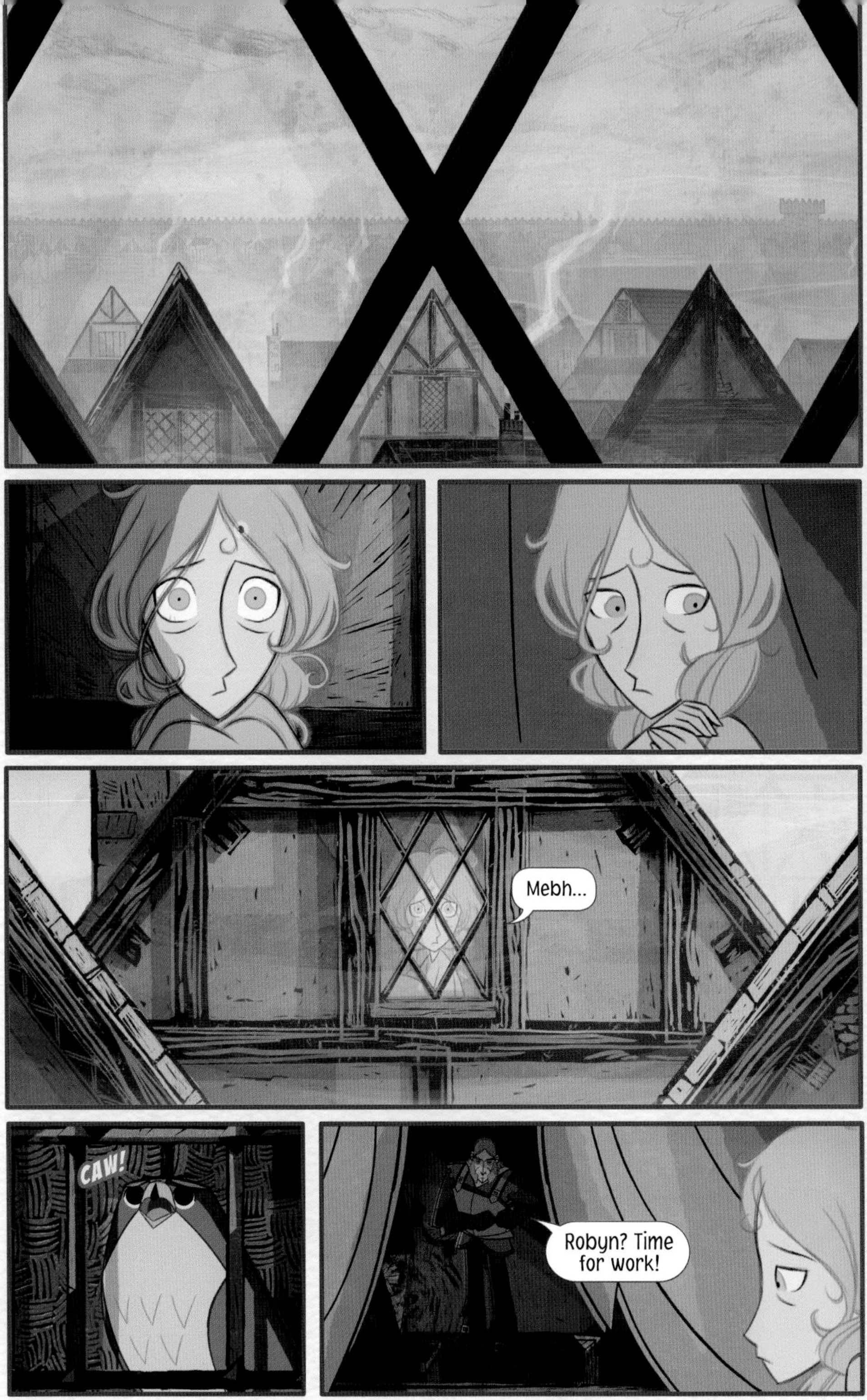

Mebh...
CAW!
Robyn? Time for work!

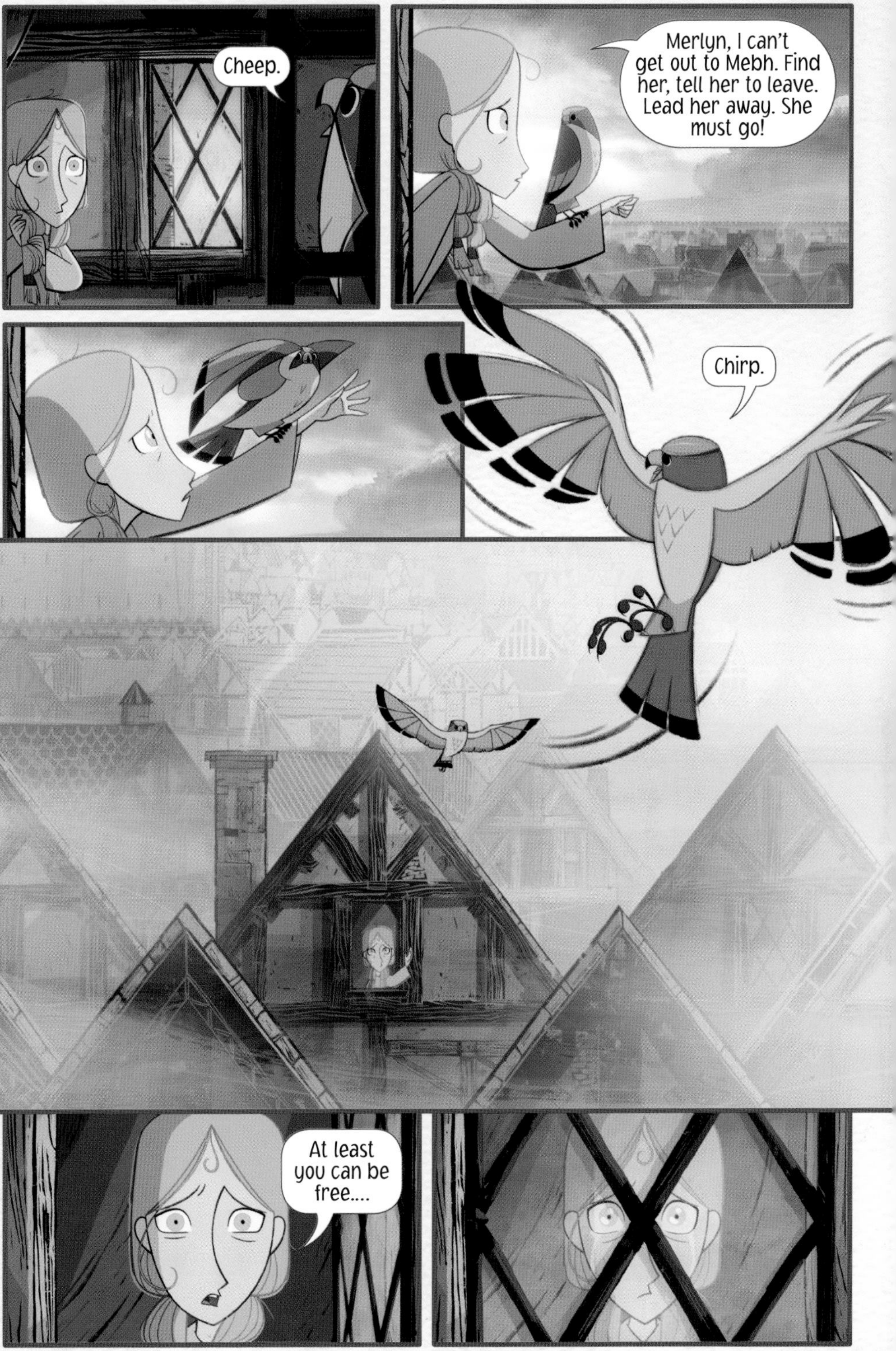
Cheep.
Merlyn, I can't get out to Mebh. Find her, tell her to leave. Lead her away. She must go!
Chirp.
At least you can be free....

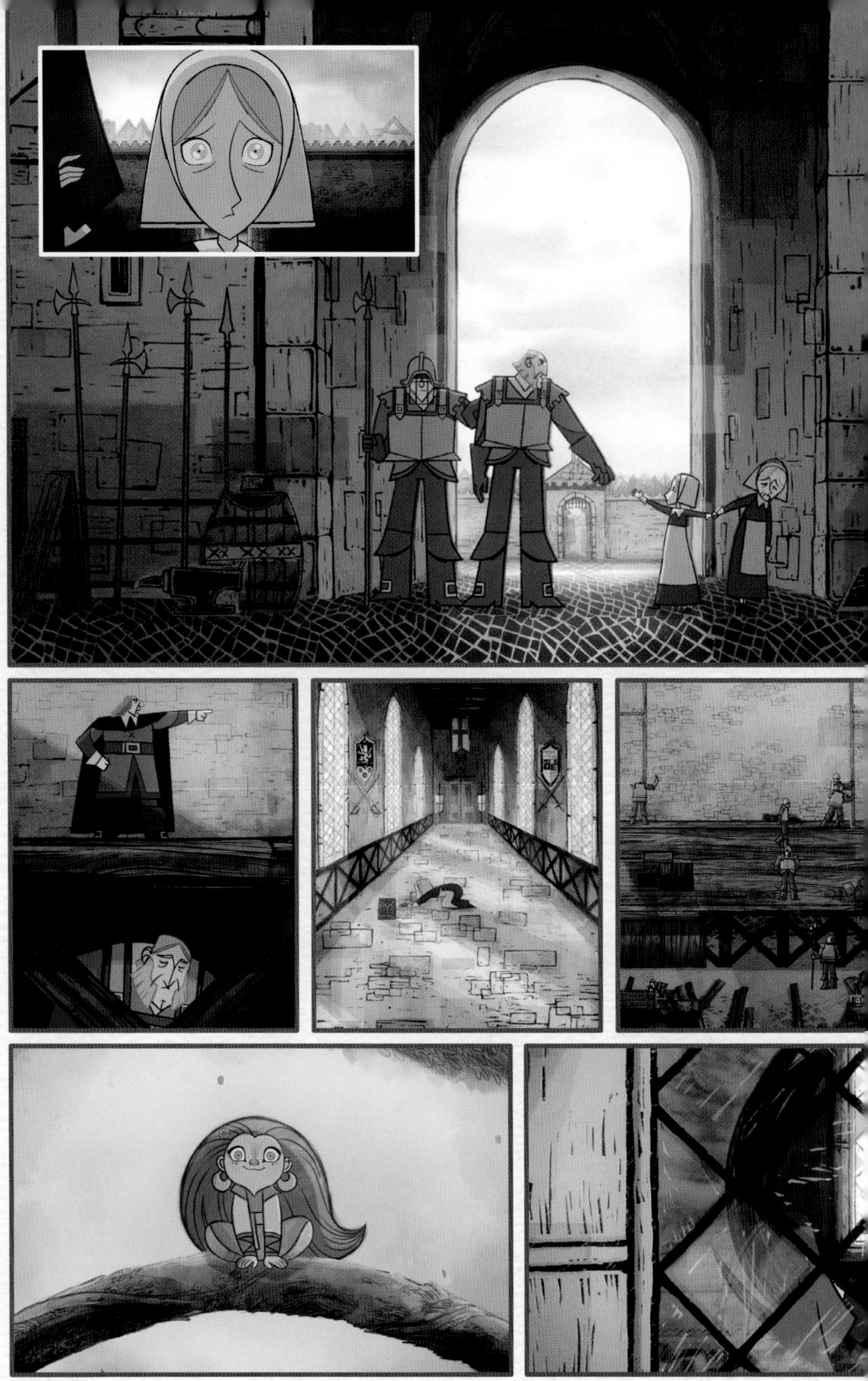

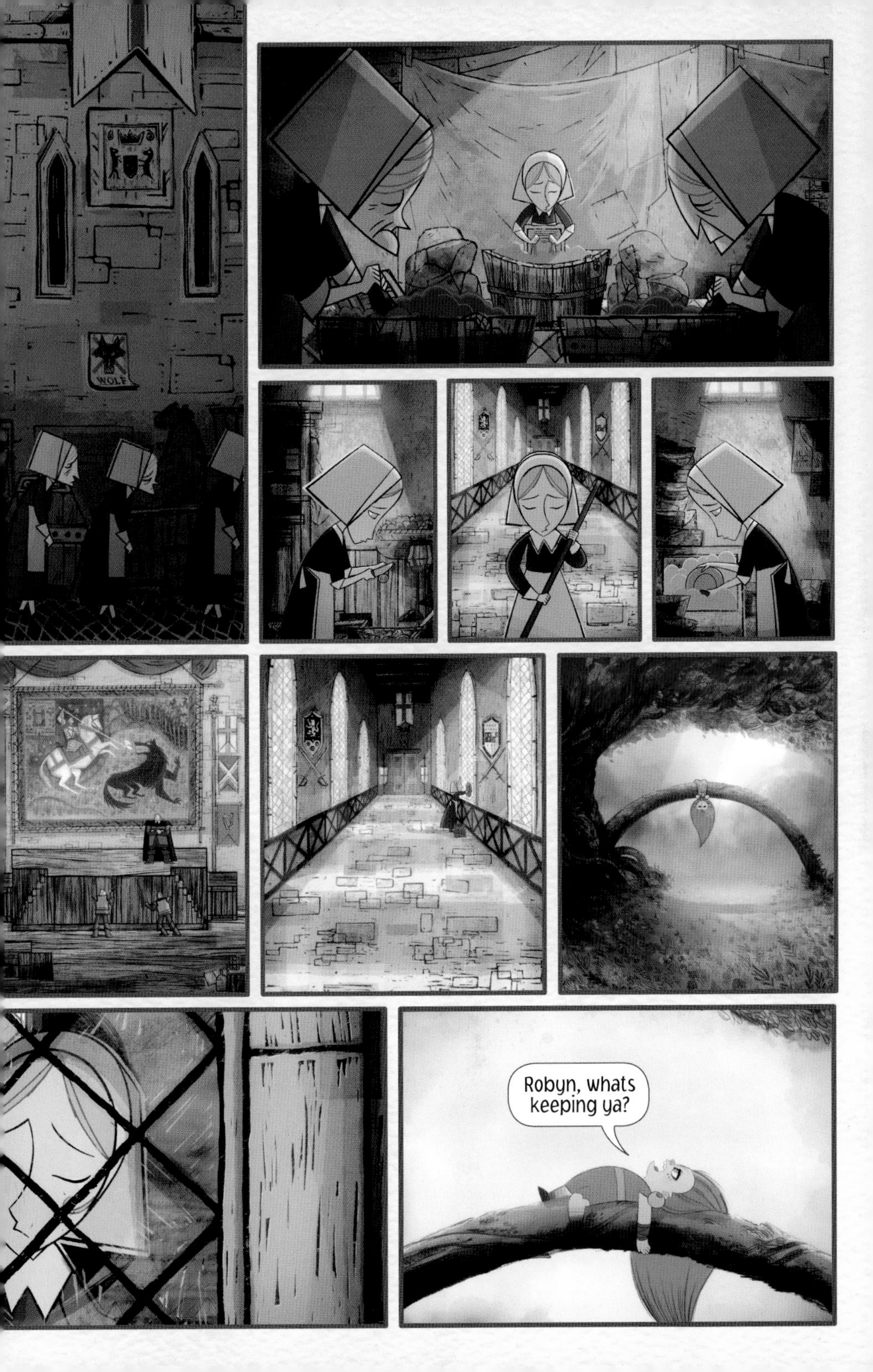
WOLF
Robyn, whats keeping ya?

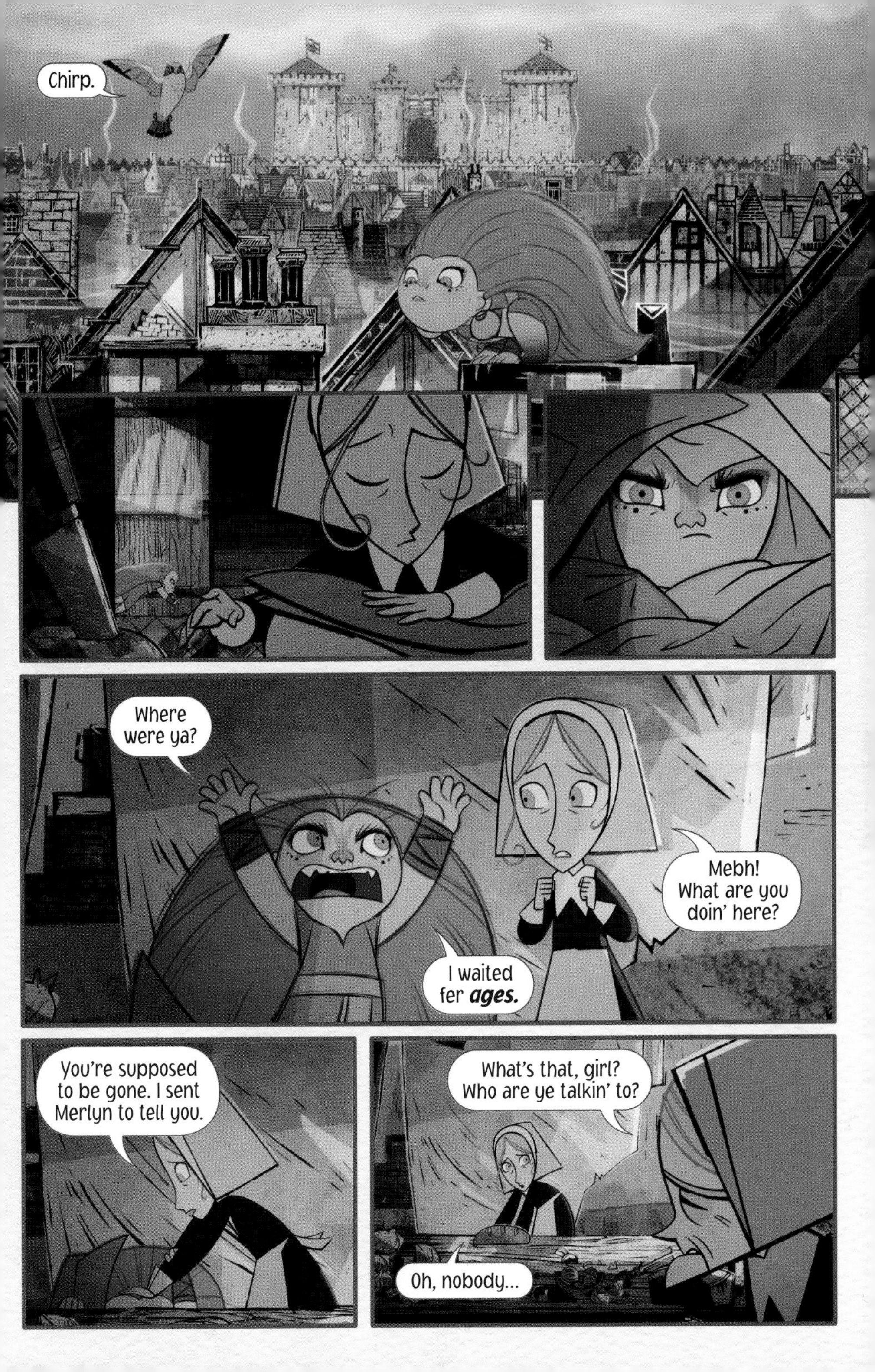
Chirp.
Where were ya?
Mebh! What are you doin' here?
I waited fer ***ages.***
You're supposed to be gone. I sent Merlyn to tell you.
What's that, girl? Who are ye talkin' to?
Oh, nobody...

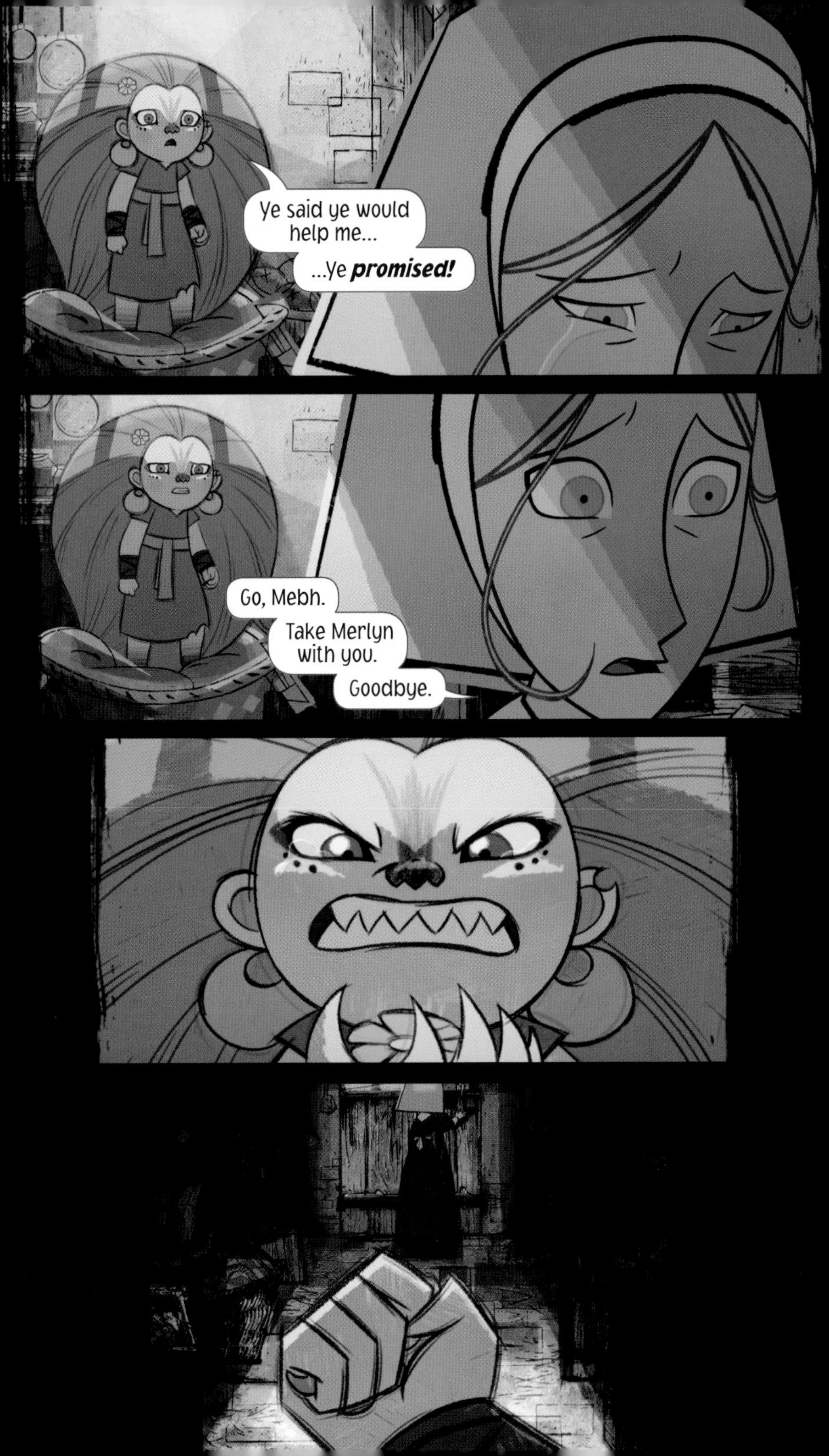
Ye said ye would help me...
...Ye **promised!**
Go, Mebh.
Take Merlyn with you.
Goodbye.

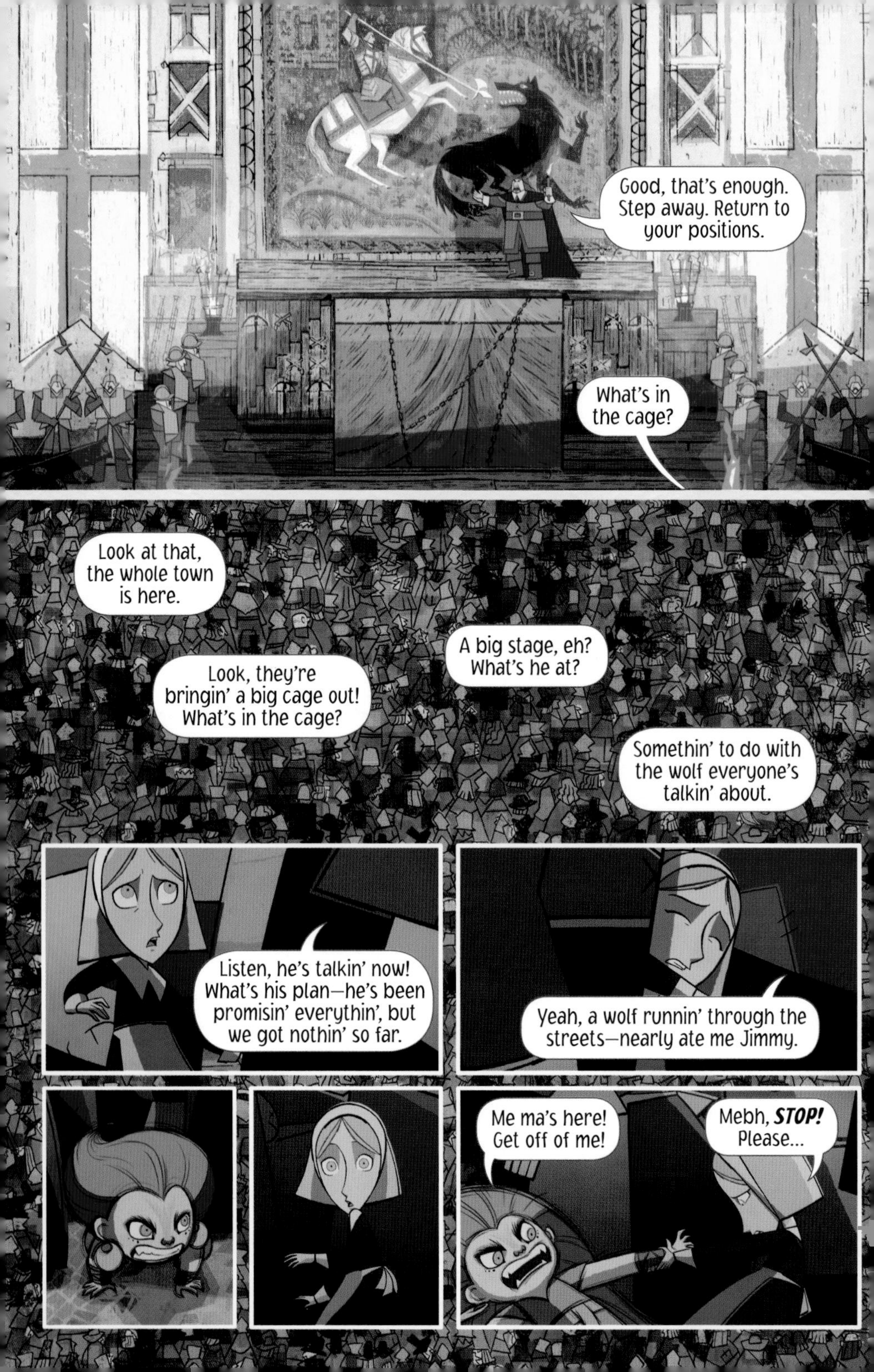
Good, that's enough. Step away. Return to your positions.
What's in the cage?
Look at that, the whole town is here.
Look, they're bringin' a big cage out! What's in the cage?
A big stage, eh? What's he at?
Somethin' to do with the wolf everyone's talkin' about.
Listen, he's talkin' now! What's his plan—he's been promisin' everythin', but we got nothin' so far.
Yeah, a wolf runnin' through the streets—nearly ate me Jimmy.
Me ma's here! Get off of me!
Mebh, ***STOP!*** Please...

No...

He has got a wolf... look at tha'.

Kill the wolf!

Kill the beast!

Kill it!

Send it to hell!

KILL THE WOLF!!

Enough! You have nothing to fear from this beast.

Now. Open the gate.

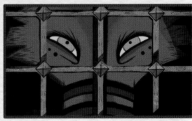

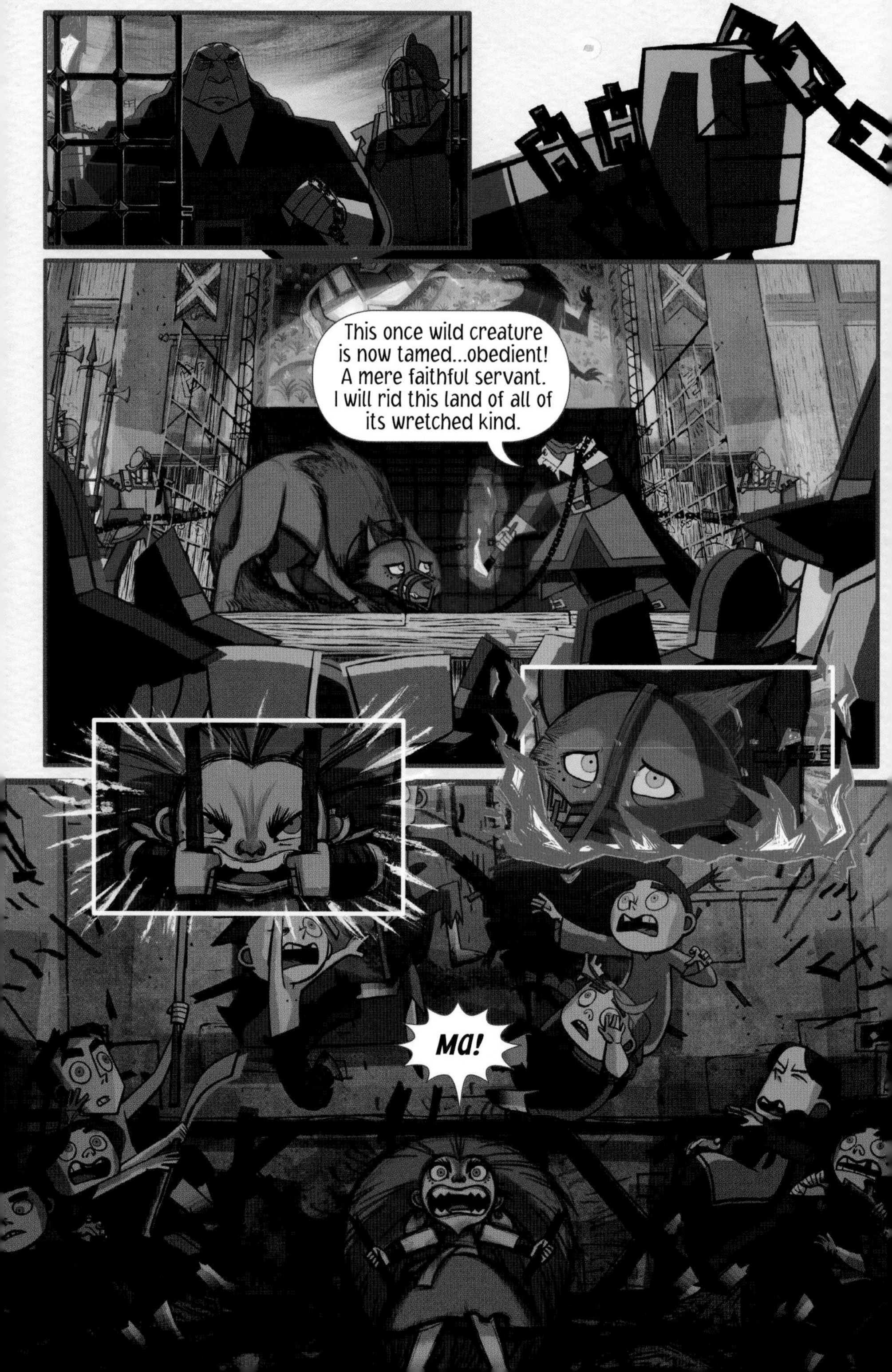
This once wild creature is now tamed...obedient! A mere faithful servant. I will rid this land of all of its wretched kind.
MA!

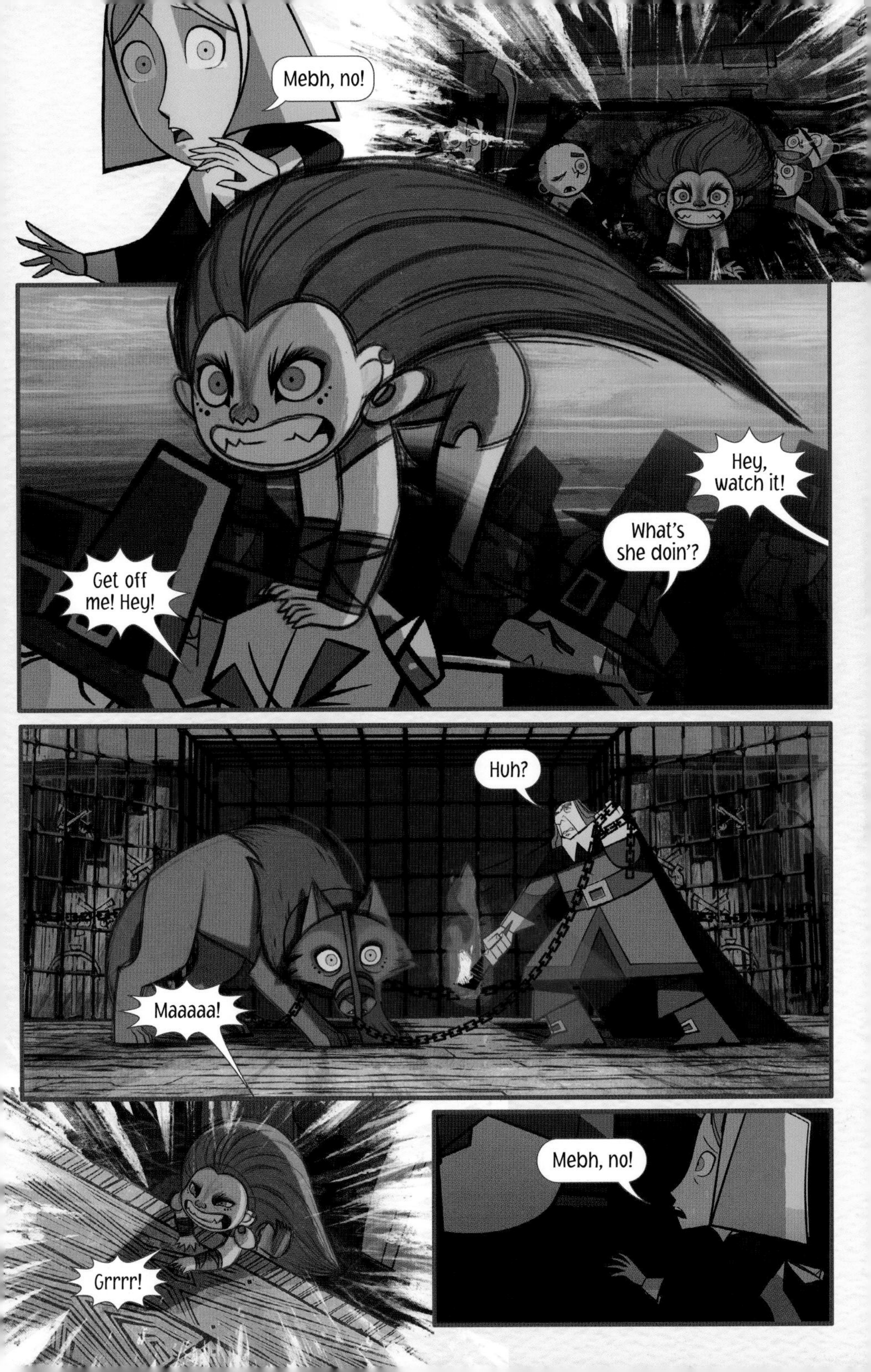
Mebh, no!
Get off me! Hey!
What's she doin'?
Hey, watch it!
Huh?
Maaaaa!
Grrrr!
Mebh, no!

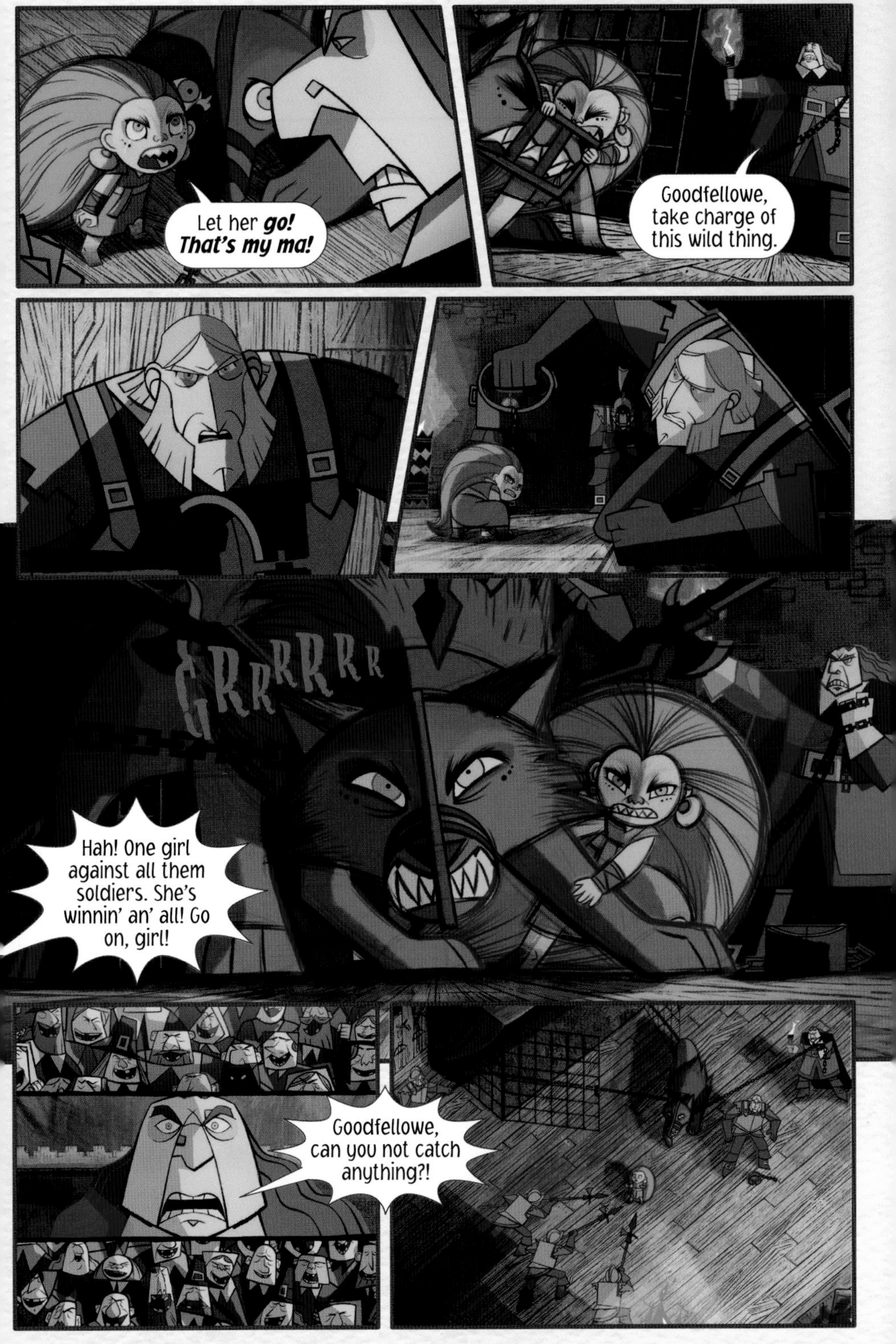
Let her ***go! That's my ma!***
Goodfellowe, take charge of this wild thing.
GRRRRRR
Hah! One girl against all them soldiers. She's winnin' an' all! Go on, girl!
Goodfellowe, can you not catch anything?!

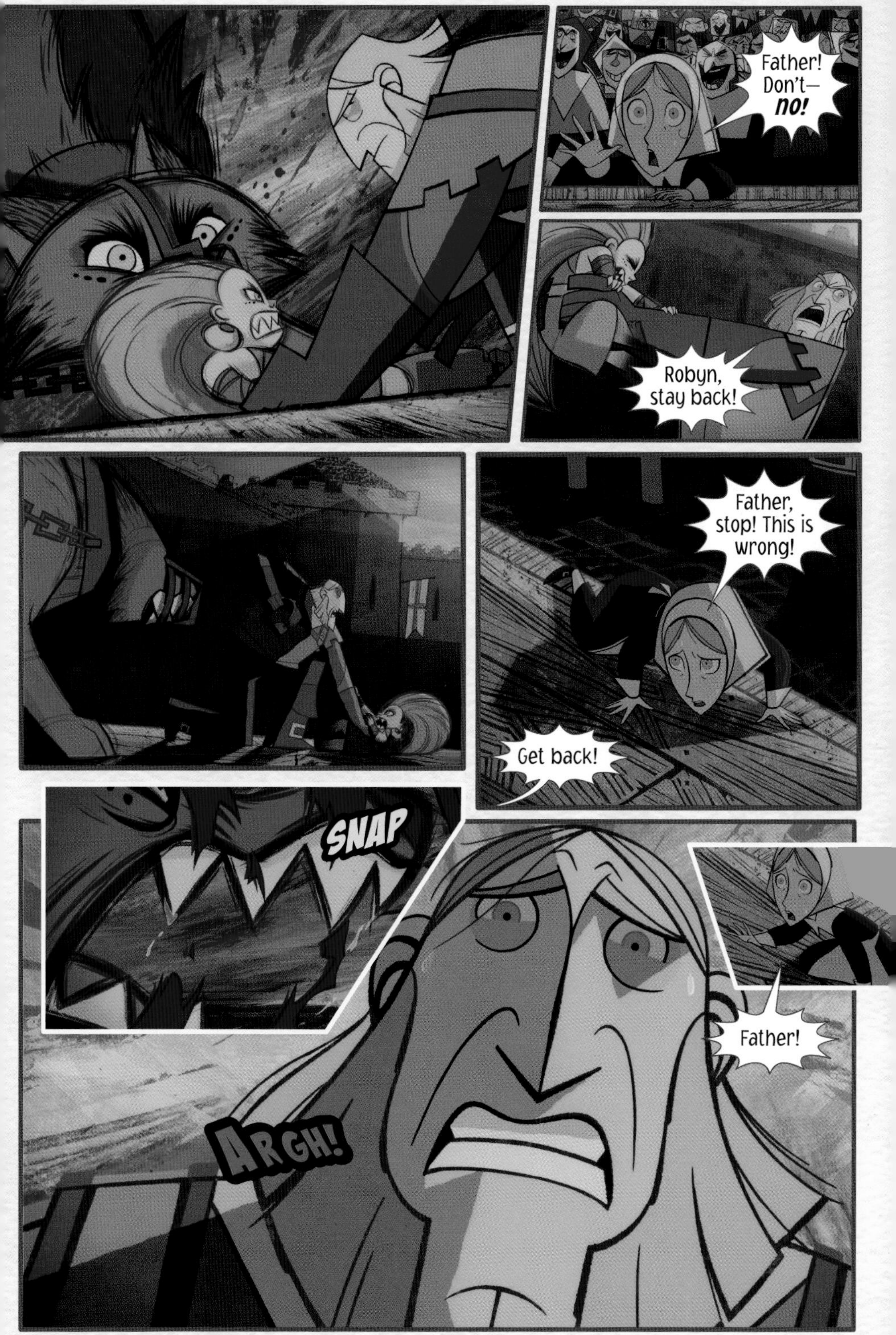
Father! Don't—
no!
Robyn, stay back!
Father, stop! This is wrong!
Get back!
SNAP
Father!
ARGH!

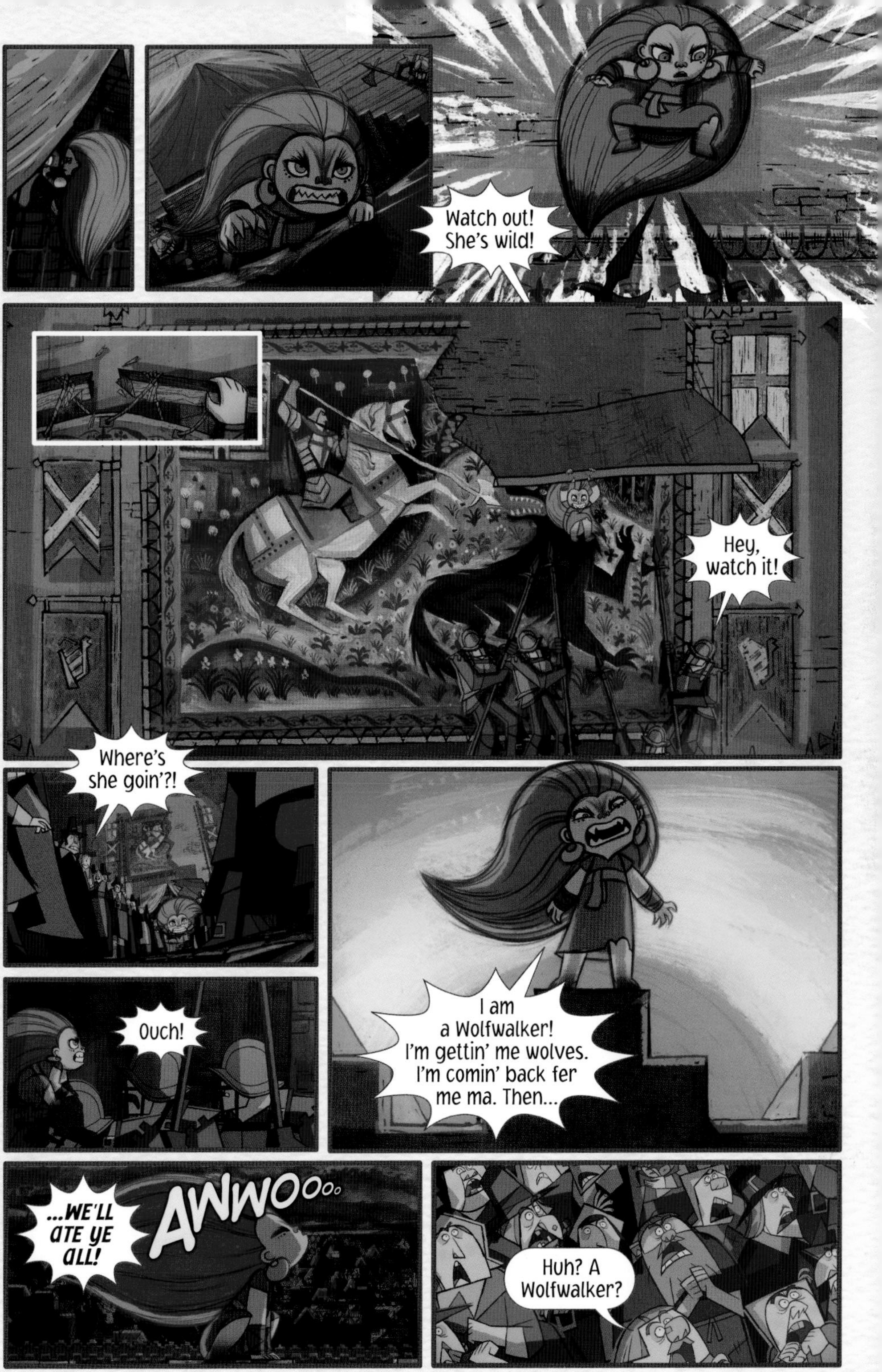
Watch out! She's wild!
Hey, watch it!
Where's she goin'?!
Ouch!
I am a Wolfwalker! I'm gettin' me wolves. I'm comin' back fer me ma. Then...
...WE'LL ATE YE ALL!
AWWOooo
Huh? A Wolfwalker?

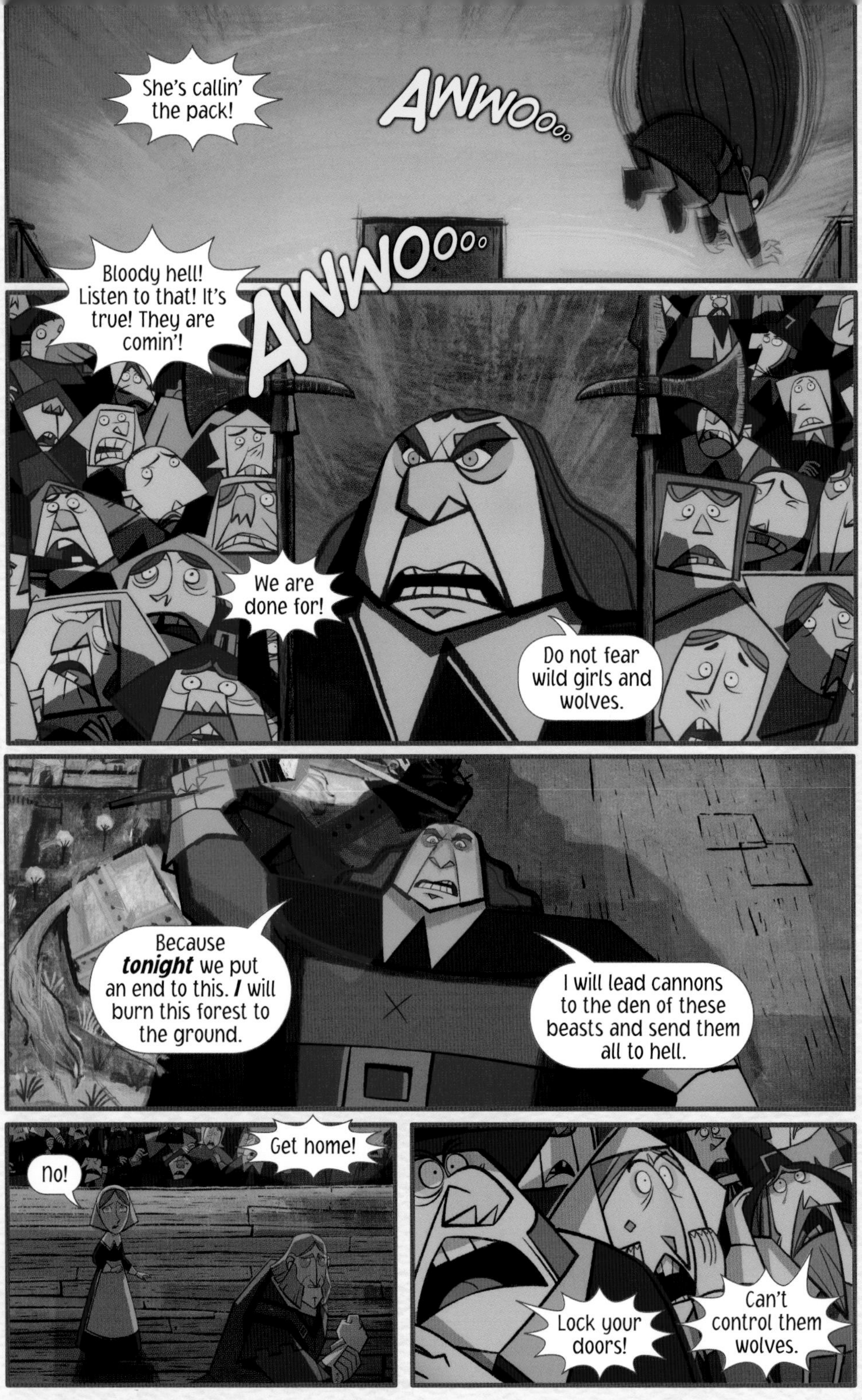
She's callin' the pack!
AWWOooo
Bloody hell! Listen to that! It's true! They are comin'!
AWWOooo
AWWO
We are done for!
Do not fear wild girls and wolves.
Because **tonight** we put an end to this. ***I*** will burn this forest to the ground.
I will lead cannons to the den of these beasts and send them all to hell.
No!
Get home!
Lock your doors!
Can't control them wolves.

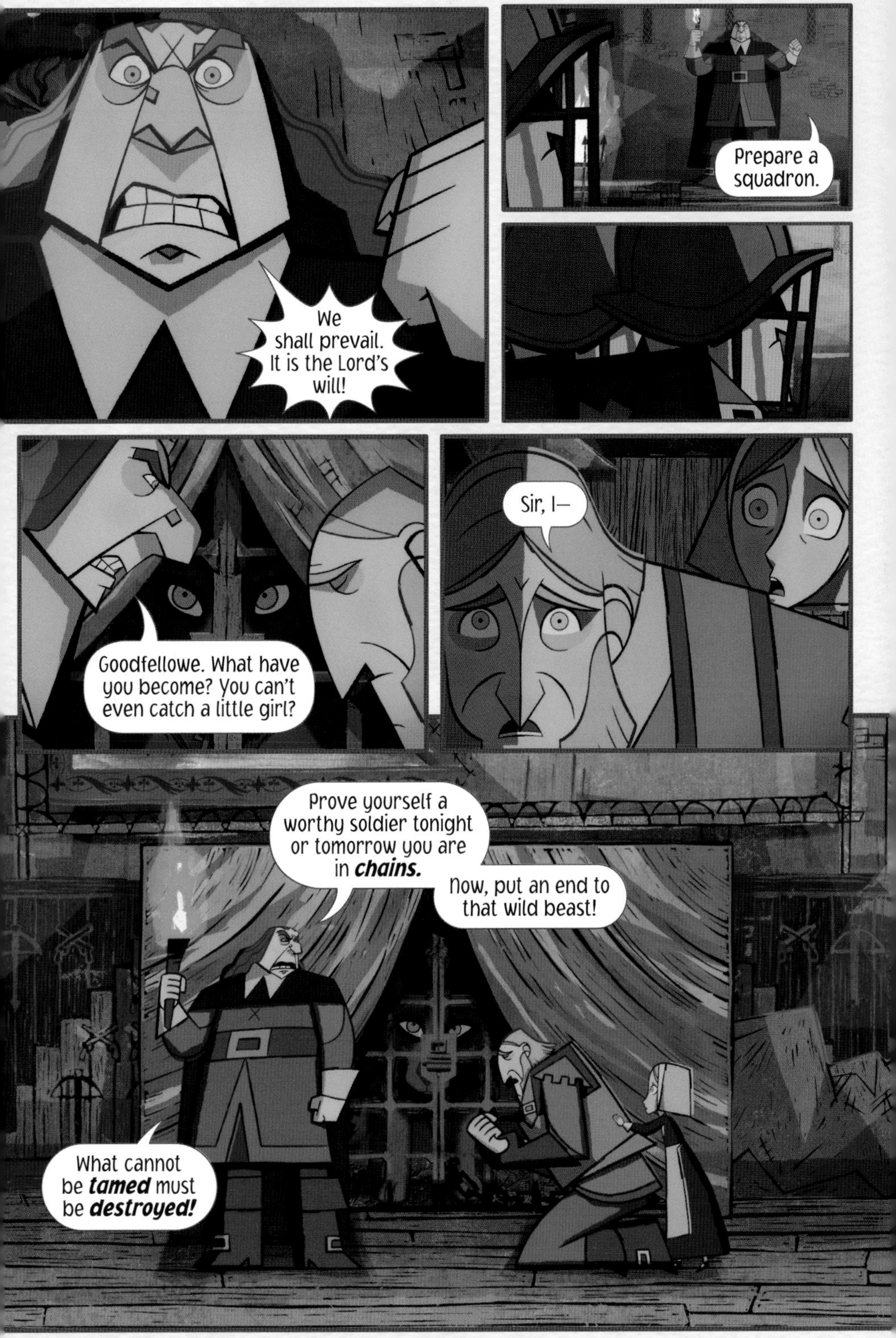
We shall prevail. It is the Lord's will!
Prepare a squadron.
Goodfellowe. What have you become? You can't even catch a little girl?
Sir, I—
Prove yourself a worthy soldier tonight or tomorrow you are in ***chains.***
Now, put an end to that wild beast!
What cannot be ***tamed*** must be ***destroyed!***

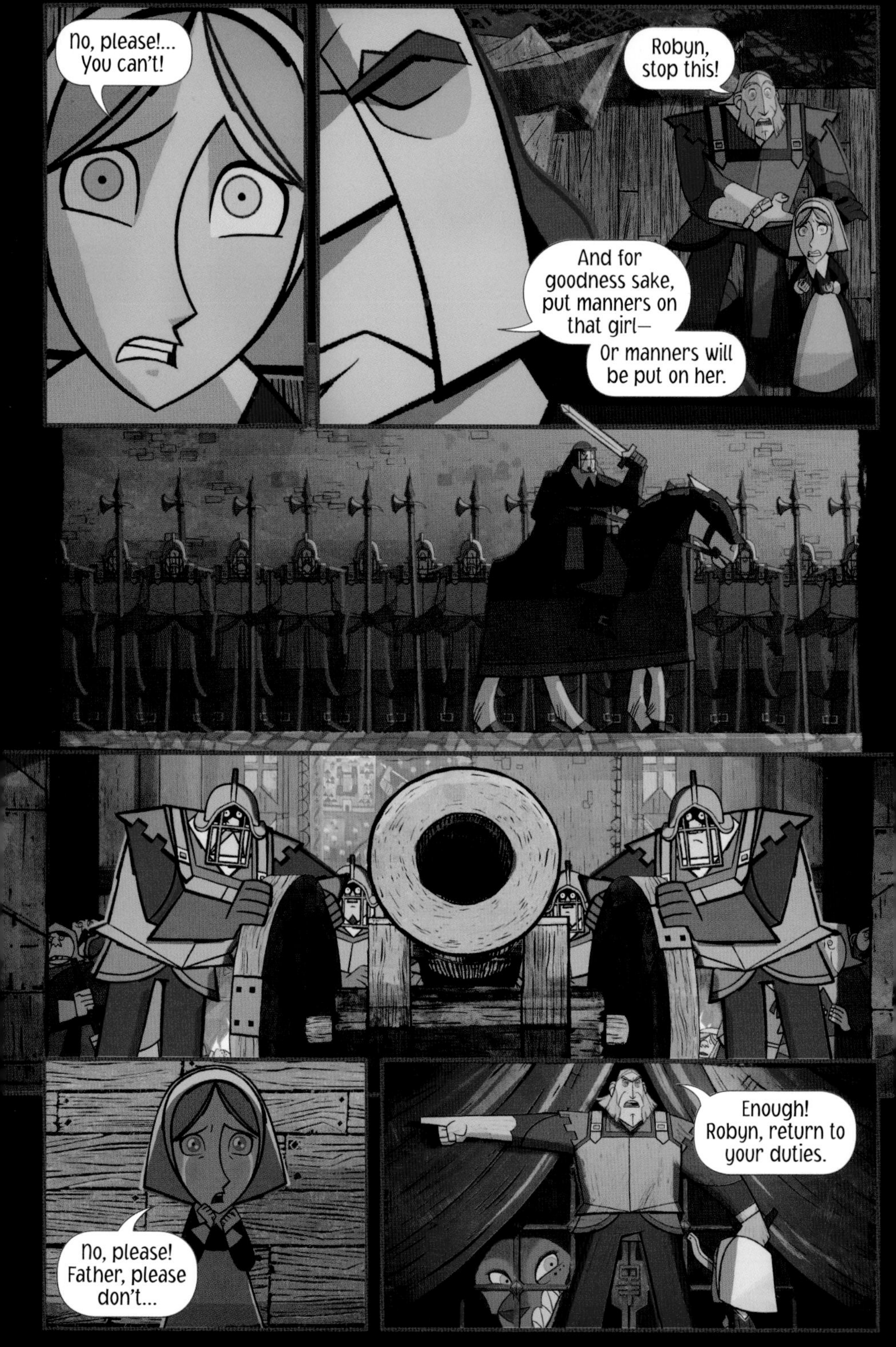

No, please!... You can't!
Robyn, stop this!
And for goodness sake, put manners on that girl—
Or manners will be put on her.
No, please! Father, please don't...
Enough! Robyn, return to your duties.

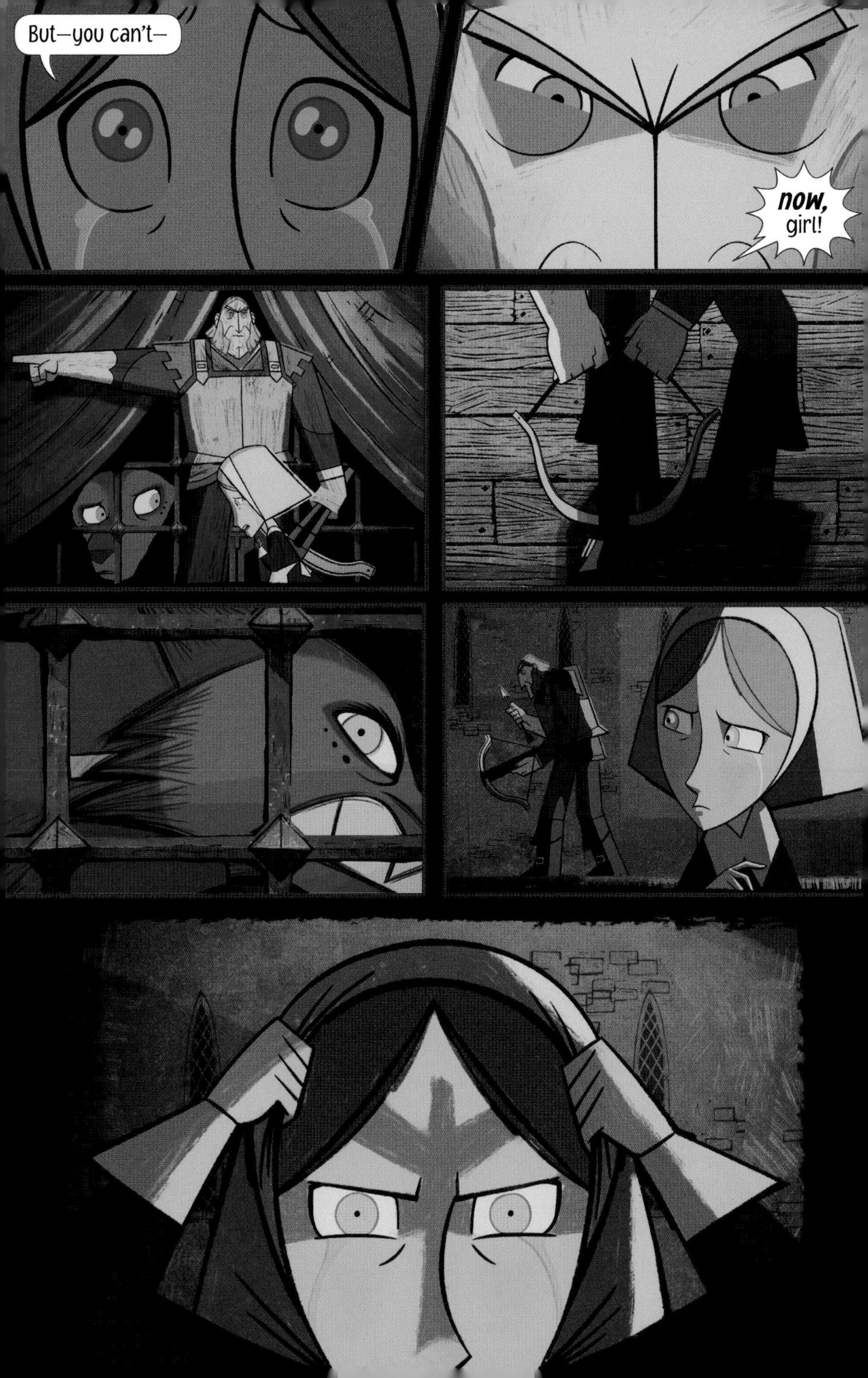
But—you can't—
now, girl!

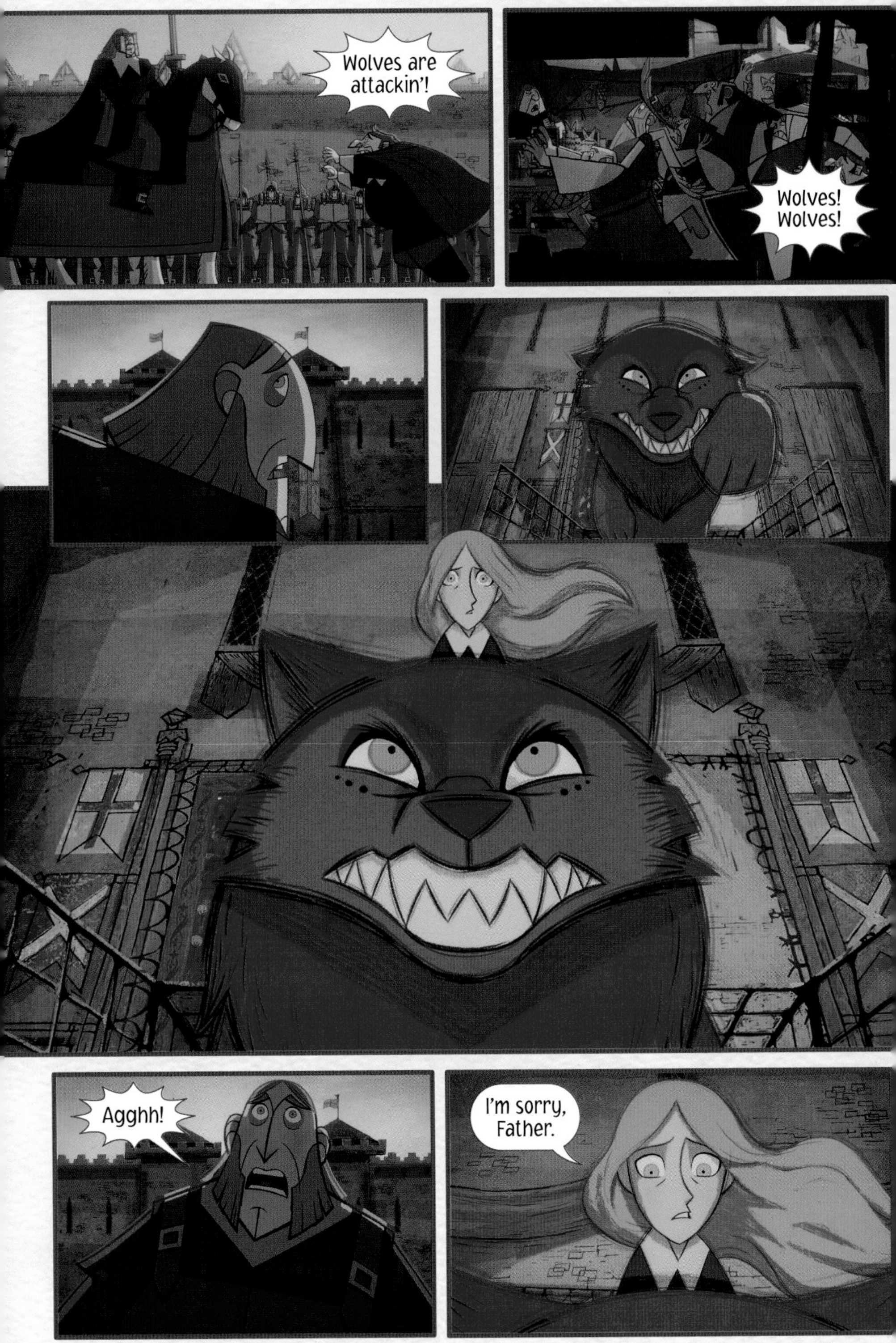
Wolves are attackin'!
Wolves! Wolves!
Agghh!
I'm sorry, Father.

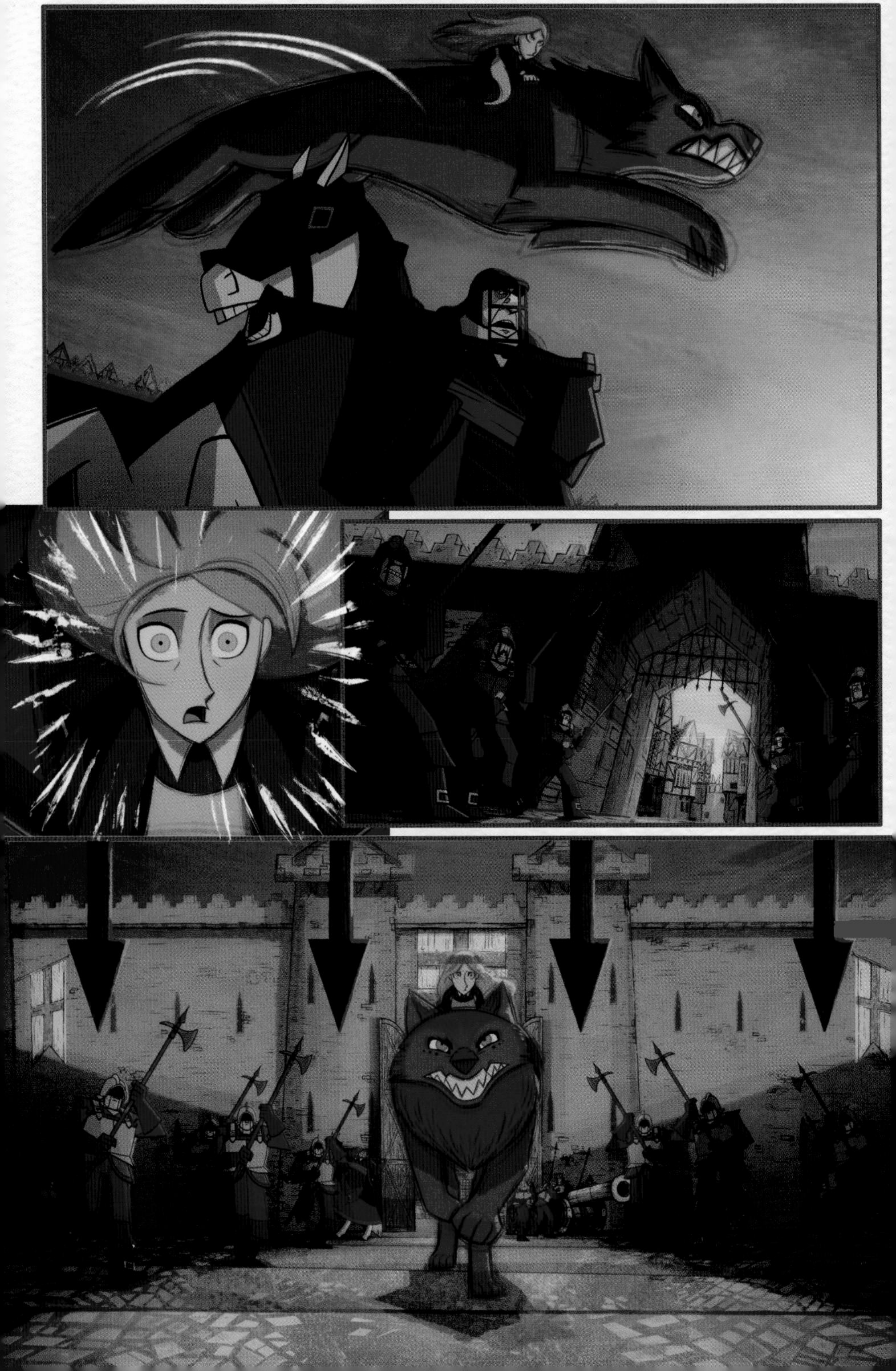

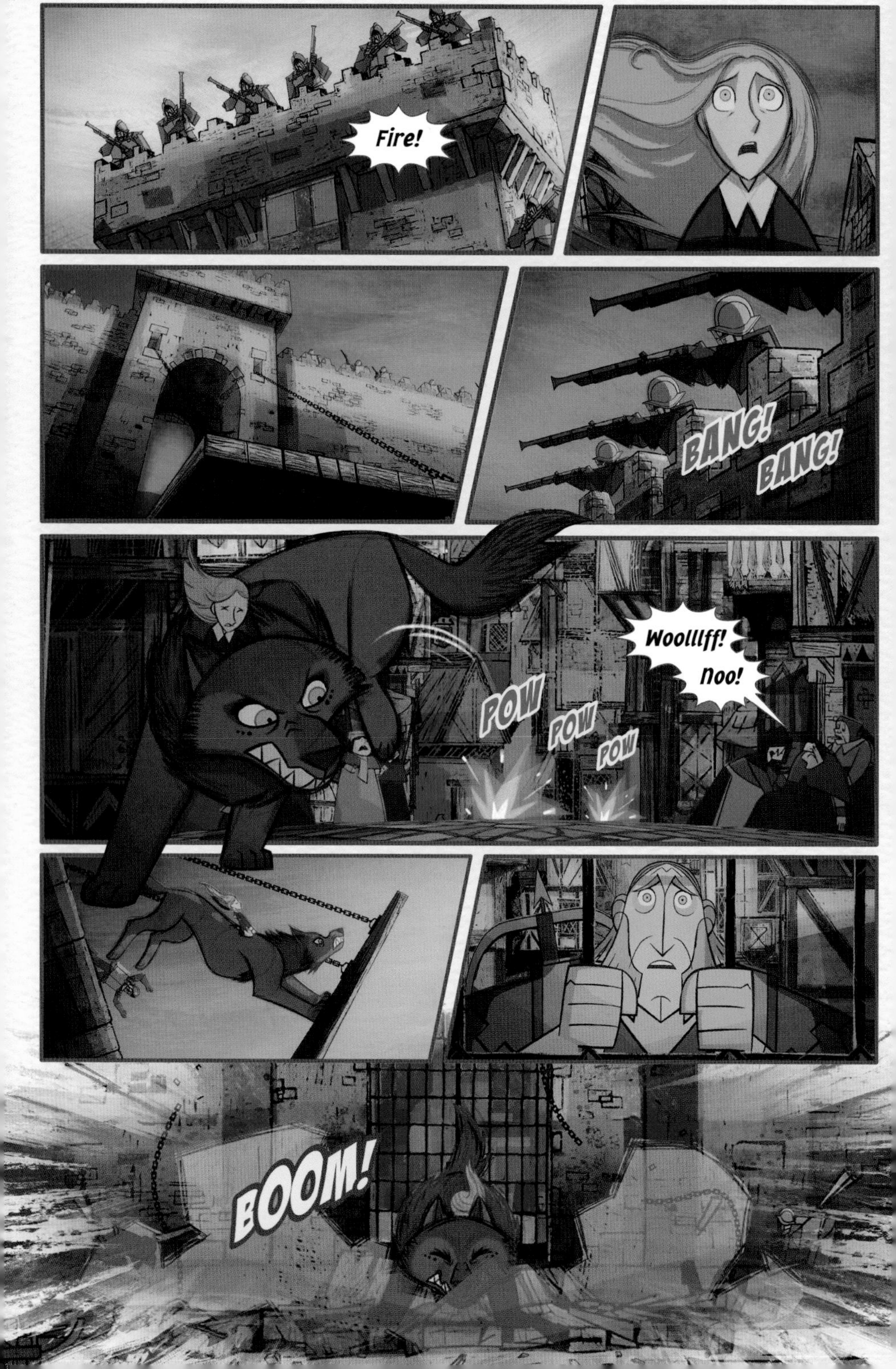
Fire!
BANG!
BANG!
POW
POW
POW
Wooolllff!
Nooo!
BOOM!

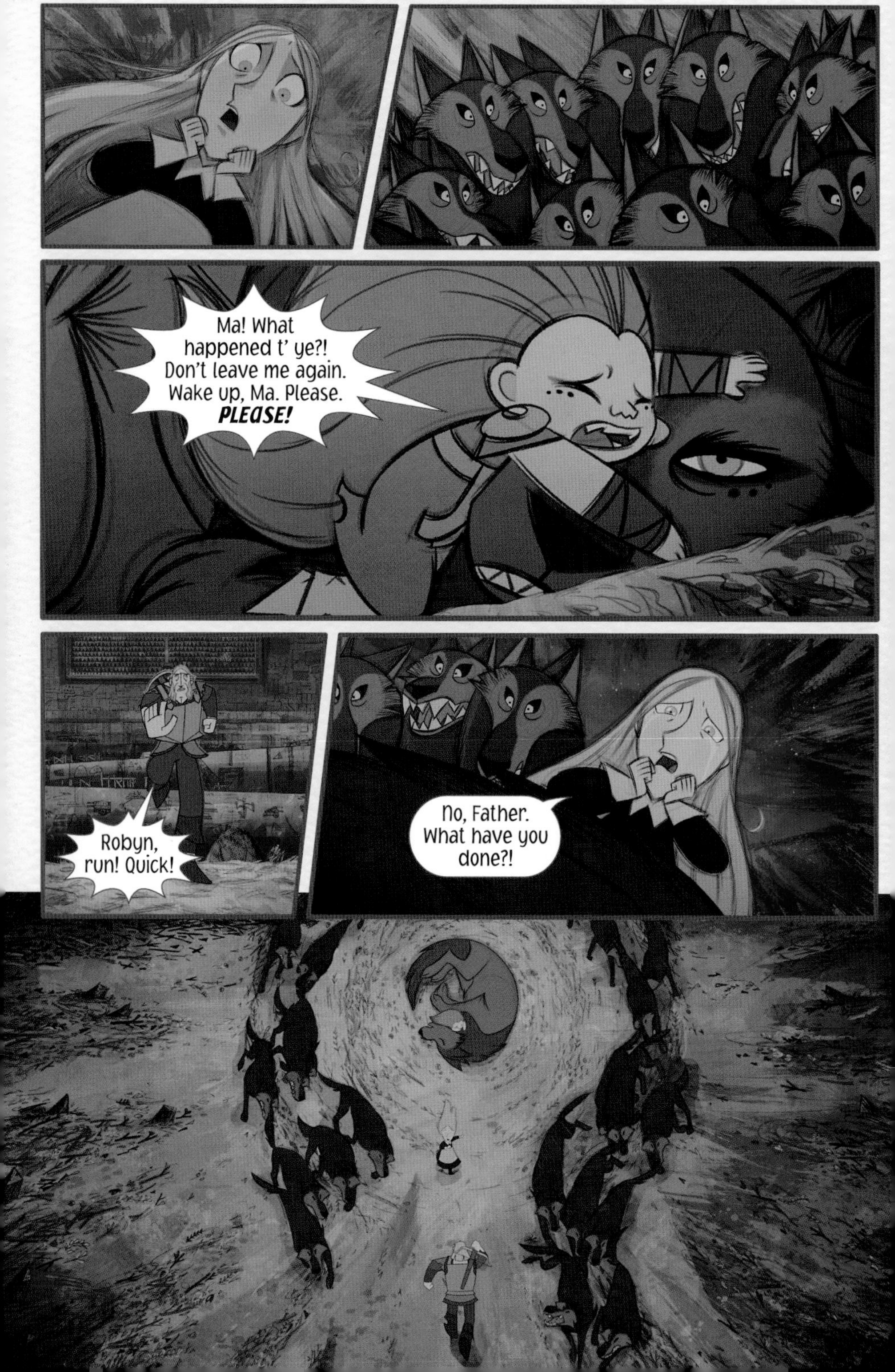
Ma! What happened t' ye?! Don't leave me again. Wake up, Ma. Please. ***PLEASE!***
Robyn, run! Quick!
No, Father. What have you done?!

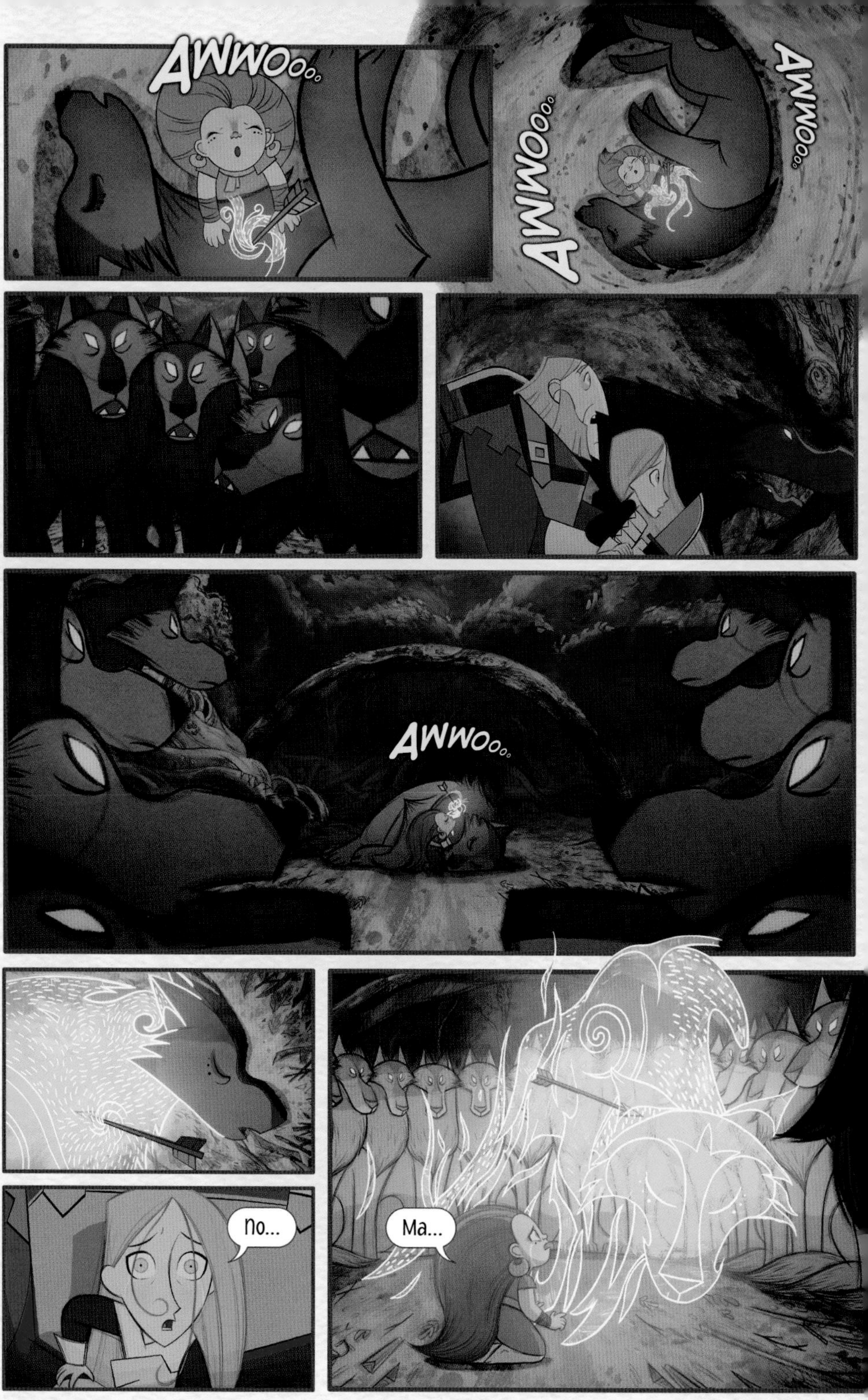
AWWOooo
AWWOooo
AWWOooo
AWWOooo
no...
Ma...

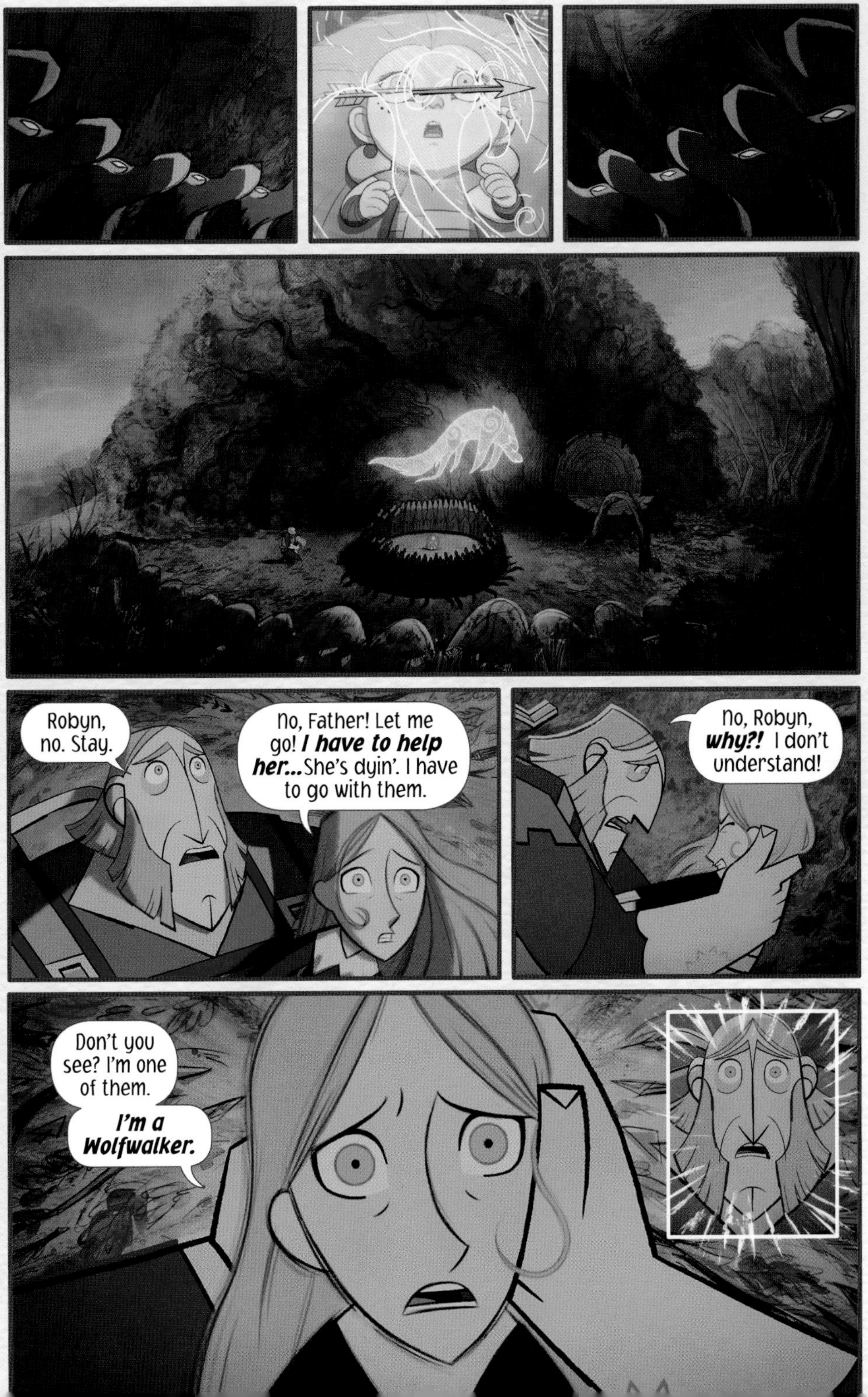
Robyn, no. Stay.
No, Father! Let me go! **I have to help her...** She's dyin'. I have to go with them.
No, Robyn, **why?!** I don't understand!
Don't you see? I'm one of them.
I'm a Wolfwalker.

No, Robyn.
Please...

I can't let
you go.

Father...

UHMMMM

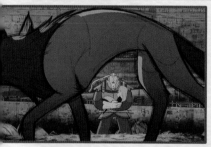

Robyn!
ROBYN!

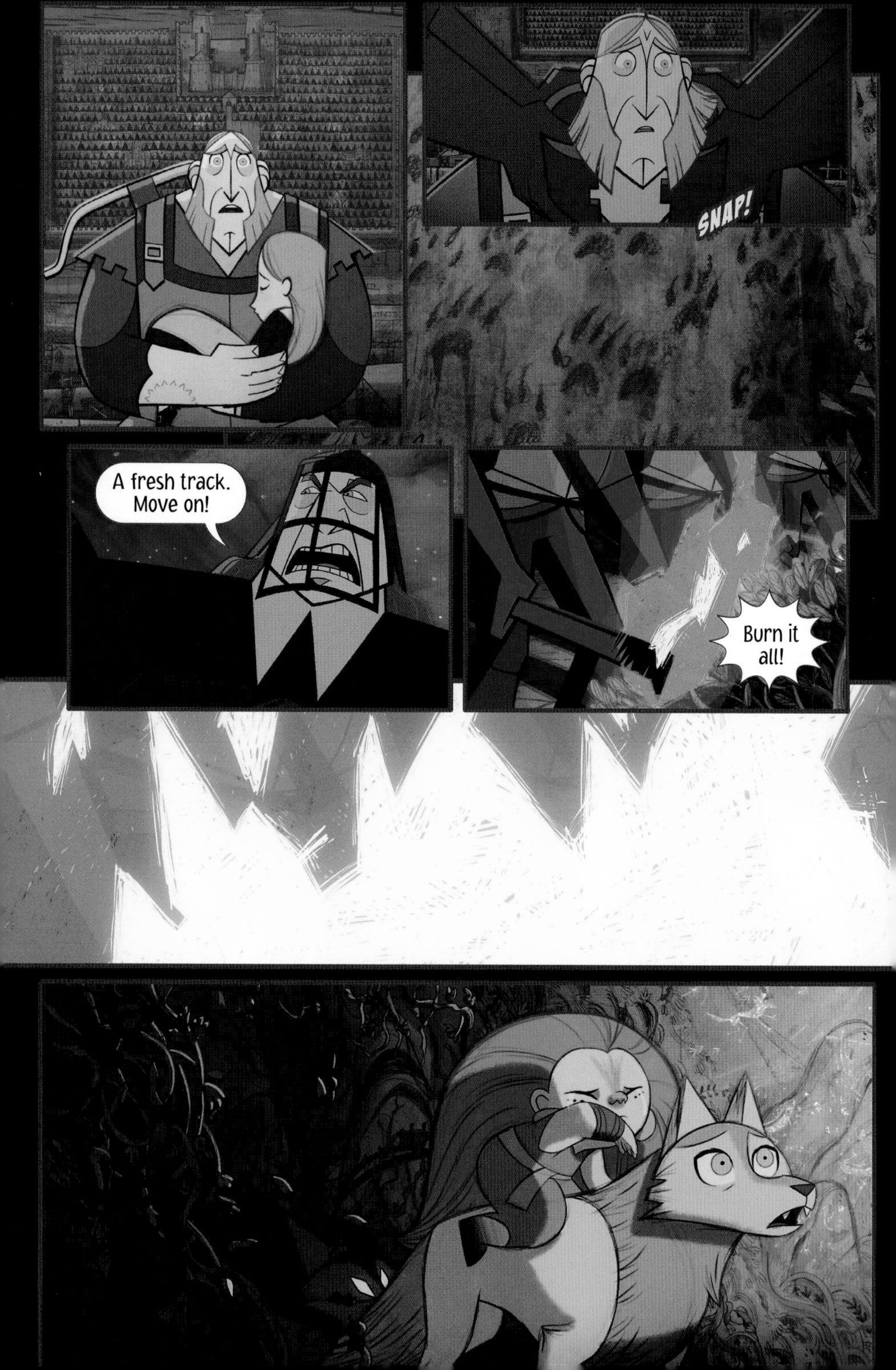
SNAP!
A fresh track.
Move on!
Burn it all!

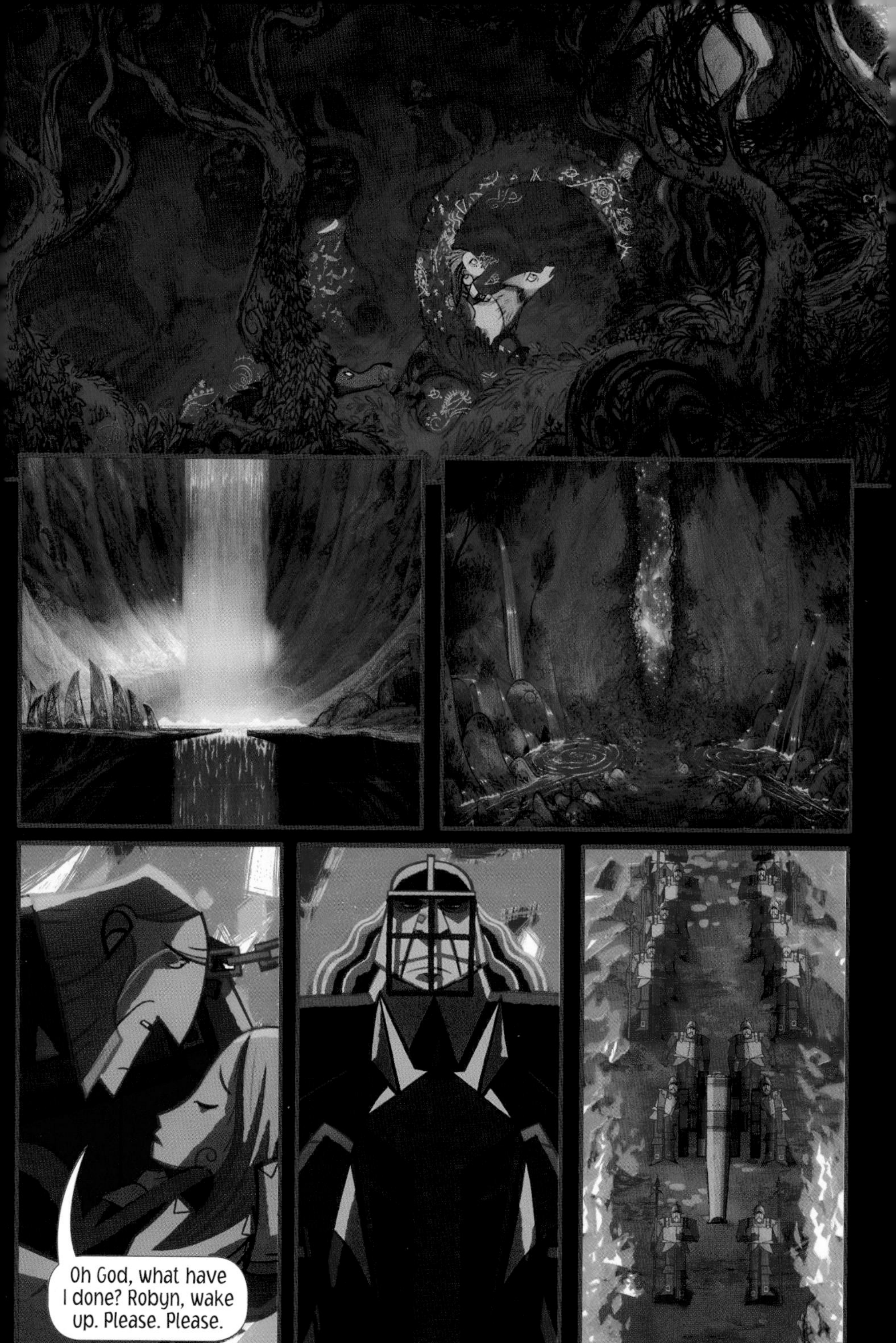
Oh God, what have I done? Robyn, wake up. Please. Please.

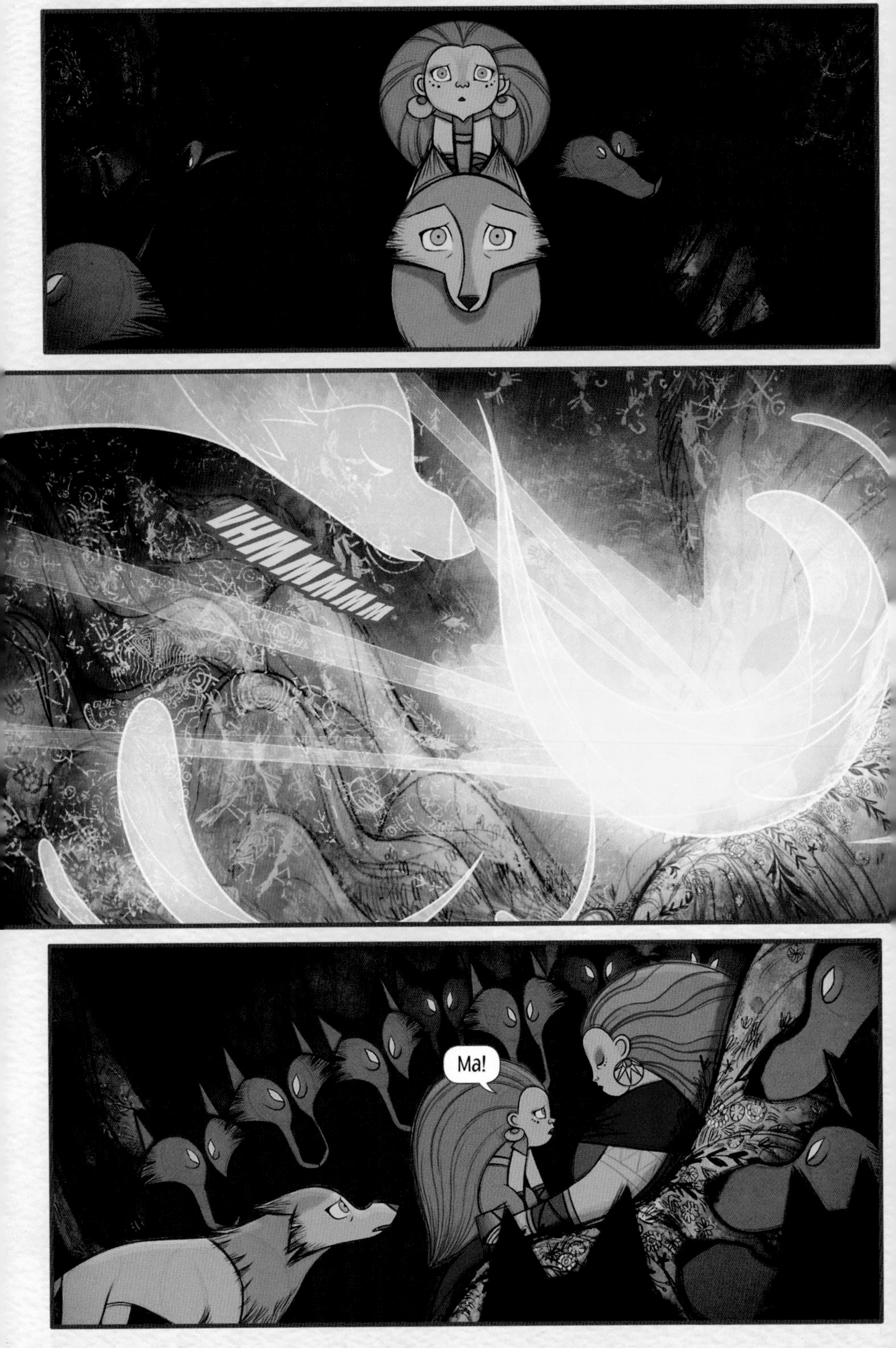
VHMMMMMM
Ma!

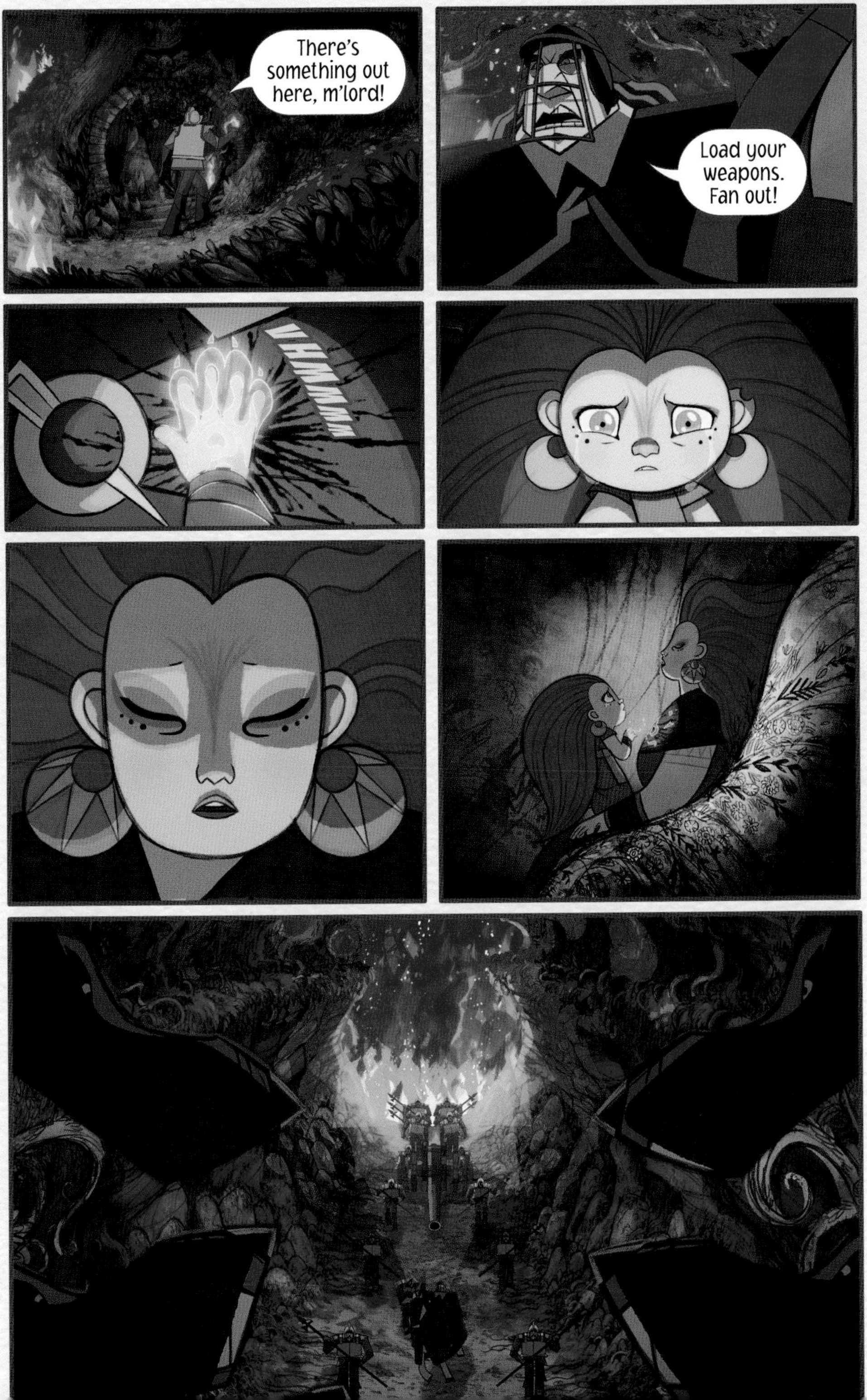
There's something out here, m'lord!
Load your weapons. Fan out!
VHMMMM

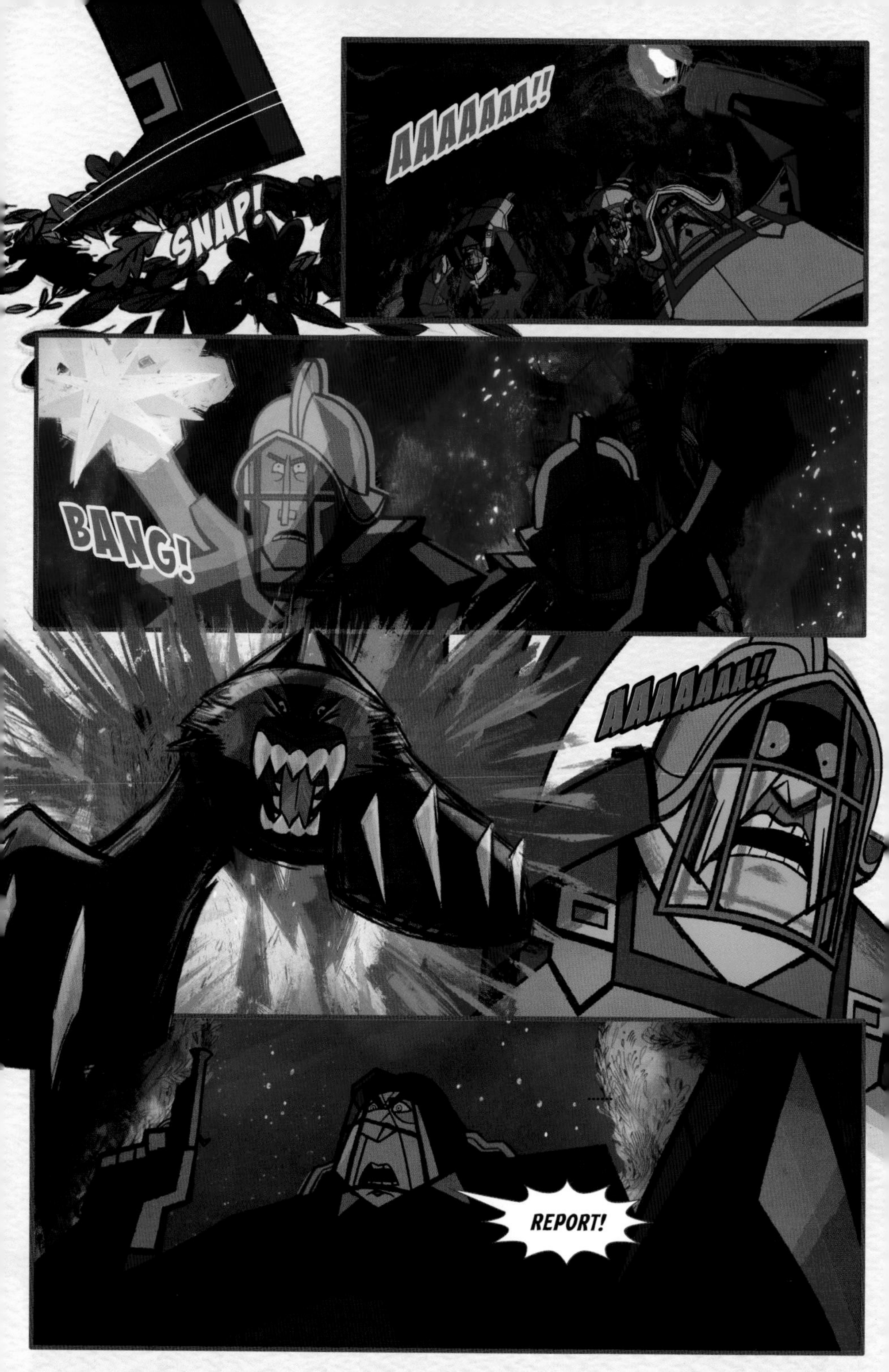
SNAP!
AAAAAAA!!
BANG!
AAAAAAA!!
REPORT!

I can't, Ma, *I can't.*
I'm not strong enough.

Please...
tell me what
to do.

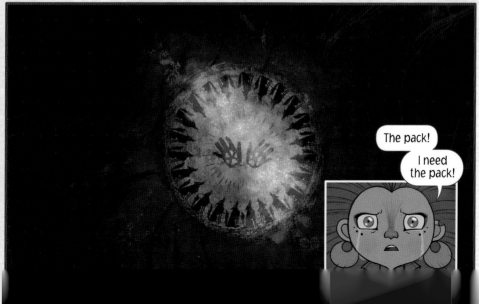

The pack!

I need
the pack!

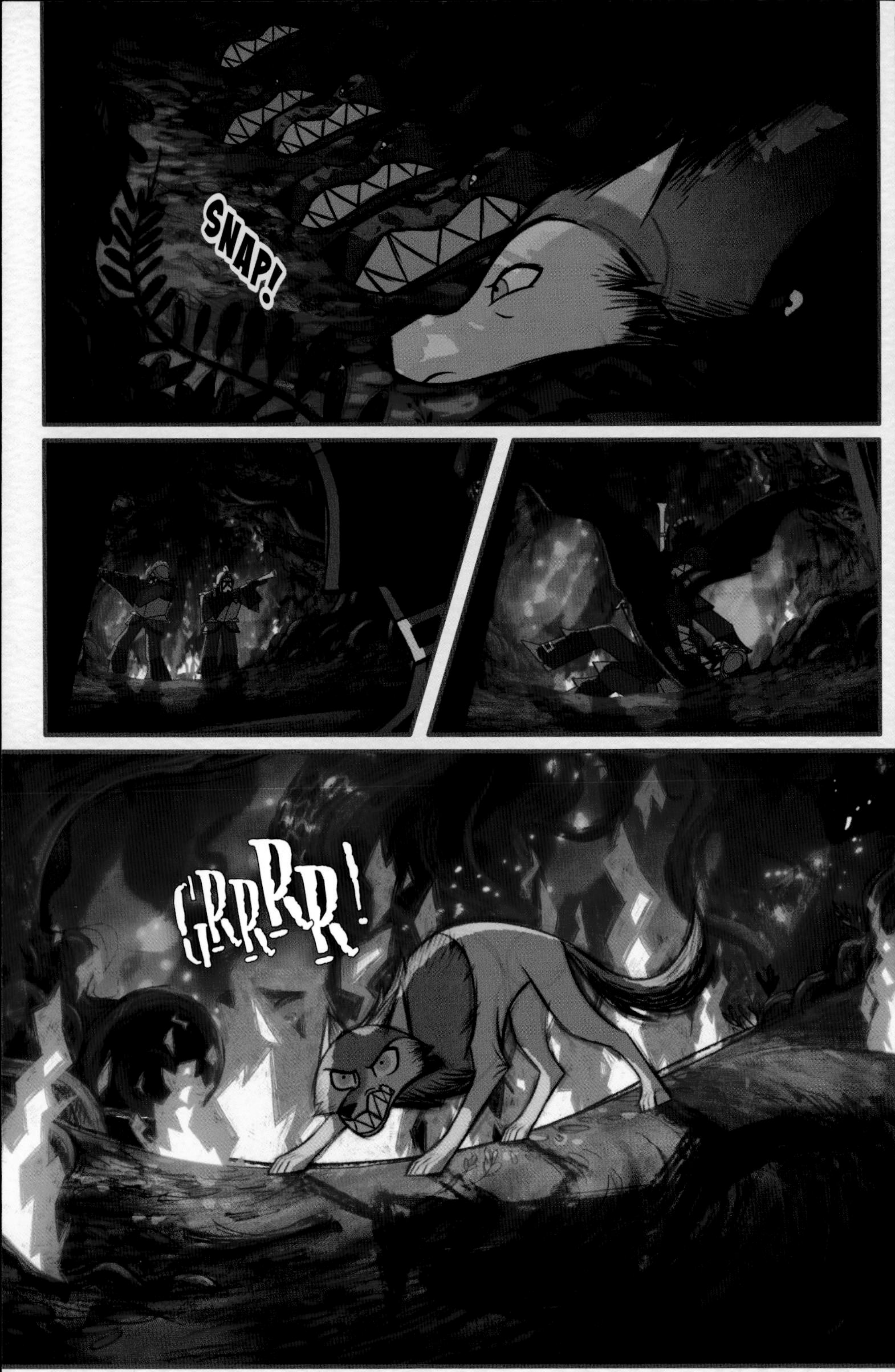
SNAP!
GRRRR!

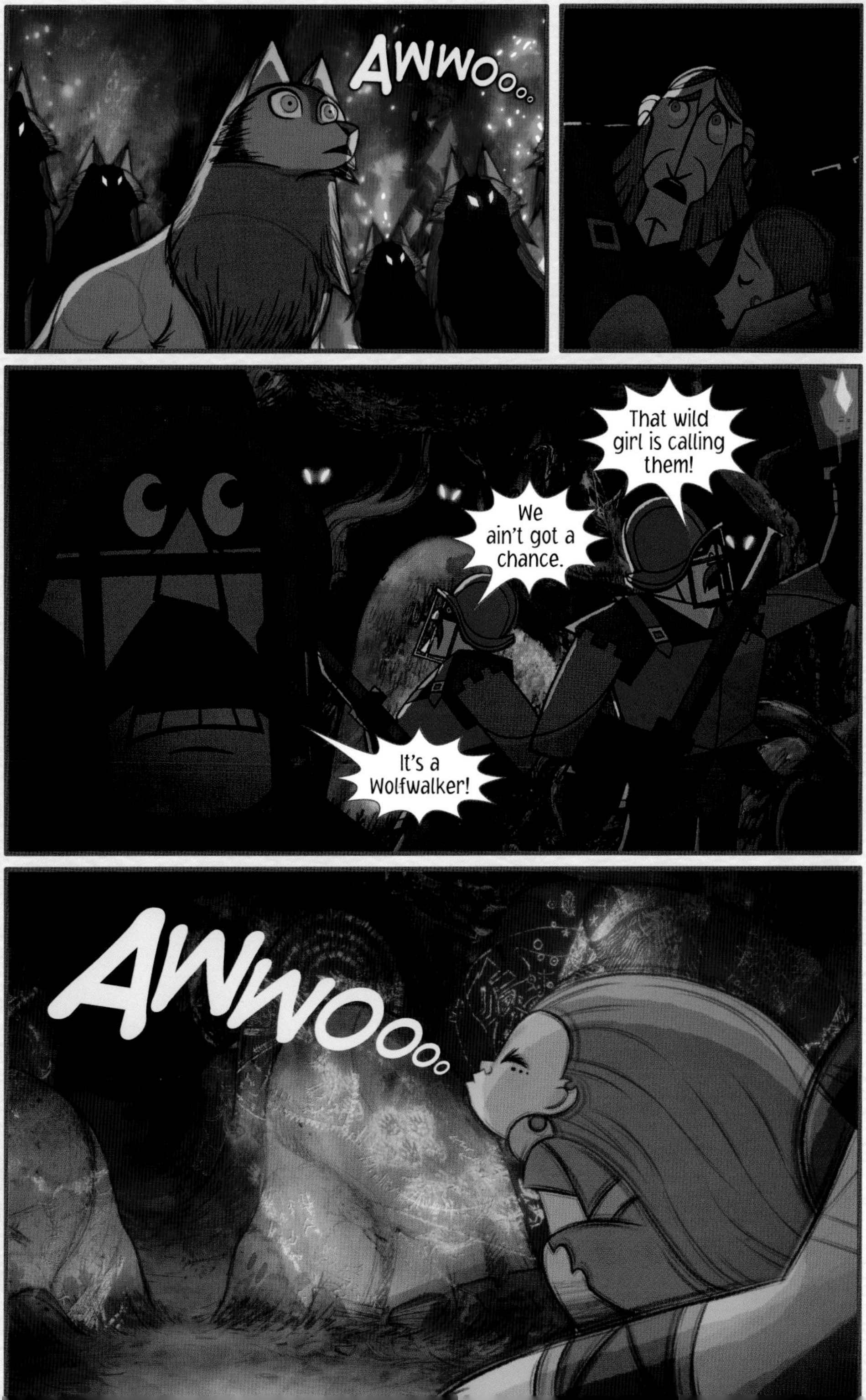
AWWOooo
That wild girl is calling them!
We ain't got a chance.
It's a Wolfwalker!
AWWOoooo

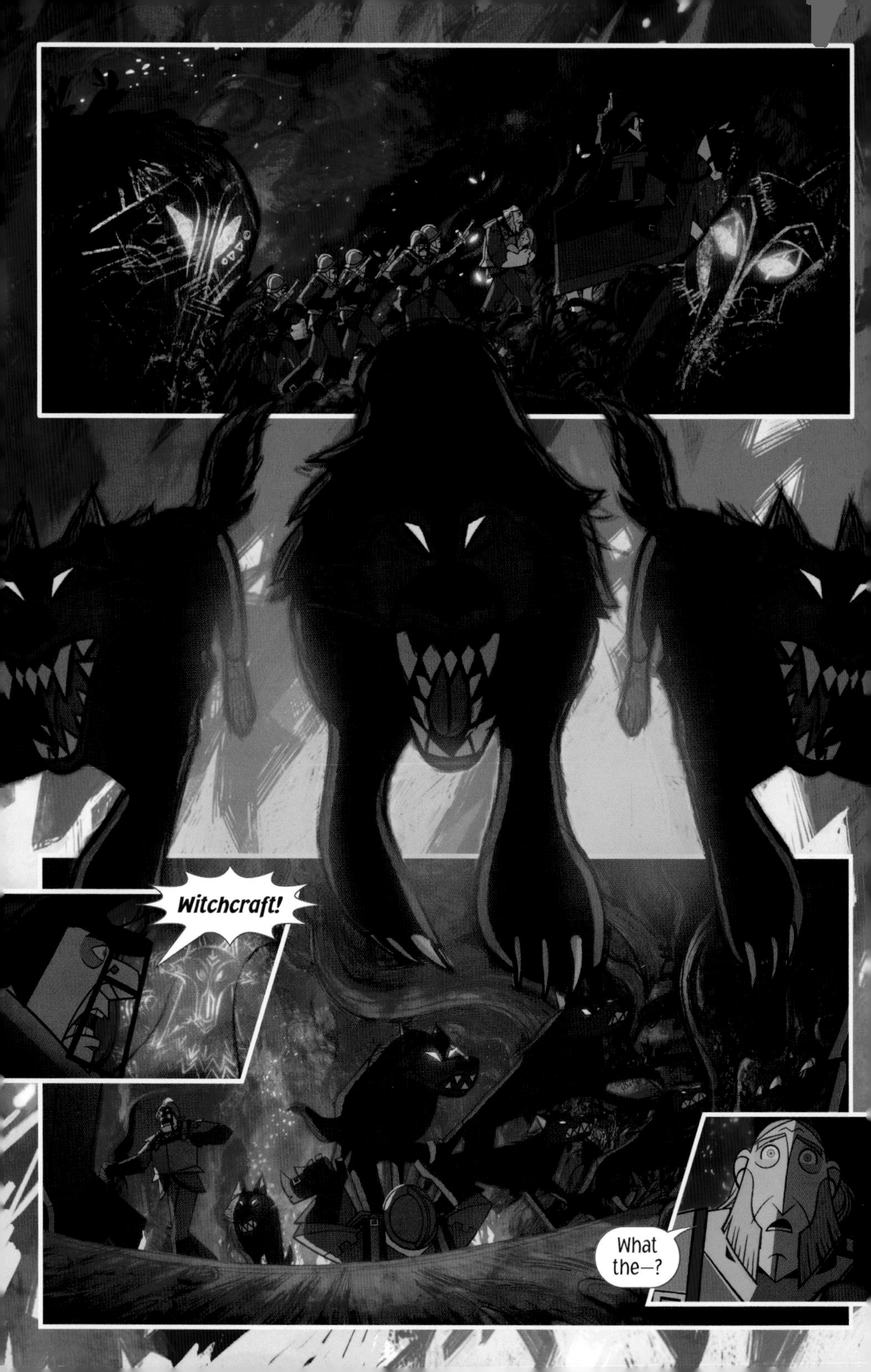
Witchcraft!
What the—?

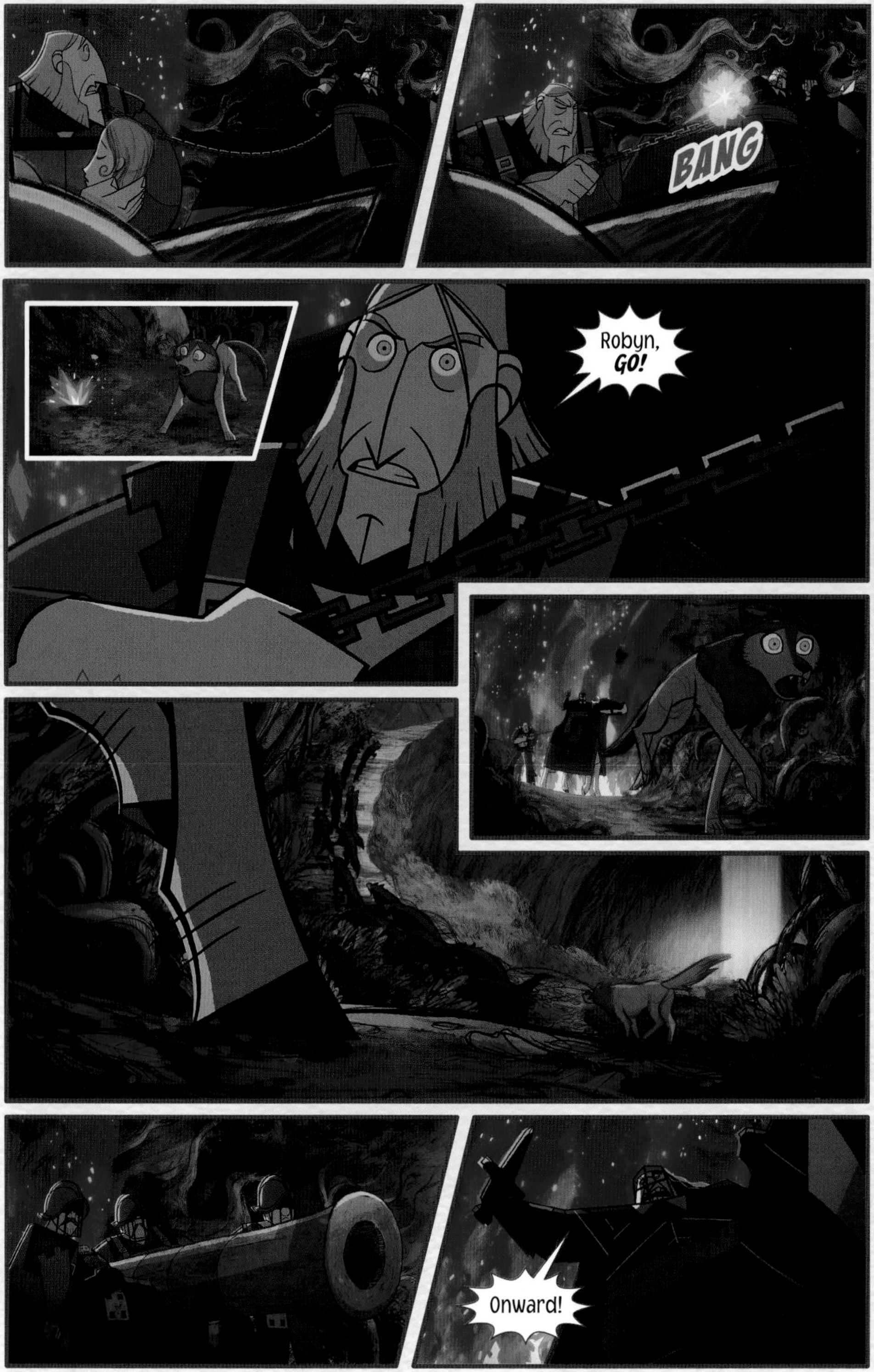
BANG
Robyn, GO!
Onward!

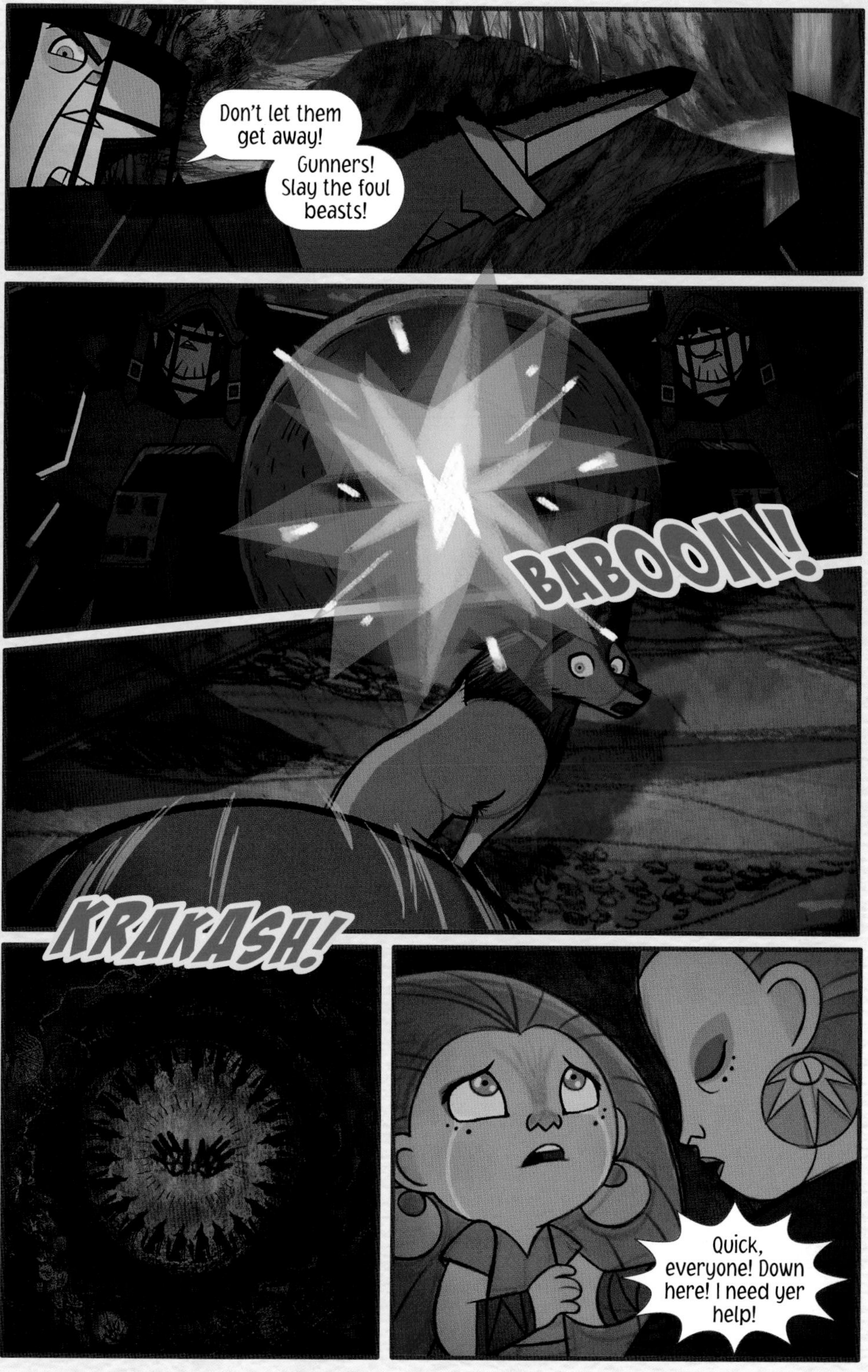
Don't let them get away!
Gunners! Slay the foul beasts!
BABOOM!
KRAKASH!
Quick, everyone! Down here! I need yer help!

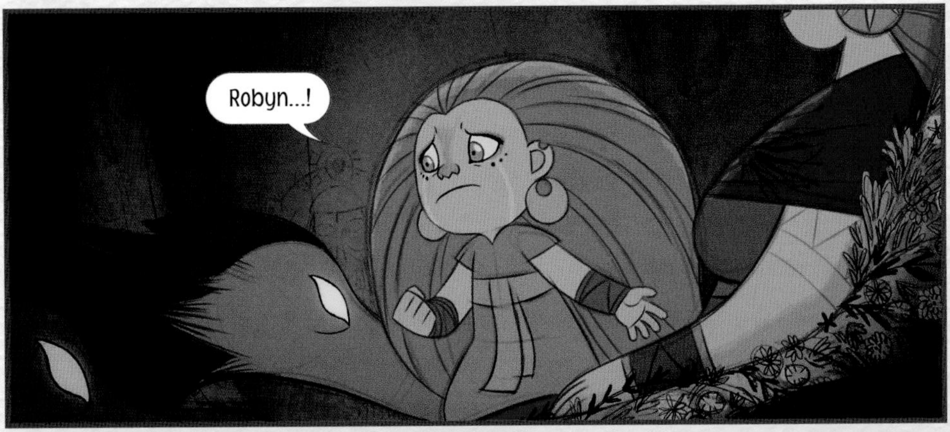
Robyn...!

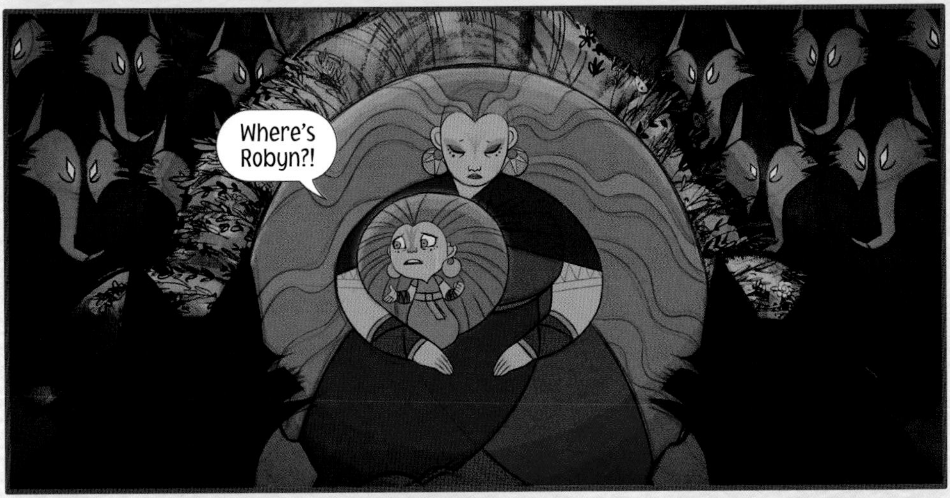
Where's
Robyn?!

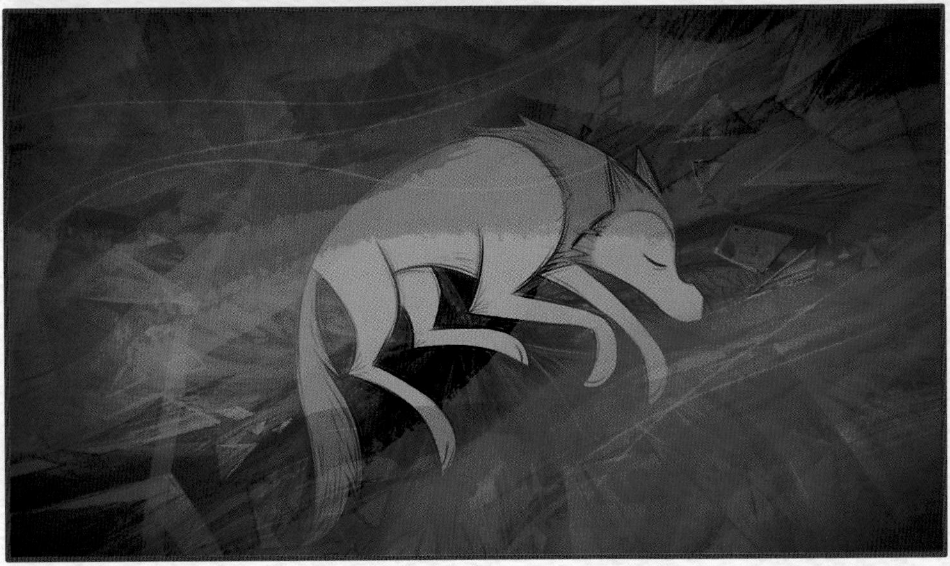

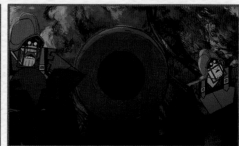

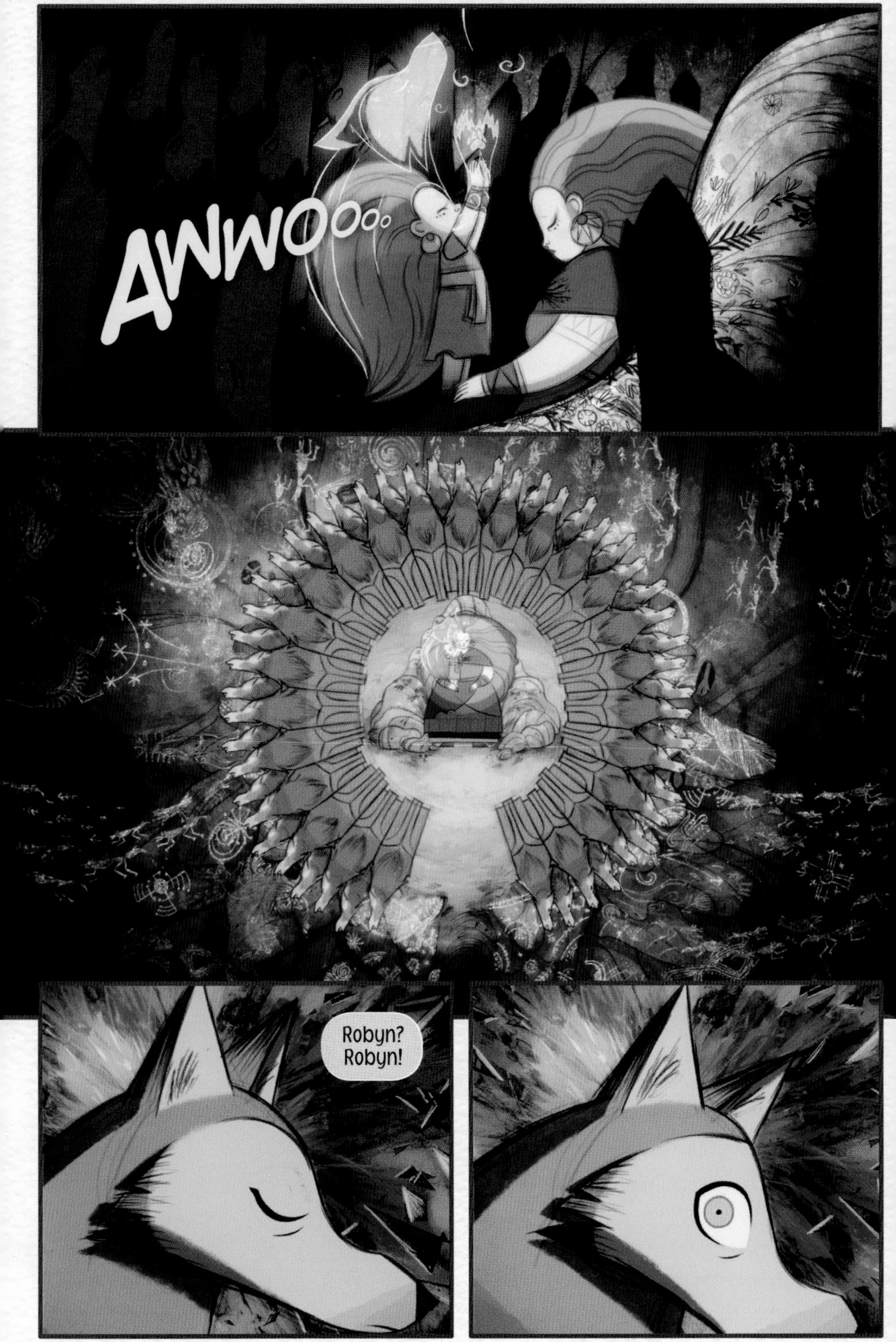
AWWOooo
Robyn?
Robyn!

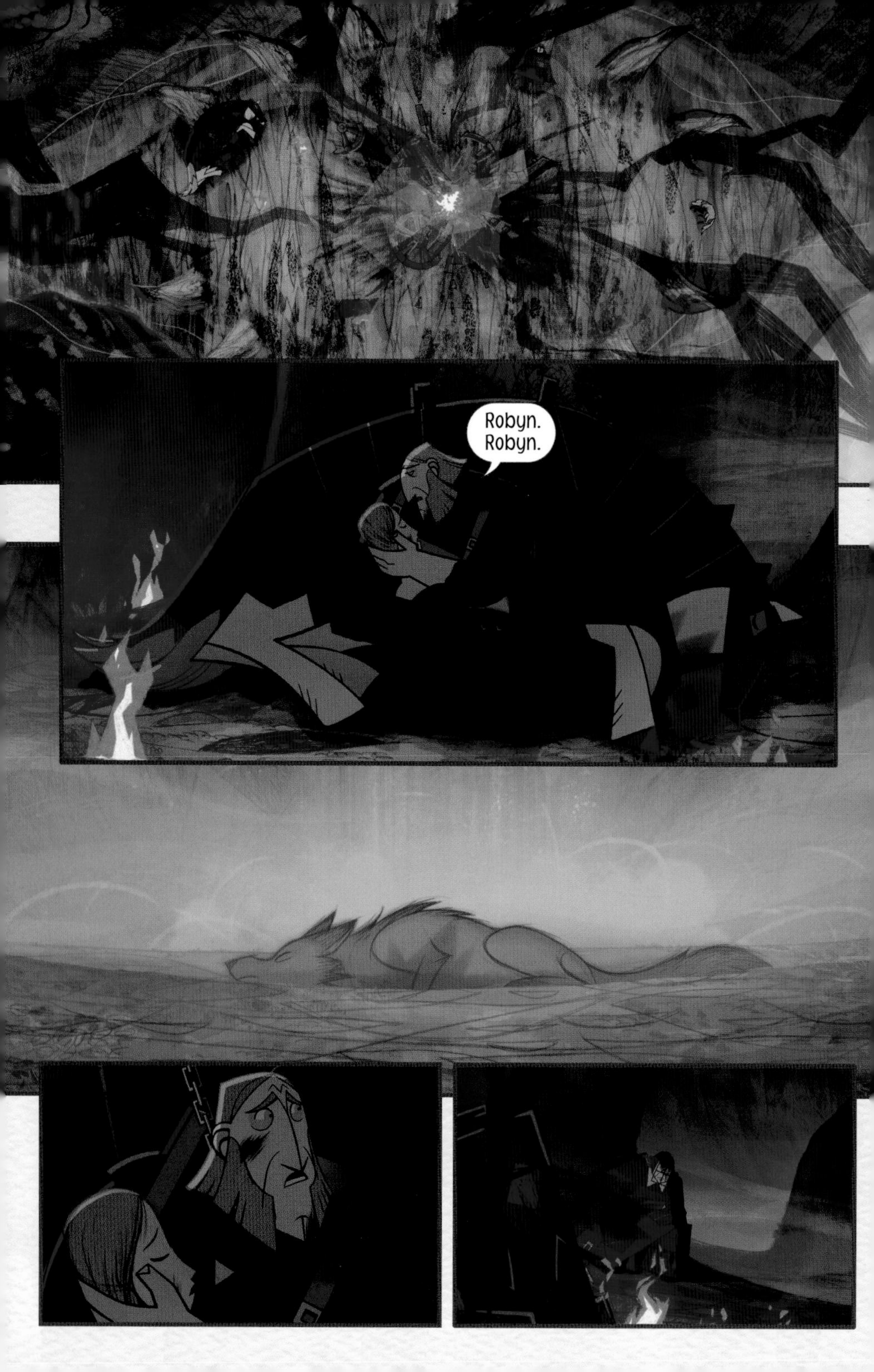
Robyn.
Robyn.

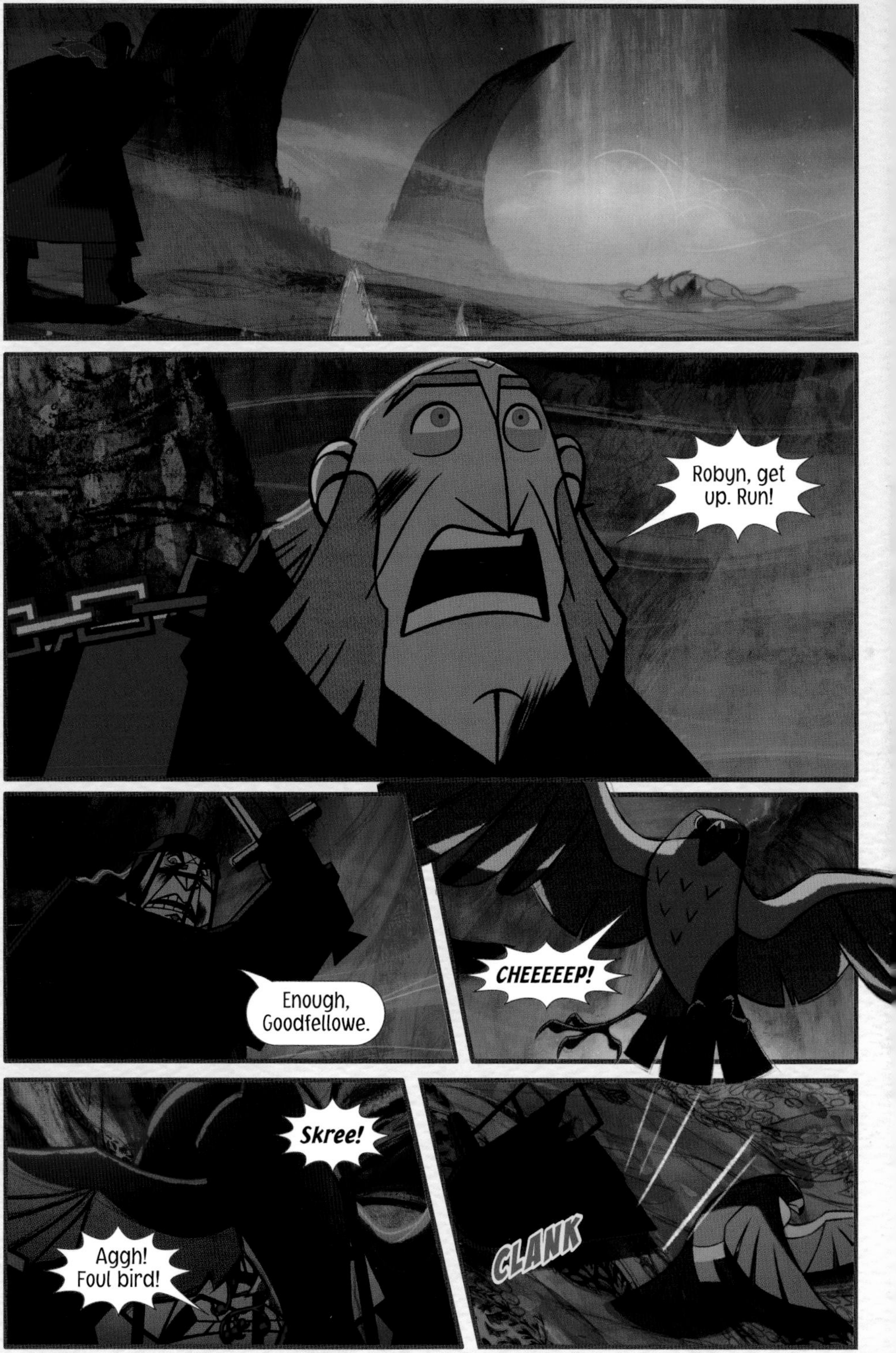

Robyn, get up. Run!
Enough, Goodfellowe.
CHEEEEEP!
Skree!
Aggh! Foul bird!
CLANK

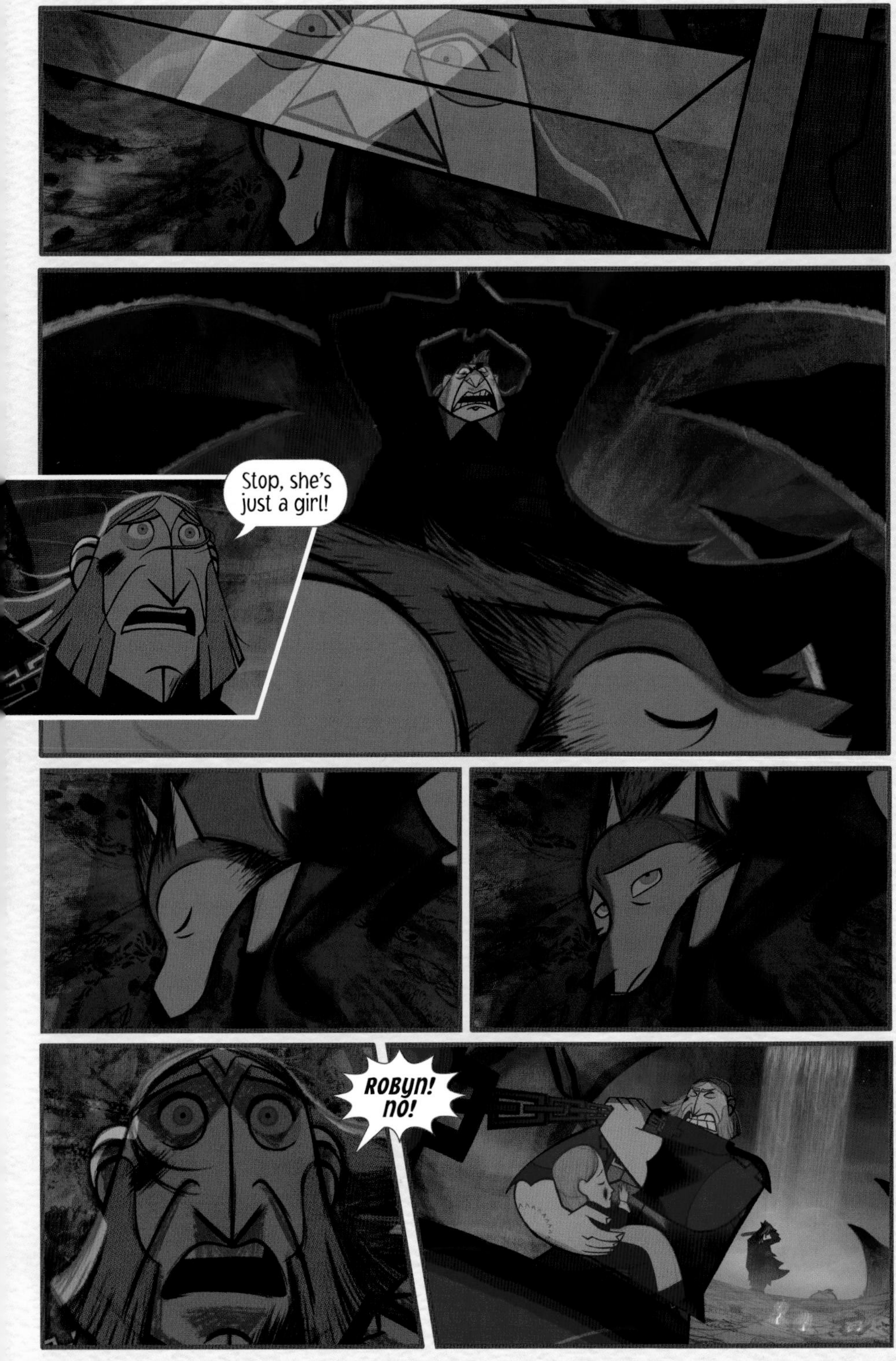
Stop, she's just a girl!
ROBYN! NO!

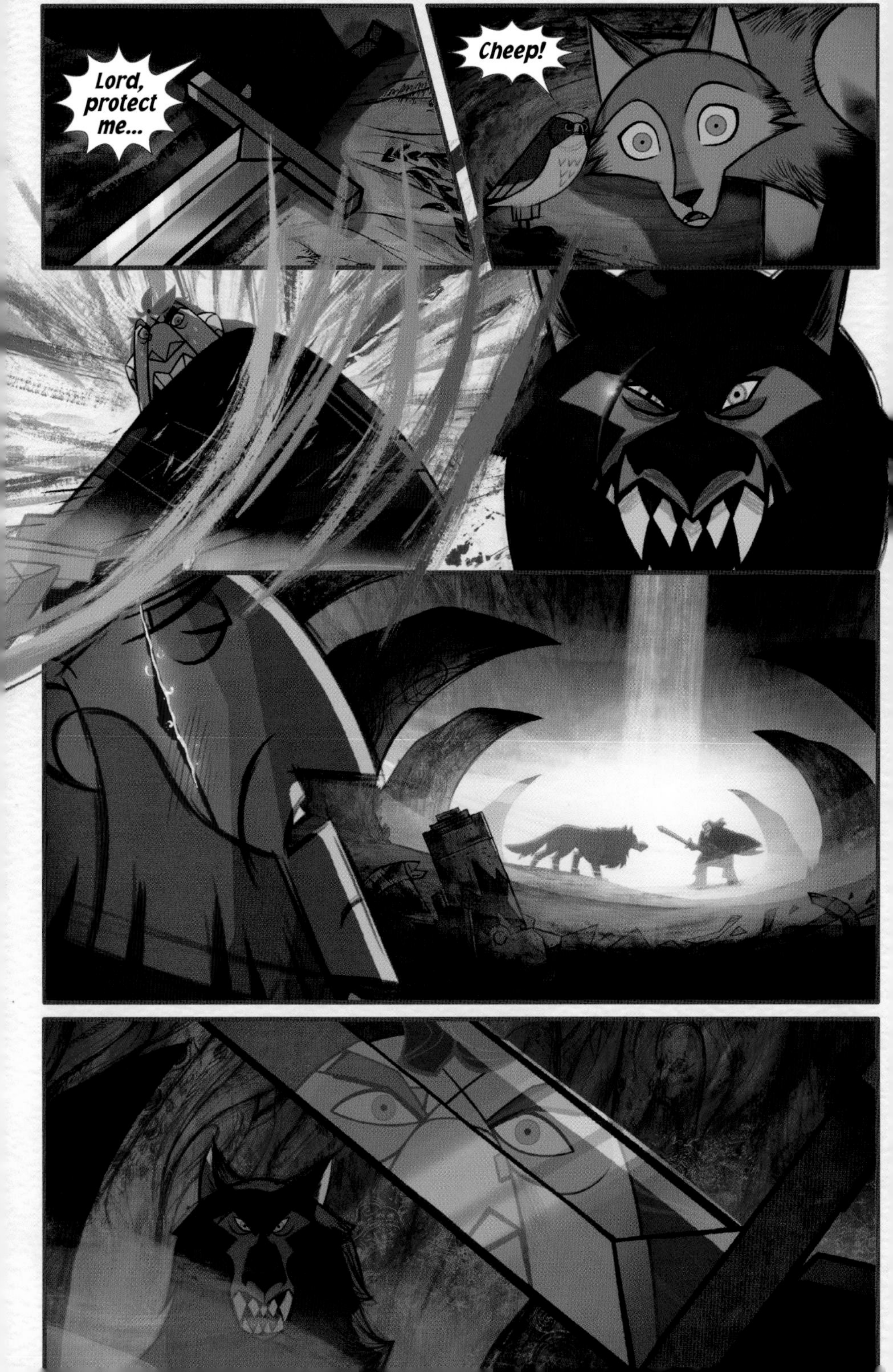
Lord, protect me...
Cheep!

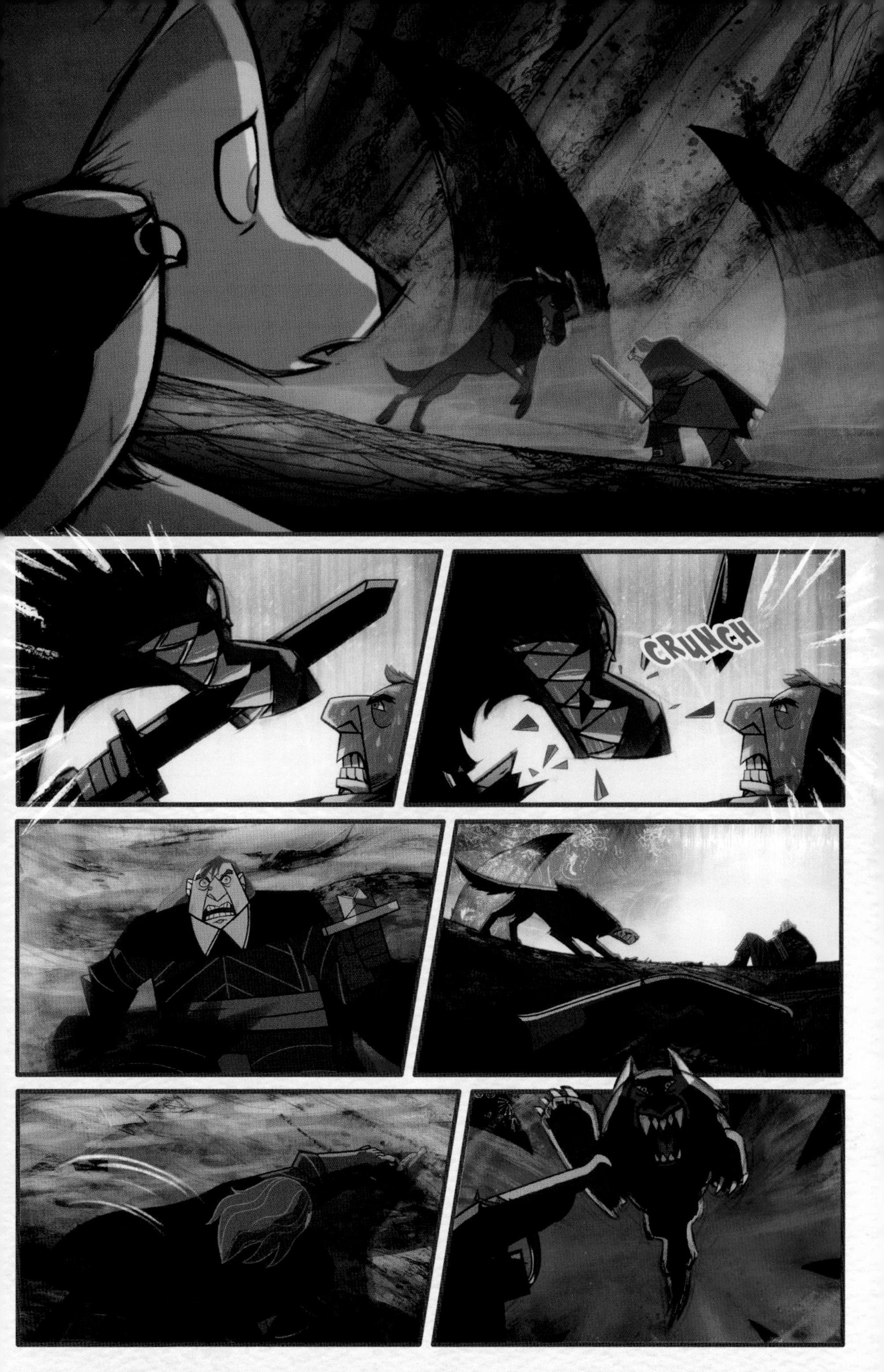
CRUNCH

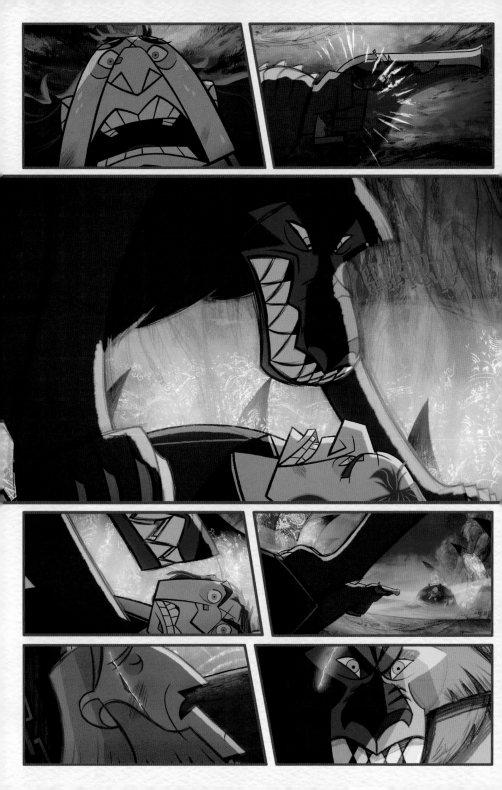

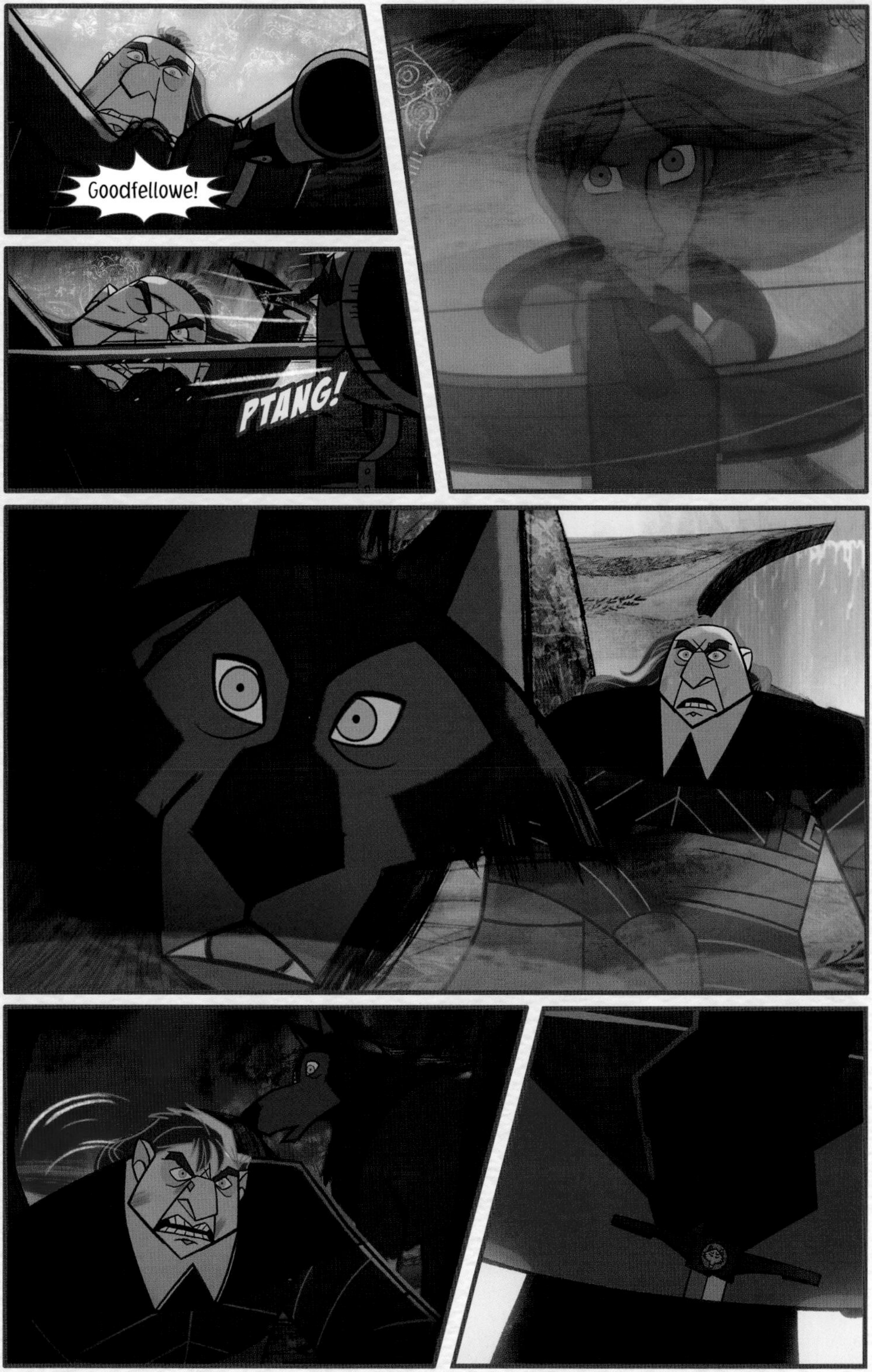
Goodfellowe!
PTANG!

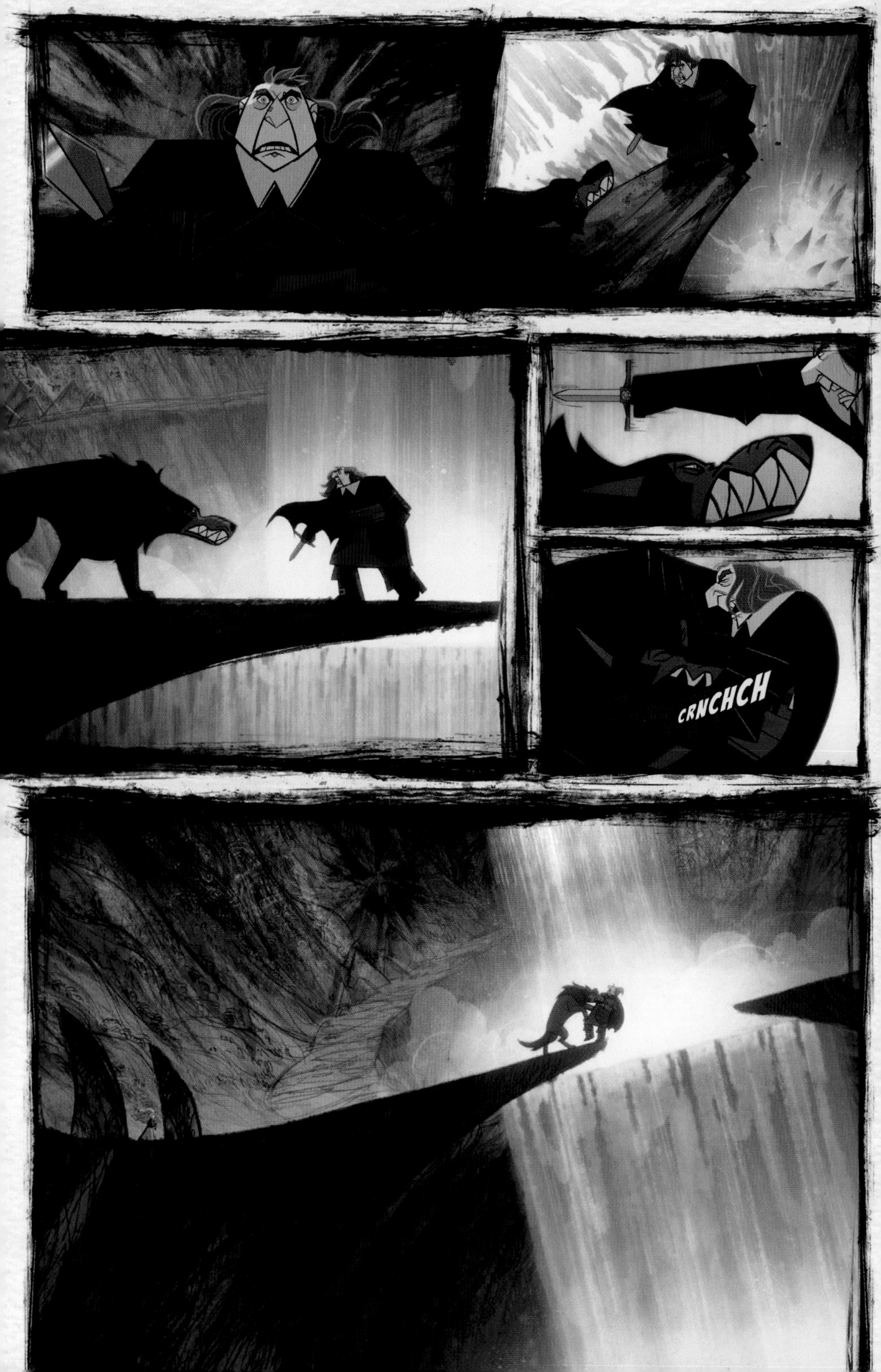
CRNCHCH

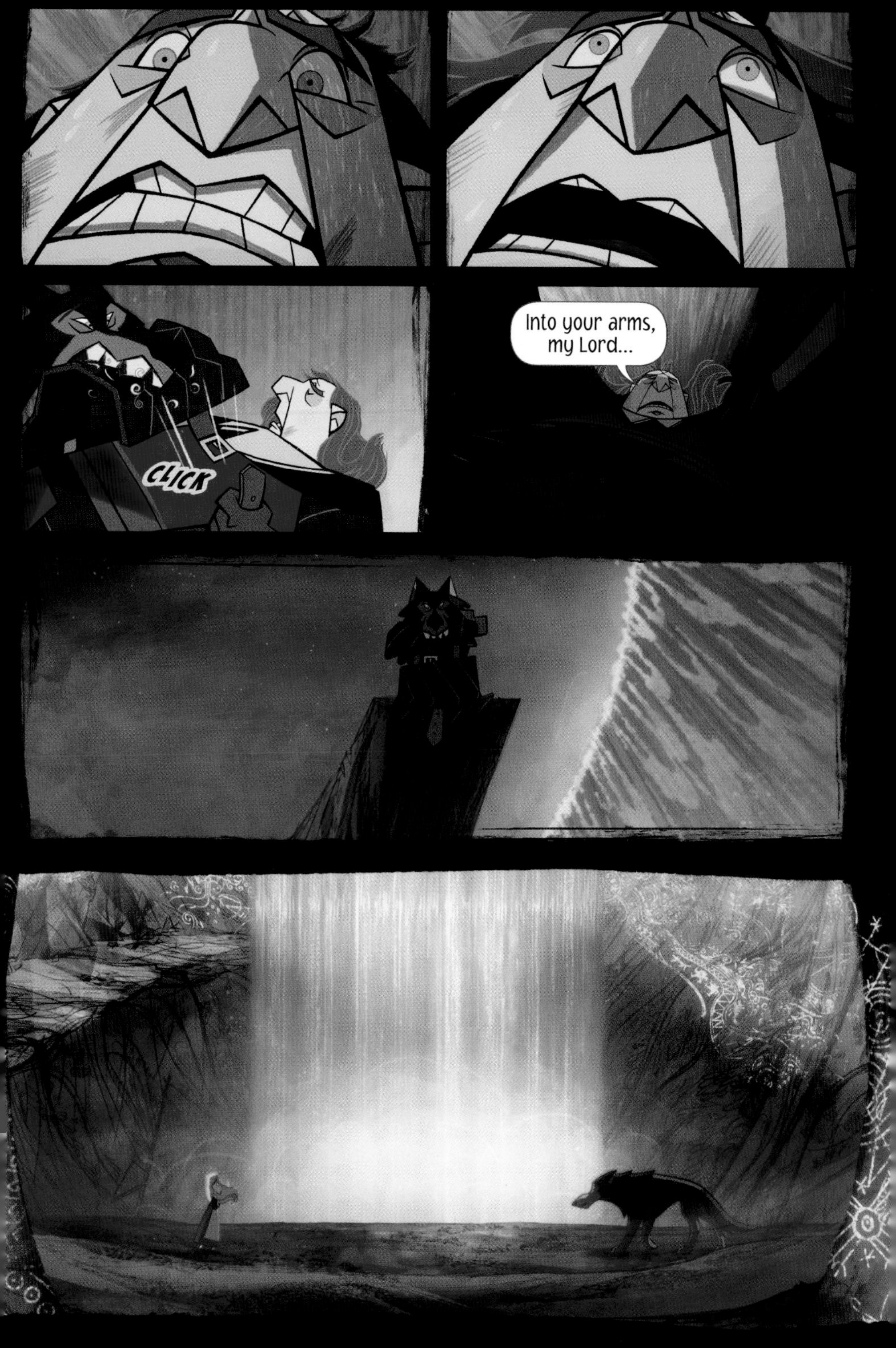
CLICK
Into your arms, my Lord...

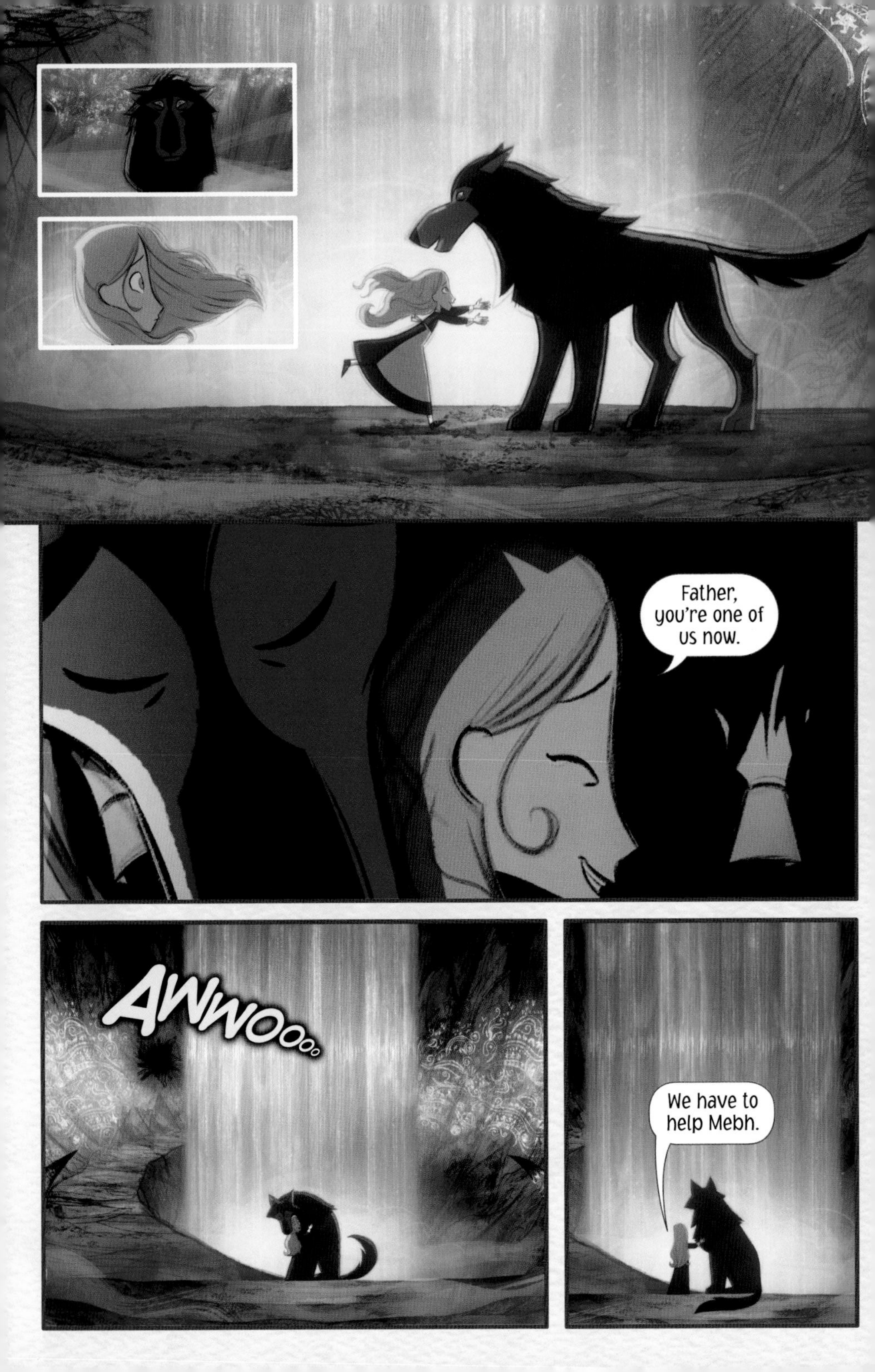
Father, you're one of us now.
AWWOooo
We have to help Mebh.

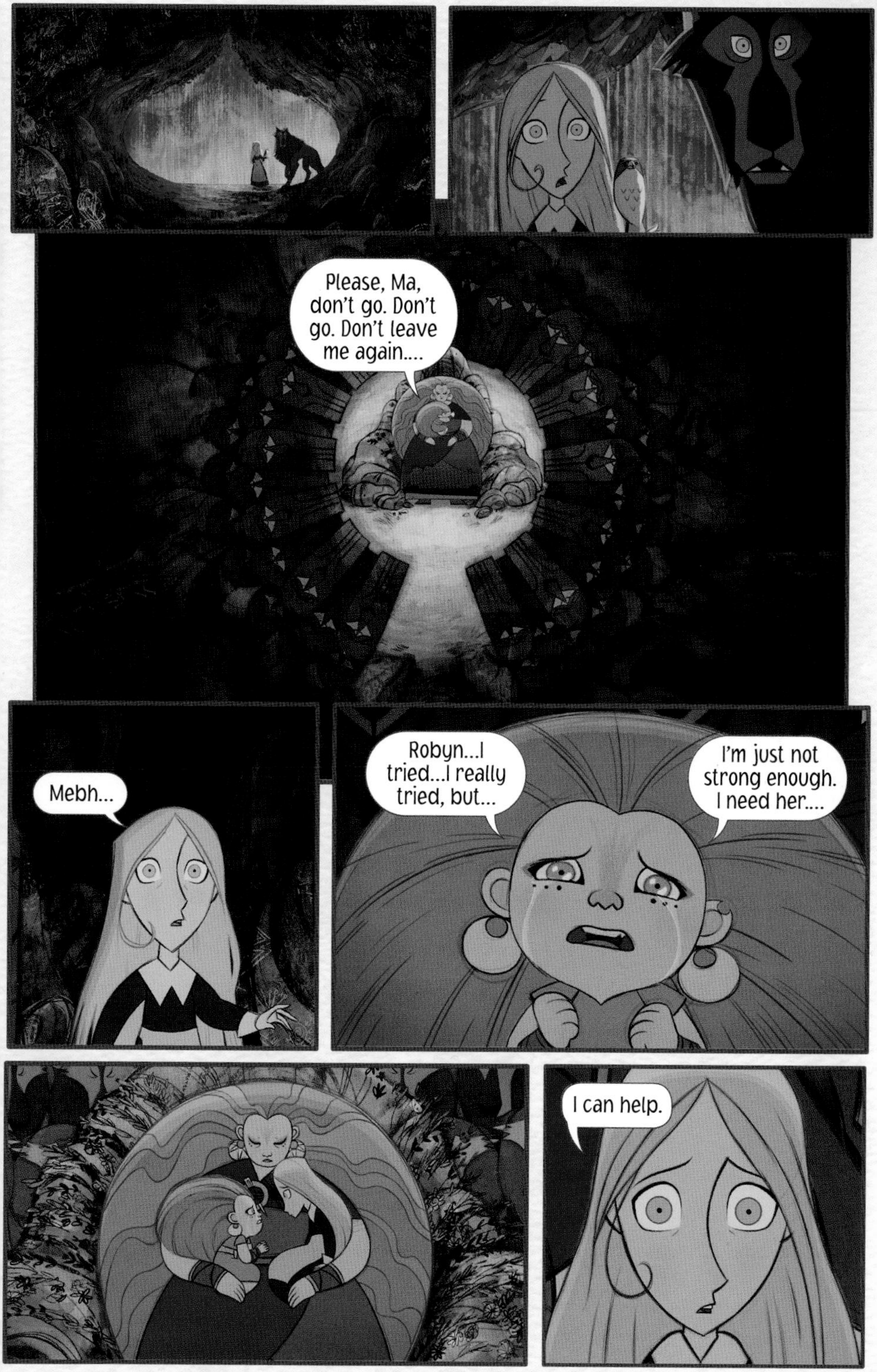
Please, Ma, don't go. Don't go. Don't leave me again....
Mebh...
Robyn...I tried...I really tried, but...
I'm just not strong enough. I need her....
I can help.

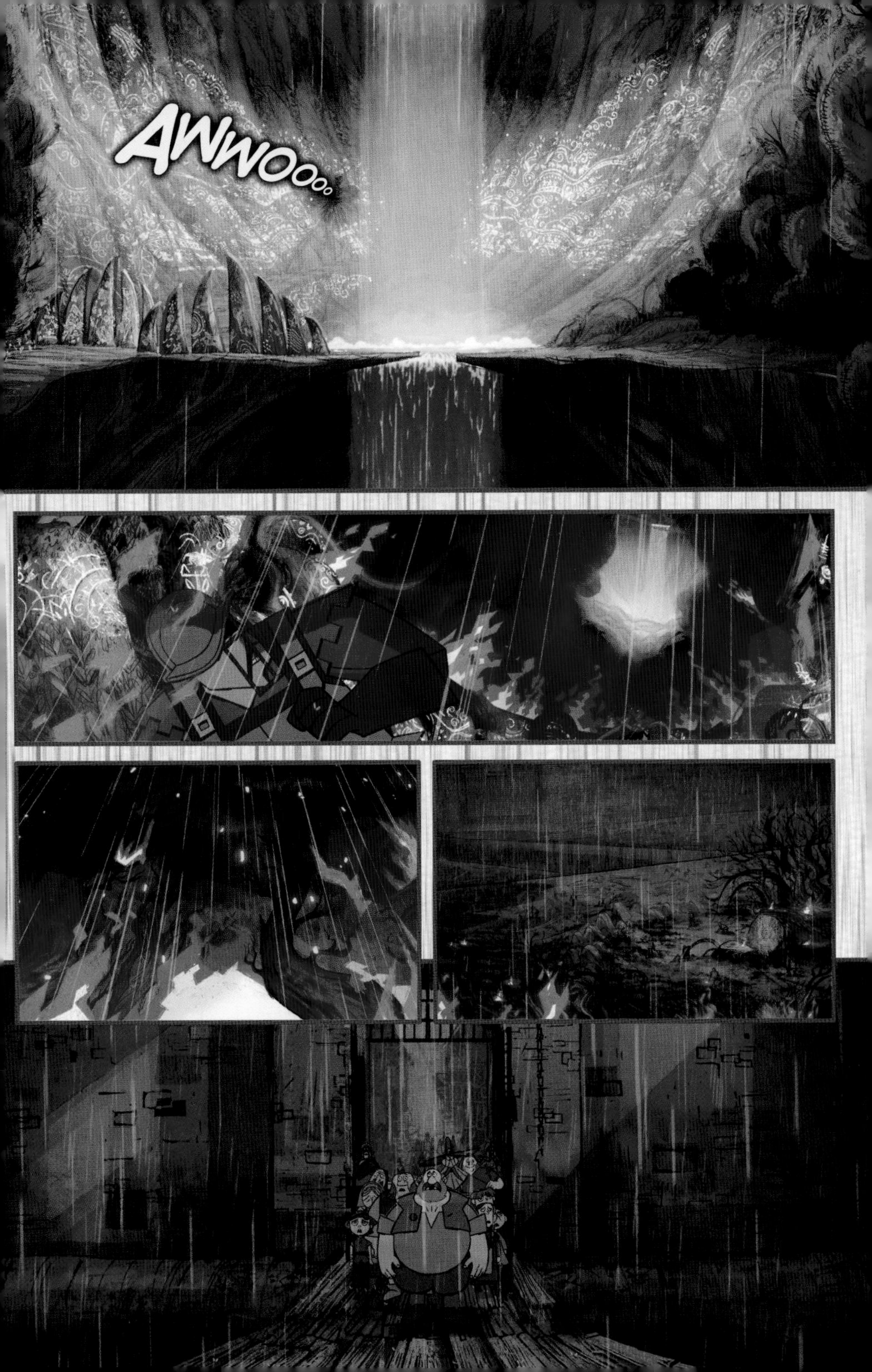
AWWOooo

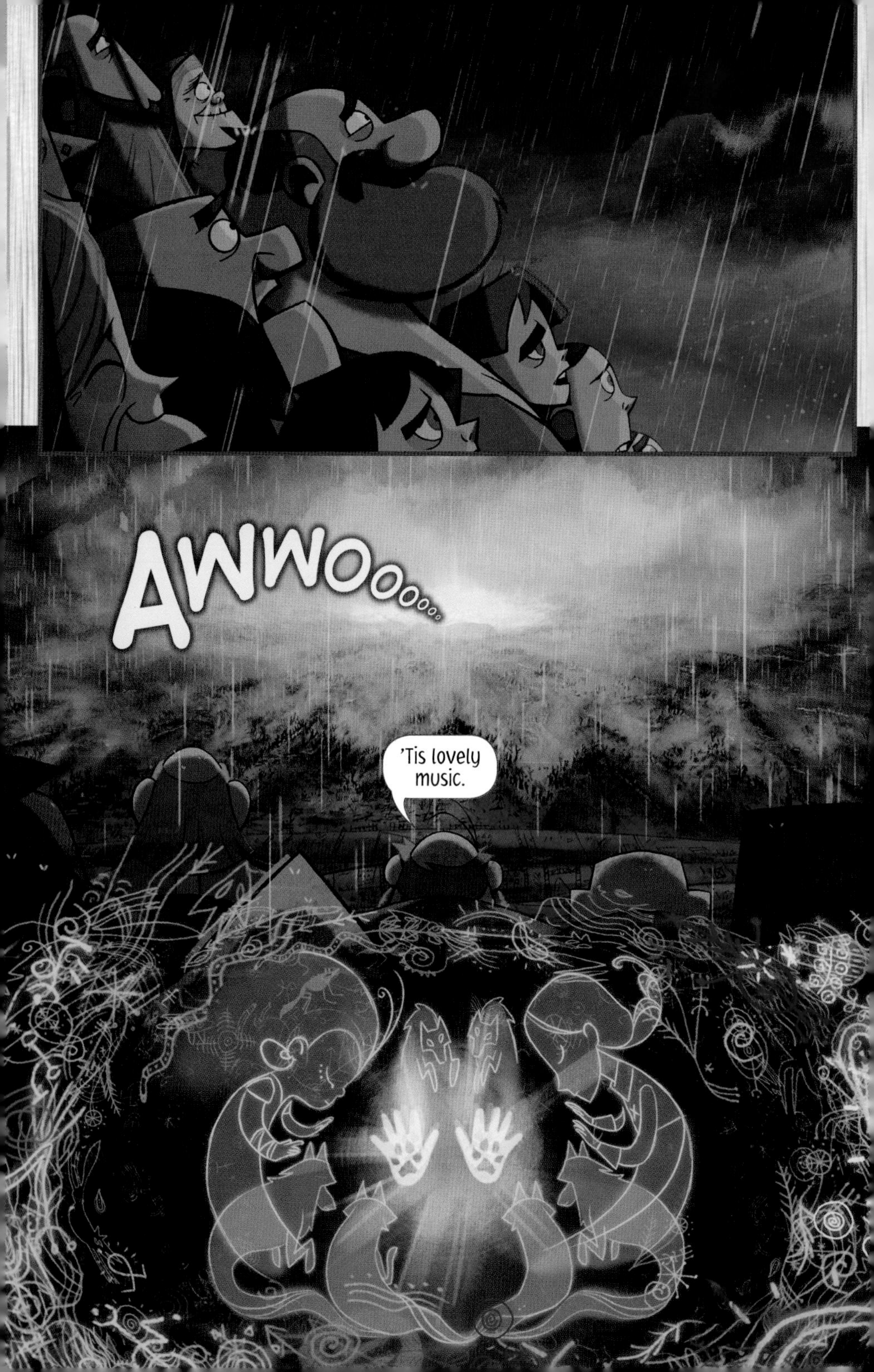
AWWOooo...
'Tis lovely music.

Haha!

Thank ye, *mo chara...* My friend.

Father?

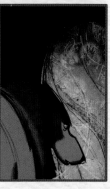

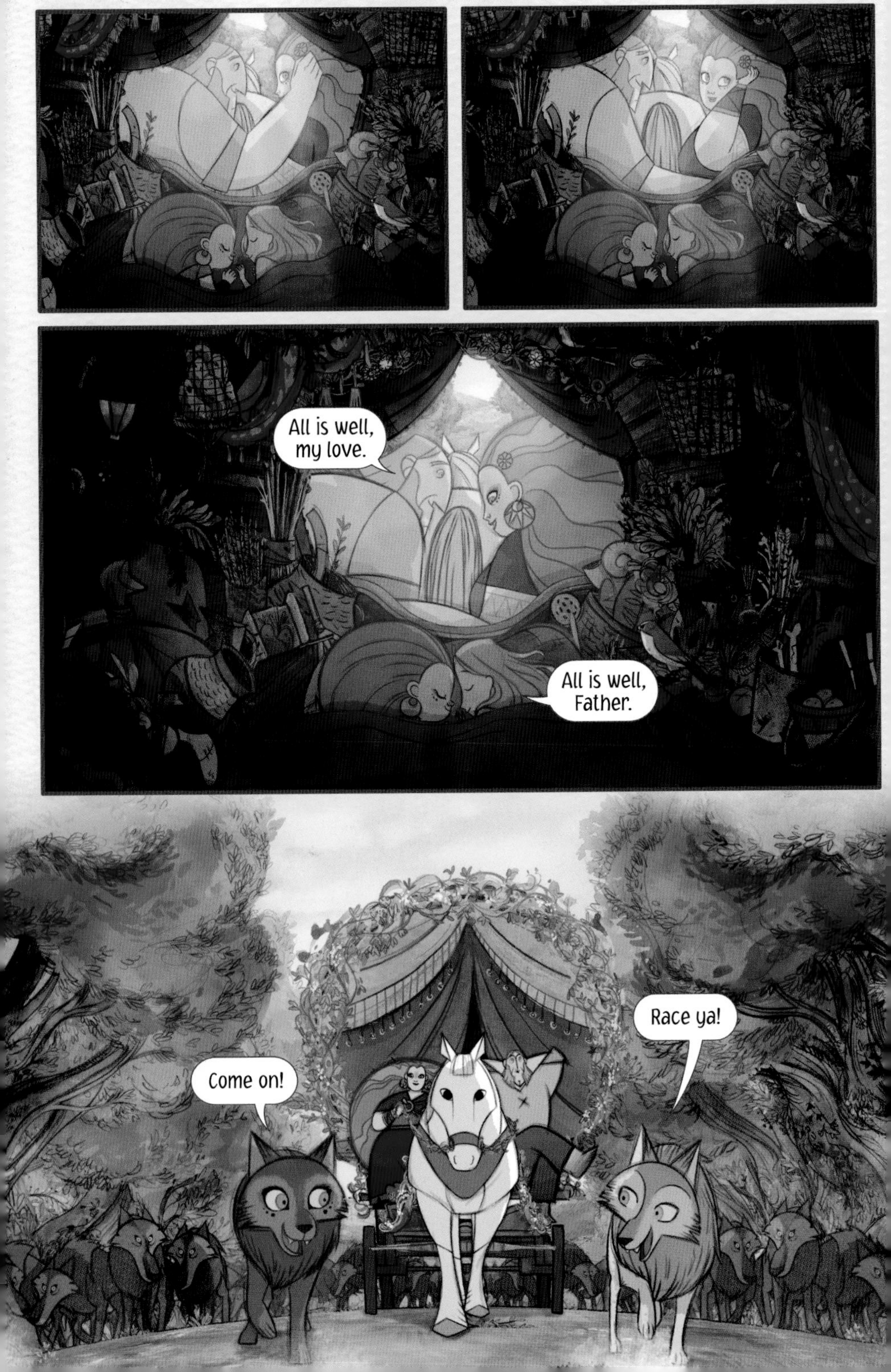
All is well,
my love.
All is well,
Father.
Come on!
Race ya!

Dylan Vaughan

Tomm Moore is the cofounder and Creative Director of Cartoon Saloon. Tomm directed *The Secret of the Kells* and *Song of the Sea*, both nominated for the Academy Award for Best Animated Feature.

Ross Stewart has been painting, illustrating, designing, and working in animation for over twenty years. Ross has worked on three Oscar nominated movies: *The Secret of the Kells* (Art Director), *Song of the Sea* (concept artist), and *ParaNorman* (visual development). He has also illustrated books and literature for a variety of publishers. He is a nature lover and would gladly sit under an oak tree all day long.

Tomm and Ross codirected *WolfWalkers*, their latest feature film.

Anna Stark

Samuel Sattin is a writer and coffee addict. He
is the words behind the Glint trilogy, *Bezkamp,
Legend,* and *The Silent End.* His work has appeared
or been featured in *The Nib, The Atlantic,* NPR,
and elsewhere. He holds an MFA in Comics from
California College of the Arts and has a creative
writing MFA from Mills College. Residing in Oakland,
California, he sometimes teaches at the California
College of the Arts and lives with his wife/assassin
and two cats.

Acknowledgments

As a fan of graphic novels from an early age, the visual language of the medium has been a part of my work as a director since the beginning. For *WolfWalkers*, Ross and I drew inspiration from many of our favorite creators and even incorporated graphic novel-style compositions and scene layouts into the film itself, so it was especially exciting for me to be part of adapting our film to the page. We even added some original pages detailing the movie's backstory and the legend of the Wolfwalkers as a bonus to the readers.

I would like to dedicate this graphic novel to the amazing crew who worked with us on the animated feature *WolfWalkers* since so much of their artwork is the basis of everything you will see in the book. I would also like to thank Megan, Rachel, and everyone at Little, Brown Books for Young Readers for their patience and enthusiasm for this adaptation, especially Ching, who made such beautiful layouts and did such a wonderful job designing the book.

Not forgetting, of course, special thanks are due to Sam Sattin, who has done such an excellent job of adapting the script and film for this graphic novel and our team in the Saloon: Desirée, Brian, and especially Maria, who was the not only super fast on the adaptation pages and the original artwork we created for this book but is also one of the most talented artists with whom I've had the pleasure of collaborating.

—Tomm Moore

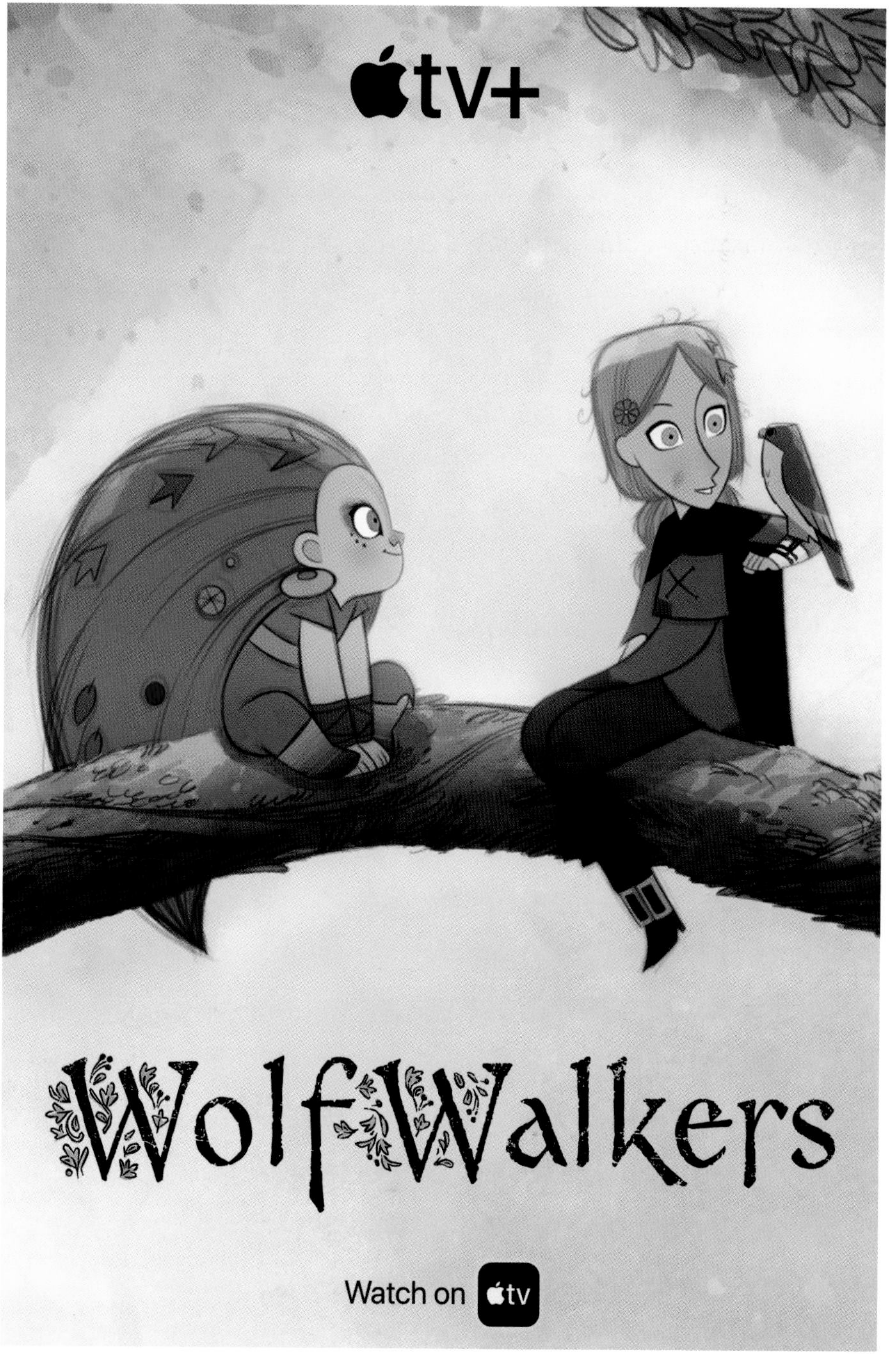
tv+
WolfWalkers
Watch on tv

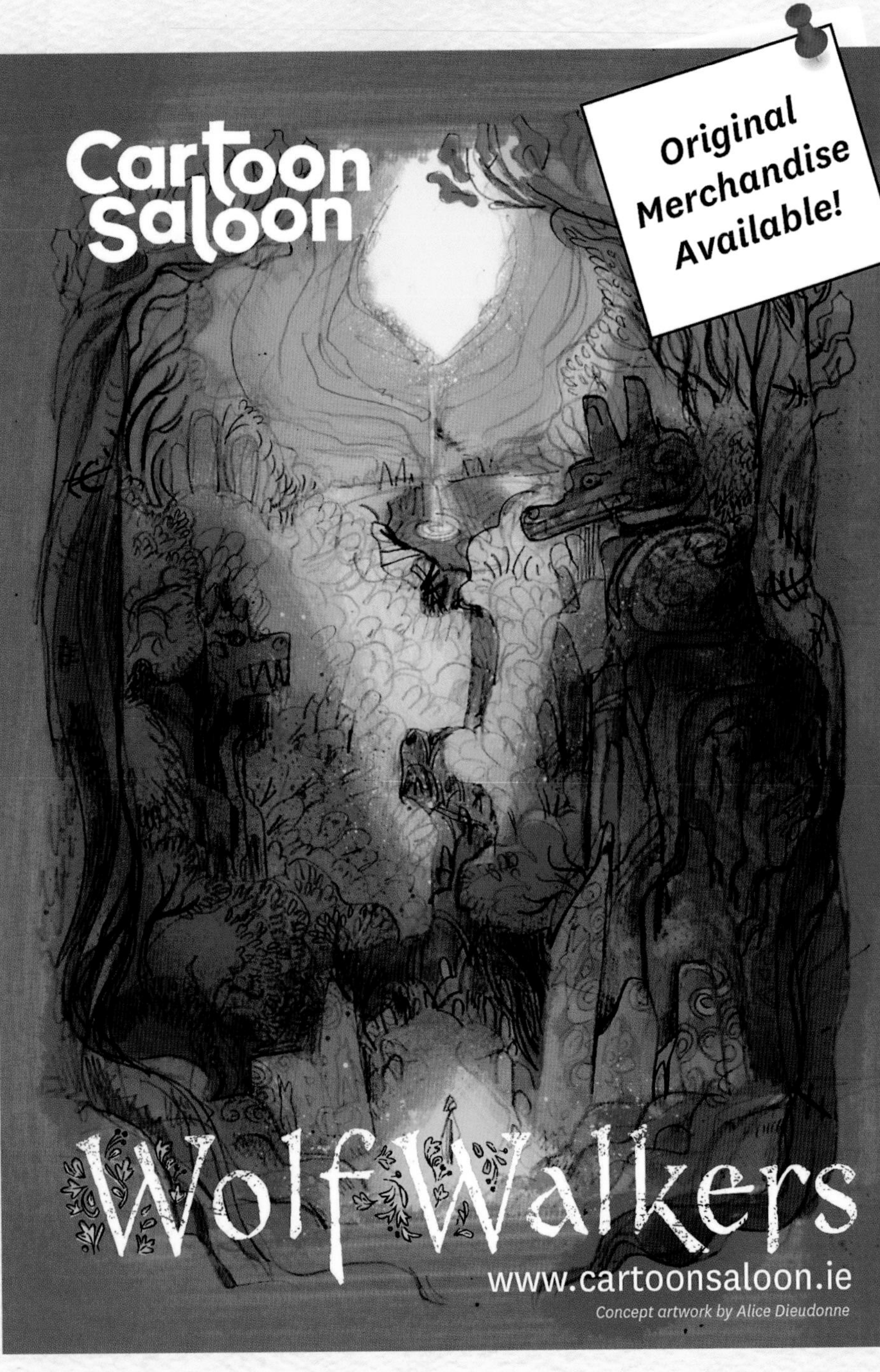
Cartoon Saloon
Original Merchandise Available!
WolfWalkers
www.cartoonsaloon.ie
Concept artwork by Alice Dieudonne